Anthea Syrokou

The Greek Tapestry

Cover Design by BespokeBookCovers.com

Anthea Syrokou
The Greek Tapestry
ISBN-13: 978-0648157434

antheasyrokou.com

For my Family

The Greek Tapestry (Julie & Friends, Book 2) can be read as a standalone or as part of a series, following on from the delightful Eventually Julie (Julie & Friends, Book 1). In this latest book, it's Maria's turn to take centre stage. Joining her are many exciting new characters, as well as some familiar and popular faces from Book 1.

Eventually Julie (Julie & Friends, Book 1)

Julie has had enough! At 27, she feels overwhelmed with the "shoulds" her family pile on her, and an office job that she detests. It doesn't help that she's carrying her "baggage of unfinished business" with her, weighing her down even more ... making it impossible to see clearly and dig herself out of the rut her life has become.

When she finally decides to take action, a chance encounter presents her with an opportunity to deal with her messy past, so she sets off to Paris to find the answers that can set her free, and live a life full of meaning and passion. Julie loses herself in the sights and smells, and in the beauty of travelling in one of the most romantic cities in the world. She opens her heart to love, and begins to be true to herself ... until she discovers a secret that sets her right back to where she began; uncertain about life — about love!

When Julie arrives back home to Sydney, she needs to make some serious decisions, or risk missing out on true love ... and finally having the career she always wanted.

Join Julie and her delightful and witty friends on a journey of fun, adventure, and passion. Set in and around Sydney, as well as London and Paris, Eventually Julie is a "finding yourself" romance that deals with being stuck in a rut and eventually finding the right ingredients to live a life that is true.

"This has been one of the nicest books that I have read all year! Chick Lit at its finest I'd say!"

Whispering Stories Book Blog

"I liked how the story flowed smoothly and kept the interest until the last page. I really enjoyed it and I'm eagerly waiting for the next book in the series."

Liina reads

"Author Syrokou writes in a clear and compelling way and her scenes of Paris and London are vivid and dynamic."

Readers Review Room

"A good read. I need to read more by Anthea!"

The Rambling Boho

"A sweet, light-hearted chick lit book that will remind you of Eat, Pray, Love in the best ways possible."

Comfy Reading

CHAPTER ONE

"I don't understand why you had people attend two church ceremonies. The guests are probably so tired by now."

Maria Reyes rolled her eyes and looked at her husband, Antonio. He was holding their baby boy, Thomas, gently in his arms. She couldn't wait to take Thomas out of that ridiculous christening outfit. Maria thought it resembled a Greek dancing costume from the moment she saw it. Her mother had made sure that the christening was steeped in tradition — Greek tradition. Thomas' godmother, Cassandra, one of Maria's closest friends, had no say in the matter once Maria's mother insisted on helping with the usual godmother duties, which quickly became grandmother duties instead. It was bad enough that she and Antonio had even agreed to have a traditional christening in the first place, without her mother taking over and making the whole experience stressful. She was relieved that Antonio didn't hear her mother's judgmental words. Things were already tense between them.

"Mum!" Maria gave her mother an unforgiving glare. "You're going to upset Antonio."

"Like he didn't upset me when he had you 'living in sin'," Mrs Salas continued. "I guess I should count my blessings that he agreed to baptise Thomas in the first place. Everyone was talking about us. I mean, you're having a christening when you *just* got married. You've taken our good name and ..."

"*Mum* ... this isn't the time for this," Maria pleaded. "All the guests are coming out and Auntie Despina is right behind us."

Mrs Salas turned around and managed an agonisingly fake smile. Maria thought that her mother's cheeks would be permanently scarred from the force of it. She had her "party face" on again. She always ensured that she gave her best performance, and she refused to let the rest of the cast and crew ruin it. Maria and Antonio's acting contracts were already being reassessed, because according to the star of the show, they had broken all the rules of tradition once Maria had been *with child* but *with no wedding ring*. Her mother's life was always one extravagant stage performance after another, and she needed plenty of praise and applause from relatives and family friends, especially if they were Greek. Mrs Salas believed Maria's behaviour reflected badly on her, and pressured her daughter to fit into the traditions she found so important. As a result, Maria often felt that she was being forced to run for President of the Hellenic Society, or for a Greek Orthodox sainthood.

"Effie ... it was a lovely christening," she heard Auntie Despina say to her mother as they watched their footing on the steep steps of the Greek Orthodox church that hot summer's afternoon. "It was interesting to see the Catholic ceremony as well. So you're going to a restaurant for the reception now ..."

"Um ... yes, Despina. I wanted to invite all of you, but you see, my daughter and her husband have other ideas. You know how kids are these days. They have their own ideas about everything."

"Well, they were both wonderful ceremonies anyway," Despina continued, glancing over at her husband.

"Thank you," her mother replied, her cheeks almost cracking from her plastered smile.

"See, I told you," she whispered loudly in Maria's ear once Despina and her husband were out of earshot. "You should have invited everyone to the reception afterwards. They think that we don't want to spend money on them."

"What are you talking about? She wasn't upset at all, and what kids are you talking about? Antonio and I are both nearly *thirty*."

"Did you see the way she looked at Spiro? They were upset that they weren't invited."

"She *always* looks at her husband like that. He looks like he's walking with his eyes closed. She probably wanted to wake him up. Anyway, let's just get this day over with already!"

"Why didn't you wear that beige dress I bought for you?" Her mother looked with sudden indignation at her outfit. "How can you wear such a bright-coloured outfit to a christening? Your hair is already so bright. Didn't you see what they were wearing at Prince George's christening?"

Maria pursed her lips. She was so close to losing it. She smiled at some of her guests, and tried desperately to keep the perspiration from ruining her makeup. Sydney was in a heat wave, but her mother's words were making her scalding anger reach volcanic proportions. It was as if lava was running through her veins.

"Again with the dress?" Maria whispered angrily. "You already had a go at me for that ..."

"You really need to grow up and dress your age. You look like you're at that hippie thing ... Wood ... something," her mother continued; her scathing eyes scanning Maria's orange bohemian dress with utter repulsion. Maria felt those hostile, dangerous eyes would fire daggers and tear the dress to shreds.

"Woodstock? I look like I'm at Woodstock? Thank you for the compliment," she replied, tossing her rich, auburn-red hair defiantly as she eyed the photographer, who was organising people so that they moved close together for a shot of the whole group. Maria could feel her mother's disapproval as she smiled at Antonio, moving away from her and closer to him and their baby boy. She looked into Antonio's pleading eyes and his tight jaw. He was onto her. He could sense that her mother was getting to her again.

"Say *haloumi*!" she heard the photographer say.

"*Haloumi*!" the group chorused.

3

Great! That's all I need; a cheesy photographer who thinks Greek-Australians eat nothing but Greek food, she thought to herself.

"Say *dolmades!*" he continued.

"*Dolmades!*"

Nicki straightened her magenta-coloured dress. She had made an effort to wear the brightest colour she could find. She wanted to show how happy she was for her younger sister at the christening of her baby boy — her precious nephew.

"Hey, are you sure you're all right, honey?" her husband Marco asked her as his arm made its way around her waist, pulling her into him.

"Yes, I'm fine. I'm so happy for my little sister. She's come so far in her life. Let's get in the photo. We're going to miss it." Holding Marco's hand and moving him along with her, Nicki gently pushed her way through many relatives and family friends she hadn't seen for years, smiling at them as she passed by. She wanted to be near Maria in the photo.

"Okay, one with your lovely sister and her handsome husband!" the photographer shrilled as Marco placed his arm firmly around Nicki's waist, sneaking an affectionate kiss on her head. Nicki could feel her husband's adoration. She giggled slightly as he whispered into her ear, "Did I tell you how beautiful you look?"

"Hey Marco. Save that for the hotel, okay? Looks like it'll be their turn next ... for a little *bambino*," she heard her cousin, Angelo, call out.

Nicki's smile quickly faded.

"It's okay, Nicki. Don't worry about them," she heard Marco softly whisper.

"Say *nappies!*" screamed the photographer, a little too enthusiastically, and with a click of the camera, Nicki's face gave way to a heavy frown. *Where did Maria find this clown?*

4

she thought. *He must be a replacement. Maria would never intentionally stand for such nonsense.*

The reception was held later that evening at a cosy restaurant by the sea. A relatively small group had joined Maria and Antonio, and was spread out across a few tables. Maria and Antonio shared a table with several close friends and relatives, including Marco and Nicki.

Marco offered Nicki a glass of wine. Nicki looked at Marco in shock, her wide-eyed stare immediately scolding him. Why was he offering her wine when he knew they both had to remain fit and healthy? He knew what was at risk. She could see the pain in his eyes the moment she looked at him. She knew what he was thinking — that it was tough for her; that he wished he could click his fingers and make the pain go away. He was always able to fix any problem. He had learned firsthand from his dad who had worked his way from nothing, arriving in Australia from a village outside of Naples with only a suitcase at the ripe age of sixteen, to buying most of the houses in their street. From his father, he learnt that *nothing is impossible* — you could start with nothing, and with hard work and dedication, you could achieve anything. Marco would repeat this to Nicki often; it was an important part of his childhood. But he couldn't fix this. Their problems weren't just bricks and mortar. Feelings were involved: her dreams — their dreams. She watched as he was just about to pour the wine. *"Marco. What are you doing? You know we shouldn't drink alcohol,"* she whispered into his ear.

"I just thought, one drink won't …" Marco began. Seeing Nicki's concerned expression, he quickly put down the bottle of Riesling and grabbed the sparkling water instead.

"That's better," she said. "We have to be careful. Anyway, I think I'll be the first to congratulate the happy family."

Nicki stood up from her seat. "Congratulations to my sister and her handsome husband. You've made the most adorable baby. I wish nothing but the best for you," she said, her face beaming with pride. She continued her speech, noticing Marco looking at his plate from the corner of her eye. "I'm so proud of how far you've come, and you make the most wonderful parents."

"Honey, I think that you've made your point," Marco said while gently nudging her to sit down.

"It's okay, Marco," Cassandra, Thomas' godmother, softly said from across the table. Nicki watched their private interaction. Cassandra's fiancé, Connor, looked at her with gentle, compassionate eyes. She knew what they were thinking, but knew they both meant well. They were merely concerned.

"Thank you so much, Nicki. I'm sure you'll spoil him rotten," Maria replied, giving her an affectionate smile.

"Nicki!" their mother shouted out from across the long table. "That dress is so beautiful on you. The colour really suits you!"

Maria's jaw dropped. She looked at her mother with unwavering eyes. "You just said that I shouldn't wear bright colours."

Mrs Salas sighed. "Always ready to argue, Maria. Don't you think that the colour suits your sister?"

"Yes, I do but that's not really the point now, is it?"

"Well, you're the mother of the child … it's different and your hair is so bright already."

"Really?" Maria challenged. "I bet if Nicki was christening her … um … I mean …" Maria instinctively looked at her sister.

"It's okay, Maria," Nicki interjected.

"Effie, both my daughters look beautiful. They always do," their father, Mr Salas, interposed, nervously looking at his older daughter.

"Mr Salas is right. You both look beautiful — whether you're wearing bright colours or not! That's what I think anyway. Don't you, Marco?" Antonio smoothly added.

6

"I definitely do," Marco replied from across the table. "We've married the most attractive and intelligent sisters in Sydney," he said, and kissed Nicki on the lips.

Maria and Nicki rolled their eyes. Maria was thankful for Antonio and her dad's save. She had to be careful with what she said to Nicki. "That's laying it a bit thick, don't you think? You're right though, we are a great catch," Maria said, laughing as she wiped a crumb of vanilla cake from Antonio's face.

Marco leaned over and kissed Nicki on the lips again. Nicki met his olive green, determined eyes with her own. She knew that he was trying to display his affection for her. He knew that the day would be emotionally draining, and wanted to provide her with all the support he could. "Why don't we sneak off early? I have something special planned for us back at the hotel," he suggested. "Come on. We don't want to waste the harbour views that came with our hotel room. We'll be back in Melbourne before you know it."

Nicki looked at the kids in the laneway. With one swing of the bat, they all cheered with excitement.

"You're out!" one of the players, a young girl, yelled. A feeling of nostalgia washed over her exhausted body. She couldn't wait to take her heels off. She imagined herself wearing sneakers and playing freely like the kids were doing, with no obligations — just a bat, a ball, and a few laughs amongst good friends. The little girl inside her wanted to come out again. *Life seemed so simple back then*, she thought, sighing heavily. She wondered if she would ever have one of her own, and watch her or him play on the street. Her mind went back to childhood, as she remembered a time when she and Maria used to play out on the street with their friend, Dimity.

"Why can't I have a turn to bat?" she heard ten-year-old Maria in her mind.

"You're too young. This bat's for older kids," Nicki had told her.

"We should have brought the little bat that I still have in the garage, so Maria can have a turn too," Dimity had offered, looking at Maria with regret.

"As if I can't use that bat!" Maria had protested. "I'm probably better at it than both of you."

"Dimity and I need to go and finish our art project, anyway."

"I love art. Can I help you with that then?"

"It's a tapestry. It's hard to make. Maybe when you're older ..."

"It's not fair!" Maria had cried. "No one lets me do anything. Mum tells me to stay with you and you don't let me do anything. When I'm with her, I have to do whatever she tells me to do. When will I do what I want?"

"Don't you have to finish your homework from Greek school?" she had reminded her younger sister.

"It's not fair," Maria had complained. "Why do I have to go to Greek school? You only went for one year. Why are you always allowed to do whatever you want?"

Nicki smiled at the memory as she stepped into their hire car. She turned to look at Marco as he turned on the ignition.

"Why were you offering me wine?" she asked him. "You know that the doctor said we shouldn't ..." She looked into Marco's cautious eyes. "I mean don't you care about our chances? It's like you're giving up. I thought nothing else mattered."

"Of course I haven't given up, Nicki. I will never give up on our family — on us." He leaned over and kissed her on the lips. He then looked at her with intent. Nicki felt his fingers stroking her smooth, perfectly made-up skin. They then worked their way through her mid-length, silky, buttery-blonde hair.

"Let's go. After tonight, you'll never ask me that question again. I have a good feeling."

A glimmer of hope suddenly comforted her heart. They were still on the same page. Everything would be okay. She and Marco would make sure of it.

CHAPTER TWO

Dimity grasped the cricket bat tightly in her hands; the unforgiving sun on her back weighed her down as she practised her swing on the dry grass. Her sun-kissed skin was crying out for moisture, and she knew that she would pay dearly later. The slight redness on her chest already began to sting as she straightened her sun hat. How she wished she had thrown on her kimono wrap on top of her tank top before the damage was done.

"Come on Mum!" Olivia yelled.

Positioning the bat on the ground, Dimity looked from her daughter to her husband, Malcolm, through squinted eyes. Everything seemed hazy as the intense sun cast a bright light in her path. The heat intensified as she waited for the first bowl. Malcolm began to run and with one quick motion the ball came flying towards her. Dimity swung the bat with great force and skill, and with one huge hit, the ball was airborne. Her eyes instantly combed the field, which stretched towards the beach, waiting to see where it would land. A golden retriever began to bark playfully as the ball neared its direction.

"*Wow*!" a few long-haired teenage boys cried out from where they sat on their skateboards on the footpath, looking on. "*Woohoo!*" they called out, whistling and yelling as though they were at the Sydney Cricket Ground.

Samantha, her eldest, ran up to her. "Mum, those boys are cheering for you. They can't believe how good you are. You're a legend, Mum."

"Well, your mum wasn't in the softball team for no reason," Malcolm said with pride. "I take my hat off to you, Madam. You have excelled yourself." He took off his cap, and bowed gracefully.

Dimity began to laugh, and couldn't help but admire Malcolm's athletic physique. He then walked over to her and planted a playful kiss on her head as he hugged her. Then he picked her up by the waist and spun her around as though she was the player of the day.

"Malcolm ... stop! Are you crazy? You know what the boys ..." Before Dimity could finish her sentence, she heard the teenagers whistling.

Olivia appeared beside her sister. "Mum, those boys are whistling at you and Dad."

Malcolm smiled at his daughter and then looked at Dimity. "Relax, Dimity. Maybe I'll teach them a thing or two about romance," Malcolm offered. "The things they see these days ... they wouldn't have a clue ..."

"Okay, now you're making us sound like we're old," Dimity laughed. "Is that how sexy industrial designers are supposed to talk?"

"What's this about sexy interior designers?" Malcolm challenged. "How are they supposed to talk?"

"Well, I'm beginning to forget. I gave up that role a while ago."

"That may be true about the latter part but you definitely didn't give up the sexy part. I know, I have a *feel* for such things, as a designer and most importantly as a husband," he continued, smiling. "Besides, you're always a designer at heart. It's always with you. Seriously Dimity, you're quite the batswoman. I mean, you're exceptionally good."

"It's not just the softball," Dimity responded. "It's all that continuous cricket I used to play with Nicki and Maria in our street when we were kids. We played every day after school. Those were the days. Okay, now I'm really sounding ancient. I guess sport makes me feel like I'm young and free again, and I'm able to keep up with you two," she said, looking at her daughters. "Although, your dad and I still have it going on, even if we're both nearly in our mid-thirties."

"Yeah," Malcolm said. "We're the coolest parents at your school, and don't let anyone tell you otherwise."

Dimity smiled as her daughters rolled their eyes.

"Why don't we go get some fish and chips and eat it at the boat," Malcolm suggested. "I'm sure your mum would love to have a break from the kitchen. She's been cooking so much since we arrived."

"That sounds great. I'll go and put a bottle of Riesling in the fridge," Dimity replied, as they began to pack the cricket gear and shake their beach towels vigorously to rid them of any leftover sand.

Dimity walked back carrying the beach bag. She watched as Malcolm and her daughters raced each other to the main house, each of them carrying something in their hands. Seagulls hovered over them in the hope for food, and the golden retriever joined them, milling about their ankles. She recognised the dog as the neighbours'. They would often see him when they came to visit her parents.

Dimity breathed lightly and contently as she admired her surroundings. The south coast was full of beautiful, crystal clear beaches and was the perfect getaway every summer. The fact that her dad owned a boat was a bonus. It was their family time, away from the clutter, routine and responsibilities that came with raising a family. Dimity breathed in the smell of the ocean. The salt in her hair made it feel rough and wild. She loved that feeling — of traces of sand on her skin, of a sense of true freedom, without worries about perfection or trivialities. It was a nice change. She sighed at the thought that it would be over all too soon.

"Come and grab some salad, Dimity," her mother motioned to her. Dimity grabbed her plate and squeezed between Olivia and Samantha to reach the salad on the table. Malcolm poured wine as the wind began to disturb the corners of the white tablecloth on the small table at the deck of the boat, threatening it and everything upon it.

"I caught a flounder the other day," she heard her father say to Malcolm.

"We'll have to get some fishing done before we leave," Malcolm replied as he made his way down to the kitchen area after noticing Olivia didn't have a fork.

Dimity eyed Malcolm's mobile phone, which was ringing persistently on the table. She hesitantly picked it up. She didn't feel like talking to his work associates. Lately, she'd felt so far removed from the design world — a world she had become so accustomed to and felt so comfortable in. So many years had passed since she severed ties with it.

It wasn't one of Malcolm's work associates calling; it was Sylvia, his mother. Walking hastily towards the kitchen area, she called to her husband from the top of the small, winding stairwell.

"It's your mother!"

"Can you get that, Dimi? I'll be there soon," he called back.

Dimity answered. "Um ... hi ... Sylvia." She would ensure Malcolm had his phone on him next time. "He can't talk right now. Yes, I'm fine. Excuse me? I'm sorry ... I can hardly hear you. It's slightly windy on the boat and everyone is talking so loud. Yes, we're on the boat eating dinner." Feeling every muscle in her body tense, she listened to her mother-in-law's reply. "It's fine! We always love eating on the boat," Dimity continued. "It's near the shore. Yes, we always have life jackets when we take it out to sea. My dad knows all about that!" Dimity rolled her eyes as she spoke. Where was Malcolm? How *long* did it take him to get a fork! She was usually okay with his mother's remarks, but lately, they were beginning to get to her.

"Olivia and Sam are on school holidays. They're only in primary school ... they don't have homework in the holidays. Yes, we're having fish and chips. My mum does eat it every now and then, and other food that isn't organic at times, but I don't think eating healthy food is exactly a bad thing …" Dimity struggled to catch her breath. Her words were, once again, lost on her mother-in-law. She could feel the heat in her face as her anger began to surface. She tried to steady her breathing. She felt like she was drowning; like she had dived into rough waters — head first — with no life jacket. A feeling of relief washed over her as soon as she saw Malcolm climbing up from the stairwell.

"Anyway, bye! I have to go. Malcolm's here." Malcolm grabbed the phone and gave her a reassuring smile.

Thank God he'd arrived before she really lost it. He had rescued her once again — as he always did when it came to his mother's interfering ways.

"Yeah, the girls are having the time of their lives, as usual. They're so lucky to be able to spend most of the holidays here. They absolutely love it, and I can't believe how much salad they're eating with their mains. Mrs McKenzie is quite the healthy cook."

Dimity looked at Malcolm as he spoke; his wavy, almost black hair slightly covered his eyes as he leaned over the table to pour the rest of the wine. Her chivalrous husband always thought of her. She gave her parents a knowing smile. They smiled back. Her dad comically raised his hands as though he was in shock. Malcolm also smiled, noticing Mr McKenzie's antics as he continued to speak to his mother. He had become part of her family. He was okay with it all. He knew that his mother would often go too far, and was happy to oblige in taking her down from her high horse.

"Thanks," she said when he hung up. "You're off the hook. You managed to arrive just in time." She planted a kiss on his lips when her parents weren't looking. She knew Malcolm would have no hesitation in displaying affection in front of her parents, but it was a bit too much for her comfort. She didn't want to entice him. She couldn't control him at times. Dimity thought it must be such a relief to spend time with her carefree parents. In his eyes, Mr and

14

Mrs McKenzie were practically hippies — an easy assumption to make when comparing them to his parents, the uptight and righteous Mr and Mrs Stewart.

Later that evening, Dimity leaned on Malcolm's chest after taking another sip of wine. The button of his white linen shirt was undone and she could feel his skin on her face. The smell of coconut-scented sunscreen lingered on it. They had taken the rest of the wine and sat by the beach that evening on the jeep while her parents got the girls ready for bed. It was their quiet time.

A chorus of cicadas pierced Dimity's eardrums as they began their nightly performance. The continuous singing quickly merged with the sound of the waves crashing to the shore, creating a soothing atmosphere.

"Stefano called earlier. He wanted to fill me in on the industrial design conference in Munich later on this month," Malcolm said. "There's also the Amsterdam conference in July … Or is it an exhibition? I'll have to look it up …"

Dimity felt her chest tighten. "Malcolm, let's just enjoy the view," she quickly suggested. She breathed in the salty breeze as she leaned on his chest again.

"You're right! I love that we're able to have our 'alone' time." He stroked her face, pushing back her wind-blown beach hair, and kissed her gently on the lips. "You're so cute … all messy and wild-looking."

"Look!" Dimity exclaimed. "There's a stray kitten near the jetty. Poor thing. Maybe we should give it some sorbet," she suggested, her heart melting as she picked up the sorbet that she had placed beside her, scraping the last of it from the dessert glass with her spoon.

"Dimi … you can't save every animal, or every person that needs help. I mean, you nearly made me stop to make sure that possum was okay on the freeway. You're too sweet for your own good, you know that? How could I not love that about you, though?" He kissed her on the lips again.

"Besides, it seems that someone has beat you to it," he said, looking at a family tending to the kitten.

Dimity smiled at him. She then looked at the stray kitten. He was right. She couldn't save every animal or person that was neglected. But she couldn't help it; it was in her nature. Growing up, her father always gave free legal aid to many clients who couldn't afford it. Dimity remembered one particular client who had a cat — one that she definitely couldn't feed herself. As a ten-year-old, Dimity had figured that the woman didn't even have money to feed herself. She looked so lost — so sad and so lonely. She lived with her children not far from Dimity and her family, and she often saw her walking through the neighbourhood with a look of dejection and sadness upon her face. One evening, Dimity had overheard her father telling her mother that the woman's husband had left her and she had no one to turn to. He had also left her with a huge debt to pay off. The woman hadn't worked for years and she had no idea how she would look after herself and her children.

The next day, Dimity had walked over to the woman's house, and offered her all the money she had saved in her piggy bank. The woman smiled at her with tearful eyes, and patted Dimity's shiny hair.

"Thank you dear but I don't need money right now," the woman had told her. "Keep it and buy something special for yourself. Money is important … but it's belonging somewhere that makes people happy. Feeling loved and appreciated can make a person feel like they have all the money in the world, and you definitely know how to make someone feel that. You've managed to bring a smile to my face with your kind gesture. Don't ever lose your humanity."

Dimity felt a tear stream down her face at the memory.

"We should have some more sorbet. What do you think?" she asked Malcolm, coming out of her momentary trance and surreptitiously wiping away the tear. She stood up from the jeep to reach for it in the esky.

16

"Sure. Why not?" Dimity could feel his eyes combing her body. He stroked her waist with his hand as she moved towards the esky.

She could feel Malcolm's eyes looking at her with admiration. She knew he wanted her to feel loved and appreciated. He had been going from one conference to another lately, always far from her and the girls. She didn't want to remind him that he had also mentioned something about a conference in Amsterdam in July. She didn't want to focus on that now. She would take one overseas trip at a time. His career was so demanding. They were lucky if they got to see each other at all during the week, and needed this time alone.

Dimity handed Malcolm his dessert glass, refilled with sorbet. The wind caused havoc with her hair as she tried to take a bite. Leaning on his chest again, she sighed contently. Feeling safe in his arms, she repressed the slight melancholic feeling that threatened her peaceful state. She tilted her head up and looked up at his face.

"I love you, Malcolm," she said.

Malcolm smiled at her. "What brought this on?" He kissed her on the head as she nestled against his shoulder.

"I don't know … I feel so happy being here with you right now … with you … and with the girls. It was such a perfect day. Let's promise each other that we won't stop having moments like this, okay?" Dimity looked into Malcolm's searching eyes.

"It's okay Dimi … that's all we need really, isn't it?" he said, stroking her hair. "We just need each other and everything else will fall into place. I love you Dimi … so much. Sometimes I think I'm the luckiest man alive."

CHAPTER THREE

Six Months Later

"You know, you could stand to lose a few kilos," Dimity blurted out. The words instantly sliced the air of the already cold atmosphere. She couldn't stop herself, even after seeing her mother-in-law's horrified expression. "I mean, the food you cook isn't exactly healthy. It's full of butter, and don't get me started on the amount of oil, not to mention the white rice and pasta which feature so heavily in most of your meals."

As confident as she appeared on the outside, Dimity was a mess on the inside. She didn't know what to do or say next as she stood at the end of the dining table that she had taken particular care to decorate, in order to impress her guests, who were all now looking at her in shock. She didn't dare look at Malcolm.

A minute must have surely passed — yet not one word from anyone. Dimity couldn't take it anymore. She had to do something. She was positive everyone thought she had lost her mind. She couldn't stand the awkward silence any more. Gaining an ounce of strength, she finally spoke.

"Anyone for dessert?" she managed.

Everyone sat staring at their plates. She cast her eyes around the table and met Malcolm's. He was the only one looking at her. His jaw was tight. His blue eyes seemed cold and distant. After meeting her gaze, he too looked down at his plate with disappointment on his face.

"We bought a delicious cheesecake from the patisserie down the road," Dimity continued defiantly, knowing her mother-in-law would frown at the fact that she didn't make it herself.

She made her way to the kitchen, still feeling the stares of the five shocked people in the dining room, which included Malcolm's parents Sylvia and Stanley, his younger brother Alex and his Aunt Marianne. Her legs trembled as she stood behind the bench in her designer kitchen. She was ready to continue with the third act of the evening. She was surprised she was able to walk at all. Usually, she would feel relieved by dessert stage, knowing that the end of the evening was imminent, and applauding herself for nearly surviving yet another dinner with guests she forced herself to tolerate. Whenever they were in Sydney, they always expected to be invited for dinner.

Dimity felt a familiar hand on her shoulder. Malcolm stood next to her, looking at her inquisitively for a second before helping her with the dessert plates. When she looked into his confused eyes she felt sorry for him.

"Who wants coffee?" he called out to the guests, who had overcome much of their shock and were now chatting again, cautiously.

Surprisingly, Dimity began to feel empowered as she walked back into the dining room, staring at them as she did so. She suddenly felt that she was the teacher and they were her nervous students. They anxiously waited for her to hand out the dessert plates, the same way a teacher would hand out papers in an unexpected quiz. *They definitely look unprepared,* she thought. She had really surprised them. She wondered if they would hang around to eat the cheesecake.

"Well, I could do with a slice," Alex said wickedly, and slightly too emphatically, eyeing his mother as he spoke. "Pass me a slab, Dimity. I could stand to put on a few kilos. I've been *too* healthy lately — no white bread or white rice for me. I'm actually eating quinoa. It's actually a lot healthier than rice, even than couscous. Barley is okay too. You know what quinoa is, Mum, don't you? Most of the celebrities eat it."

Alex was always ready to try and get a reaction from his mother. Even though he was twenty-four, he still acted like a cheeky eighteen-year-old. He was intuitive, though, and to Dimity it felt good to have an ally sitting across from her.

Although the words had come out of Alex's mouth, her mother-in-law was glaring at *her*.

"That's it! I've had enough," cried Sylvia. "I can't breathe. Where are my pills? I need my pills. My blood pressure has gone up." She began to frantically search her bag. "Stanley!" she commanded her husband. "Please, help me find my pills." She thrust her bag towards him, her face flushed.

"All right, don't panic Sylvia. They're in here somewhere." Stanley half-heartedly looked for the pills, sorting through the various bits and bobs in the voluminous handbag.

"Quick, get her some water!" Her loyal sister Marianne was almost hysterical. "Are you okay? Don't worry, we'll get you back to the house. Maybe it's the food you ate. She's not allowed to eat too much salt ..." Aunt Marianne instantly glared at Dimity, "... or be under any stress for that matter."

Malcolm quickly rushed to his mother's side, helping his father look for the pills. Everyone looked on with grave concern — everyone, that is, except for Dimity. She was left standing alone, looking guilty, dessert knife in hand. She was used to feeling alone lately. Dimity caught a glimpse of herself in the shiny tiles of her designer kitchen, dressed in her designer cocktail dress and expensive mid-heels, still holding the dessert knife. She felt like everyone was avoiding looking at her. She looked guilty and she *was* guilty, knowing her words would have instantly attacked her mother-in-law like a stab to the heart. Funnily enough, she didn't care what they all thought of her at that moment. The fear had subsided. The only thing that hurt her was that Malcolm had left her to side with them, *again*. When did he stop defending her? Just a few months ago, he would have rushed to *her* side.

"Dimity, *please*, bring her some water!"

Malcolm's accusing tone instantly brought her back from the trance into which she had fallen. He looked out of place amongst the guests, who, apart from Alex, she found dull and uninspiring. Malcolm was sophisticated in a rugged, cool way. He was also very intelligent, not to mention creative and handsome. In a daze, she poured some water from the filter, suddenly worried if the sudden health scare wasn't an act, as she often thought it was. A "boy cried wolf" scenario ran through her mind as she hurriedly handed her mother-in-law the water. Sylvia took it from her hesitantly and cautiously.

"Don't worry, Mum. It's not poison," Alex said, smiling at Dimity.

"Perhaps you should lie down on the couch," Dimity found herself suggesting. She was back to being the accommodating, dutiful host and daughter-in-law. She began to sense that she had gone too far when she caught Malcolm's questioning gaze. He really looked confused and hurt.

"That couch isn't comfortable. I need to go home. I can't breathe here. I need some air," Sylvia gasped.

"It's ergonomically designed," Dimity replied, admiring their purchase, which had been shipped from a Melbourne studio to their home in the affluent eastern Sydney suburb of Rose Bay. The contemporary design of the couch worked beautifully with décor in the rest of the house.

"*That* thing? A park bench looks more comfortable than *that*. Malcolm, please drive me home. I'm sure you didn't choose or design that. Your taste always puts comfort first. It's a lot less presumptuous. You really are a great designer. Your father and I are so proud of what you've accomplished. This beautiful house is proof of how far you've come," she stated in a matter of fact way.

Dimity couldn't believe her audacity. She had almost fallen for it this time. She definitely wasn't short of breath when delivering such well-thought-out and heavy praise for her son, and ensuring that Dimity's contributions were not at all mentioned. She was thinking very clearly, Dimity thought; in fact, *too* clearly.

"Well, you seem to be feeling better!" Dimity was fuelled by anger once again.

"What are you talking about? Look at how pale she looks. In fact, she's trembling all over," Aunt Marianne retorted. "Sylvia, don't worry, I'll call one of the girls to drive you and Stan back to the house. They both live close by anyway."

"No, no, I don't want to bother your girls. They're busy with their jobs and their own lives. I'm sure they're all extremely busy. Malcolm will take me home."

Dimity couldn't believe it. Sylvia knew that he was catching an early plane for Amsterdam the next day for the industrial design conference and exhibition.

"I need to help Dimi clean up. Is it okay if Alex takes you?" Malcolm queried.

Alex shrugged. "Sorry bro, I've got the bike today."

"Malcolm is catching an early flight tomorrow. He has to finish packing and also spend time with the girls before he leaves!" Dimity exclaimed. "Anyway, how much did you drink?" She looked at Malcolm, hoping that he would pick up on her cue, even though she knew that he only had one glass of wine.

Aunt Marianne eyed the kitchen and then looked at Dimity. "Didn't Malcolm just get you a new German-designed dishwasher?"

"I'll take you home. I can take Aunt Marianne home too. It's on the way anyway," Malcolm offered. "I've only had one glass of wine. I'm not over the limit. That's okay with you, isn't it Dimi?"

Before she could answer, he headed to the hallway to grab his coat.

"*Dishwasher?*" her father-in-law questioned abruptly. "You don't need a *dishwasher*. You've got two grown *girls* that can

22

help you. It's good for them to start knowing their way around the kitchen from a young age. Where are those two anyway? We haven't seen them for a while. They just ate and then disappeared."

"They're on the computer. Sam is helping Olivia with her proj …"

"Again on the computer? It's not good for them to be stuck all day on the computer. Kids these days have no social skills."

"They have a project to complete, and exams to study for." Dimity insisted on being heard — to no avail.

Her father-in-law continued his rant. "It's also not polite to just leave the dinner table like that. You really need to teach them …"

"Here's your coat, Stan. Thanks for coming over." Dimity smiled between gritted teeth as she heard Malcolm approaching.

"Finally found my keys," he said, innocently. He'd missed out on hearing his father criticise his daughters yet again, and his outdated beliefs about gender roles.

"Dimity, dinner was great as always. You've excelled yourself again," Alex said in a loud voice. "I'm not just referring to the food," he whispered in her ear. "Tell that uptight brother of mine to chill. He'll give industrial design a bad name. It's supposed to be a cool job."

"Thanks Alex, I'm glad you enjoyed yourself," Dimity replied, giving him an appreciative smile.

Dimity rushed them out before they could say anything else, avoiding Malcolm's gaze as she did so.

The door finally closed, the same way the curtains would at the end of a dramatic play. It was quiet in the space of a minute, except for some murmuring coming from Olivia's bedroom. The girls hadn't come out to say goodbye to the guests, and Dimity had chosen to ignore her father-in-law's demands, conveniently neglecting to tell them that everyone was leaving. She looked at the kitchen. Plates and half-filled glasses were all over the kitchen bench. She walked over to the sink, ready to commence the task of tidying up, which she usually enjoyed, finding a satisfaction in placing things where they belonged, and relishing the time when things went back to normal and the house was once again peaceful. She usually enjoyed the process, but she wasn't in the mood that night. She angrily stacked the dirty plates and, with one motion, tossed them into the sink. She then went to her bedroom and threw herself onto the bed. She buried her face under the pillow and screamed. Then she began to sob indulgently. She sobbed for a while. She felt like she was a fifteen-year-old girl again, the last time she had felt so hurt about life and her circumstances.

CHAPTER FOUR

Nicki felt as if she was drowning in tears as she sat on her bed, staring at Marco in disbelief, a nagging angst beating deep within her chest. Lately, she felt like the more she tried to swim to shore, the more the waves knocked her back, tumbling her further down into the deep.

She looked at Marco. "What are you saying exactly? What do you mean, 'It's all right'? It's not all right. Nothing will be okay if we don't continue trying …" Nicki hugged her waist tightly, her robe blanketing her fragile, quivering body. The slightly drawn curtains revealed a ray of mid-morning sunlight, which illuminated part of their bedroom that Sunday morning.

"What do you want from me, Nicki?"

"*What do I want* from you? What sort of question is that? You know what I want from you. How could you ask such a thing?"

"We're going around in circles. It's all we talk about … all we think about. Don't you see, our life has become about what we don't have?"

Nicki sat at the end of the bed, and hugged her robe even more tightly. Its warmth made her feel safe. Her heart began to ache again. She felt a pain in the pit of her stomach.

"It's okay, Nicki. It'll be okay."

"I know it will be okay. Why do you keep saying that? It's as though you're giving up." Nicki knew she was talking in circles. Her eyes were blurry, and her tears stung her face. Nothing looked clear anymore. Half the time, she felt that she was walking with her eyes closed. It was as though her thoughts had no guidance; they were chaotic; anarchical.

"Nicki, I haven't given up for years. Especially these last few months; we've become consumed with it. I'm just saying we need to step back and just have some fun. I mean,

25

don't you see, by not giving up, you're giving up on *us*. I'm tired, Nicki. We don't even know what we're doing anymore … how to talk to each other. You've forgotten who you are; what we are together. I mean, when was the last time we went out and had some fun?"

"*Fun!* Is that all you can think of? How to have fun? Do you think I'm not tired? I'm emotionally drained, but I'm not giving up. I'm never going to give up on our dream."

Nicki could feel her tears forming again quickly. She couldn't remember a day in the last few months she hadn't cried. She looked into Marco's olive green eyes. They looked almost child-like; vulnerable. She couldn't help him. She had nothing to offer him. He was right. She didn't even know who she was anymore, or who they were as a couple.

"So what do you want from me, Marco? You want me to go out and dance or eat at a fancy restaurant and pretend everything is okay? Is that what you want? Well, I'm sorry, but I can't do that. Nothing will make me forget; nothing will rid me of this pain I carry with me every single day. *You're* tired? *I'm* tired. My body knows how tired I am. My heart feels as though it'll explode."

Nicki could feel his confused, defeated stare from across the bed. She felt so fragile, as though she would break at any moment. Marco walked over to her and sat next to her. "Nicki, it will be okay. You're going to make yourself sick, and then what?"

"Stop it! Stop saying that it's going to be okay. What are you really saying with that? It's as though you're giving up. I'm never going to give up. Do you hear me? *Never* ever … I'm *never* going to give up on our child."

He began to stroke her hair, as he had so many times before, when she needed comforting, and when they were happy — with each other, and with their life. Nicki felt the strength of his arms as he held her close.

"We'll get through this. We just forgot who we are together; how we work. We just need to give it a break for a while … not talk about it … just let it come naturally. We need to see things more clearly."

"*What?*" Nicki shrieked.

She looked into Marco's hurt eyes as she abruptly pulled away from him. The look in his eyes was one she didn't recognise. It tore right through her heart — the look of defeat. He *was* giving up. He was giving up on their plan. She was losing him. She finally spoke. "I see things clearly. I see that you would rather think of other things than the one thing that I always wanted, that would bring so much joy into my life … because you've obviously failed at that task," Nicki said, shaking all over. She could see the hurt on her husband's face, and she could feel vindictiveness consume her.

"Nicki, I didn't say that," Marco placed his hand on Nicki's heavy shoulder. He had faced many of her meltdowns and the insults that marked them. That's what she would call them — meltdowns — every time she apologised later, when he would eventually give her the hope that she needed. Time would give her hope, and they would be on the same page again. But it felt different this time. She couldn't breathe. His eyes were betraying her; they revealed the decision he had made — the decision he had made without her. It was too much. She didn't want to hear another word from him. "Get your hands off from me!" she screamed.

"Nicki … calm down!"

"Stop telling me what to do, or how I should feel! You're just like the rest of them. 'Don't worry, you'll have a baby girl or boy in no time.' 'Keep practising. You'll get it right, you're both still young.' Here's a good one. I've heard this so many times: 'Just enjoy your freedom while you can. Once you have a kid, you'll be wishing for the days when you were single.' 'It will happen — these things usually happen when you least expect it.' Well, I'm sick of it. I'm sick of the looks, the whispering, the pity, the tip-toeing

27

around the subject. I mean, do you notice the silence that suddenly descends upon the room when we enter, thinking they've fooled us, that they weren't just sharing baby photos and gushing over how cute their kids are? Well, if anyone is tired of it all, it's me. I thought you were on the same page, but you're obviously not. You're just like the rest of them. The way you look at me, the pity in your eyes. I've had as much as I can take. You want to give up on our dream. You're wrong Marco — for me, giving up on the one thing I wanted … *that's* giving up on us. I want out of this *circle*. You can go and have your fun — without me. I apologise for ruining your life with my problems. Yes, *my problems* because you obviously don't care — I'm beginning to think that you never did."

"Nicki, where are you going?" he called out, as she leapt up from the bed and headed toward the door.

"It's over, Marco. Whatever this is — I can't do it anymore. It's over. It was over a long time ago, when you began to look at me the way you're looking at me now — the way everyone looks at me!"

Feeling his confused stare upon her, she stormed out of their bedroom, shooting him one final glance. He was sitting on the bed with his face in his hands. He didn't run after her this time. She knew he wouldn't. She knew that he was out of words; he didn't know what to say to make her feel better. He didn't know how to make himself feel better — to fill the void in his heart. She saw the tears stream down his cheeks through his thick, unkempt brown hair that had fallen forward, partially concealing his unshaved face. Nicki knew what he was thinking: this was the first time in his adult life when he truly believed he couldn't fix things. Even the complex renovation projects he worked on were never too much for him, the always confident housing project manager. But the cracks were too deep in their domestic project; its walls were weak, it had too many leaks, and it was all wired wrong. Nicki knew that her soulmate had given up on them, and wondered if their foundations had ever been strong.

She picked up the pace and stormed out of the house. She needed to breathe again — to feel again. She couldn't rely on him anymore. She had been so hopeful that it would be their year — their turn — but it had been six months since Christmas already, when her nephew had been christened. How many more months and years would she spend waiting? She knew that Marco was right, and that's why she didn't want to look at him anymore. All they were now to each other was a constant reminder of what they couldn't have together — what they may never have together.

She suddenly heard the laughter of children from the house next door. Nicki could smell sweet red capsicum cooking on the grill. *Another Sunday barbecue,* she thought. The grandparents were probably visiting again. Her eyes rested on the front porch of their own Edwardian house. It had so much character and old world charm. Nicki had thought it was the most romantic house she had ever seen. Their real estate agent had told them they were lucky to have purchased it for the price that they did. It was close to St Kilda beach, and the local primary school was also nearby. Marco had known it was a gem; his father had taught him well about investing for the future. She had felt so lucky to be with someone so savvy. They had so many dreams and hopes for their life together in their romantic house.

"Wow, we finally got it? You mean it's actually ours?" Nicki had exalted. "This is the perfect house for us Marco, and it's ours. Can you imagine, living near the beach, dropping off our kids at school … I mean it's a ten-minute walk."

"It's also full double brick. You know what? This calls for a celebration," he had said. "Remember that Italian restaurant that had you beaming with memories of our wedding, that one in the beautiful little town in Tuscany, with the wishing well?"

"Yes?" she had replied, her heart racing with anticipation.

"Perhaps you should close your eyes," he had said as he slowly guided her through the entrance of the house towards the garden.

"Open your eyes," he had exclaimed.

Nicki opened her eyes, her breath catching in delight. "It's a wishing well! Just like at that restaurant; just like the one at our wedding!" she had cried, jumping with joy, wrapping her arms around him. "How did you have time to organise this?"

"I told you if you married me, your life would be full of surprises," he had said, his olive skin glowing under the patio lights, his eyes filled with pride. "Together we'll make sure this house is full of surprises and sweet, beautiful memories," he had said as he handed her a gold coin. "This I promise you."

"What's this?" she had asked.

"It's a special coin ... you know ... wishing wells and coins tend to go together? You can be the first to make a wish. So, go on Nicki, make a wish," he had continued playfully, his eyes fierce with ambition, hope and conviction.

"I have three wishes. Is that okay with this one special coin?" she had asked, smiling.

"Anything is possible Nicki, that's what I've learned in life. Nothing is impossible. If you want something, you work at it and your wishes will be granted," he had said as he twirled her around and then grabbed her in his toned arms, kissing her passionately.

She looked at the house — *their home*. It had appreciated greatly since then; it *was* a good investment, for the future, the one that was supposed to include laughter from *three* cute ... *No ... I can't do this anymore*, she told herself. She wiped away yet another tear, and quickly made her way back into the house. She didn't want to have to rescue another ball, and pass it over any neighbour's fence *again*. The young family was always playing a game of soccer that usually spilled out into the street. She didn't want to pass back a Frisbee, or a ball, or a balloon or any toy — only if it was to pass it back to her little ... She couldn't think like that anymore. She had to make plans.

CHAPTER FIVE

The sun burned the cement underneath Dimity's sneakers. She could feel the heat on her back becoming more intense, but she refused to move from the bench upon which she had decided to sit almost an hour earlier that Sunday morning in July. Her white linen shirt and orange and beige-coloured sun hat did their best to shield her from its ferocity, but they were no match for its strong rays. Despite this, Dimity refused to move. She was too engrossed in the activity around her. She felt as though she was a spectator and she liked the sense of carefreeness that came from watching something exciting and new. She was witnessing a spectacle she hadn't seen for a long time from behind the lenses of her designer sunglasses, right from the comfort of a park bench — and a surprisingly comfortable one at that.

There were people laughing, sitting in the sun, eating, drinking, catching up, and just simply being there — being present. Others were in the Bavarian Club bistro, while the rest were out enjoying the sudden and unusually warm winter weather. They looked relaxed and content. At times, Dimity would hear some German words thrown into a conversation. Most of the people had German accents. From what she could make out, it was some sort of get together that perhaps occurred consistently, at a given time, just for the simple reason of catching up with friends and loved ones. She had become part of it — not by invitation, but by chance.

After having dropped off the girls at yet another birthday party at one of their friend's houses on the other side of the large park, she had decided to take a stroll and think in solitude, when she stumbled upon the bench situated right outside the Bavarian Club. Its patrons were spilling out into the park. At first, she didn't know if she should be there —

if it was a private function —but no one seemed to mind, so she just sat and observed, instantly drawn into the soothing ambiance. *How can people be so mellow?* she wondered. It almost looked like a hippie festival from the 70s, as people were mostly dressed in relaxed jeans, floral dresses or loose-fitting shirts. Probably, however, there were no hallucinogens involved. She had never seen people so present, centred and engaged in what they were doing in the moment. People smiled at her as they passed her. Strangely, she felt that she belonged there. She wanted to belong there. It was such a carefree, kind, and festive atmosphere — a huge contrast to the atmosphere the night before.

The previous night was a surprise even to Dimity. She hadn't planned on attacking her mother-in-law to that degree, but even *she* had her limits. The evening had started pleasantly enough. Dimity tolerated Sylvia's "observations", as she often did. She had tolerated her comment that her salad had too much balsamic vinegar. Then, as she had run her fingers through her hair in frustration, she had endured Sylvia's comment that she had a grey strand hidden amongst the other long, dark, ash-brown ones, and that she, with her freshly dyed almost black hair, and her sister, Marianne, who sat in her seat proudly with her freshly dyed blonde hair, hardly had any. Dimity's explanation that the ash tint in her hair was intentional was, of course, ignored. Apparently they never coloured their hair and they were both well into their sixties. She let that one slide too. *They must be chameleons*, Dimity had thought to herself, as their hair colour seemed to "naturally" change every time she saw them.

She didn't flinch at all when Sylvia told her that she needed to feed her daughters more "real, proper food". She kept it together even when Sylvia told her that her friend's daughter-in-law apparently solely looked after her kids, cooked every meal, worked, and even managed to paint her house in its entirety — without her husband's help — and that she managed to make a mosaic coffee table as well, because that was how *amazing* she was! Dimity had nearly lost it then, but simply retorted with, "She did all those things at the same time? That *is* amazing!" Sylvia, of course, had no response. Dimity had still kept her cool. *They'll only be in Sydney for a while*, she had told herself. *They'll be back in Brisbane soon. At least they have their own property in Sydney and aren't staying with us*, she had reassured herself. But she couldn't control herself any longer. She couldn't control herself when she heard the words that followed.

"Is this another one of your mum's recipes? It looks like it is. No wonder you and your sisters are obsessed with organic this and that. You know, she shouldn't worry so much about how slim she is at her age. It can age you. My face hardly has any wrinkles and your mother is younger than me and …"

That's when it happened; when Dimity couldn't sit idly and ignore another cruel remark aimed at not just her — but her mother! The thing that hurt the most though was the fact that Malcolm didn't say anything. He just went along with his mother's rudeness as though it was okay. Why did he think *she* was the one that was out of line? Why didn't he defend her the way he used to? It was only six months since their holiday on the south coast. The last few months had been crazy. Malcolm was the busiest he had been in a long time — his brand had become huge; he always had new clients to meet; he was always in demand.

When he had come home later that evening, she was still in bed. She could hear him loading the dishwasher, and she could also hear him tidying up the kitchen. She heard him enter their bedroom but she pretended to be fast asleep, even when he had kissed her on the cheek. She felt too let down by him. In the morning, she had helped him with some last minute packing, without uttering a word. They had said their goodbyes half-heartedly, repressing what they really wanted to say.

"Like I've said before, you could join me on these trips …" he began, but stopped when she had digressed and alerted him of the time, urging him to leave before he missed his flight.

The first time they had laid eyes on each other was so precious — so romantic. Dimity had just started working at an interior design firm as an assistant. Her role entailed researching and placing orders for the head interior designer, for homewares, lamps, artwork, paintings, rugs, and furniture. Casually perusing through one of the many company interior design magazines at her desk one day during her lunch hour, her eyes were caught suddenly by an article featuring a group of up-and-coming, young industrial designers, under the caption, "The Young and the Creative". They were posing suavely next to their award-winning pieces. She was immediately drawn to one of the designers, to his smile and his kind, sexy, dark blue eyes. He looked hungry, driven, and so handsome. He also looked so proud of his achievements. He was sitting on a contemporary timber side table; one leg elongated, while the other pointed inward. He had one hand on the table, as though he was caressing the fine quality of the wood, appreciating its raw beauty.

The article had mentioned that he was twenty-five-year-old Malcolm Stewart, and that he was one of the new industrial designers to look out for. Some of his designs were being displayed in the "Young Designer" exhibition in Amsterdam, where he had spent his last year working with internationally renowned industrial designers. It also mentioned that he worked with environmentally friendly, renewable materials, and tried new innovative processes that were pro-conservation. The more she read, the more she wanted to know. She was twenty-two-years-old, and had just completed her degree in interior design. She had willingly worked long hours to pursue her dream of working as a designer and, one day, to be involved in projects with some of the world's best hotels and restaurants. Her heart had raced as she read the article. She felt inspired, and sheer jubilation at the realisation that she was working in an industry with such creative people — true artists.

"There are some great new industrial designers coming out of Australia in that magazine," said Meagan Watson, head designer and Dimity's manager at the time. "They're true inspirations. That Malcolm Stewart guy is really innovative. He won an award in Amsterdam recently."

"Yes, he sounds really talented. They all do. I mean some of these pieces are really bold," Dimity had responded, feeling slightly embarrassed that she had also been impressed not only by the designs, but also by one of their creators.

"That's what makes them stand out from the rest — they're unique products that challenge old conventions and old methods of design. The industry is really seeking unorthodox and daring new pieces right now, more than ever."

That same afternoon, after Dimity had placed an order for a Moroccan dining table for a client's executive apartment, Susan, another designer from the team, had called out from her desk. "Dimity, Meagan needs you to go to one of the studios nearby and take a look at the designs. She wants you to find out all you can about them and tell her your thoughts. The new client is really keen to have something really contemporary. He's into the Australian made products and is looking for something new." Susan walked to Dimity's desk and handed her a slip of paper. "Here's the address. Thanks! I've got a four o'clock, and have to run." She had briskly made her way to the lifts before Dimity could ask any questions.

Some time later, Dimity had arrived at the address and opened the glass entry door of the furniture and lighting studio. As she had cautiously stepped in, her eyes scanned the small studio. She noticed some really exciting pieces. As she walked over to a cool and fun looking sun-bed, a familiar table caught her eye. It looked exactly like the table in the magazine. It *was* the table from the magazine! It was the table from that designer, Malcolm Stew …

"Oh hi, sorry I didn't see you there," were his first words. "I was at the back working on one of my latest projects." He had then taken a few steps closer to her. "So I see you're looking at that table," he had continued, before looking straight into her eyes.

Dimity had been speechless. His eyes were a deeper blue in real life. They were mysterious, seductive. She had found herself staring at him. She wasn't prepared to meet such a handsome, cool designer. She hadn't even freshened up that afternoon. Did she even have any lipstick on? She always wore her dark fuchsia lipstick back then; it would always bring out the colour in her pale green eyes, and do wonders for her honey complexion.

"Yes, I've seen it before … I mean I recognise it from the magazine," she had responded self-consciously.

She had taken another glance at the table, not having been daring enough to continue looking up into his eyes. He must have been over six-feet-tall, she had speculated, as she had to look up at him even in her mid-heeled boots, which added a few inches to her five-foot-eight stature. He had looked so cool and confident. He was wearing denim jeans, but not just any denim; the designer denim that really cool people wore. He also had a t-shirt on with some message on it about art, and a loose shirt thrown on top, just to add to the element of coolness. Dimity was so glad she had chosen to wear her black velvet jacket on top of her floral dress. Together with her ankle boots, she coincidentally also looked really hip.

"Oh, you must be talking about the article where I'm portrayed as this really happening, new designer. Yeah, they wanted me to lie down on a few of these tables lined up together, like I'm a super model. They had to settle for what they got — me sitting down looking really thoughtful."

"Well, I thought you looked really … I mean, the photo is really professional," she had responded, smiling awkwardly.

"Well, thank you," he had said, giving her the most friendly and beautiful smile she had ever seen.

Dimity had glowed in the warmth of that smile. "I'm here to look at some of your work. I work for an interior design firm just a few streets away from here and one of the clients wants something completely new," she said. "Oh … and my name is Dimity."

"Well, in that case, my name is Malcolm," he had said as he reached out for a handshake.

"I know," she had quickly responded, instantly feeling the cool, firm grip of his masculine hand.

"Oh … from the magazine, that's right," he had said as he looked at her with intent. There was something in his eyes, something that had made Dimity feel close to him.

"I hope it wasn't too difficult to find this place. I've just opened the studio and I haven't had a chance to put a sign up with my name yet. I know, it's not really business savvy of me. What can I say? I'm a designer, not a business man."

"No, it wasn't too difficult," she had replied, wishing that he did have a sign with his name on it, as she would have been more prepared. Susan hadn't even written his name on the note she had handed to her. She really wished she had re-applied her lipstick. "Anyway, if it's all right with you, I'll just take a look at some of your work," she had said, taking on a professional air.

"Sure, I'd be honoured," he had responded, that warm smile appearing on his face again. "How about I grab two coffees from across the road and we can take it from there?"

"Sure, that sounds great," Dimity had replied, elated.

It had turned out to be more than great. They talked for hours in his studio, and then at a hip restaurant close by. Dimity hadn't been able to stop smiling. She couldn't help herself when she was drawn to someone. She found it hard to not be friendly, and to remain distant. It had been a lot more difficult with Malcolm. She knew that she was being way too friendly for a work meeting. Dimity also knew from that night, that Malcolm Stewart was not only an up-and-coming industrial designer, but everything she wanted in a man.

"Hi, so what part of Germany are you from?"

"Excuse me?"

"Which part of Germany are you from … or is it Austria?"

Dimity finally snapped out of her trance. She looked at the tall, young man who was standing in front of her awaiting her response.

"I'm from Dusseldorf," he said.

"Um … I'm not actually from Germany … or Austria," Dimity said awkwardly. "I just went for a walk and I just decided to … um … is this a private function?"

"No, well, not really. You're free to stay. A lot us meet here on Sunday. Some just moved from Germany to Australia and don't know that many people. I guess it's a way to help each other out, make some connections, you know, and feel included."

"Oh … that's really noble! People need that in life. They need to feel like they're part of something …" Dimity said, feeling each word.

"Anyway, do you want to join us for some food and beer? It's such a warm day. Everyone's coming out to enjoy the hot weather while it lasts. I guess we could thank global warming for that."

"Oh, no … thanks, but I have to pick up my daughters from a party. My husband's on his way to Amsterdam and there's so much I have to do …" Dimity stopped herself from continuing. Why was she telling a stranger all this? It was something about the whole atmosphere. A comforting feeling of belongingness enveloped the space, and it was as though time stood still for these people, coming together to simply enjoy each other's company. Everything else could wait. The most important thing at that moment was eating, engaging in conversation and enjoying the glorious sun. *To feel so free would be wonderful,* Dimity thought, enviously.

"Amsterdam is a really beautiful city. I've been there a few times myself. Have you been?"

"No, I haven't. My husband has been there many times. He's also been to Munich, Berlin, Milan, Paris, Prague, New York, London — even Dusseldorf. There's an Academy of Fine Arts there also, isn't there? He went there too. He's travelled quite a lot. In fact, he's always travelling. His job demands it."

"Oh, that sounds interesting. So, what do you do?"

"Me? What do I do? Um … I guess I make sure everything is okay until he gets back." She smiled half-heartedly. "Someone has to keep the ship afloat, I guess …"

"'*Someone has to keep the ship afloat*'," the tall young man repeated thoughtfully. "I guess *someone* does."

"Boris, are you coming?" one of the older women from the group called out. "We're about to start eating. Tell your friend to join us if she wants."

Boris nodded. "Would you like to join us?" he once again asked.

"Thanks, but my daughters are waiting for me. Nice to meet you anyway … Boris."

"Remember … Sorry what was your name?" he asked, before joining the group.

"Dimity," she said, smiling.

"Remember, Dimity, sometimes you need to jump into the water … you know, swim a little bit. You'll be surprised to discover that the ship can survive without you," he said, looking back at her.

Dimity looked on as the suddenly wise young man named Boris re-joined the group. Each of the group walked at a leisurely pace, their hair glistening in the warm sunlight, laughing rhythmically, acknowledging other friends and relatives as they made their way to an outdoor table that was abundantly laden with food and drink. She was certain that the conversation around the table would also be abundantly *rich* and *warm* and *healthy*. Dimity looked at them regretfully. She longed to be with people who accepted, challenged, embraced, and appreciated her — she wanted to feel again.

CHAPTER SIX

Later that Sunday night, at a popular restaurant located in East Sydney, Maria breathed heavily. She was tired, and couldn't wait to get back home to her beautiful baby boy, but here she was, stuck at an impromptu party with Antonio. It was impromptu for Maria, simply because she had completely forgotten about it, although Antonio had reminded her that Sunday morning, and the night before, and apparently a few other times during the week. Maria's mind was always pre-occupied lately. It was very difficult balancing a one-year-old and a business, especially when Antonio's job as a graphic designer seemed to suddenly include her as well. Ever since they got married, she had been invited to all his work-related social events — not that she hadn't been before, but now she was expected to attend. She was starting to feel that she was part of the team, although there were some unfamiliar faces sitting across from her that evening. *That's all I need, to have to introduce myself again and be the centre of attention,* she thought. The last thing she needed was to have everyone who didn't know her wanting to know everything about their attractive and talented Chilean colleague's wife; well, that was how most of the female colleagues referred to him, and even some of the male ones. She wouldn't have minded it that much, as she really wanted to do it for Antonio, but her feet were aching from working all day at Eventually You, her shop in the city which sold organic lifestyle products, including candles, facial scrubs and incense burners — anything healing and organic, even tea and coffee. She didn't always work on Sunday, but one of her part-timers was off sick so she had to help out. Sunday was always left for her precious little one, and Antonio. Besides, she would be taking holidays in a day — after doing some much needed stock-taking.

As she sat back in her seat, having inspected the view of the city from the veranda of the restaurant, she wished she had brought some organic, healing butter lotion home with her for her aching feet.

"So Maria, Antonio tells us that you own your own business?" asked one of the women sitting across from her.

"Yes, I do. I sell certified organic, lifestyle products. The shop's called Eventually You, and it's situated in the city, on Pitt Street." Maria decided to take advantage of her chance to advertise.

"That sounds so exciting. I might drop in one day. So, please tell me, what do you use on your face? It's flawless. Is it a moisturiser from your shop? Your skin tone looks amazing, and it brings out the green in your eyes."

"Maybe it's your Mediterranean background. You're Greek, right?" the other woman interjected.

"Well, I have a Greek background but I was born here …"

"Oh, I just love Greek things," the second woman continued. "I just came back from Greece. It's so beautiful there. The islands — Paros, Mykonos, Zakynthos, Kos … Don't get me started on how sexy the guys are, and the food is to die for."

"So, do you make *pastitsio*? I would love a recipe from a Greek person; you know, the authentic way," the first woman then asked.

"Well, I don't really cook that much Greek food. I mostly cook organic, vegetarian food. I also eat a lot of Thai, Indian …"

One of the men decided to join in. "What about stuffed vine leaves and *moussaka*? Surely, you make that. I love Greek food too."

43

"Well, my mum made it when I was young. She and my dad own a restaurant … anyway, like I said, I'm more into …"

"I once went to a Greek nightclub," another of the men cut in, "and you know they actually *did* throw plates. They actually do it in some of the clubs. Greeks definitely know how to party. Have you been to one of those clubs, Antonio?"

Maria took a sip of her wine. She wasn't much of a drinker, but she really needed a drink right then. It was as she had predicted. The whole conversation had been steered in the usual direction — her Greek background. Her business accomplishments, of course, had completely been pushed to the curb. It wasn't that she wasn't proud of her background. She just hated being labelled, especially when she was born and raised in Australia. She didn't understand the fascination. For Antonio, it was different. He actually was raised in Chile and had moved to Australia five years ago. Maria, however, never thought of herself as Greek. She just thought of herself as a woman trying to succeed in what she was passionate about. She hated the restrictions that a defined label would impose on her as a person. All her life, she fought to shake off that image — the stereotype of an Australian with a Greek background.

After completing her degree, she refused to work at her parents' Greek restaurant. She wanted to start her own business — something that was hers; that she felt passionate about. She was tired of her mother's expectation to adhere to every Greek tradition when they were growing up. Life suddenly became one big obligation — Greek dancing, Greek school, Greek this, Greek that. To Maria, being Greek became synonymous with obligation. The two words meant the same. She had detested being told what to do since she was a child, and still resisted her mother's controlling nature.

Maria was always amused when she recalled some of her childhood antics. She vividly remembered the time when she was eleven-years-old, when she had to take part in a Greek dance performance with her dancing group. She couldn't believe that she had to wear a traditional Greek dancing costume. She felt so stupid. Deep down she admired the embroidery, and the sequins on the dress, but she didn't admit that to her parents. Her mother had been so stressed to get there on time. Her older brother, who had embraced the grunge look wholeheartedly, had even made an effort and stepped out in a stylish suit, as the performance was to take place in one of the grand venues in the city. Nicki was also wearing her favourite pointy shoes that were in fashion at the time, and had even straightened her usually tousled blonde hair.

Everyone made sure they were ready, but she wouldn't leave her bedroom. The asphyxiating smell of hairspray and perfume coming from the hallway had made her stomach turn. She sat defiantly on the floor, in the corner of her room. The smell of hairspray always evoked anxiety for her. She fittingly associated the strong, toxic smell with having to attend something she didn't want to be part of. She could hear the pandemonium and the cacophony from the safety of her room, as everyone tried their best to be ready on time.

"Where are my shoes?" her sister had called, frantically.

"Effie!" her father's voice had boomed from her parent's bedroom. "Where's my white shirt? I can't find it anywhere!"

"I just ironed it … it's still on the ironing board," her mother had answered from the bathroom.

They were finally all groomed and ready to head out to the car when they realised someone was missing. They gathered curiously outside Maria's bedroom. Her father had knocked on the door.

"I'm not going anywhere in this stupid dress. I look like a clown!" she had called out.

"Maria, you look so beautiful," her mother had tried to reassure her. "You're wearing the best costume from the whole group because you're the lead dancer for the *Zorba* and the *Hasaposeviko*," she had pleaded.

"No, I look silly. I don't want to go. I never wanted to do Greek dancing. I wanted to have tennis lessons," she had challenged.

They had pleaded with her for a while, until she had grudgingly agreed to go, mainly because her father had told her they wouldn't be going to the beach with her cousins the next day, as had been promised, if she didn't abide. Besides, what would they tell her teacher? Her sister had also promised to give her one of her necklaces that all the cool older girls were apparently wearing.

They had finally arrived at the carpark. Maria hadn't said a word throughout the drive. She didn't want to go and she couldn't believe her feelings weren't being considered, again. Just as they all were about to exit the car, she impulsively ran her nails through her black, opaque tights. She pulled them until a huge hole had formed, followed by a long ladder that went right down to her ankles.

They didn't get to see her perform that night. They didn't go to the beach the next day either. Maria didn't care because she never saw another Greek dancing class again, as much as she sometimes secretly enjoyed them. It just wasn't her choice to do the classes, and she *had* to have a choice. She instead had tennis lessons, as she innocently convinced her father one day that she really wanted to be a tennis player, and that she was really committed to it. Her father had given in to her wishes. He had secretly told her that he didn't want to do half the things Effie made them do either. He too would just rather go to the beach, or watch the cricket.

The rest of the night turned out to be quite pleasant. Maria was back in favour with the women that she had temporarily let down due to her unwillingness to share Greek recipes. It turned out that they both had toddlers, and they shared stories and photos of their cheeky tykes.

As fun as it ended up being, Maria was now happy to be resting her head on Antonio's shoulder, who was behind the steering wheel of Maria's hybrid car. She could finally relax! She felt so content. It had been a busy twelve months. Planning a wedding a few months after having a baby, and then a christening straight after, had definitely taken its toll on her. She had only been going out with Antonio for a few months before she fell pregnant. It had been a surprise to both of them. It was also during a time when their relationship had been tested, when she didn't know if he would be moving back to Chile to help his family recover financially from an earthquake. Everything had happened so fast but they were also so in love. After Thomas was born, they had planned to get married. In fact, they had been engaged for months before Thomas was born. Maria, however, decided not to disclose this information to her mother. She was fed up of hearing that they were "living in sin" and that they didn't do things like that where she was brought up. Maria refused to give her the satisfaction. She had only told her sister and her closest friends, Cassandra and Julie.

Antonio placed his arm around Maria as he unlocked the front door of their Victorian terrace house in North Sydney. He turned to face her and then softly kissed her on the lips. He then kissed her more passionately.

"I've wanted to do that all night," he said in a soft voice. "Thank God Thomas has been sleeping through the night lately," he continued. "We can have some 'alone time', especially now that we've got a few weeks off from work."

"It'll be good for us to take it easy for a while. We've been flat out for so long. I'm just glad I have reliable employees to help out with the shop. Anyway, we better go inside. Lucky for us that our son has such a generous godmother

47

who is always willing to babysit him. Cassandra has been a lifesaver."

"After you, Mrs Reyes," he teased as they stepped into the pleasantly warm hallway.

"Why thank you, Mr Reyes," she responded, smiling.

CHAPTER SEVEN

The next morning, Maria tied her black apron around her waist in the back storeroom of Eventually You. She was ready to do some stock-taking and place orders before she went to help Nicki unpack. Her heart ached at the thought of her sister. She couldn't believe that she would be living with her in a few hours. Nicki had been frantic on the phone when she had called her from Melbourne airport that morning, talking between sobs. She had left him. She had left Marco — her one and only true love.

Maria breathed in the pleasant scent of the vanilla candles she had lit and strategically placed around the shop. She fought back a tear that was threatening to escape. Just as she was about to commence her work, her attention was diverted to her mobile phone. She had a text message from Cassandra informing her that their friend, Julie, had called her and was really enjoying her work trip in Amsterdam. Her mind then went to Julie. She couldn't believe how her career had taken off. She was travelling more than ever. She was proud of her for finally pursuing her dreams. Julie had been in a rut for a while when the three of them shared the terrace house just over a year ago. *Europe,* she thought in wonderment. It had been a long time since she had travelled overseas.

Just as Maria was about to turn on the coffee machine, she started thinking about the time she'd spent in Greece. She hadn't wanted to go. She was eleven-years-old. She didn't want to leave her school, her friends, and her beautiful bedroom where she spent hours playing, not to mention her tennis lessons. She had everything she needed in her home in Sydney. Of course, she didn't have a say in the matter, and so her whole family had suddenly been plucked from their federation house in the inner west of

Sydney and deposited in a village in Greece, just outside the town of Ioannina. Back then, her parents were just starting to think about opening a restaurant and wanted to learn everything they could from an uncle who'd run a successful hotel and restaurant back in Greece. And so their Greek adventure had begun.

They had spent a year there before moving back to Australia. Maria had attended one of the English tutoring schools. Nicki had just turned sixteen and had to complete her studies via the Distance Education Scheme. At first they had both been miserable and had missed their school and neighbourhood friends terribly, especially Dimity, who had become part of their lives since they had first become neighbours and went to the same school. Although Dimity and Nicki were the same age, Maria had also become part of their group. It was an easy way for her mother to ensure she always had a chaperone.

Their brother John had also decided to join them in Greece. He had also deferred his studies and worked as an English tutor to gain some work experience. Eventually, after a few months, they all became accustomed to the Greek way of life. Maria and Nicki made new friends, helped out at their uncle's restaurant and hotel, and swam in the crystal clear ocean. The family often met up with the locals for lunch or a late supper at the many *tavernes*. They also stayed for a time with relatives on her mother's side — Uncle Pavlo and Auntie Irene, and their daughter, Aliki — in a town called Agrinio, two hours away from Ioannina, which was another interesting experience.

While in Greece, Nicki had been inspired career-wise and had decided that she wanted to pursue a career in tourism. She worked a few hours a week at one of the local travel agencies in Ioannina and fell in love with the industry. She would even get to go on all the tours of the town, the nearby island, and the villages surrounding Ioannina. She also helped out in the office, which was situated on an ascending road that led to the most breathtaking view of the lake.

The move back was hard for both of them, as their parents had sold their family home in Sydney after renting it out for a year, and they had moved to Melbourne, where their parents had opened their restaurant. She missed the life they'd had in Sydney before they had moved.

"Now we don't even know where Dimity lives. She's not even in her old house anymore. We don't even have her number. It's not fair!" Maria had wailed.

"I wonder if she tried to contact us? Everything was fine before. Now, we'll never see her again!" Nicki had cried.

They had spent weeks blaming their parents for losing touch with Dimity.

Maria flinched as the phone rudely interrupted her thoughts. She grudgingly answered it, feeling that she couldn't possibly talk to customers without having had her coffee fix.

"Maria. I called you at home but no one picked up the phone," her mother scolded. "What are you doing at work again? How's Nicki? I can't believe what she's doing ... leaving Marco like that. You kids, these days, leave the moment you have a problem. It's not right!"

Maria cursed herself for answering the phone. She almost bit her lip, as her anger began to take hold of her. "How can you judge her? She obviously needs some space to sort out her feelings. It's been a tough few years. The *last thing* she needs is your judgment."

"I guess you'll brainwash her the minute she arrives ..."

"What are you talking about ... 'brainwash her'? I *want* her to be with Marco. They've always been great together."

"I don't know what to say ... it's not right. Marriage isn't easy. It's hard work but you don't just give up. This isn't like Nicki. She was always the level-headed one."

"What's that supposed to mean? I can't believe you're using Nicki's separation to have a go at *me!*"

"She should have stayed with me if she wanted to sort her feelings out."

"Oh yes, she would get some great advice from you … sprinkled with a dash of judgment and a *baklava* on the side."

"How can you talk to me with such little respect? And what would you know about marriage? You're practically a newly-wed … thanks to Antonio having you living in …"

"Don't you *dare* start with that again!"

"What will you tell her? Are you going to preach your bohemian, hippie values to her?"

"Mum … enough! I'm not in the mood for this. I've got a lot of work to do."

"Maybe if you went to the Greek Sunday school at the local church, you would have learned the value of structure and restraint …"

"Restraint to be yourself … to follow your dreams … is that what I would have learned?"

"I have a headache. I don't want to talk about this anymore. How's Thomas? Who's looking after him?"

"Antonio is looking after him, you know — *his father.*"

"Well, he didn't answer the phone when I called."

Maria took a deep breath, trying to steady her breathing. "Well, maybe he just couldn't get the phone because he was changing Thomas' nappy, or maybe he was out in the garden, or perhaps he took him to the park. There are *so many* possibilities. Besides, we do have mobile phones," Maria said, feeling the heat course through her body.

"So Antonio's looking after him on his own? Does he know that kids at that age need structure? They need to have nap-time, play-time, sleep-time, and not to just stay in the park or in the garden all day?"

"Of course he knows what he's doing. What sort of a question is that! So the fact that we've read so many parenting books doesn't count for anything?"

"*Parenting books?* In my day, we didn't need books to tell us these things."

"Well, that must be why the world from when I was a child until the present, has become such a *wonderful place*. Every parent knew what they were doing then. Everyone turned out to be *so* well-adjusted. It must be because the parents in *your day* didn't read any *parenting books!*" Maria screamed down the other side of the line, feeling every muscle in her body tense.

"Maria, there's no need to be saraca ..."

"*Sarcastic?*"

"I know the word. I did do some English classes when I came to Australia. My customers at the restaurant always tell me my English is so good. It's a Greek word, anyway. Most of the difficult words are from Greek words. Anyway, I can see there's no getting through to you. How's my cute grandson? Has he learned any new words? I miss him all the way from here in Melbourne."

"Well, apart from *mama* and *dada*, he knows *bye* and *hi* and a few other words," Maria said as she tried to restore her breathing. *Why do I always manage to be lured into her minefield?*

"Well, I hope you'll teach him some Greek words too."

"We will ... *eventually*. Don't forget that his father is from Chile. Anyway, let's concentrate on English first. I don't want to confuse him."

"Toddlers are like sponges. They soak in everything. It's never too early to learn Greek. As they get older, it's harder to pick it up. By the time he's in Greek school, he'll know so much."

"*Greek school?* Who said anything about *Greek school!* I'm not going to bombard him with Greek school. He won't have time for his own interests. If he wants to, he can learn

Greek, *if* they offer it as a language in high school. Should I also enrol him in Spanish school *as well?*"

"*Maria*, just because you don't want anything to do with your Greek background, it doesn't mean your son won't either. He might be proud of his Greek *and* his Chilean background."

"Who said I'm not proud of my Greek background? I'm just against all the formalities. *I am proud.* It doesn't mean that I had to do everything your way just to be Greek."

"If you're proud, you would encourage Thomas to learn about his background. All I wanted for all of you is to learn about where your parents came from. We knew we would make Australia our home because we loved it here, and we were able to settle here. A person should also know where they came from though, shouldn't they?"

"They should learn as much as they *want* to. You enforced it," Maria continued, fuming again. She calmed down when she heard a knock at the door. It was Stacey, one of her part-timers who would also help her with the books and look after the shop whenever she took time off. "Anyway, I have to go now. Stacey just arrived and I have to open the shop. Say hi to Dad for me."

Maria hung up the phone, feeling relieved that her mother lived in Melbourne. She would be adding her input on all matters Greek, and all matters parenting as well if she lived in the same city. *How dare she accuse me of not being proud of my Greek background! How dare she tell me how to feel and how to live my life … even now, when I'm a grown adult, and a successful businesswoman as well. Doesn't that count for anything?*

Maria finally walked towards the glass front door of the shop. She breathed in the vanilla scent, needing to be healed from all the negative energy. She had tried so desperately to live in the moment, to be a holistic person. "*Not proud of my heritage*," she muttered before opening the door.

"Oh, hi Stacey,"

"Hi Maria," Stacey responded, entering the shop.

Maria looked at the little travel agency situated opposite Eventually You. It had suddenly caught her attention. The poster of Stonehenge that had been there the past few weeks had been replaced with a picture of a small, white Greek Orthodox church. She felt that it was talking to her; luring her to admire its magic. Memories of the Greek tapestry Nicki and Dimity let her contribute to making instantly came to mind. The sea in the background was breathtaking — so blue, so enigmatic and infinite. She remembered weaving the same deep blue colour into the tapestry, each thread straying from the rest, finding its own path, then coming together as a whole in the end, creating something magnificent. The contrast between the white church and the dark blue sea on the poster was just as emphatic — it was majestic. *Not proud of my Greek heritage*! she scoffed.

***

"I can't believe how many things I forgot!" Nicki exclaimed, later that afternoon in the North Sydney terrace.

Maria looked at the suitcase with a bewildered heart. Did her sister even know what she had done? Was she even thinking clearly?

"I need this time, Maria. I know what you're thinking. Believe me, I've been able to read people's minds for a while now. Most communication is done without talking ..."

"I just think it's all a bit sudden. I mean, you have an argument and you just leave? Have you thought everything out? And I know all about reading feelings and all that. I did live with Cassandra when she was in the middle of her counselling studies. She and Julie would drive me crazy when I didn't reveal my feelings."

"I can imagine how intense it would have been when Cassandra started dating Connor — another counselling student in the mix. I'm sure it was fun, though. I mean, you always had your analytical girl talks with Cass and Julie, from what I remember you telling me. Anyway, we'd better organise the sleeping arrangements. I have to arrange to send some of my things to Sydney as well. I don't want to go back in *that house* …"

"It was intense, *and* fun," Maria said, recalling an image of Cassandra and Connor studying together in the dining room. Maria stood silently. She didn't understand her sister's feelings or her actions. She and Marco had been so in love. *That house?* she thought to herself. How could she talk about their lovely home with such contempt? Her heart went out to her … and to Marco. She knew things were bad, but she never expected her to leave her husband. Nicki's behaviour was so erratic. Maybe she could talk some sense into her, now that she would be temporarily living at the terrace with her, Antonio, and Thomas. But how would she cope with seeing their happy family?

"I also have to call work," Nicki sighed. "I'm sure I'll be able to get a transfer. Working in the travel industry for so long has definitely helped me make connections. I'd love to work close to your shop in the city. Maybe I should start looking for an apartment there. I always dreamed of working and living in the city. How glamorous!"

Maria sensed that her sister was on a caffeine high. She was talking and planning things much too quickly. It was odd.

"*Apartment?* Nicki, don't you think you need to take a step back? You just need some time on your own to think. Anyway, at least you're not close to Mum right now. I mean, living in the same city with her would have been a nightmare. You need your space … to sort your feelings out."

"She's not so bad. I don't let her get to me like you do."

"That's because she doesn't interfere in your life as much as she does with mine, although I'm sure she won't approve of your actions … leaving Marco like this. Just be warned," Maria continued, remembering the conversation she had with her mother earlier. "You'll be off the hook soon enough, though. Everything's my fault usually. She doesn't think I can look after myself. It's just like when we were young, and she wouldn't even let me go anywhere without you. You and Dimity used to chaperone me everywhere."

"It is strange that she doesn't let up when it comes to you," Nicki commented. She mused. "*Dimity* ... I wonder what she's doing with her life. It's strange how we severed ties with her so suddenly. We were all so close. It's funny how life turns out." Nicki looked at her suitcase again, tears forming in her eyes.

"Nicki ... is there anything I can do?"

"Don't worry about me. I'll be all right, and I promise you, I'll find an apartment soon. I won't intrude. I mean, I didn't even know you were both taking time off from work."

"Nicki. It doesn't bother me. I guess it will be like old times ... having all those girl talks in this house, the way I used to with Julie and Cassandra, before they moved out and let me and Antonio move in permanently."

"Anyway, I'd better start unpacking once and for all. *Oh no!*" Nicki exclaimed. "I can't believe I accidentally took one of Mum's vintage evening bags!"

"What bag? Oh ... *WOW!* It's beautiful. I never knew Mum had such eclectic taste. It's almost something that I would buy."

"It's from Greece ... from when she was young. I borrowed it one day for a work 60's themed dress-up party, but never ended up using it. Mum doesn't even know I borrowed it. I had thrown it at the back of my closet and forgot about it."

"It's so unique. I guess silver mesh was all the rage back then." Maria looked at the accessory with intrigue. "I'll go and make us a cup of organic tea," she called out as she made her way to the kitchen, down the hallway, with the bag on her shoulder. Catching a glimpse of herself in the long, antique mirror, she stopped to admire the bag, which shimmered wildly like silver glitter. Maria unzipped it. She wondered how it looked inside. To her surprise, she saw that it wasn't empty. There were a few folded up pieces of gold and blue cardboard neatly placed in the side sleeve. Maria took them out as she walked towards the kitchen. *It must be a dance invitation for some Greek community thing that Mum and Dad are members of,* she thought to herself. She was right — they were invitations — but not for any Greek community dance. They were invitations for her cousin Aliki's wedding in Greece, *and* one for her baby's christening, *and* another for Aliki's parents' wedding anniversary — Nicki and Maria's Uncle Pavlo and Auntie Irene.

Why would Mum not have mentioned this? Maria thought. She had become close to Aliki when they lived in Greece. She would have loved to have gone to at least one of the functions, or to at least call and offer them her best wishes. Maria's chest tightened. She became increasingly angry the more she processed it. Her mother should have told her about the invitations. It was so strange. She always forced her to get in touch with her Greek heritage — her relatives, where they grew up — and yet she hadn't told her anything about the invitations. Her cousin would think she wanted nothing to do with her. What Maria really couldn't believe was that her mother hadn't mentioned Uncle Pavlo and Auntie Irene. She hadn't talked about them for years, but they too had always been close, back in Greece. She had to find out why. She would call her after she got Nicki settled. Something didn't add up.

CHAPTER EIGHT

Dimity stared at the boats as she walked past the jetty at a quick pace. They looked so peaceful floating in the calm water, which glistened in the sunlight that blanketed it. The gentle waves created a lovely mosaic effect, and it almost looked like the water had been sprinkled with silver glitter. As she looked over to the other side of the bay she saw a seaplane coming into land. The whole vista was so peaceful. She had decided to go for a walk after dropping the girls off at school, and after having helped out at the school office, as she always did on Monday and Thursday morning, along with the uniform shop on Wednesday, the occasional school disco, and other fundraising events throughout the year. She needed to devote her energy into her fitness, as she didn't know how else to fill the emptiness she felt inside. Usually she had a goal to strive for: the girls to finish the school term, exams to be over, going away for the summer holidays, Malcolm to return back from his trip ... That would usually keep her going; keep her hoping. She was always expecting that there would be something behind the curtain — something for her, after waiting for each goal to be met.

Lately, she felt that there was nothing to wait for, that there was nothing behind the curtain except more waiting. She kept thinking that once all the goals were met, she would be happy and it would be her turn, but that still hadn't happened.

It had now become Malcolm and his career on one side, and her looking after the girls on the other side.

Her mind drifted to their second meeting. Dimity couldn't believe that Meagan had wanted her to meet with the handsome *Malcolm Stewart* again. Apparently, the client who was interested in his work knew a lot of people in high places and some of them were interested in purchasing his pieces for their businesses and their homes. They were also eager to become clients with the firm she worked for.

Dimity had made sure she was prepared this time — not that everything hadn't turned out okay the first time she saw him. She had never expected to have had a *business dinner* with him. This time Dimity made sure that she was wearing one of her most flattering dresses, one that accentuated her long, slender, toned arms, and her svelte waist in an unassuming way. She had complemented the sophisticated dress with knee-high statement boots that were very avant-garde at the time, and a studded leather bracelet, revealing her inner rebel. She wanted this hip, new designer to know that she was in his league. She had let her long, dark hair fall free, and applied her favourite fuchsia-coloured lipstick. After a spray of her floral-citrus signature perfume, Dimity was ready for business.

She had opened the door to his studio, and was immediately taken aback by how drawn she was to him. He looked so cool and confident as he talked to a customer. The moment he had noticed her, he had given her a smile and had motioned with an informal hand gesture that he wouldn't be long. It immediately communicated that he knew her and that she wasn't just a customer, or just any business associate, even if it was only their second meeting. The moment she'd looked back in his direction, after having momentarily looked away, trying to pretend that she was looking at a chair that was next to her, she had realised he was still looking at her. She had instinctively smiled at him. He'd returned the smile, then immediately looked back at the customer.

"Sorry to keep you waiting," he had finally said after the customer left. He had then given her the most intense of looks. Dimity knew he liked what he saw. His eyes had said it all, and she could feel his appreciation. Usually she wouldn't make anything of it when men looked at her, but there was no mistaking the look that he had given her.

Moments later, they were sitting in the coffee shop across the road. Dimity had filled him in on the buzz that some of his designs had caused, and told him that he was quite a sensation.

"So, what are you passionate about, Dimity? What are your plans? I know you're an assistant at the moment, but where do you want to go from there?" he had asked with genuine interest.

"My plans?" she had asked, taken aback. "Well, I guess the plan is to get my break and be part of the Interior Design team," she had replied when she had regained her composure. "My dream has always been to eventually work on big commercial projects like hotels or restaurants. I realise it's very competitive, but I know I can do it. I just need to keep working hard and learn as much as I can. It's just so exciting working in such a creative and innovative industry. I pinch myself sometimes ... I can't believe how much I love this industry!" she had responded enthusiastically, momentarily looking at him, realising that the entirety of his face had been taken up by the sexiest and warmest smile. His eyes had looked like they were dancing. She couldn't hide her elation. There was something about him; she wanted to confide in him.

"Sorry," she had said, embarrassed about how forthcoming she had been.

"Sorry? What are you sorry about? The industry needs people like you. I mean ... I feel inspired just listening to you talk. I feel like starting my next project as soon as I get back to the studio. If we don't dream, we have nothing to aspire to. Don't ever stop pursuing your dreams," he had told her gently, looking into her eyes. Dimity had broken the stare. She couldn't believe how fast her heart beat when he looked at her. He was supposed to be a client, but the way he looked at her was so seductive that he felt like

61

someone more. She stared back at him, and he held the gaze, smiling warmly once again.

"Anyway, we'd better get back to work," he had continued. "Do you think our *meeting* is over?"

She didn't know what was happening. She had many meetings before but she usually couldn't wait until they were over. This time, she didn't want it to end.

Dimity stopped at the lights. She smiled at the memory with a heavy heart. She crossed the road and stepped into a cosy coffee shop situated on the corner of her street. She needed a coffee fix. As she took her coffee and thanked the shop owner, who knew her by name, her heart filled with heavy regret when she saw a couple sitting at a table sneaking a quick kiss while their little boy coloured in a picture earnestly, his parents looking on proudly. They looked so happy, enjoying life and creating special moments together.

A few minutes later, Dimity stepped into the wide hallway of the home she and Malcolm had designed together. She walked thoughtfully across the white marble tiles, sipping her coffee as she entered the formal dining room. She had never used it for its intended purpose, always opting to use the smaller dining room next to the kitchen instead. Dimity often enjoyed sitting on one of the chairs in the formal dining room, looking out into the tranquil garden.

She found it fascinating that the garden always had some colour amongst all the green. Depending on what season it was, new flowers would blossom in different areas, offering their unique beauty to the rest of the garden. Just when certain varieties of flowers finished their turn making the garden look beautiful with rich and vibrant colours, other varieties would blossom and bloom. Each species of flower would re-emerge again next season, having another turn at creating beauty. Splashes of red and purple were now having their moment in the sun, creating a lovely, poetic picture.

The dining room was so peaceful. Dimity was always waiting for the right time to use it — a time when she would invite guests who respected her. She imagined hosting her ideal dinner party on the long, rectangular timber table Malcolm had made. She held it in high regard, so it was only fitting that her guests also respected it and everything around it. Images of passionate, heated debates on subjects such as art, design, politics, and music would fill her mind. *One day*, she kept telling herself. *One day* she would have guests like that; she would have the life she had always wanted.

The stillness of the room and the whole house began to create a melancholic atmosphere. *How did I end up feeling so isolated?* She had vowed to never end up like this — that she would never give up her career and her dreams, that she would never have the look in her eyes that conveyed a deep-seated loneliness, just like the look the woman her father had helped had in her sad, tired eyes all those years ago. But here she was, in an almost too perfect house, in a beautiful affluent suburb, with no one to share it with. Malcolm was away *again*. The girls were always busy with their friends and their own lives. Her sisters, Andrea and Luca, were working interstate. Even the friendships she had made with the other mothers at her daughters' school were slowly disintegrating, as the transition from primary to high school would slowly and inevitably put an end to the daily drop-offs and pick-ups, as many students would soon make their own travel arrangements.

The silence was interrupted when her mobile phone rang. Dimity jolted; the sound seemed very loud at that time of the day, when silence engulfed the house.

"Hi Dimity."

Dimity paused. She was momentarily taken aback. The familiar male voice had an unusual, distant tone.

"Dimity, it's me, Malcolm. I'm just calling to see how you're doing. We didn't get to talk much before I left. So … how are you and the girls doing?"

"We're fine, I guess. I'll have to pick them up before you know it, and get started on dinner. My parents are coming over tomorrow so I guess that will be good for them. They might not feel so lonely."

Dimity knew full well that the girls were far too busy to feel lonely. The last thing she wanted was to appear like a nagging housewife. It was too pathetically clichéd. She still had her pride. Dimity was surprised that he was calling her at that time. It must be the early hours of the morning in Amsterdam. Why wasn't he asleep?

"I know it's hard for them — for all of you," he said after a long pause. "If you don't stay on top of your game in this business though, it's easy to get left behind. Anyway, I feel really bad, but I need to tell you that we have to extend the trip for a few more days. It turns out that one of the buyers for the new lighting line is in Eindhoven, so it would be great to meet with him since I'm already in the Netherlands. I need to discuss the line with him. It's one of our old clients, Stefano. I've been doing business with him for so long … I don't want to let him down. I'm really sorry, Dimi. I didn't know how to tell you. He wants to meet me in Amsterdam in a few days."

"Don't worry," she said, almost too quickly. She couldn't believe what he was telling her. How many times had she heard that before? There was always a good reason for *his* career, *his* aspirations, *his* everything. Who was he talking to? It was *her*, Dimity, the designer that he was so in awe of. She knew too well that if *you don't stay on top of your game, you'll be left behind.* Her whole life was like that, let alone her career. How would she ever get back to the level she'd been at when she had just started making her mark on the industry? How dare he make her feel like she was some lonely housewife who couldn't make it when her husband wasn't around. She would not allow Malcolm to think about her like that.

"I'm fine, Malcolm. *We're* fine. You don't need to worry about us. Just get some sleep. I can handle it. Everything's fine."

"Are you sure?"

"Yes, I'm positive," she said confidently, and hung up the phone.

That afternoon, as Dimity drove her Audi Q3 out of the school carpark, her daughters strapped in the back and ready to head home, Samantha, who was eleven, a year older than Olivia, enquired, "So when is dad coming home?"

"He'll be gone for a few more days. He'll probably be back on Sunday."

"So is he bringing us anything?" Olivia asked enthusiastically.

"I'm sure he'll bring you some souvenirs for your rooms."

"Souvenirs?" Samantha cried. "I want a cool leather jacket like the one Amanda has. She got it from Europe. She wore it at the school disco last time!"

"We have leather jackets here," Dimity replied, raising her voice slightly. "You can get them when the sales are on. You don't need to get one from Europe. Besides, I just got you that denim one you said you 'had to have'. Your dad and I have bought you girls so many clothes lately. I didn't have half of what you have when I was young. I certainly didn't go to a private school either. Money doesn't just get handed to people, you know?"

"I just wanted to say it's from Europe. I know you can get them here. We never told you and Dad to take us to a private school. I'd rather have the jacket," Samantha continued. "You have so many expensive things in your closet anyway. Do you even really need all those clothes? I mean ... it's not as though you go anywhere lately, or work."

"Every designer outfit you see in my closet was on sale," Dimity responded, her blood pressure rising. "Yes, I do have a lot of clothes, and maybe I don't go anywhere now, but I used to. A lot of those clothes I bought with the hope that one day I might work again, and maybe one day I'll start going out to grown-up places, instead of devoting every ounce of energy to you and your father."

Nothing she did was appreciated. She recalled her mother-in-law emphasising that Malcolm had renovated the house alone, when in fact Dimity had contributed significantly, losing sleep over certain decisions, such as whether they should do the floors in marble or Portuguese limestone, checking the contractors were working on plan, and simultaneously making sure everything ran smoothly on a day-to-day basis so that everyone else could actually strive to do their best.

"Mum, it's just that we don't understand why you don't go out anymore. If I had all those clothes, I would want to show them off. You and dad used to always go out to cool parties when we were little. Even in photos, you looked like you were a cool couple. Anyway, why don't you work? We never told you not to work. It's not as if we can't catch the bus to school. Aren't you a designer?"

They were right. They did attend cool parties when the girls were young. Her heart began to ache again as she pulled into the driveway, and turned off the ignition. "I'm sorry for raising my voice at you two," she said, turning to face her daughters. "I just get tired sometimes. It's hard trying to do everything when your father is always away."

"Why don't you ever go with him?" Olivia asked. "Dad always asks you to go with him. You always say you can't."

"Yeah, why don't you? It's not like we can't look after ourselves," Sam added.

"What are you talking about? You're in primary school. Catching the bus is one thing ..."

"You could ask Granddad and Grandma to mind us. You always say no. Besides, it's fun staying with them. Granddad goes cycling with us and he even takes us fishing," Olivia continued.

"Well, they're coming tomorrow, so I have to organise the guest room."

"Whatever!" Sam said, suddenly losing interest in the conversation and finding it in her iPod instead. She jumped out of the car and scanned through the list of songs. Olivia soon followed her when she heard her favourite song playing.

"Try and finish your homework before dinner you two," she called after them, "and if you have any projects, it's best to get a start on them now …"

Later that evening, Dimity began to prepare the guest room. She had poured herself a glass of Merlot and began changing the sheets, after making sure there were fresh towels in the ensuite. She was relieved that her parents were staying. She heard her mobile ring and hurried to the kitchen to answer it. She missed the call, but soon a text message came through. It was from Malcolm:

"Have a nice night, Dimi. I love you and I miss you."

She felt a tear roll down her cheek when she read the words. She walked back to the guest room, drunk with emotion. She stopped when she noticed a piece of furniture that had meant so much to her. It was the side table that she had first seen him thoughtfully sitting on — the first time she laid eyes on him when she was a young, wide-eyed assistant. He was now her husband — the man that had looked back at her from the page of a magazine, the man who she thought was the sexiest, most intelligent, coolest up-and-coming industrial designer, who had instantly seduced her with his smile and his casual attitude. The table also symbolised a turning point in their relationship. She remembered the moment vividly.

Dimity had walked into his studio one Friday afternoon. She wanted to let him know that the client was happy with how efficiently the orders had been placed and delivered. He was wearing a cosy looking sweater that made him look like a poet. He had looked up from the counter, appraising her more seriously than he usually did. As she continued telling him how great everything had turned out, he had walked over to where she was standing, so he was up close. She could feel his presence — the heat between them.

"So you came all the way to tell me that?" he had said, his eyes smiling.

She had sat down on the table that had been featured on the magazine, taken aback by his question.

"Well, that and the fact that I won't be working with you for a while ... well, of course you're on our list and we will definitely need you for other clients. I mean your designs are so innovative and you're one of the ones to watch out for," she had quickly added.

He had sat next to her on the table. He then smiled at her as though he could sense the effect he was having on her.

"You're right about something. Everything turned out great, and I'm glad you came over here to tell me that because if you had just called, I wouldn't be able to do this." He leaned closer to her, and stroked her hair gently. Before she knew it, he was kissing her softly on the lips.

When their lips parted, he had looked searchingly into her eyes. His were serious. She could feel the warmth of his breath as he stroked her hair again. He finally spoke. "I know this isn't exactly professional, but I've wanted to do that since the moment I saw you. I thought you were the most gorgeous woman I'd ever seen. Dimity, you can't deny what's happening between us. You can feel the chemistry, can't you?"

She had looked up at him. The warmth of his hand holding hers was enough to make her tremble all over.

"I can feel it … I mean, I've felt it from the moment I saw you," she had replied, feeling that she couldn't keep up the charade any longer.

Dimity smiled in between tears as she looked at the table that had marked the beginning of their relationship. What had happened over the last couple of months? Surely they could get the spark back. She couldn't let their relationship suffer anymore. It had been so long that she had let him touch her; she always made excuses.

"I can't now, Malcolm. I've been helping Olivia with her project all evening," she had said hastily, when he had pulled her close almost three months ago, kissing her on the shoulders as she got ready for bed.

She couldn't be close to him, not after he had just told her that he had to go on another trip — that time to Milan.

"You wouldn't believe what your mum said to me when she called," she had told him earlier, before he had told her about the impending trip. "She actually said that your cousin has chosen 'such a lovely colour scheme for her apartment. It isn't clinical at all, like a lot of white houses are these days.' She said I should get some ideas from her …"

"You smell nice Dimi … you know that perfume drives me wild …"

"Malcolm … not now! I'm tired," she had interrupted irritably. "Not now, Malcolm!" she had said again, slightly raising her voice, when he had uttered the words she'd heard so many times.

"I have to go away next week. It's a really important client. Of course, you could come with me … I mean your parents keep asking to help with the girls but you never take them up on their offer. It would be good for us, Dimi …"

"*Really, Malcolm*? I mean, is it really that easy to just drop everything and just fly with you to the other side of the world? Oh … I forgot … I don't actually *do* anything … well, according to your mum I don't. Oh yeah, she called earlier and suggested that since I don't work, I can take them to visit some of their friends and relatives here, since they're going back to Brisbane soon. I just have to work at the school, and take Samantha to that important piano concert she has been practising all year for … I guess those things aren't as important!" she had yelled as she stormed to the bathroom, feeling his hurtful stare as she slammed the door behind her.

Dimity touched the smooth timber surface of the table. Noticing that a drawer was jammed, she reached over to close it. The key was stuck in the drawer that was usually unlocked. The only person who would use it other than her was Malcolm. He must have tried to lock it that rushed morning before he left. Curiously, Dimity tried to unjam the lock, careful not to ruin the table. With one sudden jolt, the drawer flung open, freeing a page from a magazine, and some pamphlets. She looked at the page from the magazine. Her eyes became fixated on a photo of Malcolm laughing with a pretty young woman. They were at one of his work parties. They looked like they were having fun, like they had been interrupted for a quick photo in between laughs. Dimity admired the woman's unusual yet stylish outfit. Her eyes scanned the other sheets. It was some information regarding the woman. Her name was Julie Canei. She worked for one of the well-known interior design companies.

Dimity's heart sank. She had an awful feeling in the pit of her stomach. She remembered Malcolm's call. He had still been awake, even if it was the early hours of the morning. *I'm being ridiculous*, she told herself. He probably locked the information away so the girls wouldn't throw it out or use it as scrap. But it had been years since they would do such things. Plus, he had asked her to go with him that morning.

Although, he wouldn't have expected her to accept his offer — she never did. Maybe she should have considered it more. She looked at the photo again. They looked so happy together — they were on the same page literally and figuratively, the way she and Malcolm used to be when they attended design parties. *No. Malcolm wouldn't do that to me, or to the girls. We've just lost each other for a while. He wouldn't cross the line.* She felt a twinge of pain on the left side of her body. Remembering the way Malcolm used to look at her, how much he loved her — there was no way he would throw that away.

Grabbing her glass of wine, she walked upstairs and made her way to the balcony. *Why don't I go with him on his trips when he asks me? Maybe he needs me as much as I need him,* she speculated. She had to do something! She remembered his smiling eyes looking at her, the way they shared their sorbet together that beautiful day on the south coast. She couldn't throw that away! She looked out into the distance. The stars looked so magical. Their omnipresence evoked deep emotions within her. She felt she was part of something bigger — something extraordinary. They reminded her that there was more to life than just existing — there could be magic and sparkle. Her mind went to the bizarre morning she'd had at the Bavarian bistro. The ubiquitous, positive energy that morning was extraordinary. She also remembered the words from the philosophical young man she had been so fortunate to meet.

"The ship can survive without you," he had told her.

Yes! The ship can survive without me, she thought to herself. *It can stay afloat. Boris is right. I have to jump out of the ship. I have to swim!*

***

In a five-star hotel somewhere in Amsterdam, Malcolm Stewart stared out at the morning sunlight from the balcony of his suite. He was standing there shirtless, still in his boxer shorts, staring searchingly at the sky. After having gone for an early morning jog, needing desperately to have an outlet for his frustration, he had headed for the shower, but changed his mind and instead stepped out onto the balcony. He looked at the city below him, then back at the morning sky. Once again, he was experiencing everything alone. There was a void in his heart. Something was missing.

He walked back to his room, feeling depleted. He hadn't slept at all when he had hung up the phone after talking to Dimity. He had just tossed and turned for most of the night; even pouring himself a scotch from the minibar to heal the emptiness he was feeling. He looked at the king-size bed he had been sleeping in — in the only room that had been available. It was too big for one person. It had been almost two months, if not more, since he had touched her. Now, she would always withdraw from him. He couldn't go through life without that passion. Malcolm felt that the love of his life was slipping away from him. She was becoming someone he didn't recognise. Even the way she had spoken to his mother wasn't like her; God knows his mother deserved it, though. When had the relationship between his family and his wife become so toxic? It was as though she was pushing them away the same way she was pushing him away. The only person she would connect with was his younger brother, Alex, but everyone got along with him.

He looked at the clock despairingly. He had to shower and get dressed. He had to meet with Julie Canei, one of the interior designers, before yet another exhibition, this time at the Academy of Fine Arts. He used to feel so excited to attend all the industrial design events. Lately, he felt that it didn't mean as much to him as it used to. He used to share it with Dimity. He needed to share his world, his vision with someone. He couldn't continue living with a constant void in his heart.

CHAPTER NINE

Maria looked at the photo of her friend, Julie Canei, in the interior design magazine, as she waited for her mother to answer the phone. Nicki had been looking at it earlier in amazement and had left it on the kitchen bench with some work travel brochures. An attractive man was next to her, holding a drink. His name was Malcolm Stewart. Maria had heard of him. He was apparently a big name in the industrial design world.

Her mother finally answered.

"Why didn't you tell me about the invitation for Aliki's wedding and the christening for her son, and God knows what other invitations you've been keeping from me?" Maria blurted out. She could hear her mother's breathing; the silence amplified the tension between them.

"Maria ... is that the way to talk to your mother?"

"Why didn't you tell me? You're usually the first to tell me to attend other functions — anything with the word 'Greek' in it ... Why not this? I mean, it would have been the perfect opportunity to go to a Greek wedding, with *Greekness* all round — the islands, the ancient sites, exploring my heritage. Why would you not even mention that, especially when I know Aliki?"

"I didn't tell you because I knew you wouldn't go. You despise everything I tell you. Anyway, how do you know about the invitations?"

"Nicki accidentally brought one of your bags that she had borrowed from you with her. There was also a wedding anniversary invitation for Uncle Pavlo and Auntie Irene. What exactly are you referring to when you say I *despise everything* you tell me? Oh ... you mean my Greek heritage. Is that what I despise? I despise you interfering in my life, judging everything I do. The way you treated Antonio in the beginning was unbelievable …"

"Are you still talking about that? Everything's fine. We've been great with Antonio. He isn't upset with us."

"Yes, it is fine because we had a precious little boy. That's what our 'living in sin' did. It created a precious human being. Not everything turns our wrong when it's not under your control — under some planned agenda. I would have loved to see Aliki again. She was actually quite close to me and Nicki. We had already lost our other friends, especially Dimity. We obviously had no choice then, but we do now. You should have told me about the invitations. You should have told me *and* Nicki. It was up to us to make that decision. Why would you keep it a secret, whether we went or not? It doesn't make sense."

"After all these years, you're still going on about losing your friends?"

"Yes I am, Mum, because these things can affect a person; to the core. You can't control my life anymore. Tell me … why didn't you tell any of us? Even John doesn't know."

"*Maria* … I'm not going to be spoken to like this. Besides, you loved the time you spent in Greece. Even now, you and Nicki talk about how wonderful it was. As for the invitations, I told you why I didn't tell you. I don't want to talk about this anymore. I'll talk to you when you calm down. *Bye!*"

Maria stared at the phone with her mouth agape. Her mother had *hung up* on her. There was something off about the whole thing. It was nonsensical. She would always show them all the other invitations from Greece. Why not these ones? *Why isn't Mum talking to her brother and his wife, Irene?* She hadn't thought about it before, putting it down to losing track of them. To deliberately hide the invitations in a bag she hasn't used for years meant that she didn't want anyone to see them.

74

Deep in thought, Maria leaned over the kitchen bench, and reached for her favourite cup and saucer in order to make some herbal tea. She looked at the interior design magazine again. She then flipped through it and found the page with Julie on it. She smiled back at her friend, who stood next to the world-renowned industrial designer. They were at a work party in the photo, and now she was in Amsterdam meeting with him while attending yet another design exhibition. *She's lucky that she has such an understanding and supportive boyfriend*, Maria thought, acknowledging Malcolm Stewart's sex appeal. Julie was always travelling; even having missed Thomas' christening, which Maria knew she greatly regretted. She was so happy for Julie — for finding a career she loved, for being in a long-term healthy relationship. She then looked at the travel brochures next to them. Mesmerised by the images, she placed the cup and saucer on the marble bench top. There were some majestic pictures advertising the Maldives. Her eyes then scanned the next brochure. It was the image she had seen behind the display window in the travel agency across from her shop — the same church, the same magnificent blue backdrop, the divine waters of the Aegean Sea … Santorini. Her heart felt tight with frustration. Her mother had dismissed everything she said, like she knew best, just like she always thought she did. She had to find answers. Enough was enough! She would call the shots this time. Perhaps it was time to discover her parents' homeland again and find some answers. Perhaps it was finally time to go back to Greece.

***

Dimity was driving on New South Head Road in the Eastern suburbs of Sydney, deep in thought. She stopped at the traffic lights and couldn't resist looking at the beautiful view of Rushcutters Bay. She suddenly felt hopeful, and energised from her sudden plan to take action and salvage the relationship that years ago seemed unbreakable. She wanted to feel that connection again — that unspeakable desire, and the chemistry between them.

She was driving home after picking up some *baklava* from a delectable Greek cake shop in Double Bay. Her parents had arrived earlier that morning from their house in Jervis Bay on the south coast, and she wanted to serve some dessert with the coffee after brunch. They were so eager to help her with the girls. Her mother thought it was so romantic that she would drop everything and spontaneously surprise Malcolm. She still had a lot of packing to do and to ensure that she had everything she needed. She placed the *baklava* further back on the seat in case it fell when she drove off. The enticing smell of the syrup pleasantly permeated the air, instantly conjuring up wonderful memories from her childhood. A sense of nostalgia filled her heart from the familiar aroma.

It was a hot summer's afternoon in the late 1980s. She was eight-years-old and she was walking home from school with her older sisters, Andrea, who was twelve, and Luca, who was fourteen. They had just stepped out of the milk bar at the end of their street, and Dimity had just sunk her teeth into an orange and mango ice block. Andrea had insisted that her Double Chock ice cream was heaven on earth, while Luca walked along casually sipping her milkshake. Dimity could hear Madonna's *Material Girl* playing from a car radio. The Pet Shop Boys soon followed, and they all tried to sing along to *You Were Always on my Mind*, as Dimity and Andrea ate their ice cream, and Luca sipped her drink. Maria could feel the perspiration on her body. The sweltering heat was unbearable that afternoon, and she couldn't wait to get out of her school uniform and into her swimming costume, and stand under the sprinkler in the backyard. Just as they were approaching their house, Luca had noticed a family moving into the house across the street, just a few houses away from their own. Dimity looked at the blonde girl, who looked to be the same age as her. A younger girl was on a tricycle, and a boy who looked like he was Andrea's age was carrying some boxes into the house.

"Mum," the blonde girl had called to her mother, looking in Dimity's direction. "That girl is wearing the uniform that I have to wear at my new school."

"Oh, so it is!" her mother had responded, holding a white box in her hands.

They had crossed the road to meet the new family. "Hi," Luca had said. "I'm Luca McKenzie. Yeah, my sister goes to the local primary school. Are you going there too?"

"Yes, she starts on Monday," Dimity's mother had answered. "She's in the third grade."

"Hi," Dimity had greeted the girl. "My name's Dimity. Some people call me Dimi. I'm *also* in the third grade. I can show you around the school on Monday if you like, and introduce you to all my friends."

"Thanks," the new girl had said, shyly. "My name's Nicki."

"My name's Maria!" the girl on the tricycle had yelled, confidently. "I'm going to school next year," she had continued as they all greeted her with a warm smile.

"We actually live in number 28, the house over there, across the street." Andrea pointed it out.

"It's great to meet new people. We don't know anyone in this neighbourhood. Nicki was worried that she wouldn't make any new friends. Would you girls like to try some *baklava*?" The girls' mother had asked with an accent. "I'm Mrs Salas."

"It's a yummy *glyko*," Nicki had told them, slowly coming out of her shyness.

"Yes, it is. *Glyko* means 'sweet' in Greek," her mother had explained.

When Dimity had taken the first bite, she couldn't believe how sweet it tasted. She hadn't tried anything like it. She had eaten it so quickly. "Don't worry Nicki. I'll make sure you make a lot of friends," she had once again reassured her, as she savoured the taste of the sweet in her mouth.

"You're in great hands with my sister. She'll make sure you fit in," Andrea had also reassured Nicki.

Dimity had told her mum the minute they walked through the door. She was so excited that she had a neighbour going to the same school as her. They could all walk to school together, they could ride their bikes in the street, they could do homework together, and visit each other all the time.

Dimity smiled at the memory as she passed Lynn Park in Rose Bay, turning into her street. She pulled into the driveway and turned off the ignition. Entering the house, she walked down the wide hallway and headed straight for the kitchen when she placed the *baklava* on the bench. She heard her parents murmuring on the veranda, so she stepped out to join them. The garden looked so glorious, its splashes of colour surprising her again. Her mother had already set the outdoor coffee table and had laid out the food, which consisted of gourmet sandwiches with smoked salmon and capers, couscous salad, and a vegetable frittata. As she walked towards them, her mother offered her a glass of iced tea with a slice of lemon. Dimity loved that her mum looked after herself. She was so fit and she took pride in her appearance. Dimity would often even lend her some of her outfits. They were similar in height, and she always wore her brown hair in a sophisticated bob.

"Thanks Mum," she said as she sat on the lounge chair next to her dad.

"This looks deliciously healthy. Thanks for setting the table for me."

"No problem, Dimi. I know you have a lot of packing to do anyway."

"This does look lovely," she said once again, looking at the healthy food neatly spread out on the table. "I wonder what Sylvia would say," she said quietly.

"Sylvia?" her father queried. "How are she and Stan? I haven't seen them for a while." Her father was a fair and sociable man who always tried to give everyone the benefit of the doubt. She knew that she got her kindness and generosity from her parents. Malcolm would often tease her that he had to protect her from herself because she was too sweet and forthcoming with people. *Except for his mother*, she thought ruefully.

"Oh, they're okay, I guess … you know, still offering their *lovely* advice on everything I do and making sure I'm aware of any imperfection I may have. Apparently being into healthy food is not a good thing, because I'm starving my girls and we'll age quickly. It's a *bad thing* that my girls don't eat processed foods or bleached flour."

"Oh … Dimity! Try not to worry about what Sylvia says. You never used to worry about things like that. I remember you would just laugh them off. Sylvia makes her 'observations' on everyone, not just you."

"Yes, I know that she does it to a lot of people, and that she's one of those people that can get away with it, but lately she's been almost callous. It's as though she wants to intentionally undermine me. I really don't know how someone as cool and intelligent as Malcolm is related to her. Both his parents are so judgmental. The only thing he gets from his mum are her blue eyes. I admit, she's attractive, especially in photos from her youth, which she proudly keeps showing to everyone. He definitely gets his strong jaw from his father. I'll give them that. Personality-wise, they are so different. They are so obviously cruel. If it wasn't for Alex being at the dinner on Saturday, I don't know how I would have got through the night."

"What about Malcolm?" her mother asked her as she handed her a plate of salad.

79

"What about him?"

"Well, he supports you too, doesn't he?" her mother asked with concern in her voice.

"Well, I don't know. He used to. I don't know," Dimity replied with a slight quiver in her voice as she flicked her soft fringe away from her eyes.

"Well, I'm glad you're going on this trip," her mother continued. "Couples need to be reminded about what made them fall in love with each other. It's hard balancing a family with a career, without neglecting each other."

"It's just that ... I can't believe how distant we've become with each other lately. Sometimes I feel like I shouldn't complain. I have everything I need for myself and my family, but I feel so ... I don't know, empty sometimes, and really lonely. I used to connect with him so much, and now ... it's as though we don't even see each other. I don't know how we meant the world to each other, and now ..."

Dimity felt her father's hand on her shoulder. "Don't worry, Dimi. Just go and visit him. Things have a way of working themselves out. All marriages need work and effort."

"Thanks Dad," she said, leaning her head momentarily on her father's shoulder. She was so grateful her parents were there. A feeling of relief washed over her. She was glad she had confided in them.

"Anyway," her mother said, "I've never seen any man admire a woman the way Malcolm admires you. He was so in love with you, and still is. I think you just need time on your own. He's a really good man for you. He would do anything for you. That's what we thought from the minute we met him. Also, speaking of Sylvia, don't you remember what she told us the first time we met her?"

"What?" Dimity asked curiously, remembering what she had said about her mother, but not wanting to mention it; not that her mother would really mind, the way she was dismissing Sylvia's rudeness. Besides, her mother was as beautiful as ever.

"She said that her son is so lucky to have found a beautiful, intelligent, and genuinely caring girl like you, and that she had every faith in you and Malcolm as a couple."

Dimity's heart nearly stopped. "Sylvia said that — *about me*?" She couldn't remember her mum telling her that. She had probably not paid attention at the time, feeling confident in her marriage, and not caring what anyone else had to say. Back then, they only had eyes for each other. Nothing else mattered, especially trivialities. Their love was above all that.

"Yes, and I never forgot it. I wasn't only happy that you had met a man that adored and loved you so much, but that his family had also accepted you with open arms."

Dimity needed a moment to process what her mother had said. She would never have believed it if someone other than her mother had told her that Sylvia actually said those kind words about her. Still, it didn't excuse her current behaviour. Her mother-in-law had become so spiteful towards her over the years that Dimity imagined Sylvia herself would probably not believe she had ever uttered anything nice about her daughter-in-law either.

"Anyway, you'd better continue packing. Go and be with your wonderful husband. You both need this time. Don't worry about the girls. We'll look after everything. It's about time you let someone help you. Like I've been telling you for so long, you can't do everything on your own. Being a mother doesn't mean you should never do something for yourself. You and Malcolm would always make sure you spent time together. You can have that again." Her mother gave her a reassuring smile.

"Okay, then, I'd better start packing after we have coffee and some *baklava*. Malcolm won't even be in the Netherlands for much longer, but I know he has no urgent projects after that, so I'm hoping we can extend our stay in Europe."

"That sounds wonderful," her mother said with the same reassuring smile.

"The *baklava* sounds good too," her father added.

***

Maria had been packing frantically. She never realised how hard it was to pack for an infant. It was Tuesday morning and they would be leaving the next day. She had to plan a trip to the other side of the world in the space of a few hours. She didn't mind how tired she felt. All of a sudden she wanted to go to Greece. She had become more attached to the idea the moment she planned their itinerary, with her sister's help. She had to find out why her mother deliberately kept the information from her.

Antonio had been in shock when she told him. "You want to go all the way … *to Greece*, just because your mum kept some invitations hidden from you?"

"It doesn't make sense, though. I mean, knowing how relentless my mum is about me getting in touch with my background … don't you think it's odd?"

"It is odd," he had said, "but all the way to Greece, just like that? Do you know how much planning is involved?"

"Don't worry. Nicki will help us. She's in the industry. Besides, when else would we do it? The timing is perfect. You have time off from work, and you finally convinced me to take time away from the shop. It's been a hectic year …"

"*Greece* …" he had looked at the brochures sceptically. "It *would* be nice, and it *is* summer over there." Antonio had finally come around, growing more excited as they discussed which places they should visit.

Just as she and Antonio had become used to the idea, Maria suddenly realised that she would be abandoning her sister at the worst possible time.

"Go … don't worry about me," Nicki had insisted.

"But … I feel bad leaving you," Maria had said. "You know," she had then said, jubilantly, "You could come with us. It would be so much fun. Besides, what would you do here on your own? It may give you a different outlook."

"Maria. Really, I don't mind. I need time alone to process everything, plus, there's work. I just appeared at your doorstep without warning. I don't expect you to babysit me. I just needed somewhere to think."

"Are you sure? Well, if you don't come with us, I'll get Cassandra and Connor to check up on you. They might be able to help you — without any judgment."

Cassandra and Connor, with all their counselling skills, are the perfect people to help Nicki with her problems, Maria thought, easing her guilt. She would ensure they looked out for her.

The trip couldn't have happened without Nicki's help. She had been a godsend, and seemed to welcome the diversion. She immediately began making calls.

"So are you going to visit the house in the village near Ioannina, and where we lived in Agrinio, with Aliki?" she had asked. "It would be weird to go back. I wonder how everything looks now … now that we're older. You know, living in Greece was a great experience for us in many ways. It gave me the insight into what career I wanted to pursue, but when I look back, it also made me realise that relationships don't last forever. Sometimes circumstances can ruin the strongest bonds," she said sullenly.

Maria's heart ached. She wanted her sister to be happy again. Just as she wondered if she was allowed to pack some of her organic baby products in her handbag, she heard Thomas crying. Antonio had gone out to get some last minute things for the trip. Maria hoped Thomas wasn't teething. She walked into his room as she heard the phone ringing. She hastily answered it.

"Hi Mum. I can't really talk right now. Thomas is crying. I have to settle him."

"So Nicki tells me you're going to Greece? Are you sure you'll be able to travel so many hours with a small child? I'm really surprised. Since when did you want to go to Greece?"

"Mum, I can't talk right now," Maria said, putting the phone on speaker mode and struggling to calm Thomas, who was restless after his nap. Of course she would be opposed to the idea — she was obviously hiding something. She would soon find out what it was when she talked to Aliki.

"Well, anyway, what do I know?" her mother continued. "You hip, young mothers know everything these days, but it could be hard on him. Anyway, since you're going, I want you to buy some gifts on your father's and my behalf to give to some of our relatives. You're visiting your uncles and aunts and cousins, aren't you? They'll be offended it you don't. It would also be a good idea to take Thomas to the church I used to attend as a girl."

Maria's jaw dropped. She had heard every word her mother had said. It didn't make sense. She suddenly didn't have a problem with her going to Greece, and now she wanted her to visit everyone? What exactly was going on? Whatever it was, Maria didn't care. She had to go to Greece, to finally see it again with her own adult eyes. Something had always been missing in her life; she felt that Greece had the answers she needed, to make her feel whole, to stop resisting life. Thomas miraculously settled as she walked around the room with him.

"I thought you were concerned about Thomas getting tired," she challenged. "So it's okay to drag him from the city to the village to the islands now? Our relatives are scattered all around Greece."

"How can you travel all that way, and not see everyone?"

Just as Maria was about to answer, Thomas began to cry again.

"Mum, I really have to go now. Can't you hear Thomas crying?"

"You have to go and give them some gifts on our behalf? *You have to* … your father and I will transfer you the money."

"Oh, *I will Mum.* I will visit *everyone.* In fact, I plan to visit the churches, the museums, and as many monasteries as I can, and that's because *I want to.* Don't worry about the money. It's on me," she replied, trying desperately to find a comfortable position for Thomas.

After hanging up the phone, she looked at Thomas. "How dare she tell us what to do … again," she said to her son, who looked at her blankly. "We'll see so much of Greece, and we'll make sure we visit everyone — including Aliki. Just try not to cry so much." She looked at him with a hopeful look on her face before giving him a big hug. *I will find out why Mum is being so mysterious*, she told herself.

CHAPTER TEN

Malcolm Stewart took long casual strides as he walked back to his hotel room after having spent the afternoon having a late lunch meeting with his team. As he walked, a small studio with artwork in the front window caught his attention. He couldn't believe that it had all started for him in a small studio similar to this one, which stood humbly amongst other big name shops in the street. Now he was in Amsterdam again. The city never ceased to amaze and inspire him, with its breathtaking and intricate canal system, its architecture, its history, and the city's love of design and art. It was definitely unique. He was staying right near Centrum *Spiegelkwartier* — an art hub home to many art shops, antique dealers, and quirky, hip cafes. So many times he had imagined holding Dimity in his arms, sitting together in one of the many boats in the canals, gazing in wonderment at the breathtaking views. It had all started for him in Amsterdam. It was here he had won his first prestigious award, paving the way for a successful future. The award had led to the feature article about young up-and-coming industrial designers in which he was included. It had also led to him opening up his studio, where he first met Dimity.

Now, he had become bigger than he ever thought he would be. His brand had branched out on an international level as increasing numbers of commercial and private clients wanted his designs, leading to mass production and his own furniture range. It had also meant keeping up to date with the latest technologies and adapting to new methods, finding different ways to manipulate wood, to prototype, to experiment with textures and form, and to play with aesthetics. The industry was evolving at a quick pace and he felt that he had to change and move with it. He always wanted Dimity and himself to be part of each other's creative worlds, to challenge each other and admire each other's successes. But though he had found success, he never envisioned his life with Dimity to be like this. They practically lived in separate worlds, and that feeling remained even when he was home with his family. It had felt more and more like this of late.

Malcolm walked over to a nearby bench, needing to process his feelings. *We used to be such a happy family,* he thought as he sat down. He was immediately drenched in calming sunlight. He thought of how he felt when she had told him she was carrying his child — their child. He had felt blessed.

He recalled a night years ago, one of the most sacred he had spent with her. They had been married for a few months at the time, though it felt like they were still on their honeymoon. One of his friends from the industry who had been working abroad had decided to have a reunion, inviting friends that they hadn't seen for a while. They were asked to bring their partners. Excited about the prospect of spending a weekend together at the Barossa Valley in South Australia, they eagerly accepted. It was the perfect, romantic getaway, with friends, good food, wine, and each other. It was also a chance to spend time together before Dimity commenced work on a prestigious hotel project; she had been ecstatic about being part of the project team.

Dimity hadn't met this particular group of Malcolm's friends. The house they had all rented was perched on a hill overlooking one of the region's many vineyards. She had been helping in the kitchen, preparing drinks and some snacks to accompany the wine, laughing with his work associates and their partners as they all shared stories about their design escapades. Malcolm had been playing a game of cards with one of the guys in the lounge room, occasionally glancing in her direction through the open kitchen, admiring her as she mingled with the others.

He had looked away from his game and smiled at her from the lounge room. She had caught him looking at her and had stopped what she was doing. She smiled back at him. They both knew what the other was thinking. The heat from the room had increased in ferocity; it wasn't just from the lit fireplace. She looked so sexy and irresistible in her floral dress with thin spaghetti straps. It was similar to the one she had worn when she had first entered his life. Not being able to control his desire anymore, he walked towards her and looked intensely into her eyes. He instantly felt the heat from her hand when he held it gently. She smiled at him, staring at him without talking. She had felt it too.

He had led her out of the room into the hallway. As they walked towards their bedroom, he had stopped and kissed her gently on the lips. She had responded and began kissing him more intensely. When they heard murmuring close by, they had both stood still, hugging each other, breathing deeply as though they were being tortured. "We better go to our room," he had said. As soon as they entered, he had turned her around gently and began kissing her passionately. He had then whispered in her ear, "You are so hot tonight. You're driving me crazy." She had smiled at him. She then began to unbutton his shirt, in between kisses. It was one of the most intense nights they had ever had. Marriage had only deepened their connection.

Malcolm smiled at the memory as he sat on the bench, feeling the need to remember how strong the connection had been between them. They had created their first precious child that night — their daughter Samantha.

"Hi, you're Malcolm Stewart, the industrial designer." A young woman was looking at him, eagerly awaiting his response.

Forced back to the present, he instantly sat up straight. He was used to getting stopped by eager young women who at times treated him like he was a rock star.

"Yes, I am. You're familiar with my work?" he asked through squinted eyes, not wanting to disappoint the young woman. He genuinely liked encouraging new designers. He just needed to weed out which ones weren't just interested in his designs.

"Well, I love looking at design magazines. I'm not really in the industry. I just had to see you in person," she continued, still smiling at him. "So, if you need someone to show you around, I grew up here …"

"That's okay," he responded politely as he stood up. "I have a meeting I need to attend. Thanks anyway," he said, and then began to walk away, smiling to himself.

Looking at his watch, he walked briskly past the shops, stopping once more to admire the little studio selling artwork. He caught a glimpse of a man coming out of the back room. His top was splattered with paint. He saw himself, the way he used to be — free to create, doing what he loved.

Back at the hotel, still deep in thought, he stepped into the elevator. He really did need to get ready for a conference call and then make some notes for tomorrow's meeting with Julie Canei. He didn't want to disappoint her. She was one of those designers that genuinely loved what she was doing. He could relate to that. He had been surprised by a familiar passion and appreciation for the design process. She was also attractive, in a sweet way. As the lift opened, he stepped out of it, acknowledging a woman who was smiling at him, letting him step out of the lift before she stepped in. He really needed to be with Dimity — he needed to connect with her again. He hoped it wasn't too late, and that her erratic behaviour was a temporary phase. But as he remembered how she had attacked his mother at the dinner party, he wondered if he had already lost her.

CHAPTER ELEVEN

Dimity was sitting in the departure lounge at Sydney Airport. It was Tuesday evening and there was no turning back now. She was going to try and reconnect with Malcolm again. She couldn't hide her exaltation about the trip. She had told Alex about her plans to surprise Malcolm. He thought it was really great, and said that he wished he could find a girl like her, and that Malcolm was so lucky to have her. "So he better start treating you right again," he commented.

Dimity had enquired about how his parents and even Aunt Marianne were, curious to see if they had said anything about her behaviour at the recent dinner.

"So you mean you want to know if they think you're an utter bitch who wouldn't know a frying pan from a Stella McCartney dress?" he had asked.

"Well, yeah," she had responded.

"Relax," he had said. "They'll get over it, and that auntie of ours ... I thought Malcolm was arrogant lately, but she definitely gives him a run for his money. I seriously don't know how I'm related to all of them. I'm just lucky to be the youngest and get away with everything. You know, if you didn't say anything that night, I probably would have. Seriously, I don't know who they think they are sometimes."

"You still didn't answer my question, Alex. Does that mean, yes? They did say that about me? I wouldn't be surprised. I mean, I may have come down a little harsh. Your mum isn't even overweight and I must admit, it is beneath me to pick on someone's weight. I was being spiteful. She did hurt my feelings, though."

"Don't worry about them. Yeah, I'll admit, they were stunned, but I've never seen them so tongue-tied in my life. Anyway, go be with that brother of mine. You know, I can't believe how into himself he's become. Ever since he's become this *big shot designer*, he's really changed."

"I think we both have," she had said, knowingly.

Dimity instinctively checked if her mobile and boarding pass were in her bag. She had finished the rest of her packing after she and her parents had their coffee and *baklava*. Even her daughters helped her when they came home from school, picking out outfits that they insisted all the models in the magazines were wearing. Samantha, who was in Year 5 and in the middle of a reproduction topic in her Physical Education and Development class, even tried to suss out if it was a second honeymoon for her and her dad, giggling with her sister as she asked.

She had kissed the girls and her mum and dad goodbye, before Samantha reminded her not to forget to purchase the promised leather jacket. *They sure start young*, Dimity had thought, although she was reminded of her days wearing her Wham t-shirt, studded cut off gloves, and Madonna inspired virgin bangles, and the teased hair inspired by Bananarama she and her sisters used to have. She had been barely ten years old. Dimity and her sisters wished that her mum *had* intervened back then after looking at old photos of themselves at their parents' house every Christmas. They all declared that they looked like clowns. Luca's eyeliner had been applied so heavily in one of the photos that she looked like she belonged in one of Alice Cooper's music videos.

"Excuse me," Dimity said to a man who looked to be in his thirties as she tried to get to her seat by the window. As she finally sat down, placing her handbag on her lap, she acknowledged the man with an apologetic smile. He was seated right by the aisle, leaving a seat between them. He smiled back at her and she couldn't help but notice that he was very attractive.

"So, are you going away on business?" he politely asked, giving her another friendly smile.

"No, I'm going to Amsterdam for a vacation," she answered, matching his smile. Her heart was racing so fast; she was nervous with positive energy. She felt like she wanted to share her plan with the world.

"That's where I'm heading. We should catch up and see the city … you know, two Australians in a foreign place," he enthusiastically suggested.

Dimity was taken aback by his proposition. She never really knew if someone was hitting on her. The man was still smiling at her as the seat belt light went on.

"Well, looks like we're in luck. No-one's sitting in the seat between us," he said leaning closer to her side.

"I'm meeting my husband there … in Amsterdam," she added, sensing that the attractive man sitting next to her was getting a bit too friendly. "My parents are minding the kids. We have kids … *together*," she continued, in case he didn't get the picture.

"Oh," the man replied, his smile fading.

After an awkward silence, the steward enquired if they would like headphones and the attractive man sitting next to her instantly accepted them. He then placed them on his ears, and gave her the *look*, which could only mean one thing. It was the "don't think that I'll be talking to you for the rest of this flight" look.

Mid-flight, a few martinis and one Bloody Mary later, with the attractive and now unfriendly man contentedly fast asleep next to her, Dimity's mind began to wonder about simpler, more innocent times. Feeling emotional from the alcohol, she pondered about her childhood. Staring searchingly into the clouds, her mind drifted back to the time she had met Nicki and Maria. It had been a fun and exciting time, when life suddenly became one big adventure. They did everything together. In the beginning, they played together at the local park. They walked to school together and walked home together, meeting Dimity's sisters at the bus stop midway, where the high school kids were dropped off. They would stop at the milk bar and treat themselves to cinnamon doughnuts and a milkshake, or an ice cream on the really hot days. If they were really hungry, they would stop at the Greek hamburger shop owned by Maria and Nicki's uncle.

Homework had even become fun as they took turns visiting each other and completing it together. Mrs Salas would always serve them the most delicious Greek food, and she would often make mouth-watering sweets. They would also team up against Nicki and Maria's older brother, John, telling him to turn down his music when it got too loud. Maria was always with them, and even became one of Nicki and Dimity's "clients" when they pretended they ran a hair and beauty salon.

Whenever Nicki and Maria would visit Dimity's house, Mrs McKenzie would cut them a bowl of refreshing fruit and they would sit at the outdoor patio and eavesdrop on Dimity's older sisters as they sat on the banana chairs and talked about boys. The younger girls would giggle quietly behind their boat-shaped watermelon slices so that Andrea and Luca didn't see. Nicki had even come along with Dimity and her family on many of their fishing trips on Mr McKenzie's boat. Maria would protest when her mother would tell her that she was too young to join them. She would hear screaming coming from the Salas house when Maria would have to attend a Greek church function instead.

As Nicki and Dimity became teenagers, and Maria officially a tween, they had so much fun sitting in Maria and Nicki's backyard, talking about which boy they found the spunkiest at school. During that time, they welcomed the loud music that blared from John's room. He was heavily into grunge, and they would pretend they were in the mosh pit of a concert. At Dimity's house, whenever Luca and

Andrea weren't around, they would sneak into their rooms and try all their clothes and accessories.

They had become inseparable. Dimity and Nicki shared most of their classes at school. Art was their favourite subject and they would eagerly plan what their next painting or collage would be as they were often assigned to work as a team. Their art teacher had been amazed at some of their work. Dimity remembered the time when they were in Year Ten when the class had to make a tapestry. It was one of the things they had to do while studying art history. They were fifteen at the time and had begun to take their art very seriously. They worked on the tapestry together, both in class and every day after school, in between doing their other homework. Mrs Salas had shown them some of the old Greek tapestries she had, which inspired them.

"How are we supposed to make ours look like that?" Nicki had cried.

"I'm sure we can do it," Dimity had offered. "Ours will look even better. The Salas and McKenzie girls can do anything!"

"Yeah!" Maria had also enthused. "We can do anything! I'll also help. I love art." She had looked at them with hopeful eyes.

"You can help me in the kitchen with the *loukomades*," Mrs Salas had interjected. "They're for the church excursion tomorrow."

"I wanna help Nicki and Dimity. I can't go with you to the excursion *or* help in the kitchen …"

"Okay, you can help us," Nicki had intervened with a worried look, knowing too well that Maria and her mother would end up in a screaming match. "We do need all the help we can get. I'll mind Maria. She can hang out with us tomorrow," she had added confidently, meeting her mother's apprehensive eyes.

"Yeah, don't worry Mrs Salas. We'll mind Maria. My sisters and my mum can also check up on us. We'll be okay,"

Dimity had added, taking pity on her young friend. Mrs Salas always dragged Maria to so many Greek church events.

"I think this picture would be perfect," Nicki had continued, pointing at a picture of a white church perched on a hill overlooking the Aegean Sea. Mrs Salas hesitantly left them to carry on, allowing Maria to contribute.

"*Yeah!* I can be part of the team, and I don't have to go to that *stupid* ..."

"Yes, my little sister. Consider yourself hired," Nicki had interrupted as she heard her mother hovering around, obviously unsure about her decision.

The tapestries Mrs Salas had shown them led to conversations about travel, and how amazing it would be to live on a Greek Island. They had kept their promise and allowed Maria to pitch in, letting her work on a small section of the sea. When they had finally completed the tapestry, both their families and their teacher were left speechless. Dimity found it fascinating that although they strayed with different colours and in different directions, it all came together in the end, as one complete and beautiful picture. They had all contributed their own beauty to it and everyone couldn't believe how professional it looked — so much so that it was chosen to be displayed in the school office for a few months. Once they could take the tapestry home, Dimity had let Nicki and Maria have it for a while, after which it was her turn. They all decided that they would always be together in life, even when they were married. Their kids would grow up together and they would go on family vacations together. They were all truly best friends.

"Excuse me. Do you want coffee or tea?" the man sitting next to her asked, as the steward awaited her response. He hadn't talked to her since their earlier conversation. She had been so caught up in her memories that she hadn't even heard the question.

"Yes, I'll have a coffee. Thanks."

"Here you go." He helped pass the coffee to her. "Looks like you were a million miles away," he said. "Pardon the pun," he quickly added.

"Yes, I was … and the pun was actually funny," she said, surprised at his sudden change of heart. "Not long now," Dimity continued as she looked at the map on the screen. She followed his suddenly friendly cue. "Looks like we're nearly in Hong Kong," she added, noticing that he had consumed as many alcoholic beverages as she had — if not more. *That explains his change in attitude.*

"So, you're meeting your husband in Amsterdam? Is that what had you in the clouds? Sorry," he said, looking shocked. "I can't believe I did that again. Believe me … I don't usually talk like this. I'm usually very eloquent with the English language. I'm an English professor. I'm going to Amsterdam to see the House of Anne Frank. After getting my students to read the book so many times, I thought I'd go and see it for myself."

"Wow," Dimity managed. "I'm intrigued, and I too am usually more eloquent. Generally, I use more creative words than *wow* too," she added, smiling and suddenly feeling the need to impress him with her vocabulary. "Yes, I'm meeting my husband. I'm actually surprising him."

"Oh, he isn't expecting you?"

"No, he isn't. I hope he's thrilled to see me and everything works …" Dimity once again got ahead of herself.

"Everything works out for you?" he continued. "That's what you wanted to say, isn't it? Well, I'm sure he'll be thrilled to see you, and if it doesn't work out, you can still meet me in Amsterdam," he added, smiling cheekily. "I'm just kidding. Trust me, it *will* work out. He'd be a complete idiot to give up someone as beautiful and charming as you."

"Well, thanks for the compliment, and I hope you're right."

"Oh, I am right. You broke my heart the minute you told me you were married."

"Oh …" she said, smiling. "I have a feeling you say that to a lot of girls."

"No, I don't," he said, looking back at his magazine.

Dimity smiled to herself and looked out of the window. He was right. It had to work out. *Malcolm will be so happy and surprised to see me,* she thought excitedly. *His work obligations will be over soon and we'll have the second honeymoon we never had. We'll only have eyes for each other! Besides, it's true — he would be a complete idiot if he gave up on me.* She needed to hear that. She needed to feel like a desirable and interesting woman again. She'd take the compliment. She needed to get her confidence back — now more than ever.

***

Nicki stared at the house she grew up in. She had to see it again, to remember the laughter and the dreams — her life before it became so complicated. She had always felt safe in their home as a little girl. Her boots made a clacking sound as she stepped onto the rough asphalt in the laneway — the same laneway where she, Maria, and Dimity would play cricket. The lemon tree her father had planted was still in the garden after all these years. It had weathered all sorts of elements, and there it still stood, strong as ever. She remembered the overhanging grape vine, the *klimatia,* in her mind. She could hear laughter as she imagined her parents, Maria and herself, eating the fresh figs from the fig tree as they sat on the table under the *klimatia;* hearing John's loud music blasting from his bedroom window.

She then walked over and peered into the front bedroom window. She noticed a man working on his computer. It was the bedroom where they would sit for hours, talking and listening to music, doing homework together, convincing Maria to do her Greek school homework, telling her that it was useful to know another language, as her mother had instructed them to do as the "wiser" and "older" girls. It was the room where they used to play hairdressers, where Maria was their client and they had almost ruined her thick, long hair when a brush stubbornly entangled itself between strands of brunette. It was the bedroom where their mother would bring them homemade *baklava* or shortbread biscuits, *kourabiethes*, while they made their tapestry on the loom — thread by thread. She remembered the blue — how striking it was, how excited they had been that it would depict the beauty of the Aegean Sea.

"The weft threads are the only ones that are seen," she had told Maria and Dimity. "The warp threads are needed to allow the weft threads to do the work. See how the loom keeps the warp threads firm, to allow the interweaving of the weft threads?"

"Yes, they're all needed to make the picture; even the one's behind the scenes, like a play, I guess," Dimity had said, sceptically.

"They're all a team ... the loom, the weft and warp threads," Maria had said, proudly, as she began to get the hang of it. "Like we are," she had added, excitedly.

Nicki turned to look at the McKenzies' house across the street — number 28. Nicki remembered how she loved trying on Andrea and Luca's clothes when they were out: studded belts, leather jackets — the coolest clothes she had ever seen.

A white furry cat with green eyes suddenly caught her attention. She smiled at it as it stretched its agile body.

"Come on kitty. I have some milk for you," she heard Dimity's voice in her mind. "Come on kitty. You can stay here. You don't have to sleep alone — in the cold streets." The cat had hesitantly approached the entrance of the house; one of the many cats that Dimity had lured. She and Maria had looked on with excitement.

"Are you inviting another cat to live with us?" Mrs McKenzie had called out.

"It's hungry. I'm just feeding it and then it'll go away."

"Dimity ... you know once you give them milk; they'll never leave."

"Dad always helps people ... like that sad woman ... the one with the cat. *She left*," Dimity had challenged.

Nicki looked at a car being parked across the road. A few minutes later, a woman stepped out of it — right in front of the McKenzies' house. She helped a little boy out from the back seat. Nicki instinctively smiled at her. She looked at the little boy looking with jubilant eyes at the cat. He then held his mother's hand and crossed the road. Nicki watched them enter their house — the house that friends and relatives used to refer to as "the Salas house". Breathing heavily, she tightened the belt of her brown anorak and passed the old milk bar where they used to frequently hang out after school, that used to always smell of cinnamon doughnuts. She could almost taste the cinnamon on her lips. It was now a depressing discount shop. Lifting her collar against a sudden chill, she continued walking towards the car.

CHAPTER TWELVE

"Antonio, please ... can you help me with Thomas' pram? I don't know how to fold this thing, especially with these flat shoes. It's as though I have no shoes on. We have to board soon, and we haven't even gone through customs."

Maria had been frantic all morning. She wasn't used to travelling with a child. Deep down she could still hear her mother's words and she did feel nervous about travelling from place to place with a one-year-old. "Breathe in, breathe out," she'd advised herself all morning. "I'm a holistic, present-centred person. I own a shop full of healing incense oil, and scented candles ... and new-age CDs. I can handle this calmly and efficiently."

"It's okay, Maria. We'll get there." Antonio methodologically placed the luggage on the conveyer belt, looking at the woman working behind the counter apologetically.

"Don't worry so much, Maria! Remember, you might run into one of your customers. They won't believe anything you have to say about how relaxing the organic herbal teas are," said Cassandra, the proud godmother, who held Thomas and gave Nicki a knowing look.

Nicki had volunteered to drive Antonio and Maria to the airport, and Cassandra and Connor met them at the international terminal. Nicki looked at Connor. He was taller than she remembered. She had last seen him at Thomas' christening. She had been in her own world that day. He reached out his hand to officially greet her. "How are you, Nicki?"

"I'm okay ... I guess," she answered self-consciously, as he studied her with his kind aqua-blue eyes. He seemed to genuinely want to know the answer. Nicki awkwardly flicked her hair away from her face when she then met

Cassandra's concerned eyes. It was as though they could sense her denial … everything was far from okay.

Maria then continued. "I am relaxed on the inside, and if I didn't have to talk to our beloved mother, who wouldn't stop reminding me to visit everyone on her list of relatives, I would have had time to have one of my herbal teas," she added, looking from Cassandra to Nicki.

"Well, at least you're doing something exciting. Do you believe my stubborn sister who resisted doing anything that was considered Greek, practically all her life, is actually going to *Greece*?"

"Well, I hear this wouldn't be happening if it wasn't for you, Nicki," Cassandra said. "I can't believe you organised the trip so quickly. How are you doing anyway? It's been a while since we've seen you." Cassandra looked at her thoughtfully.

"What are older sisters for? Besides, I wanted to see what our mum would think. You've probably noticed, as one of Maria's closest friends, that my sister tends to do the opposite if someone dares to define her," Nicki continued, smiling.

"It would be great to catch up. Neither of us have clients this morning, so why don't we have a coffee after Maria and Antonio leave, and this little cutie of course," she said, lifting Thomas in the air and kissing him on the nose.

"Sure, why not? I'm not working yet anyway," Nicki said, patting her little nephew on the back. Connor gave her a warm smile. Perhaps she needed to talk to an expert.

"Coffee sounds great right about now," Maria said, checking her tote bag for the tenth time that morning, in case she forgot anything she needed in the plane for Thomas.

"Well, at least you're going somewhere romantic together, and you've got this little guy …" Nicki trailed off, her eyes tearing.

"Oh Nicki ..." Maria hugged her sister. "I'm so sorry. Here I am going on and on about how stressful it is to pack ... I'm sorry ..."

"You don't need to be sorry for everything. I'm so happy for all of you. You have a beautiful boy, who I adore, and a very handsome and creative husband," she said, smiling at Antonio. "I'm so proud of my little sister. It's not your fault for any of this. I'll be okay. Anyway, I'm glad I'm in Sydney. Now I can be closer to you and Thomas," she said as they walked away from the luggage check in area.

"And away from Mum," Maria added, smiling at her.

"Well, thanks for the compliment," Antonio interjected, giving Nicki a sincere hug.

"One more question before you leave our shores. Did you buy the gifts that were on Mum's list? I mean, you're really losing your rebellious streak if you did," Nicki enquired.

"Well, kind of. I got the gifts that I wanted, from *my* shop; gift wrapped with the company logo," she said, laughing. "The business is online now; you know? Might as well get it out there as much as I can!"

***

Dimity boarded the next KLM flight in Hong Kong, greeting the steward at the entrance as she made her way to her seat. The now charming professor waved to her from his seat, and she reciprocated before moving further down the aisle to her own. She sat down, and fastened the seat belt. She then opened her bag and took out her phone. She scanned through her photos until she saw his face. Malcolm's eyes were smiling; so were hers. He had her arms around her, and he looked proud and content. They were so in love at that wedding, which was for one of Dimity's distant relatives. It was one of her favourite photos and was taken a while ago; before they began to lose each other, and before she began to realise that she had made a big mistake in leaving the career she loved so much. She needed him back in her life. She so wanted to be the happy family they used to be.

Hours later, Dimity grabbed her luggage from the conveyer belt, and quickly made her way towards the taxi stand at Amsterdam Airport Schiphol. She was amazed at how contemporary the airport was. It was more like a museum of modern art. There was actually a very impressive art gallery in the airport itself, as well as some of the finest restaurants of the sort that would usually be found in a hotel or the main part of the city. As a particularly interesting lighting fixture caught her attention, she instantly thought of Malcolm; imagining how he would analyse the lights and unique chairs and tables scattered throughout the airport whenever he would go to Amsterdam. She stood there for a while, admiring how beautifully the light fixtures hung in the contemporary space.

As she continued walking towards the glass exit doors, she smiled at a familiar looking man. It was the Australian English professor. He was getting into one of the taxis when he had noticed her. She waved back to him. She was glad he turned out to be a nice guy. After all, it wasn't his fault that he found her irresistible and had been heartbroken when she told him she was married. Dimity smiled to herself as she remembered his words. She suddenly felt feminine and confident. Just being out in the world made her feel sensual and beautiful. She had changed her outfit in the airport restrooms, which had been as clean and well designed as the rest of the extremely busy airport, as if they belonged in a very clean five-star hotel. She had opted for a beautiful pair of relaxed-fitting grey marle pants, and a matching tailored cami. She completed the look with a pair of espadrilles, a long silver necklace, and a silver cuff on her wrist. She also messed up her silky hair a bit, to create a tousled look. She knew Malcolm always thought she looked sexy with her hair slightly wild. The sudden warm weather they were having in

Sydney had done wonders for her complexion, creating a deeper honey glow. With a retouch of her deep pink lipstick and a spray of her floral-citrus perfume, she was ready to try to rekindle what she and Malcolm had lost. The plan was to go straight to his hotel and surprise him.

Dimity stepped out of the taxi. She was standing in a street lined with many shops and restaurants. She ran her eyes along one of the main canals nearby, observing the cars and bikes parked diagonally along each side, and imagined herself and Malcolm in one of the boats. *Maybe later in the evening,* she thought, feeling her heart racing, unable to control her excitement. *I'm actually in Amsterdam!* she thought with excitement. *I actually did it.*

She walked closer to the hotel near Centrum *Spiegelkwartier,* and looked around, taking in the beauty of the city, marvelling at the old buildings juxtaposed with the very new architectural designs. She noticed that many were repurposed apartment buildings. She realised why Malcolm kept insisting that she go with him on some of his trips. "Why are you so opposed to getting some help?" he had asked her impatiently one day, when he showed her his itinerary for another planned trip to Amsterdam, which also included a stop in Milan. "It would be a great chance to travel together … to spend time together — just you and me," he had pleaded.

She walked towards the five-star hotel, feeling beautiful in her choice of outfit. The glass door opened automatically and she smiled at the doorman as he greeted her. The fabric of her cami felt so soft and sensual on her skin. Her espadrilles made a slight pitter-patter sound as she took gentle steps on the marble floor; her slightly flared pants floating freely; caressing her skin as she walked through the foyer. She came to a halt, her eyes wide open in disbelief. It was so beautiful, from the marble floor and walls, to the contemporary gold pendant lights and floor lamps, the avant-garde chairs and designer rugs, all perfectly positioned within the enormous space. She breathed it all in. This was what she had always aspired to do one day — to work on a large scale interior design project in a prestigious hotel like the one in which she was now standing.

After a short while, she snapped out of her state of adulation, and realised she had no inkling of where Malcolm might be in the hotel. Dimity had managed to get Alex to call and discretely find out any information. He had found out a room number without too much trouble. She began walking towards the lifts, her heart racing with excitement to see him, and to surprise him. She wanted to see love in his eyes again. As she continued walking, she passed a lounge and bar area. The room looked so cosy and alive with people talking, drinking, and enjoying the piano music. She could hear high and low-pitched voices from segregated conversations, intertwined with the gentle clinking of cutlery on porcelain plates, and fine crystal glasses periodically placed on polished glass tables. The aroma of walnut liquor awoke her senses, as she neared the bar. The cosy space had such a sophisticated, worldly vibe to it. She felt inspired as she scanned the room.

Suddenly she noticed a sophisticated looking man in a denim shirt sitting with his back to her, running his hand through his hair. It was him — it was Malcolm. She knew that look a mile away — the confidence, the thick, soft, almost black wavy hair, the way he casually sat back in his chair, and the watch with the brown leather strap she had given him on his thirty-fifth birthday. It was *him*. She instinctively began to walk towards him. She was so excited. Just as she was about to surprise him by running up and planting a kiss on his cheek, he laughed. She immediately stopped walking. He was with someone. As he momentarily moved his head, taking a sip from his beer, she noticed a pretty, sophisticated young woman sitting across from him. Her light brown hair shone in the illumination of a floor lamp next to her. She was holding an iPad in her hands and she was also laughing. They looked like they were speaking their own language — they were both so animated, so passionate about their conversation. The woman was smiling at him as she picked up a glass of wine. It was *her* — the woman in the magazine she had found in the drawer of the side table.

Dimity didn't know what to do. Was it the right time to surprise him? She suddenly felt like an outsider, as though she didn't belong there in their creative world. She used to be in that world too, once upon a time. She used to smile wholeheartedly; immersing herself in her work. He used to look at her the way he was now looking at the young woman. She could see his eyes now as he picked up a notebook and sat on the chair beside the woman. They were so seductive. Even after so many years of marriage, she would at times lose herself in them. His neat beard made him look masculine and sexy; it had grown out from its usual stubble. Instinctively, she moved closer towards them. They were still smiling, as though sharing a private joke. She *did* have a right to be there! The man that was sitting there so suavely was her husband. He had wanted her to be there — with him. She could still feel her heart racing, but it was now heavier. She was determined, however, to do what she set out to do.

"Malcolm," she said quietly as she moved to stand behind him.

He spun around. "Dimity?" He looked shocked. "What on earth are you doing here?" His voice was deeper than usual. His smile faded, as he stood up with a perplexed look in his eyes. They didn't look as warm as they usually did. They looked hurt — almost afraid.

"I thought I'd surprise you," she replied awkwardly, feeling the woman's curious stare. She felt like she was talking to a stranger, rather than her husband. The way he was looking at her was so seriously, so formal.

He stood up to face her. Dimity tried hard to suppress the feeling that threatened to spill over into her heart — the feeling that Malcolm wasn't happy to see her. He was still in shock, she reassured herself. Of course he wanted her there. But as much as she told herself that, she couldn't help but feel that he was trying to steer her away from the woman, as if she had interrupted something important. She got the feeling that he was embarrassed of her being there.

"Dimity … is everything okay? Are the girls okay? I'm just so stunned to see you here. What's going on?" he continued, taking her by the arm and leading her to a quiet part of the foyer.

Dimity was taken aback. He hadn't even kissed her. She had travelled all this way, and he hadn't even kissed her. He was looking at her like she had lost her mind. She felt irritated at the feeling of his hand on her arm.

"Malcolm, I came to surprise you. Aren't you glad to see me? Why are you looking at me like there's something wrong with me?" She suddenly stopped walking. She needed to hear what he had to say.

"I'm just shocked," he said, looking deep into her eyes. "This isn't like you," he continued, talking softly so no one would hear.

"That's what makes it a surprise — the fact that it isn't something I would usually do. Why are you looking at me like that?" she asked again, looking into his questioning eyes.

"It's just … you haven't been yourself lately," he replied.

"What are you talking about? I don't understand why you're acting like this," she said. Her heart felt even heavier. She felt like he was breaking it piece by piece with his accusing, questioning eyes.

"You know what I'm talking about, Dimity … the scene with my mother. I mean, you were so callous and vindictive. It just isn't like you. You haven't been yourself lately *at all*."

He had now led her to a quiet conference room. Dimity felt like he was looking at her in the way a nervous parent would at a defiant child who was threatening to throw a tantrum in public. She couldn't believe what he had just said. He had the audacity to look at her like that, after what he had accused her of? *How dare he say that I was the callous and vindictive one! Was he even at the same dinner?*

"How can you say that when you saw how much your mother hurt me? Didn't you hear the cruel things she said about me? She insulted me *and* my mother. It's bad enough that you didn't defend me at all. I mean, you just sat there looking at me like I was out of line when she's been out of line *since we got married*!" Dimity responded, raising her voice.

"Dimity … please, *calm down*. A client might see you." He reached out to touch her shoulders, to calm her.

"Who exactly are you worried about? The pretty woman you were having a *meeting* with? You both looked like you had a lot of important things to discuss. That would explain why you were laughing so much." Dimity fumed. Tears streamed down her cheeks. She was breathing quickly, feeling that she had to gasp for air. This wasn't how she had envisioned things. He was supposed to greet her with a passionate kiss and a warm embrace. He was supposed to be over the moon that she was there to spend time with him!

"Her name is Julie," he said with a serious look on his face.

"What?" Dimity's heart sank. He was being so protective of this woman.

"The woman you're referring to; her name is Julie … And what are you talking about? Now you're being childish. She has nothing to do with our problems, so please leave her out of this. You can't just blame the world, Dimity. You've been acting erratically and distant for months now … and why did you just emphasise the word *meeting*? Just what are you accusing me of?"

"You know what I'm accusing you of. Didn't we have the same type of *meeting* when we met? Didn't you used to look at me the way you're looking at her, instead of this look you're giving now? It's almost as though you don't want me to even be here, as though I'll embarrass you or even ruin your plans." Dimity trembled all over.

"Yes, you're right. I was looking at her with admiration, but not for the reasons you think. I was admiring her passion, her drive and optimism — qualities that I had admired about you. Julie reminds me of the reasons I fell in love with you. Lately, I don't even know who you are anymore. I don't know where that kind, warm, passionate and determined woman has gone, the one who used to forgive people, and see the good in them and the world. As for my mum, you haven't exactly been friendly with her over the years. You used to find her observations funny. They only became more intense because you completely disregard anything she has to say."

"Stop it! I don't want to hear any more." Tears ran down her cheeks. Each word he uttered felt like a dagger in her heart. "I can't believe you can be so cruel. I tried to do everything for you, for our family. I've put my career on hold so I can ensure you and the girls are able to prosper and achieve your best. Do you think I don't miss being that passionate, optimistic woman I used to be? Now, instead of appreciating all the sacrifices I made, you just stand there and make me feel like I'm worthless?" Dimity couldn't stop crying.

"Oh, don't put that on me Dimity!" he said with a tight jaw. "I never told you to abandon your career; I never told you to mind the girls without any help. How many times did I talk to you about getting help so you could pursue your career again? How many times did I tell you to join me on my trips so you can get some inspiration and follow your dreams? Anyway, you need to calm down. You're shaking all over. I don't want to upset you anymore. Let's go and talk in my room. We can get something to eat." He placed his hands on her shoulders, suddenly looking worried.

"*Leave me alone!* Don't worry … I won't embarrass you. I know that's what you're worried about. I can't believe that you're blaming me for everything. I did so much so you can be where you are today. I didn't want to ruin your career. You were *Malcolm Stewart — the up and coming designer*. I hadn't even made my mark yet. I was close though; I was being considered for a design project with one of the major hotels. They knew that I was so eager and capable of doing it. I had proven myself when I became part of the design team. That never happened though. I was left behind again. I knew deep down you didn't think my career was as important as yours. I knew that everyone expected me to step aside and let your career take off. I mean, the industry adored you — you were the one that could change the industry with your innovative ideas."

"Dimity … What are you talking about? I was so proud of your accomplishments. That's why I fell in love with you; you had determination in your eyes, not only for your work, but for finding happiness in life. I wanted you to succeed, and to have it all," Malcolm said, trying to touch her face.

She recoiled. "Really, Malcolm? You say you wanted me to succeed in the industry. Well, if you wanted me to succeed, then why would you have been so careless? Why would you have not even considered what it would have done to me? I mean, the timing was unbelievable. I was about to be accepted as one of the interior designers for a major project in a new *five-star hotel for God's sake!*" She was almost hysterical now, looking at Malcolm straight in his genuinely perplexed eyes. "You know what I'm talking about, Malcolm. *That night* … the night when you said that I was driving you crazy, the night when you couldn't keep your hands off of me at the Barossa Valley. Remember I had told you that we need to be careful. Well, you insisted that it was all okay. Well, it wasn't okay, was it — the next thing I knew I was pregnant, and *we had just got married!*" Dimity said angrily. He was hurt. He looked like someone

110

had knocked the air out of him. His jaw was so tight; his shoulders so tense. He had moved away from her. Dimity couldn't stop. She knew she was being vindictive but she couldn't stop. There was so much hurt inside her; so many repressed feelings.

"Was that your plan — for me to stay home while you furthered your career? I mean, you knew they were about to offer me the job; and then they didn't. All of a sudden, I was assigned to run errands, and place orders again. I was back to being the assistant. The minute Meagan found out I was pregnant, do you know what she said to me? She said she would have to give the job to Susan because it would involve a lot of travelling ... and then do you know what she said? *'Go back to that handsome husband of yours. Everyone is talking about him. Tell him we might need some of his pieces from his furniture range for the hotel project.'* That's what she said to me."

Dimity finally stopped. Malcolm looked so serious. She could almost see the vulnerable little boy in him.

"Have you finished?" he finally asked, softly. "Well, I'm glad I know where we stand now," he continued, staring at her intensely.

"You didn't even care that my career took a beati ..."

"Just stop! I've heard enough!" His voice was louder now — angrier. "I don't know who you are anymore. You're right! I couldn't resist you that night. You were this beautiful, sweet, determined and confident woman I had fallen so hard for. Now, I realise you're different. That woman would never have uttered those words to me. Oh, you're definitely still beautiful; there's no doubt about that. But it was your warmth and kindness that made you irresistible. I apologise for showing you how much I loved and desired you that night. It won't happen again, because I can't pretend — I can't touch someone that I don't even know. I'm not made like that. I thought there was hope for us. When I saw you standing there in the bar, I was shocked, but the shock began to wane, and I thought we could try to work things out and spend time together, but things are worse than I thought, Dimity. I don't even recognise you. No one's ever hurt me the way you've just hurt me now. And you've changed. All I see now is an attractive woman in designer clothes, but nothing else. Your kindness and heart are gone." He looked her straight in the eye as though he wanted her to feel each word. His eyes brimmed with tears.

Dimity stared back. The crease between his eyebrows became deeper as his words left an imprint in her heart. This wasn't how she wanted things to turn out. She couldn't listen to him anymore either. She didn't want him to keep looking at her with such disappointment; she couldn't handle it. She had to get out. She could hear murmuring from outside. A man entered the room with a laptop. Other people also entered the room. They were preparing for some type of conference. Dimity fixed her hair and wiped her tears with her hands. She couldn't embarrass Malcolm like this. He was well known in Amsterdam. She didn't want to be there with him anymore, anyway. They had hurt each other so much. Her heart was aching to the point where she couldn't breathe.

"I have to get out of here," she said, holding her bag tightly. "Sorry for ruining your meeting with … *Julie*," she said as she struggled to breathe.

"Where are you going?" he asked, concerned.

"I don't know. I can't be here though. I have to go," she said, walking quickly towards the door of the conference room. She was now heading towards the exit of the hotel, passing the lounge and bar area. The woman named Julie was still there, sitting at the table and typing something on her phone. She looked up briefly, then lowered her head once more after catching sight of Dimity's expression. Dimity kept walking, tears streaming down her face. Her silver cuff felt tight and began to hurt her wrist. Her clothes suddenly felt uncomfortable. The fabric didn't feel soft anymore; it didn't make her feel sensual. She felt stupid and angry with herself — for giving up everything! She never accepted help from anyone. She just accepted her circumstances and convinced herself that she couldn't have it all. But It was impossible to have it all; someone would miss out. It was never her turn though. *When will it be my turn?*

"Dimi." She heard Malcolm's voice. "Dimi ... *please stop!*"

"What do you want?" She turned and saw him marching towards her.

"Where are you going? You can't just leave like this. We have to talk. You can't keep shutting me out," he pleaded with her, frazzled.

"I'm sure you can do without me. You were just fine before I came, laughing and enjoying yourself. Sorry for ruining it all for you! Besides, there are a lot of attractive women in this hotel. I mean, if that's what you only see in me, then I'm sure any of them will be happy to be in the company of Malcolm Stewart. I mean, you're practically a rock star in this city. If you're looking for something more though, I'm sure *Julie* can offer that passion and creative enthusiasm that I don't apparently have," she said, turning away again, making her way to the exit. She then stopped abruptly and turned around to face him again. "Malcolm," she called out.

"What Dimity?" he asked standing still, taking deep breaths, nervously awaiting her response.

"You know ... I just wanted to surprise you ... I wanted to spend time with you in Amsterdam ... like a second honeymoon. I really thought you wanted it too," she said between tears, looking intently into his vulnerable eyes.

"Dimity ... wait," he called after her as she turned away from him, walking out into the street. She momentarily turned around and saw that he had bumped into an older woman. He let her pass. Dimity walked straight towards a taxi that was waiting outside the hotel. She saw him walking out into the street as she placed her seat belt on in the taxi.

"Amsterdam Airport, please," she told the driver.

"*Dimity*," she heard his desperate voice as he raced towards the street. It was too late. The taxi pulled out of the curb, leaving him and all the hope she had for them as a couple behind. She looked at him with genuine regret as he ran his hands despairingly through his hair. She then looked out at the street she had admired just an hour earlier. Covering her eyes with her sunglasses, she let the tears stream down her face, and allowed herself to feel the pain.

Dimity couldn't get her head around what had just transpired. She replayed it all in her mind. *How could it all have gone so wrong?* She was so angry with him. She couldn't believe what he had said to her; his words were so cruel and cold. Part of her wanted to teach him a lesson and meet with the English professor who had been so taken with her. He *was right!* Malcolm was a *complete and utter idiot* for having not worked things out with her. Perhaps she should take him up on his offer. She could play that game too! The other part of her felt so sad for him. He really looked so hurt when she blamed him for her having to give up her career. That night had meant so much to him — to both of them. She never regretted it. She loved her children so much, and she couldn't resist him that night either.

Still, it was true. She did have to give up a lot in terms of her career. She didn't feel as valued as an employee after she had announced that she was pregnant. Being a part-time employee had made her feel like an outsider. She had been overlooked for the important projects, and once again, she had felt that she had been left behind — to hold the fort while everyone else prospered in their roles.

Now she was being told that it was all her fault — *her choice!* When did she have a choice? It just happened, without any warning. She had also been told that she had no passion, no determination; that she had become vindictive. Well, enough was enough! It was her turn to shine, her turn to have a place in the sun! She did so love him, though. She had hurt him deeply — to the core of his being. But right now she had to put that out of her mind, and carry on.

As she walked into the airport, her eyes became teary as she remembered how excited she had been to surprise him. She never anticipated that she would be leaving so soon — alone.

"All I see is an attractive woman in designer clothes."

She remembered his cruel words as she sat on one of the chairs in the international departure lounge. Her heart felt like it had been shredded into pieces as she replayed them in her mind. He didn't see the "kind, passionate woman" he had fallen in love with. *"I can't touch someone that I don't recognise — I'm just not made like that."* Dimity couldn't bear the pain she felt in her heart. How could the man who was supposed to love her so much want to hurt her so badly? She didn't want to remember his words anymore — or the look of disappointment in his eyes. The way he had looked at that *Julie* woman, and the way he had looked at her … She couldn't take any more heartache.

In between tears, she looked at the departure list. London, Madrid, Athens … Her eyes instantly rested on Athens. Soon, clusters of people would be waiting to board the plane, off on vacation to Greece. She was overwhelmed with fear and confusion; just like a small, frightened girl. *What am I going to do now?* she thought, as a bout of anxiety made her chest tight. She looked at the rows of cities again. They looked like rows of hope for a better life … for fun … another chance … a turn in the sun.

An image of herself walking home from school when she was fifteen entered her mind. She was on her own. Andrea and Luca were at university. Nicki and Maria hadn't gone to school that day, and she couldn't wait to pop over to their

115

house to find out why they had been absent. She hadn't seen Nicki or Maria waiting outside their house in the morning for their usual walk to school, and when she had knocked on the door, no one had answered. She had wanted to discuss her plans to work at the local supermarket on Thursday nights and Saturday mornings with Nicki. As she kept walking casually, she wondered if she should buy the new Smashing Pumpkins CD, unsure if John already had it. Suddenly, her heart dropped. A huge truck was outside the Salas house. She knew straight away what type of truck it was. It was a removalist truck. The Salas family were moving out of the neighbourhood! She would lose Nicki and Maria! Nicki had hinted that they were moving to Greece one afternoon when they were doing their latest art project together, but Dimity didn't think anything of it. She didn't want to believe it, so she ignored it, and Nicki didn't bring it up again.

She remembered feeling like the world as she knew it had suddenly ceased to exist. She didn't have a plan. She hadn't been prepared for the change. She had become so used to having Nicki and Maria in her life, and now she would face life without her dearest friends. All their plans for the future had just vanished. She had felt so lost, like the world was no longer safe and that she had no control over her circumstances.

As Dimity had walked towards the truck, she saw Nicki, Maria, John and their parents loading suitcases into their car. Nicki's eyes were downcast. She had looked at her friend in deep sadness. "We'll only be gone for a year ... and a bit," Nicki had told her hesitantly, trying to reassure her. Dimity knew she was also trying to convince herself. She had even planned on taking the tapestry with her since it was their turn to have it, and to convince Dimity how confident she was that they would return and give it back to her.

They had exchanged letters in the beginning. They had talked on the phone. After a rough start, Nicki and Maria

116

seemed to have adapted to their circumstances. They were doing new and exciting things with their life.

Meanwhile, she was left behind, working on a casual basis at the local supermarket on her own, and going to the same school *without* her best friends. She had always thought they would be by her side.

She waited for months, until one day she saw the "For Sale" sign outside the Salas house as she headed to work one Saturday morning. Andrea, who walked with her, had been the first to notice it. She had seen how upset Dimity had been, and had tried to reassure her, telling her that it didn't mean that they wouldn't come back to Sydney. Andrea herself had also been heartbroken because she had always had a crush on John. Andrea also began to feel sad when she realised that she would miss cheeky little Maria, who always seemed to cause drama in her family. "I *will* miss Mrs Salas' cakes: her *kataifi*, her *galaktoboureko*," Andrea had continued. "We *will* see them again though, I'm sure of it," she had added after seeing Dimity's reaction. Dimity had completely shut down. She didn't want to talk about the Salas family anymore.

Andrea was wrong — they didn't end up seeing the Salas family in Sydney again. In fact, they lost touch with them completely. After a few more months had passed with no contact, the McKenzie family was also moving — to the south coast. Dimity had tried to contact Nicki and Maria, but had lost their number during the move. She had sent two letters before they officially moved, but she never heard from them again. It had all become too hard, so Dimity had just accepted that it wasn't meant to be. She didn't care where her parents were based. Her life had lost its sparkle — its piquancy.

Dimity looked around the airport. Where would she go from here? She sighed heavily. She couldn't go back home.

She couldn't go back and wait for Malcolm *again* when she had such great hopes for them in Amsterdam.

She instinctively looked at the departure board. Her eyes scanned the different destinations until they instantaneously stopped at one particular city again – *Athens*. Her mind began to think frantically. She started feeling excited at the prospect. Could she really just take off like that? Why shouldn't she? Why should she always be that *someone* taking care of things at home? She would do it! It would be so beautiful this time of year. Besides, she had a bag full of designer clothes with her, and they were in need of being worn in a place where she would be inspired — her inner desire and beauty would complement her clothes, not the other way around. Maybe he was right. She needed to start feeling, to be more determined, and to be that inspiring woman she used to be. Well, if that was what he wanted, that's what he would get! *I'll show him just how erratic I can really be!* She was more determined than ever to regain her zest for life. Yes, she would go — she would go to Greece! *She* would be the one leaving this time!

***

Nicki stared into the distance as she sat on her bed, resting on her pillow in the guest bedroom of the North Sydney terrace house. She was holding a photograph of herself and Marco that she had found while unpacking her suitcase. She looked at it momentarily, then looked away, unable to tolerate the pain she felt in her heart when she thought of all the hopes and dreams that they had for their life together as husband and wife. She gained the strength to take another look. She looked so happy in the photo. Her pale blue eyes were so full of hope for the future and love for the man standing next to her, holding her tightly as though he didn't want to let go. His green, confident eyes looked so content, and full of love — for her, his wife and life partner. The

118

photo was from happier times, when they had planned a life full of love, and eventually a family. They would often imagine what it would be like to hear little footsteps in the hallway, or to laughingly complain about having to attend yet another soccer game — for *him*, or for *her*.

"It seems that you've forgotten who you are as a couple." She remembered Cassandra's words at the airport coffee shop earlier that morning.

"You also forgot who *you are*, Nicki … what makes you happy. This can't be the only thing that defines you," Connor had added.

She had sat back in her seat feeling vulnerable and exposed. They had seen through her pretences, her smiles, and her protests that everything was fine. That couldn't be further from the truth.

"I'm fine," she had protested. "I'm fine," she said again, until she realised the words had no meaning. They couldn't convince her and they definitely couldn't convince Cassandra or Connor. She had left the love of her life.

"You need to find yourself again … would you agree, Nicki?" she had asked gently. "Then, and only then, will you find who you are as a couple."

"That's what he said …" Nicki murmured. "Marco … He said that I have forgotten who I am … and who we are as a couple."

"He's right," Cassandra had said.

"I *am* finding myself, though. I'm looking for an apartment and I'm going to work …" she had trailed off when Cassandra gave her a questioning look.

"That's all fine, but don't rush into anything," Cassandra warned. "Work is great, but you need time to think … to find out who Nicki really is … and then to remember who you were together … what attracted you to each other."

"Work has always helped me," she had said as Cassandra looked at her sceptically. "I'm going to set up an interview with a manager I used to work with … it will be fun working

119

near Maria … like old times again, when we were young and free," she had said, overly excited, knowing that she sounded far too eager.

A tear fell gently onto the glass of the silver picture frame, landing right on the eyes of the happy woman she no longer recognised; it was soon followed by another, then another, obscuring the happy couple. Nicki had started the day feeling strong and ready to face the world, but the nights sometimes seemed unbearable. She still loved him, but they kept hurting each other. She had to let him go. Their grief had become unbearable. Now she was alone, and what hurt the most was that the hope that one day she would carry *his* child had also gone. She had lost him — the man she fell in love with, her soulmate — they had lost each other and their dream … and she had lost herself.

CHAPTER THIRTEEN

"I can't believe how annoying that guy on the plane was. I mean, you'd think he never heard a child cry before," Maria muttered to Antonio.

"Well, at least we're in the hotel now, so no-one has to hear anything. I can't believe he fell asleep the minute we walked into the hotel foyer. Besides, look at this spectacular view." Antonio walked towards the window as though a mystical force lured him there.

Maria gently sat on the perfectly made bed, careful not to wake Thomas. She enjoyed the silence of the ambient, air-conditioned room. Her sister had obviously booked one of the best hotels in the whole of Athens.

Maria's thoughts were interrupted by her mobile vibrating. "*What?*" she hissed, trying not to wake Thomas. "Is she for real? I can't believe this! We just arrived and my mother's already calling me!"

Maria gently moved the pram towards the other side of the large suite. She knew that things would get heated with her mother. They always did.

She walked towards the balcony to stand near Antonio, but stopped before stepping through the doors and into the warm Athens air.

Her mother's voice assailed her. "So how is everything going? Is Thomas all right? Are you in Athens now?"

"Yes, Mum, I'm in Athens and Thomas is all right, and everything is fine," she answered robotically. *Well, it was,* she thought, wondering what demand her mother would be making on that particular day.

"That's great! Remember, don't go to the Acropolis in the middle of the day," she advised her. "It gets extremely hot up there, and it'll be really dangerous for Thomas. It's better to go in the afternoon or early morning."

"Yes, I know, the concierge and the taxi driver have already warned us. Thanks anyway," she said, wondering what else was on her mind.

"That's good! Well, enjoy Athens. Oh … and if it gets too tiring for Thomas, you don't have to visit some of the relatives … Only do it if you can," she added. "You don't have to visit your Auntie Irene or Aliki. Anyway … don't forget to go to the church in the neighbourhood … in Agrinio and light a candle. I used to go there when I was a young girl. It's good for Thomas to get to experience as much of his background as possible, now that he's young."

"I can't believe this!" Maria said, exasperated. "I finally come to Greece and you still think you can control me … all the way from Melbourne! You still think that what I do in my life and the choices I make are bad. Why aren't you excited and proud that I'm here? Tell me, Mum. I mean … *of course* I plan on visiting Aliki, and Auntie Irene and Uncle Pavlo. It already looks like we don't care about them because of *you*!" Maria was shaking all over. She felt that her head would explode. The fatigue from the flight was catching up with her, and she tried to remain calm when she saw Thomas moving in his pram.

She noticed Antonio looking at the view with a thoughtful look on his face. She could see the tension in his square, raised shoulders. A sudden bout of guilt took over her. He had grown up in a big family, and he had learned to ignore the trivialities, the bickering. There were lots of arguments, from what he would tell her, growing up in a family with two brothers and five sisters, but they loved each other. His mother had taught them to be honourable, caring people, respecting of themselves and of others.

Antonio had become the town hero when he'd saved a woman from being robbed outside the church where they volunteered their time helping those who had nothing. He could relate to them, his family having nearly nothing themselves. He loved his large family, but they were noisy

122

and demanding, and he liked to find solace from the cacophony. He was a quiet kid who immersed himself in reading, and fantasised about travelling and design. He hadn't planned on staying in Sydney permanently, but the moment he saw Maria behind the counter of her shop he had fallen in love. He was captivated by her rebellious eyes, her wild, vibrant hair, and her philosophy of living in the moment. That's what he had told her. They wanted the same thing in life — to be themselves, to create, to be free, to really live without conditions and restrictions.

He finally moved from where he stood, walking towards Maria looking agitated. He grabbed the phone from her.

"Mrs Salas," he said with the utmost finesse. "Thomas is barely one-and-a-half years old. He won't remember any of this trip but we'll definitely fit it into our schedule. Don't worry. My mother tells me exactly the same things ..."

Soon after Antonio politely ended the conversation with Mrs Salas, Maria said in bewilderment, "Do you believe her? She thinks she can still tell me what to do, even when I finally agree to visit Greece. Nothing I do for her is good enough! Do you believe that she told me that I don't need to visit Auntie Irene and Aliki ... I mean, how daft does she think I am? Why did I even decide to come here?"

"From what I remember, we came here because it would also be wonderful to see Greece, and enjoy the time we have away from work. Remember when you convinced me?" Antonio asked as he sat next to her on the bed.

"Of course, that's why we also came here, but she's been acting so suspiciously ..."

"Did you even see where we are? Have you even looked outside the window since we got here? We have a view of one of the most famous ancient wonders of the world and all you can think of is your mother upsetting you again. Just have a look," Antonio glanced at the view as he sat next to Maria. "Do you see it? Isn't it amazing ... to be looking at the Parthenon?" Antonio turned and looked at her with pleading eyes. "I mean, we're in a five-star hotel with the Parthenon in full view and you're shaking all over, my carefree, free-spirited wife … because you let your mother get to you — again!"

"But she's telling me what to do …"

"Do you even hear yourself? Who cares? Let her tell you what to do. *You* know what you need to do. You're an adult …" he trailed off shaking his head, looking solemnly at the floor. He then turned to look at her again. "Look at how she treats me. Do I let it get to me?" he challenged.

Maria looked searchingly into Antonio's eyes. She saw the boy in him — the kind, generous boy who had saved the woman outside the local church, with his worn-out shoes that had a hole where rain would seep through, yet neglected to tell his parents about in case they had to worry more about money. Mrs Salas saw none of that. Mrs Salas only saw what she wanted to see. He was right. She needed to be stronger for herself — for both of them.

Antonio took her hands in his and met Maria's eyes. "Remember when I met you? I thought you were the most free-spirited woman. That's who you are, Maria, so let's just live in the moment. We're not going to be here for long, and yes, then we can worry about getting answers when we visit your cousin … okay? That was our plan when you were selling the idea to me. Come on, just have a look." He stood up and guided her to the balcony's large glass doors. "Do you see it? Isn't it amazing?" he mused, pointing to the view.

She looked at him, the guilt overwhelming her as she gazed into his hopeful eyes. She finally inspected the magnificent structure. Her frustration almost instantly began to subside.

"I'm going to go and have a shower after I put Thomas to sleep in the cot," he said as Maria continued to examine the view. A sudden silence engulfed her.

"Okay …" Maria replied without thinking, her eyes fixed on the historical site.

She stepped out onto the balcony, transfixed by the breathtaking view of the Parthenon perched atop the Acropolis. Calmness swept throughout her whole body. She felt that the ruins were speaking to her, insisting that she live in the moment. It suddenly occurred to her that she was breathing in the very same air that the ancient Greeks had once breathed.

"Grab a glass," Maria called out some time later from the balcony as she heard Antonio stepping out of the bathroom after putting Thomas down and taking a shower. "The bottle's on the coffee table," she continued as she took a sip of chilled white wine, breathing contently. Maria could practically feel her husband's confusion as she heard him walking towards her. The smell of herbal soap pleasantly infiltrated the air.

"In Greek mythology, they say that the Goddess Athena planted the olive tree that's on the Parthenon. Is it still there? I heard they regrew it with one sprig from the original tree," she called out, excitedly. "I studied all this in Ancient History." She felt Antonio's lips on her cheek. "Mmm … you smell nice." Maria looked up at him. His smile took over the entirety of his face. "The wine's also nice," she said with excitement in her voice as she looked at her husband, who was dressed in the hotel's white cotton robe, a glass of wine in his hand. "I thought I'd open a bottle. When do we get to enjoy a glass of wine with a view like this? I mean, we're talking ancient greatness here."

"Are you sure you're my wife? I mean, first, you don't usually drink, and I'm pretty sure you were in no mood to look at any view earlier on."

"Well, I think you *and* the Parthenon may have slightly changed my attitude. I mean … look where we are. Isn't this amazing?"

"It *is* amazing, and speaking of goddesses, the only one I see is the beautiful temptress sitting beside me. You do know that Athena was supposed to be a virgin? That's why it was called Parthenon, after her," he said, smiling.

"Yes, I know what the word means; I *did* attend Greek school for many excruciatingly unbearable years," she said, with smiling eyes.

"Well, after what we just did before we left Sydney, Aphrodite might be someone more on topic … you know, the *goddess of love and fertility*," he teased her.

"Oh, shut up Antonio!" she giggled. "Anyway, you forgot *beauty*. She was also the *goddess of beauty*. Her son was named Eros … can you imagine? You do also know that women in Ancient Greek culture were actually very powerful and dominant in the household, even if they were just assigned to do domestic duties?"

"Well, I do know of the story about the women wanting to punish their men by depriving them of love and attention. They barricaded themselves in the Acropolis, to punish the men for constantly going to fight the Spartans."

"Well, don't worry. There's no chance of that happening and I don't need an ancient Greek soldier. I can't resist my toned Latin lover standing right here, all clean and bare-chested." Maria's eyes combed his bare chest. She then threw her arms around him and kissed him passionately. "And from now on, I won't let my *ever-so-domineering Greek mother* ruin my mood. I *will* enjoy this holiday with you and Thomas, and I *will* get the answers I need when we visit Aliki. But until we do that, we have plenty of time to be alone before our little one begins to control us." She took another sip of wine and gazed at the view with content eyes. Her heart felt light as she allowed herself to live in the peaceful moment.

***

Dimity sipped her *frappe* and observed the people around her. She was sitting at an outdoor table in a shopping and café square called Plaka, escaping the unbearable heat of the sun earlier in the day. She had wanted to visit the Parthenon on the Acropolis but decided against it as she climbed the steps while gasping for air, feeling dizzy from the unforgiving heat. She had spent the night in a small three-and-a-half-star hotel, which was not what she had been accustomed to. She didn't mind. She felt young and free, not knowing where she was staying and having to settle for whatever she found. It wasn't as though she had planned any of this. She was in Greece, on her own — without her children, without her husband. Who would have thought that events would have unfolded as they did? It had not been long since she had been sitting on the park bench that Sunday morning, admiring the laid-back patrons of the Bavarian Bistro, or since the Saturday evening when she had insulted her mother-in-law. Now, she was sitting in a *kafeneio* in Athens, in a relaxed summer dress and a fedora hat, sipping a *frappe*.

The activity around her was comforting, yet she still felt uneasy being on her own in an unfamiliar place. She was definitely not used to travelling alone in a foreign city and was wary at first, but sitting in the square made her feel comfortable. Plaka was filled with energy and excitement, and had amazed her as she'd strolled along its winding, steep, rustic streets. She almost felt like she was on one of the islands or even in the streets of Cuba or Italy. The many coloured buildings in blue and yellow, pink and terracotta, and of course, the traditional Greek Island inspired colour schemes of blue and white, created a happy and friendly atmosphere and made that particular part of Athens look like an island right in the city.

She had been so excited as she had walked next to the ancient *Agora*. She had stood still and admired it before walking through Plaka's maze-like streets. She imagined what it would have been like — how the ancient Greek women, men and children would have shopped.

She suddenly thought of Malcolm. He would have been so inspired by the architecture, the archaeological sites, and the nature around her. What would he think if he knew she was sitting here amongst it all? From the reception she had received in Amsterdam, he would think she had really lost her mind. *Would he even care*, she speculated, *after the cruel things I said to him?* The thought of everything she had said began to torture her with guilt, as would always happen on the rare occasion she was cruel to someone. Malcolm was right. It wasn't like her to be vindictive. It just wasn't in her nature.

She hadn't told him where she was. He kept leaving her messages and calling her on her mobile. She hadn't responded to any of them. She had instead sent one of her own, telling him to check up on the girls, as she would not be home for a while. She also informed her parents about where she was currently staying. Her mother seemed worried and her father told her to be careful and to try and not look like a tourist. They were very concerned that things didn't work out with Malcolm. She didn't go into the details with them; she needed time to process it herself. Against their wishes, and with much protest, she also made them promise they wouldn't tell Malcolm where she was.

They, in turn, reassured her they would look after the girls and to keep them posted in regards to where she would be staying. They had also told her that Andrea had stopped by to surprise her with her new boyfriend, who she had met at one of her marketing launches. Luca was also planning to visit her from Melbourne in a few weeks. She was currently working as a make-up artist at one of the fashion shows in Melbourne.

Dimity couldn't believe she had missed her sister. In fact, she missed both of them so much — now more than ever. It was funny that, as the little sister, she was the one who had settled down, while they were leading glamorous careers, never taking the plunge and walking down the aisle. Luca had always been unconventional and never really believed in marriage. She had been in a long-term relationship with one of the fashion photographers but didn't see the point in making it official. Dimity had seen recent photos of her on one of her social media accounts. Her hair was jet black with red at the ends. It suited her lively and independent personality.

Dimity heard vivacious laughter coming from the table next to her. There were so many groups of friends and families having a bite to eat around her. Self-consciously, she adjusted her sunglasses. Feeling the perspiration on her skin underneath the stylish frames, she looked at the brochures in front of her on the small table for one.

"One *melomakarona* for the thoughtful and beautiful woman." A male waiter with an American accent smiled at her as he handed her the cake she had ordered.

"Oh, thank you," she responded, awkwardly. She wasn't used to getting all this male attention. She had forgotten what it was like.

"So, why are you alone? What's the story?" he asked her. His tone was so deliberate and not at all apologetic for its intrusive abruptness.

"I … I guess I just need some time alone … you know, to re-group … to chill," she responded, trying to speak the same language as a resident from LA, which he seemed to be from. He looked like a surfer, or some thrill-seeker.

"Big mistake!" he said looking at her disapprovingly.

"Sorry?" she questioned, taken aback.

"Don't ever admit you're alone when you're in a strange city. You're from Australia, right?" he asked in the same direct tone, as he pulled a chair and sat on the opposite end, leaning his arms on the backrest.

"Yes, I am," she responded apprehensively, not knowing how to respond. She felt like she was being quizzed and she didn't want to give the wrong answer.

"I could tell from your accent. I've been to Melbourne and Sydney a few times myself. I studied medicine there."

"Oh," she said, feeling stupid for judging him. She would have never picked him for a med student. Then again, she would never have imagined she'd be a bitter stay-at-home mum, who had completely given up on her career, and resented everyone for it.

"I see women like you all the time when I wait and bartend in the local bars and restaurants. I'm sorry to be abrupt, but you're extremely attractive. You're also a tourist, and you're travelling alone doing some soul searching, I'm guessing. You need to tone that down a bit ... try not to look so obvious ... so lost."

"That's okay," she found herself saying. How many men would she attract that would offer her advice? Was she that transparently lost? She strangely found it sweet that he actually cared about her safety. "So, how do you propose I do that?" she asked, following his cue.

"Well, for a start, you just admitted that I'm right, which you never do with a stranger. Second, don't carry a digital camera. You've got your cellular ... your mobile anyway. The travel brochures on display could also be a huge giveaway," he said, now smiling at her.

"I guess they are," she responded, smiling.

He suddenly rose from the chair and placed it back in its place. "One more suggestion," he then said. "Keep your wedding ring on. With a smile like that, all the males in Athens will be lining up to ask you out."

"Okay ... thanks, I guess," she responded, awkwardly.

Where would she head to next? What was she even doing there — in Greece, and not Amsterdam? Her mind momentarily thought of Nicki and Maria. How wonderful it must have been for them to live in Greece when they were young. Of course, it would have been easy to forget about her, if they were busy learning about the culture and the wonders of a foreign and breathtakingly beautiful country.

She wondered if they were still in Greece. She had never found out. Back then, social media was a thing of the future. She had searched for their names online a while ago, but never found anything. She even tried to search for their brother's name, John. She had come across a dentist named Anthony J. Salas who had a practice in Melbourne, but she couldn't be sure if he was related. There were many people with the same surname. She had soon given up searching for them on social media altogether. They could both even be married by now anyway, she figured, and their surnames may have changed. Besides, she had never received any response to the last few letters she had sent them. They were all different people now.

She wondered what it was like — where they had lived. She had always tried to imagine it when she had read their letters. She would be left feeling envious that her friends were doing something so adventurous. At that age, it all seemed so exciting. She remembered the address on the envelopes — a village near the town of Ioannina. She couldn't remember the name of the village. She had sent her letters to their uncle's postal address in Ioannina.

The American waiter was now at the counter serving some customers. She stood up from her chair and made her way over. "Sorry to bother you, but do you know a place called Ioannina? I was thinking of going there. I've always wanted to see what it looked like. I've heard a lot about it. It's either that or the islands, I guess."

"Sure, it's not too far from here by plane. They call it *Yannena* in Greece. Just hold on a few minutes. I'll tell you how you get there after I serve these customers."

"Sure, no problem," she said, her excitement growing. She had a plan. Now she wouldn't look so lost anymore, or feel it either.

CHAPTER FOURTEEN

Malcolm Stewart was finding it hard to concentrate. He was sitting on one of the lounge chairs in the hotel foyer, trying to focus on what the buyer was telling him. His mind had been pre-occupied with thoughts of Dimity. Where was she? Was she okay? So many thoughts had crossed his mind. He had been a mess since she left. He felt that his world had been torn in two. She had always been there, through everything, even during those times when he had felt so tired and overwhelmed with his career.

It was as if she had twisted a knife in his heart. He couldn't believe she had blamed him for that night that had meant so much to him — to both of them, he had thought.

"So Malcolm, I'm interested in buying the whole line for our new chain of restaurants. Your designs never cease to amaze me. You're always on top of your game — ahead of the rest," said Stefano, the buyer with whom he had done business with over the years.

"I guess I am," he said, coming out of his trance. "I guess I am … in my career …" Malcolm trailed off thoughtfully. He couldn't do this anymore. He had to wrap things up and find out where she was. He was losing her. This time it was different. He was where he wanted to be in his career, but at what expense? He was nothing without the love of his life — and his family. Her words kept torturing him.

"I gave up everything for you."

"So how is that beautiful wife of yours … Dimity, right? She was an interior designer wasn't she? I used to see her at all the parties. It's been so long," Stefano said, looking at him inquisitively.

"She was … I mean *she is* an interior designer — and a lot more. You know what, Stefano? It has been a long time. In fact, it's been *too* long."

"Look, Malcolm. I've been doing business with you for a lot of years and I feel that I know you personally. So I'm going to be frank with you. Work … it can be great, it can be challenging, it can even be a companion at times, but it's not family … *that's* what's important in life."

"You know, Stefano, I'm just beginning to realise that. If you don't mind, I really need to wrap this up. I haven't slept all night and I really need to take care of some things." He looked apologetically at the older man, who could obviously sense his despair.

"Malcolm, do what you need to do. I'll be in touch. Go make things right with your wife. Dimity isn't someone you can forget easily. From what I remember, she is one remarkable woman."

"I intend to, Stefano. You're right, she is a remarkable woman." *I just need to make sure she knows it,* he thought, walking away. *First, I need to find her.* He just hoped it wasn't too late for them, and that wherever she was she was okay.

Moments later, he was walking down the corridor heading to his room. He took out his mobile and looked at it again. There was still no response to his messages. The only message she had sent was one instructing him to look after the girls. She didn't give him any clue as to where she was staying. Was she even in Amsterdam? Ever since she'd left, he'd had a sinking feeling. He suddenly felt what it would be like to really lose her. Had he taken advantage of her, thinking that she would always be there, no matter what? He thought of her accusations. Did she really feel that she had given up everything? He walked into his room and over to the minibar. He opened a bottle of beer and sat on the couch that overlooked the balcony and the early afternoon sky. He took a sip. He then quickly picked up his phone and dialled his home number. No one picked up again. The girls were probably getting ready for bed and he didn't want to disturb them so late. He didn't want to alarm them anyway. Dimity had told him in her only message to him that her parents were looking after them. He then instinctively dialled Alex's number. Maybe his brother knew where she was. She could always talk to Alex. It pained him that she couldn't talk to him, and instead felt more comfortable confiding in his younger brother.

Alex answered after several rings. "Hi bro. So you finally have time to call your little brother. I'm glad to see your busy schedule permitted it. I'm actually honoured, but I'm also surprised. Anyway, I'm surprised you even have time to call me … now that Dimity's there. I thought you two would be too busy to call anyone, if you know what I mean."

"Alex, I don't have time. I need to know where Dimity is. She's not with me. I mean, she was but she left. We got into an argument and she just took off. I'm really worried about her. She was really upset. You need to tell me where she is … if you know anything."

"What are you talking about? You don't know where she is? What did you do to her? Did you upset her again? What's wrong with you? She couldn't wait to surprise you and you get into an argument with her? You know, if you're not careful …"

"Can I get a word in? Right now all I care about is finding out where she is. You can save the lecture for after …"

"Do you know how excited she was to surprise you? She wanted to spend time with you, to connect as a couple, and what did you say to her when you saw her? Did you show her how happy you were to see her? Did you take her in your arms and tell her? You know, she was the only one of your girlfriends that cared about me when I was young. She always insisted that I join her family on all their family fishing trips. She never wanted me to be left out. It's hard to find someone as sweet and generous as Dimity. When are you going to be a man and stick up for her? I'm sure there are plenty of guys waiting to step in if you can't do what a husband should do, and that's to make sure she knows how special she is. She gave up everything for you, Malcolm, and now you're a big shot and you know what you've done, you've taken advantage of her generosity, how sweet she is …"

"Alex, I know. You don't have to tell me. I screwed up. I should have done all that. I know that. I just need to know where she is so I can make things right again," Malcolm finally interjected. He hadn't been able to get a word in. Alex had nearly deafened him and he had to hold the phone away from his ear; it felt like his eardrums would burst from his brother's vitriol. For Alex to react like this, he must have known how much Dimity wanted to surprise him.

"Man, all I'm saying is she really wanted to reconnect with you. That's why I called to find out your room number. She wanted to show you how much you meant to her. I don't know what you did or said, but she must have been heartbroken if her plan didn't work. I just pray to God you weren't with some other woman or I'll come there personally and …"

"Alex, relax! I wasn't with someone else; well, not in that way. If you don't know where she is, I have to go …"

"No, I don't. Just go find her before it's too late, and put her first for once — like she put you all these years."

Malcolm hung up the phone, feeling frustrated and angry with Alex, but mostly with himself, because the more he thought about it, the more he began to realise that his annoying little brother might be right. Her words played constantly on his mind. Alex had just told him something similar. He took another sip of his beer, and then undid another button from his shirt. He took another look at his mobile. Still no response. He felt his stomach turn as his anxiety intensified.

He got up from the floor. He took another sip from his beer, and then with one sudden motion threw the bottle across the room. It shattered on the wall, and beer spilled down onto the carpet. Malcolm needed some air. Closing the door behind him, he walked towards the lifts. As he walked out into the street, he took a huge breath, and headed towards the canal. He looked at the boats and the people in them. If only he had taken her in his arms and told her how much he missed her. He would be in one of those boats, with her, or maybe even back in the hotel room, in the king-size bed, showing her what she meant to him, the way he did back then. He took a glance at his watch, the one she had given him for his thirty-fifth birthday.

His heart ached. He should have known she would have been lost if she gave up a career that meant everything to her, and now he had just accused her of having no passion.

His phone beeped. He hoped the message was from her, but it was from the interior designer, Julie Canei. She had thanked him for meeting with her during her visit to Amsterdam and would keep in touch about working with him in the future. Malcolm couldn't help but smile. He worked well with her. She was passionate and witty. They did have a good time together, talking about his line and other design matters. She seemed sure of herself — content. She reminded him so much of Dimity. They were so alike. He could actually picture them as friends.

His phone suddenly rang. He answered it immediately, seeing it was Samantha.

"Hi Dad …"

"Hi Sam, how are you? It's so good to hear from you. I miss you and your sister so much," Malcolm said. "How are you both doing? What time is it? It must be after ten now," he said looking at his watch. "Are you and Olivia still awake?"

"Olivia is already sleeping, and I was just getting ready for bed. I wanted to talk to you. Is Mum with you? Did she surprise you? She was so excited when she left. Usually she's so sad and grumpy lately. Dad … are you and Mum getting a divorce?"

"Sam, what are you talking about? Of course we're not getting a divorce. Why would you think that? Your mum and I just need to spend some time together," he said, realising his daughter didn't know anything about their mother not being with him. He felt an instant pang in his heart, and clutched the phone tighter, when he heard the concern in her voice. He also felt bad that Dimity was so sad, and that Sam had noticed.

Sam sighed. "It's just that she always seems to be thinking about something. She always just sits in the dining room that you never really use and stares at the garden. Amanda from school said that's what usually happens when parents divorce. They are always sad and they go away together."

"Sam … your mum and I … we're fine. We're definitely not getting a divorce. We love each other so much and we love being a family. In fact, I'm planning to take some time off so we can all do something together. How does that sound? I miss you and your sister so much."

"You're always away lately. Can you help me with my school project when you get back? We have to make a prototype of a toy. All the other kids are getting help, and then we have to do a presentation on it. Can you help me design it and then make it?"

Malcolm's heart filled with warmth. "When I get back, we'll start working on it straight away, okay?"

"I have to do some of it as well. I mean, it can't be that good because they'll know that my famous dad made it."

"Sure, of course you will. I'll just get you started," Malcolm smiled as he spoke.

"Okay, Dad. So you and Mum aren't getting a divorce?"

"No Sam, we're not. Your mum and I love each other too much," he said with a heavy heart. "Sam … are your grandparents still awake?"

"They just went to bed. I couldn't sleep until I called you."

"That's okay. Even though it's late there, and you should be in bed, I'm happy to hear from you. Can you get them to call me tomorrow?"

"Sure, Dad. Is it about them looking after us longer? Mum already told them that you're extending your trip and that you'll be away for a few more weeks."

"She did?" Malcolm's heart sank. Where was she? He had to know. He had to know that she was all right, and that she hadn't given up on them. "Sam, just have them give me a call, okay?"

"Sure. Dad. By the way, did you and Mum get me that leather jacket she promised me?"

"Um ... I don't think she did yet. Look ... don't worry about it. I'll take care of it," he answered, grinning.

"No, don't worry about it. I just studied all about animals and where leather comes from. I want something else, like maybe one of those cool copper bracelets that are so in right now. Amanda said that Amsterdam has some of the coolest designs. I'll get Gran to send you a photo, okay? Olivia wants one too."

"Okay. Bye sweetie, make sure you go to bed now. Say hi to Olivia for me."

CHAPTER FIFTEEN

Maria and Antonio walked slowly through the maze-like streets of Plaka. "Do you believe Socrates, Aristotle and other philosophers, poets, mathematicians, and many others of the greats would have walked the same streets that we're walking on at this very moment?" Antonio asked, exalted.

"It doesn't even look like we're in Athens. This strip is completely different to the rest of the city. I guess we can't forget where we are when we look over there," she said as she pointed to the Parthenon, which was in full view, towering over the city.

"It's like being on an island," Antonio said, inhaling deeply to take it all in, as he walked slowly with Thomas strapped securely on his chest, his little sun hat on.

"I know. The colours are so different to other parts of Greece," Maria observed. "I love how some of the houses are painted yellow and have blue doors. It's a rustic, island feel. I love how the paint is stripped off. It adds to the rustic look."

They were walking down many steps towards a long line of cosy looking shops that stretched up on both sides of the narrow, steep, busy street.

"Do you believe my mother is trying to tell us what to do again … even on our trip? I mean, she honestly thinks she can tell us where we should go. The nerve of her, especially when she's guilty of keeping the invitations from all of us. That's why I even decided to come here. How dare she try to tell me how to feel — again? I *will* find out why she lied to us though — I'll get my answers as soon as we visit my uncle."

"Maria … can you focus on what's around you, and not on your mother? Remember what we said back at the hotel?"

"You're right. I'm sorry." Maria looked at her husband with regret. He held Thomas securely, trying his best to make them all happy. *Why do I let her get to me like this, even when she's not with me?*

An invigorating aroma caught her attention. It smelled like figs, or rose, perhaps. Her senses guided her to a beautiful, almost mystical little shop, crowded with shoppers, holding paper bags with the shop's logo on it.

Maria's heart began to beat wildly. She stepped into the shop, taking her sun hat off. "I'll just have a look in here for a while," she called out to Antonio.

The small cramped space was so cosy. Healing oils, soaps, and other similar products were displayed in clusters around the shop. Maria picked up one of the soaps. She could smell the citrus. She picked up another. It smelled like Turkish Delight. As she studied the ingredients, she wondered if they used the same techniques as the ancient Greeks. The olive oil would definitely have many benefits. She then wondered if she should devote a small corner of her shop to Ancient Greece, and sell products that were rich in olive oil.

A young woman bumped into her as she perused the shop, pushing Maria close to some incense burners. "Sorry," she heard her say. Maria didn't care. Her eyes were fixated on a beautiful incense burner made of copper. She quickly walked back to the entrance of the shop, squeezing through the other shoppers. Maria instantly felt the intense heat on her face as she leaned outside. "I'll be a few more minutes. I won't be long," she called out to Antonio, who was sitting on a bench under the shade of an umbrella with Thomas.

A long while later, Maria rushed out of the shop, holding a small card in her hands. "Antonio, you won't believe it …"

"Believe what?"

"I'm going to be selling some of the products at Eventually You!" she cried. "I've got the details of the supplier, and they want to branch out. It's a great idea … to devote a whole section to Ancient Greece — my customers will love it! I spoke to them and all I have to do is give them the go-ahead and organise the payment."

"That's wonderful! Who would have thought?" Antonio stood up from the bench.

"I know! I gave him my website details. He was really impressed. I can't believe how many beautiful things are around us. This place is almost magical — the Byzantine influenced jewellery shops, the paintings, the antiques, the hand-painted icons, wood carvings, ceramics … I mean, look at this jewellery. There are so many jewellery shops with pieces that are so intricate and unique. The Greek gold also has a different, slightly more yellow shade," she continued, as she touched one of the pieces from a display stand outside another quaint shop. "Julie would be so envious — she's always been into unusual accessories and clothes."

"Just like you? I remember she always wanted to break free from others telling her what to do."

"Yes, I guess we're alike with our adventurous style. Although my style is a lot more relaxed and laid-back, and that's what I'm going to be from now on — chilled as a cucumber."

"Glad to hear it," he said with smiling eyes.

"I mean, how can I not be? Look at where all these shops are situated," she said pointing to the Acropolis again, which they could see from a distance, surrounded by many poplar and olive trees. The Parthenon looked as though it was guarding the surrounding neighbourhoods, overlooking them while they charmingly carried on doing what they were supposed to be doing as they sat in its shadow.

Some unique bohemian throws then caught Maria's attention. She felt right at home. All the products embodied spiritual healing, evolution and growth. She wanted to embrace that mantra whole-heartedly.

She caught Antonio looking at her. He seemed overjoyed that she had changed her attitude. She was definitely in her element, and she hadn't mentioned her mother in the last thirty minutes or so.

"It's unbelievably easy to get from place to place," Maria exclaimed as she walked slowly, wrapping her bolero throw around her shoulders, her long auburn hair flowing freely behind her. She had chosen to wear a white maxi dress and a pair of flat, Greek-inspired sandals. With her sombrero hat and sunglasses, she was beginning to feel like a Greek goddess herself. There were large avenues from the south and west of the Acropolis that had been turned into pedestrian streets and the walk was relaxing and effortless.

"There are also so many cafes and restaurants. How about we have a *frappe* and something for this guy before we head to the Acropolis," Antonio suggested.

"I wouldn't mind some *mezethes* as well. That means "appetisers". There is so much to choose from." Maria stopped in front of another small shop, musing at the jewellery on display. She felt Antonio's hand on her shoulder.

"You really are in your element, aren't you?"

"I just can't believe how many interesting things there are. It's like being in Byron Bay or at the Bondi markets, but on a much larger scale. The streets are full of these types of shops," she continued as Antonio turned her towards him, and kissed her gently on the lips.

"I love seeing you like this — happy and content. You look so radiant. I think Greece is agreeing with you already. I should have dragged you here a long time ago. Maybe I should be *thanking* your mother this time?"

"Careful ... you're the one who told me not to mention her."

"You're right. Anyway, I can see you can't wait to buy something. Just go and I'll find a table over there," he said, pointing to a row of tables and chairs outside a charming *taverna*.

"I don't know where to start. You're right — I better shop before Thomas becomes restless." Before Antonio could respond, she walked slowly inside the small shop, feeling Antonio's smile as she admired all the products around her.

***

Dimity marvelled at the ancient site in front of her. It had been an easy stroll back to the Acropolis from Plaka. She had eventually walked uphill, via the pedestrian street, through a strip called Monastiraki, and then along a path surrounded by woods. When she reached the top, she turned right and came across some steps that led her straight to the Parthenon. She was now standing at the south-east end of the Acropolis, looking at a Greco-Roman Temple which stood at the centre of Athens. She had found out from a group of tourists that it was, in fact, the Temple of Olympian Zeus. Whichever direction she looked at, she was left feeling humbled and moved. Who would have thought she would be standing on the Acropolis, admiring the Parthenon and the city of Athens? Emotion took over as she turned around and walked towards the sacred olive tree that had been planted in ancient times for *Athena Parthenos*.

She then slowly walked to the temple known as the Erechtheion and admired the intricate carving. Mesmerised, she continued taking slow steps through the rugged rocks that were scattered throughout the site. Their sheer size amazed her. Dimity was glad that she had been working out, because it required a lot of energy to walk around the site and really appreciate it. The scorching heat was still unbearable; the perspiration coursed down her face. Perhaps it would have been wiser to see it after five;

however, she had made it a priority to visit the Acropolis before she made plans to go to Ioannina, and hoped to also have enough time to fit in the Archaeological Museum before leaving Athens.

Now she was standing in front of the Parthenon itself. The marble, gently blanketed by the afternoon sunlight, was highlighted in gold and cream tones, as the paint had been stripped off, revealing the original marble. At times, the columns appeared to be beige, or even a rose colour. It was so liberating just being there, but she also felt sad that Malcolm wasn't experiencing it with her, as she listened to the light-hearted conversations of couples and families walking past her.

She couldn't help but look at her phone again. He had left her another message. Feeling the need to reply, she sent him a message, reassuring him that she was okay and that she needed some time for herself. She told him that it was too soon to talk; she still needed time.

He had also told her that the girls were under the impression that they were together. He still insisted that he had to talk to her. Dimity thought that he sounded really worried.

As she continued walking, taking pictures along the way, she heard a child laughing. A happy couple and their son were admiring the view of the city from the south side. The man was holding the young boy on his chest. The woman, whose lustrous hair was a rich, auburn red colour, was laughing loudly at the child's antics. Her heart felt heavy. It was just six months ago that they were that family — happy in each other's company. She continued walking, trying to not miss anything, when she heard her phone beep again. It was Malcolm. He too had left a message.

Dimity,
I know you're hurting right now and I know we both said some hurtful things to each other, but please, give us a chance. We need to

talk about it. I'll give you some time if it's what you need. I'll stay in Amsterdam for a while. I don't want the girls to worry. Dimity, I don't care about my work commitments. All I care about is you. I just want you to know that I love you so much. You mean everything to me. I know you feel the same. Please call me soon. I love you, Dimity.

Your husband, Malcolm.

"I love you too Malcolm," she softly said to herself, a tear threatening to stream down her cheek. *I do need some time though.* She once again looked at the happy couple with the small child in the man's arms. That was how she wanted Malcolm and her to be again — truly together as a couple, and as a family. She wanted to be the passionate woman that he fell in love with again — more to the point, she wanted to be the woman that *she* loved being. Now, however, she had to make plans. She began to walk back through the rugged rocks, towards the steps, feeling the perspiration on her face and through her hair. She turned around, looked at the historical site again, and took a deep breath. She said her goodbyes, knowing it was a privilege to be in its presence. Then she made her way down the steps.

***

"Hi Mrs Salas," Maria heard Antonio say that late afternoon back at their hotel room. She had just stepped out of the shower after an exciting but exhausting day at the Acropolis. They were now getting ready to go to dinner at the hotel restaurant, which overlooked it. It was beautiful seeing it during the day, but at night it looked completely different; it was illuminated with light throughout, creating a brilliant visual display. The light would change colour at different intervals, making it even more spectacular.

"Yes, we already went to the Acropolis, the Ancient Agora, and Plaka. We'll see some more of the historical sites before we head for the islands," she heard him say. "Oh …

146

we also got to try some of the desserts. Maria and I had some *kataifi* with our coffee … but I have to say Mrs Salas, as tasty as it was, nothing beats your desserts … No … it's true. Even Maria said it," he continued, looking at Maria with a smile.

He definitely knew which buttons to press. He was smiling as she glanced at him, his deep, dark brown eyes looking almost angelic as the compliments flowed. Her mother was obviously taking the bait. Maria knew that he was sincere though, and she had to agree with Antonio — it was difficult to find desserts as good as the ones her mother made. The customers at their Melbourne restaurant would have to pre-order as there was such a demand for them. Her mother still made them, and even if her staff were helping, she would oversee everything to make sure it was done right.

"No, don't worry about a thing. Just look after yourself, Mrs Salas," Antonio continued. "You know, you and Mr Salas need to start enjoying your life and relax more. I tell my mother that as well … She's fine, thank you. I called her a few days ago. She really wants to see Thomas. I might send them over to Sydney in a few months. They would love to spend some time abroad."

Antonio then turned to face her. He discretely made a gesture asking Maria if she wanted to talk to her mother. Maria immediately replied by shaking her head from side to side, and Antonio instantly told Mrs Salas that Maria was still in the shower. He finally hung up.

Maria immediately went over to kiss him. "My husband — every mother-in-law's dream son-in-law. Who would have thought, after how long they took to accept the fact that we weren't married when I was pregnant?"

"How could they *not* accept me; is the question," Antonio replied, smiling. "Let's not crack open the Champagne yet. Your mother still has a go at me every chance she gets, but I don't care what she or anyone thinks."

"It doesn't bother you at all?"

"Well, maybe just a little," he said, with a half-smile. "You know what I've learned though?"

"What has my wise husband learned?" Maria teased.

"Some people will never change, so we can't change them, but we can change how we interact with them."

Maria looked at Antonio with eyes wide open. "Wow, you certainly are the positive one in this relationship. Cassandra and Connor would probably offer you a job at their counselling practice." Maria's heart instantly felt heavy when she thought of Cassandra and Connor. She had asked them to make sure Nicki was okay. She wondered how her sister was doing.

"Well, I think I've got my work cut out for me here. I need to encourage my wife to be the carefree woman she wants to be. The worried look you've got on your face only tells me one thing — you're worried about something your mother's said."

"No. I promise it's not that. It's actually about Nicki. I hope she's okay."

"Why don't you give her a call? I'm sure she's fine, with two qualified counsellors checking up on her. Anyway, we'd better get Thomas ready for his fancy dinner. You think he's up to it?"

"I think I will give her a call, and you're right, I'm not going to waste another moment worrying about my mother's trivial concerns. Anyway, at least I didn't have to talk to her. The conversation would probably have not been so amicable. I'd better call Nicki before we go to the restaurant. I did try calling her earlier. It should be nearly midnight now in Sydney, but she said she's been staying up late. I hope it isn't because she's having trouble sleeping. She's on her own and I feel bad for what she's going through. Do you mind dressing Thomas?"

"It's cool. Say hi to her from me. Don't worry about Thomas. I'll make him look really stylish just like his dad," he said, walking into the bedroom.

"Hi Nicki … how are you?"

"I'm okay. You know, taking one day at a time. You don't have to babysit me while you're on your holiday. I don't need my little sister worrying about me."

"Don't worry. Mum has already called me so many times. Calling you is a breath of fresh air. I really want to know how you're doing."

"I went to *Eventually You* to see how Stacey is managing on her own. She seems to have everything under control. I also noticed the travel agency across from your work. You know, I might be able to get a transfer there. Maybe it's meant to be — I mean, it's right across from your shop and it's the agency I work for as well …"

"So, did you hear from Marco yet?" Maria had to find out. Her sister was planning a new life but wasn't even mentioning her true love.

Nicki paused. "Maria, can we not talk about that now? It's late. I still can't believe you're in Greece. God … it brings up so many memories of us being young … being plucked from our old neighbourhood in Sydney and flown all the way over there. It was quite an experience. Do you remember how angry we were? We didn't want to leave our house, our school, Dimity … it's funny how life works out, isn't it? One minute you're in a relationship and the next … Anyway, sorry … I'm drifting again. I tend to do that lately, don't I? How's Athens? It must be amazing being in a city that has one of the most ancient and sacred sites."

Maria had an uneasy feeling at the pit of her stomach. It was as though Nicki didn't even want to face the fact that she had just left her husband. "Nicki … please, you don't have to apologise. Remember, I'm here for you, whether

I'm on holidays, whether I'm busy with Thomas or the shop … I'm here for you."

"I know, Maria, and it means so much to me. Even John won't stop calling and is threatening to bring his wife and kids from Melbourne to live here for a while. Do you believe our cheeky, grungy brother, has become such a family man, and a dentist as well? Like I said, just when you think you know people, they completely take you by surprise. Anyway, I better leave you. I'm sure you have somewhere fabulous to be in that spectacular city. Send me some photos from your trip as you discover new places. Say hi to our cousins and other relatives from me as well, especially Aliki."

"I will, and remember to call me if you need anything."

"I will, little sister. Enjoy your time in Greece. I told you … just when you think you know someone …"

"Yes, I know … you would never have pictured me here."

"Well, I never forget how you detested having Greek dancing lessons. I remember the incident every time I wear a pair of black opaque tights," Nicki said, laughing.

"Goodnight Nicki. Try to get some sleep."

"Bye Maria. Regards to Antonio, and give Thomas a big hug and a kiss for me."

***

Back at the North Sydney terrace, Nicki stared at the phone in silence. *Have you heard from Marco?* The question lingered in her mind. She stood up from the cream armchair, nestled in one corner of the pale blue lounge room, and walked over to the desk by the window. She placed the phone down, then picked it up and looked at it again. It was another message from Marco. She didn't feel like replying. A deep fear emerged from deep within her at the thought of facing him and their problems. She didn't know how to act; who she was — who had she even become? She had been "Nicki and Marco trying to have a baby" for so many years. Marco had his life; he had his work parties, his occasional Friday card game nights, his soccer reunion games. Nicki had her dreams — her tears.

You don't know who you are anymore, Nicki. She remembered his words again. *When was the last time we had some fun?*

She looked at the contact details her boss back in Melbourne had given her. She would go to the interview tomorrow. She might be working near her sister. She had to hold onto that. *It will be okay. Work will keep me busy.* Watching people eagerly planning their next holiday always distracted her when she was drowning in tears. It always made her forget.

CHAPTER SIXTEEN

"*Efharisto*," Dimity thanked the man who helped her with her luggage as he handed it to her from the small local carrier.

"*Parakalo*. The pleasure is all mine," the man replied with a heavy Greek accent.

She was glad to be standing in Ioannina, and no longer seated in the small plane she had just stepped out of. "Slight turbulence" was how the extremely tanned steward, in her husky, seductive voice, had described the experience she had just endured for 45 minutes. This was a complete understatement. Extreme rides at amusement parks that her daughters and Malcolm had coaxed her onto seemed tamer. She placed a hand on her stomach, feeling queasy from the cheese triangle she had an hour earlier. She walked into the local airport, rejoicing in the fifteen minutes of air-conditioned bliss as she went through the usual procedures, which were becoming so familiar. She was feeling more and more like a worldly, independent traveller as she continued her solo adventure.

Dimity stepped out of the airport and waited for the driver who was to take her to the hotel where she would spend the next week. She observed the rising mountains and trees in the distance while she waited. She would make other arrangements if she wished to stay longer, or otherwise would head straight for the islands. She also eventually had to let Malcolm know what her plans were. She didn't want to think of that yet. It was too draining, and she needed to keep up her momentum.

She had called the girls and couldn't help but ask them a few questions regarding her usual concerns, such as: "Are you both up to date with your homework?" "Did you get started on all your projects?" "What time are you both going to sleep?" "Don't give your grandparents a hard time either; even if you don't like lentils or chickpeas, just eat them … they're not running a coffee shop." She had stopped herself before she reminded them to shower and brush their teeth regularly, realising she was beginning to consume herself with worry about everyone being able to even breathe without her being on board. *The ship will survive without me*, she reminded herself as she had quickly said her goodbyes to them, before they asked if they could talk to their dad. She would make excuses whenever she talked to them: he had stepped out to buy some takeout, she had told them once, as they had been eating out too much lately, having lavish dinners and lunches in Amsterdam. She had felt so bad lying to them, but what choice did she have? *'Oh by the way girls, I'm in Greece and your father is in Amsterdam because we got into a heated argument because he wasn't as happy to see me as I thought he would've been.'*

Instead, she had said, "I'd better go now. Housekeeping is waiting for me to answer the door. Okay, bye sweetie. Kiss your sister for me." She imagined how Samantha would have rolled her eyes at the fact that she had called her "sweetie", and that she had told her to give her sister a kiss.

Dimity's driver was another young, very tanned woman, who waved to her, grabbed some of her bags and began talking straight away.

"Welcome to Ioannina! Dimity, right? My name is Eleni. Is this your first time here? Well, if it is, don't worry. You can ask me any question and I'll be glad to answer. It's part of the service. I can also help you organise hire cars, or tell you about the attractions and any form of transportation you need to get around the town and the villages." Eleni opened the door to the car, letting her in. Dimity was impressed with the fluency of her English.

"Thank you. I must say, your English is really good."

"Most of us have learned English at school. I also studied in London, and I now work for the tourist board. It's a *must* in the tourist industry. So, are you from Sydney?"

"Yes, I am," Dimity replied, fastening her seat belt.

"I'd love to visit Sydney. I've heard so much about it. I have lots of relatives in Australia and Canada," she said. "It's great to see that you use a seat belt," she digressed, talking at the same fast pace. "Not many do here." She looked at Dimity in the rear-view mirror as she reversed from the parking spot.

"I've noticed," Dimity replied.

"So, your hotel is situated in the heart of *Yannena*. It's a great location. I can give you some brochures that point out the main tourist attractions and different restaurants, as well as the main shopping districts. You can actually get a boat on the lake and see a lot of the sights on the other side. Lake Pamvotida, also known as Lake Ioannina, is the largest lake of the state of Epirus, where the town of Ioannina is situated."

"Thanks. I wouldn't know where to start." She looked out at the busy city streets. The mention of tourism reminded Dimity of Nicki. She remembered she had worked in one of the local travel agencies. She wondered if it was where Eleni worked.

"So, what brings you to Greece?"

"I don't really know. It wasn't a planned trip. It just happened. I guess Greece was calling me. I've felt this connection to it from when I was young. I think I need to find some answers and this wise country with all its history could give me those I need. My name is also Greek in origin, apparently. I guess my mum got caught up in the romance of the history of it."

"Well, things that are unplanned usually turn out to be the best plans, if you know what I mean. You're right — your name is a Greek name. I think it actually stands for something. You're also right about our country. It's a great place to do some soul searching. The landscape, the history, usually set things in perspective. That's what it's usually about … perspective."

"Well, I definitely need that in my life," she said, looking out of the window again. "There seem to be a lot of young people here," Dimity acknowledged as she looked out onto the busy streets as they drew away from the remote airport with its backdrop of towering mountains.

"One of the biggest universities is situated here."

"Well, that explains it."

"It also explains the many bars and clubs," Eleni continued.

"So, there are ferries to take you anywhere around the lake?"

"Yes, you can see many historical sites — all the old Byzantine and Ottoman architecture. We're situated in the north-west of Greece across from the Albanian border, and Epirus is one of the most mountainous regions in Greece. You'll see what I mean when you take a stroll by the lake."

"I could see that the minute the plane landed at the airport. It's such a contrast to the fast-paced, hip and trendy town that I'm seeing now," she continued, as she looked at the many coffee shops, restaurants, bars, and boutiques. "So, that would mean there are a lot of villages around here, right?"

"That's right. Some people still live in the villages on the outskirts of Ioannina and drive to the town when they need to. It's a complete contrast. It's very rural and some of the old stone houses are even still standing. A lot are used for holiday houses. The younger generation are now building more contemporary houses as the older generations have passed on. Some still choose to live there. I guess it's an escape from the towns. You'll notice when we get to your hotel. It has excellent views of the lake, and the mountains behind it. Anyway, we're nearly there. You can call me any time if you need any help with travel, or advice on sightseeing."

"Thanks," she said as they turned into a steep, bumpy, winding road. She jumped in her seat as the roughness of the road caused the small car to shake slightly. It looked so spectacular. The road was no longer lined with trendy, contemporary, and old boutique shops and cafes. An enormous old stone wall that looked like it was the remnants of a castle from the Byzantine era — *Or was it the Ottoman?* she speculated — stretched along the length of the road. It was part of the hotel at which she would be staying. She began to feel excited at the prospect of staying in such a romantic place. It almost looked poetic. Her heart instantaneously ached when she realised she would be alone. It looked far too romantic to be staying there by herself. She had at first been enticed by one of the most extravagant and opulent hotels in Ioannina. It was in the brochure that the concierge in Athens had given her, but she had instantly fallen in love with the charming, rustic looking hotel she had seen in a smaller picture, next to its enormous five-star cousin. Besides, she could use the pool and restaurants in many of the hotels anyway, she had reasoned. She couldn't wait to venture out and look at some of the major hotels in the town. The brochure had showcased many interesting, unique, and decadent hotels throughout Ioannina.

Dimity stepped out of the car and took a deep breath. The view was breathtaking! The mountains actually looked like gods towering over the enormous, peaceful, and slightly melancholic lake. It was definitely a place where someone could do some thinking. It would also be a place where relationships could be mended. Just looking at the view made everything seem so trivial, with the unruly and overpowering mountains juxtaposed with the tranquillity and calm that radiated from the lake.

"I see by the smile on your face that you like what you see," Eleni said, as she handed Dimity her luggage.

"I definitely like what I see. It's just so moving, and … I don't know … infinite. It just does something to you," she said, surreptitiously wiping away the tear that had begun to stream down her face.

"Do you need more help with your luggage?"

"Oh no … I can take it from here. You've been great."

"Well, like I said, if you need anything, just call me. Here's my number," she said, handing Dimity a business card. "Is your husband joining you later?" she suddenly asked.

"What?"

"Sorry … I just noticed that you're wearing a wedding ring. I'm sorry. That was so rude of me. I just thought it's such a romantic place here … anyway, sorry."

"No … don't apologise. I don't know if my husband will be joining me," Dimity said looking at the young tour guide, even though she was really telling herself. A day had passed since he called, and she still hadn't gotten back to him. He was probably worried about her. She would call him soon.

***

Nicki looked at the picture of the Greek Orthodox church overlooking the mesmerising crystal blue water of the Aegean Sea. It would be like her second home for now, where she would work and plan holidays for many wide-eyed customers with big dreams for adventure. She was sure that she would get the job. The interview was just formalities — filling in forms, and the like. Her boss had practically hinted that the job was hers. Her role would have her oversee a small team of consultants, as well as help out with clients on occasion. She couldn't believe she would be working right opposite Maria's beautiful and mystical shop. She walked inside the office. There was a buzz of activity: phones ringing, the faint tapping sound coming from keyboards as travel consultants searched for prices, the best accommodations, and travel insurance.

She could feel the positive energy oozing from the customers sitting on the comfortable, contemporary chairs, their excited eyes fixated on images on computer screens or brochures — eyes that belonged to future tourists or honeymooners, or students deciding to have a gap year.

That was how she had met him.

She had fallen for Marco — her Italian crush, who was twenty-three at the time — while working. Marco had planned to take a few months off from university and defer his studies so he could travel Europe with his friends. She helped him find accommodation; she had organised their flights, their drivers — she made sure everything would be easy for the smooth-talking, green-eyed uni student, and his deviant friends, who wouldn't stop flirting with her. She had been smitten as soon as he began to talk. There was something about him — his confidence, his charm. He was attractive, in an unassuming way. His personality gave him a certain presence. He had a tight, slightly crooked jaw, and olive skin. Despite his tough exterior and cool charm, his eyes were kind. He was five-foot-eleven — rather tall, compared to her five-foot-six stature.

It had turned out that Marco had developed quite the travel bug, and was in fact back at the Travel Centre, where she worked in the Melbourne CBD, a few months after his stint in Europe. Apparently he wanted to travel around Australia and needed to ask some questions, not needing to book anything *just then*. As soon as she had seen him, Nicki had known that he wasn't going to be booking a holiday any time soon. She knew the reason he was there from the moment he had walked in the room, greeting her with a smile that was only for her. Then, just as he was about to walk out the door, he had asked the question that changed her life: "Do you want to go grab a coffee, or something?" She had agreed. It was nearly her lunch hour anyway. They had their coffee — and they also had the *something* — and that was chemistry, and lots of it. That chemistry had led to

158

her saying "I do" at their nuptials in a romantic setting in Tuscany, Italy. It was a storybook romance, and she had ended up marrying the handsome property project manager.

From that first coffee, Nicki knew that dating Marco would be one great adventure. He was the most exciting man she had ever met. The coffee they had that day was accompanied by him paying the restaurant's violin players for an extra performance for just the two of them.

"It was great coffee," she had said, on their way out of the stylish space, only to be greeted by the sounds of violins as she stepped onto the footpath.

"Just who are you, *Marco Rossi*?" she had asked in between laughter, her cheeks warm with embarrassment and jubilation. Marco Rossi made her feel like she was the only woman in the world. She could feel it from then — that being with him would mean that music would always be part of her life. Any shyness or resistance melted away when she was in his presence.

His marriage proposal had been just as extraordinary. "My beautiful Nicki, 'you are the sun and the moon'," he had chanted as though he was on the streets of Verona as she looked down at him from the balcony of her house, situated in a quaint suburban Melbourne street. "Would you do me the honour of being my wife, my fair lady?" Nicki had laughed uncontrollably as he mixed up his lines, his accents, *and* his literary characters. He had *passione*, he would often say. "We always need *passione* in life — *Abbiamo sempre bisogno di passione nella vita*," he would whisper seductively in her ear, making her feel like she was starring in her own version of *La Dolce Vita*. He had confidence in himself, and in life, and he brought out her confidence too.

Nicki took a deep, heavy breath. She had been carrying so much pain in her heart. It was slowly coming to the surface. *"You need to find out who you are as a person,"* he had told her that Sunday morning. Cassandra and Connor had also told her the same thing that day at the airport. *What am I doing?* she thought to herself as she combed a strand of hair away from her face. She could feel the tension in her whole body, the tightening of her chest. She had to be free of it. *I can't pretend. I can't just continue working here as if nothing's wrong. I need to do something — I need to discover who I am — to feel happiness, to laugh, to feel the sunlight on my face.* She took another glance inside the travel agency, then looked over at Eventually You. *Such an earthy, healing vibe*, she thought as she gazed at her sister's cosy, mystical shop. *That's exactly what I need — to be healed.* How could she plan someone else's journey when she didn't even know where *she* was heading?

She stepped back and turned to face the display window of the travel agency. She heard Maria's words in her mind. "You should come with us." Her eyes returned to the poster. The sea looked so infinite and so mesmerising, full of promise and possibility. She had weaved that part of the sea, thread by thread. She had weaved the sky, the white church, the magenta bougainvillaea. They had all weaved it until it became a complete and beautiful picture. She had strayed in a different direction but she would return home; she would find out who she was again, who little Nicki Salas was and how she hoped to evolve. It was time — it was time for her to book accommodation and flights — for *herself. She* needed a holiday this time.

CHAPTER SEVENTEEN

Maria gazed at the beautiful view of the crystalline sea of Santorini, with the mysterious ship in the distance that she had been looking at for the last thirty minutes or so. She couldn't seem to look away. Antonio had gone to buy a *souvlaki* in pita bread for himself, and a *haloumi* wrap for her, with a side serving of *tzatziki* for lunch. The smell of the food from all the taverns and takeout stands had conjured up memories of her childhood, and strangely, she felt comforted by the smell. Thomas was resting in his pram beside her, and he too looked content as he listened to the calming sounds of the waves crashing onto the rocks down below. She looked to the left of the many white, yellow, and terracotta apartments and villas, each with their charming cobblestone courtyard, where she could also see some cable cars and a few shops displaying canvas beach bags, and white skirts, lined up along an ascending road further away. A man on a donkey was passing expertly down the many steep steps, and she couldn't help but look their way as the bell ringing on the donkey's neck caught her attention.

"Thomas, look! A donkey," she eagerly pointed out, taking him out of the pram quickly to make sure he could see it as it made its way down the steps. Thomas began to laugh, revealing two cute little dimples. He seemed to be enjoying the different places they were visiting and exploring together. She looked over at the volcanic terrain known as Caldera on her right side, and couldn't believe she had ties to a country that was so rich in beauty and history.

"It's beautiful, isn't it?" Antonio walked down the steps that led to the courtyard adjoining their villa, holding their lunch and a few beers. Maria had agreed to join him in a beer, deciding to live in the moment. He placed the food on the outdoor table that was surrounded with terracotta pots that housed vibrant red European flowers. She had also noticed the beautiful magenta bougainvillea draped over the walls of the apartment next to their villa. The contrast of the magenta against the white walls, and the deep blue backdrop of the sea, created a happy and lovely picture that was typical of Greece. That variety of flower seemed to be blooming in many parts of Greece, in colours ranging from fuchsia, to cherry blossom, to a deep, rich magenta colour, like the one she was admiring in front of her. She breathed in the salty smell of sea air, and admired Antonio as he talked to Thomas. She couldn't believe how blessed she was to have such a beautiful family. As beautiful as the view was, she knew that with Antonio, she could be in a tent in the rain, and she would still be happy. That's just how he made her feel. He was so good for her. If only her sister could be as happy as she was, she thought guiltily.

"What are you thinking about?"

"Oh ... I'm just thinking about how happy I feel at this very moment ... with you and Thomas, and I can't help but worry ..."

"About Nicki?"

"Yes. I mean ... she had it all at one stage. She was so in love and now she's lost the love of her life. She's alone now. I don't even know if she's talked to him since they parted ways. I know my sister — all she wanted was to have a precious child with the man she loved. She wanted it so much. She would have given everything else up just to make that dream real. All she cared about was that child ... the one she only saw in her dreams. Why does life have to be so complicated?"

"Maria ... don't worry. Nicki will land on her feet."

"I know she will eventually. She's always been the one that looked out for me, from when we were little. If I had a problem at school or with Mum, I could always count on Nicki to help me. She and Marco were truly in love. Now

… she's lost her best friend, again. As cliché as it sounds, he really was her soulmate."

"Don't worry so much, Maria. We'll be there for your sister. Even John is looking out for her. I'm sure all her friends won't abandon her. They may be able to reconcile. Some relationships *can* stand the test of time. Besides, you even got Cassandra and Connor to look out for her."

"I'm sure you're right," she said, as she placed Thomas back in the pram and sat on the chair across from Antonio. "Anyway, the food smells so good," she said, eyeing the pita wraps as Antonio handed her a glass of beer.

"To true love," he toasted, and kissed her on the lips.

"To us," she smiled at him and then looked at the sunlight gently caressing the blue sea in the horizon.

***

Malcolm Stewart was deep in thought. He was sitting on a park bench watching people walk or cycle by. He had been in the Netherlands for just over a week, and she had been out of his life for nearly four days now. He stared at his mobile phone. *Where in God's name is she? Doesn't she know how worried I am?* He had given her time, but this was getting old now! How long would he wait? What about the girls? His in-laws would not even clue him in. Surely they knew where she was. She couldn't be that irresponsible and not tell anyone about her whereabouts. He was beginning to lose his patience. He couldn't stay in Amsterdam indefinitely.

As his eyes scanned the park, they fell on a young family having a picnic, instantly reminding him of happier times. He remembered their time at the south coast, almost six months ago — the night breeze from the ocean and the smell of the sea in her long, soft, lustrous hair, constantly covering her face, forcing her to hold it back with one hand as she tried to eat her sorbet with the other. She had leaned onto his shoulder, and they had sat and looked at the ocean for a while. She had then turned and looked at him. He never forgot what she had said to him.

"I love you Malcolm." He remembered looking into her green eyes as she looked at him with intent.

"What brought this on?" he had asked, kissing her on the head as she placed her head back on his shoulder.

"I don't know … I feel so happy being here with you right now … with you … and with the girls. It was such a perfect day. Let's promise each other that we won't stop having moments like this, okay?" Her eyes had looked so sincere, slightly vulnerable and emotional.

"That's all we need really, isn't it?" he recalled telling her as he stroked her hair. "We just need each other and everything else will fall into place. I love you too Dimity … so much. Sometimes I think I am the luckiest man alive."

He remembered the kiss they shared; it was so intense. He remembered the sorbet spilling all over her blouse, making its way sensuously down her neck. He remembered the shock in her face as it melted and continued to make its way down into her blouse. They had both laughed out loud. He sat closer to her and began to kiss her neck, working his way down, tasting the sorbet in between kisses.

"Malcolm!" she had cried. "My parents will see us from the window!" She had looked at him as though she was a devious teenager.

"Well, in that case, I won't continue doing what I was planning to do. I know how crazy it drives you when I kiss you over here," he had continued, kissing her and unbuttoning her blouse, tasting the sorbet as he continued to work his way further down her soft skin.

"Malcolm, I'm serious … they'll see us," she had said, giving him a look he knew so well.

"You mean you want me to stop?" he had teased.

"Yes, I mean … it's not the right place," she had said, unsuccessfully trying to suppress a smile from appearing on her face, which was practically glowing.

164

He had held her hand and scanned the area. His eyes had made contact with her father's boat.

"Malcolm ... what's on your mind? Surely, you aren't suggesting we go to the boat ..."

He had continued kissing her on the lips, then her neck and her exposed shoulder, leading her to the boat, stopping at different intervals to kiss her again. Her protests ended abruptly, having quickly been replaced with an intense look as she followed him into the boat. They had stayed there for most of the night as the boat swayed from side to side. They had then snuck back into the house, softly giggling like teenagers, slipping back into their bed, pretending that they had slept there all night.

That morning, as they sat around the breakfast table, her mum appeared very jovial.

"It was very turbulent last night. It seemed it was choppier than other nights," she had commented, looking out of the window as she spoke.

"Was it?" Malcolm innocently questioned. "We didn't realise. Dimi, did you notice anything?" he had asked her, giving her a knowing smile. She had looked down at her plate self-consciously, pretending to play with her food.

"No, I didn't," she had managed, looking up at him, and giving him a *how could you?* glare. She had then digressed and began to ask Olivia why she wasn't eating her food. He had then continued to taunt her by placing his hand on her bare knee under the table, knowing she would panic if her parents picked up on any sign that they had spent the night in the boat.

"Dimity ... are you okay?" her father had asked. He had been smiling as well.

"I'm fine. I just thought there was a mosquito on me," she had said, discretely taking Malcolm's hand off of her knee.

She had then excused herself and headed straight to the bathroom. Malcolm followed her and grabbed her by the hand, turning her to face him.

"Dimi ... relax! I was just being funny. I just think you look so adorable when you look like a guilty teenager."

"I can't believe you," she had snapped. "I was so embarrassed."

"Relax. Your parents are cool. I mean, they're practically hippies. They live by the sea, your mum is into healthy food, and she used to own a flower shop."

"So that makes them hippies, does it? My dad was a solicitor. So how does he fit into your hippie stereotype?"

"Okay, that wrecks my theory, unless I take the 'he fought for justice' stance. I mean, he always gave free legal aid to those who couldn't afford it. Dimity, sorry if I upset you. It won't happen again," he had said, trying hard not to smile.

"It better not, and I'll tell you what else won't be happening for a while ... what we did last night!"

He had just smiled at her.

"What are you smiling at?" she had asked.

"Well, if you're going to make threats, maybe it should be something you can actually commit to. I mean, you do find it difficult to resist me, don't you? I know what drives you wild, all your zones. Last night's an example of that ..."

"You're unbelievable — and full of yourself," she had said, messing his hair, unable to resist a smile.

"Do you still love me?" he had asked, looking at her innocently.

"Of course I do. I just hate that you know me so well. But you know what? I wouldn't have it any other way, because I also love that you know me so well. Although ... it's also evident that you can't resist me either. I mean, you can't keep your hands off of me."

"That's true," he had said, looking at her affectionately. She was right. He couldn't resist her.

He was torturing himself. He had to do something. He abruptly stood up from the bench and wandered aimlessly with his hands in his pockets. The small studio caught his attention again, as though it was calling him. That was how it used to be — him and his studio. He remembered the first time he had seen Dimity in it. "Sorry," he had said to her, "... for not having a sign. I'm an industrial designer, not a businessman." He looked at his mobile again — still no message from her. He had one message from yet another potential buyer who was eager to do business with him, but he couldn't deal with that now. It didn't seem important. Nothing did without her.

Without thinking, he walked into the studio. There were all sorts of interesting things inside — paints, canvasses, oil pastels, sketchpads. He needed to release his energy somehow. He had to create again!

CHAPTER EIGHTEEN

Up close, the lake looked just as mystical and romantic. Dimity breathed in the air as the white and red ferry swayed from side to side as it made its way to the Ali Pasha museum, dedicated to one of Ioannina's most notorious rulers. Eleni, the tour guide, had told her it was one of the *must-sees* while she stayed in Ioannina. She could see where it stood proudly in the distance, as proud as Ali Pasha himself would have been, she imagined. There were so many museums to see from the Byzantine and Ottoman eras in the region, not to mention so many boutiques, restaurants, and shops, both rustic and modern. It seemed that the town was divided; on the one hand, it had a contemporary aesthetic, with clean lines and precise measurements, as seen on the many new houses, apartments, and shops, while on the other, it still had its rustic charm, which filled the streets with history from a world of long ago.

It was Dimity's second day in Ioannina, and she was becoming used to her own company. She had her breakfast that morning on the Juliet balcony of her hotel room. It was peaceful and calming to sip her coffee while she became acquainted with the breathtaking view of the lake, and the enormous mountains behind it. She had ordered in, feeling lazy and realising that nothing could really beat the view from her balcony. As wonderful as she felt, her heart always felt heavy as Malcolm was always in the back of her mind — as were the girls. Their marriage was a big question mark, hanging like a cloud over her head. She felt like she had to call him after she visited the island across the lake — known as Nissi — as soon as she got back to the hotel.

The ferry finally anchored at the island. The Ali Pasha museum dated back to the Ottoman Empire and was Ali Pasha's home during his final days. Eleni had told her that it was actually a monastery where he hid for two years with his wife, Vassiliki, and to look out for the bullet hole still in the ceiling from when he had been captured by the army after years of resistance and brutality.

The sun burnt her feet as she stepped out of the boat. She began to walk slowly, musing as she observed the surreal, mystical surroundings. There were fish markets on one side with adjoining courtyard *tavernes*, while on the other side there were stalls bedecked with unique jewellery pieces that had a gypsy element to them. She was surprised to see many gypsies trying to get people's attention, who were selling electronics, flowers, and handmade shawls and blankets. She continued walking as she looked at the signs that led her to the museum. She noted the Ottoman influence as she walked along a cobblestone path where the entrance of the courtyard welcomed visitors with a cannon from the time. *That definitely sets the mood,* she thought. The history in that part of Greece was dominated by many of these sorts of historical sites, all of which emphasised Ali Pasha's rule of the region.

Dimity walked up the stairs of the museum, which was covered in old, original brick. She walked through the rooms that displayed Ali Pasha's many belongings, including a number of paintings. She was amazed to see the bullet hole in the ceiling. She spent at least twenty minutes reading all the information and taking it all in, before deciding to stroll around the markets on the island, finding somewhere to sit and have a refreshing drink at one of the outside taverns that overlooked the lake. The perimeter of the courtyard boasted terracotta, blue, and white pots with red flowers and lush green plants. Children were playing a game of soccer using a drink container as a ball, and a cat was sleeping under one of the tables, finding shade from the harsh midday sun. She looked at the cat and smiled to herself. Dimity ordered a glass of *portokalada*, which she remembered was the Greek word for orange-flavoured soda. She didn't usually drink soft drinks, but the atmosphere evoked carefree memories from her childhood — sipping cold refreshments in the Salas house, listening to Mr and Mrs Salas tell Greek stories and myths.

A couple at the next table ordered a plate of white bait and a grilled sea bass, and she suddenly felt hungry. She politely summoned the waiter again, and ordered a grilled bream with a Greek salad. She then sat back in her chair, and took a deep breath. She was glad that she had chosen to wear a chambray shirt on top of her mid-length, black, strapless summer dress. The sun was unbearable. She looked at the people around her, enjoying the parade that was unfolding as more and more people made their way across the island. She then instinctively took out her mobile, wondering if she had any messages from the girls, or from Malcolm. He had kept his word and given her some space. There were no messages from the girls, her parents, or her husband. It felt strange, not seeing Malcolm's name flash across the screen on a regular basis. She began to wonder what he would be thinking, and decided to call him as soon as she got back to the hotel. She thought he should at least know which *country* she was in. As far as he knew, she was still in Amsterdam. *I can't leave him waiting there forever*, she thought, as a twinge of guilt caused a slight pain in the pit of her stomach.

She gazed at the ferry, which danced in the waves. She was used to having the sea in her life, and it was a calming influence. Her mind went to Rose Bay, and the family home. She recalled the many times she looked at the bay and the sea with him, the wind spraying sea salt in their hair. She thought of his blue eyes looking at her intimately. She remembered his full, soft lips kissing her, his neat beard tantalising her as he stroked her neck with his lips. *I'll call him soon*, she reassured herself. As she looked at the lake again, she noticed that as poetic as it looked, it was melancholic, just as she was, even when she was feeling free and happy on her private little Greek adventure.

That afternoon, as Dimity stepped out of the boat in Ioannina, she decided to continue her day of discovery and take a walk through the busy streets. She quickly made her way back to her hotel room to freshen up, before heading back out. She walked along an old, maze-like, stone-paved alley that led her to one of the main streets in the centre of town. It was filled with noise, shops, and restaurants.

She continued walking down a wider street flanked by one of the massive medieval, stone fortress walls — the main entrance to the castle dating back to Ali Pasha's rule, known as Kastro. It was the same wall she had passed in Eleni's car on her first day in Ioannina. She gazed at the enormous clock tower built onto it, the Greek flag waving proudly atop it, and the green grass growing out from the historic wall's crevices. She crossed the road again, careful not to get run over by a scooter with a cool young couple on it. Dimity couldn't believe how fast the locals drove. The speed limit seemed to be *no* limit.

The street was packed with tables and chairs from outdoor restaurants, which were densely populated by young and old locals and tourists, sipping *lattes, frappes, freddo cappuccinos*, and cold espressos topped with frothed milk. She casually looked through the windows of boutiques, mesmerised by unique shoes, dresses, beach attire, and homewares. She noticed a sign on a shop in English — "Live & Create". She walked into the contemporary looking shop, drawn to some beautiful vases and vessels on display in one of the windows. The details and colour schemes of the visual stimuli throughout the shop instinctively caught her attention. The colours were obviously reflective of the local setting and the culture, as hues of blue, gold, brown, and white were painted creatively onto each unique piece.

She instantly felt a familiar desire while appraising their simple, unique, bespoke beauty.

Instinctively, she picked up one of the vases to examine it more closely. She wondered how it was made to look so transparent. She turned the vase upside down, and momentarily lost her grip on it. She gasped in relief as she managed to save the vase from meeting a cruel destiny, and quickly placed it back where she had found it. She turned around and felt something touch her elbow. "Oh, no!" she cried in disbelief, suddenly realising that the *something* was, in fact, an expensive looking vessel. It was too late this time. It fell right to the ground with a loud crash, all the pieces gathering around her Roman sandals. She couldn't believe what had happened. She felt so humiliated as she looked around for anyone who worked there.

"It's okay ... really. I can see it was an accident." She heard a Greek accented voice as she turned around to face a tanned man with short brown hair and blue-green eyes.

"*Then einai tipota* ... It's nothing, really," he continued. "I can make another one. Although it was one of my favourites." He looked at her intently as he spoke. "I have many favourites though," he said once again, back-peddling when her eyes grew wider and her face became warmer from embarrassment. Dimity continued to stare at him with her mouth half open. She felt like crying at the realisation of what she had done.

"I'm so sorry," she finally managed. "*Signomi*," she continued, remembering some Greek from the time she spent at the Salas house.

The man smiled at her sudden attempt at speaking his native language.

"You know some Greek, do you?"

"I had some Greek friends back in Australia when I was young. I'm really sorry for breaking such a beautiful vessel. It was so intricate. You actually made it? It must have taken you so much time."

"I don't look at it that way. The time I spend on making things is never a waste. The process of making something is as rewarding as the end process. I always learn something new with each piece I make. New things can always be made if you have inspiration … a bit like life is — ever-changing, evolving."

Dimity just smiled. There was something about the way he spoke. It was as though the philosophical words just rolled off of his tongue without much thought, like a poem.

"Well, in any case, I'd like to pay for it," she responded. "I just wouldn't feel right about it." She placed one of the broken pieces on the shelf and reached into her mini tote bag for her wallet.

"That won't be necessary," he immediately interjected. "I only let customers pay when they purchase something they love, that will bring a sense of joy, or evokes a hidden desire, or even a point of view — at the very least a conversation. Most of my designs are influenced from this town — its history, the mountains, the lake, as well as the exciting nightlife and, to some extent, the politically-minded youth. The contemporary element is influenced by the role the youth play in changing the town, and stamping their own identity on it from their own time."

"I noticed that as soon as I looked at the colours you chose. The rough surface on many of the vessels seem to reflect the rugged terrain of the villages, and the old architecture from the Byzantine era," she said excitedly.

"You're right. I am inspired by geography, and architecture. I'm very impressed."

"Well, my husb … I mean, I used to work as an interior designer, so I've worked with many industrial designers and artists. I guess I've learned to speak their language," she responded, stopping herself from hiding behind Malcolm once again. She, Dimity Stewart, was an interior designer in her own right, and the more she began to say that, the more she might actually start believing it again. This was her time after all. She also didn't feel the need to highlight that she was married. She liked where the conversation was heading, and she didn't want any communication block to ruin the flow.

"You know, if you really feel bad about not paying, there is another way you can help."

"Oh … which way is that?" Dimity asked, feeling slightly uncomfortable. Just what did he have in mind?

"You can sign up for my design lessons," he continued, pointing to a sign at the front counter.

"Oh …" Dimity said, relieved. She was about to dismiss the possibility, knowing that she wouldn't be in town that long, until she took a few steps closer to read the sign. "So you teach people to make something as unique and amazing as the pieces you have on display. Why would you want to give away your secrets?"

"Well, the process isn't completely a secret. It's what an individual creates that can be unique. You know … some people surprise themselves … and I get to earn a bit on the side. The lessons are right here at the studio and we sometimes go to my other studio in one of the villages near Ioannina to be inspired by nature."

Dimity looked at the list of names. Hesitant at first, she then took the pen in her hand and began writing her name.

"Dimity," he said. "I think your name is Greek in origin."

"I think it is, although there has been some debate about it."

"My name is Stavros," he said, offering his hand for a firm handshake. "Nice to meet you. We meet here tomorrow at 11am. See you then?"

"See you then Stavros," she said, smiling as she released her hand. She walked out of the shop, stopping momentarily to take a deep breath, before walking out into the hot, busy street. She didn't know what it was, but something felt right about what had just happened, as though it was what she needed at that point in her life.

Hours later, Dimity stumbled into her bedroom. She was exhausted from her first full day in Ioannina. After leaving Stavros' shop, she enjoyed a walk around the lake — what was known as a *peripato* in Greek — followed by a late ten o'clock dinner, which seemed to be quite a reasonable and acceptable time by the locals. The *you shouldn't eat dinner after seven o'clock* rule had obviously been ignored by the Greeks, yet many seemed to have bodies worthy of a *Sports Illustrated* cover. Perhaps a salad at ten o'clock was the norm for those trim and athletic looking girls and guys. Dinner at a restaurant for a family with young children late in the evening was also perfectly fine. Who needed to go to sleep early when they could sleep in the middle of the day, *siesta* still being the norm throughout the country? Dimity was just fine with it. It all seemed perfectly relaxing. She had decided to order some white bait, which seemed to be popular, and light, along with a salad. The white bread dipped in olive oil might have tarnished the healthy label she had placed on it, but what the hell? Some carbohydrates couldn't hurt once in a while. She had to chill out sometimes. She had become rather uptight with her regimens and schedules over the years, feeling that she had to have control over some aspect of her life.

It seemed like everyone was out, taking a night-time stroll, pushing prams, or walking dogs. There were street performers on every corner — puppeteers, *bouzouki*-playing buskers, a busker with a pelican — all entertaining the many passers-by. On the other side of the restaurant she could hear the ongoing beats emanating from the many nearby nightclubs. Dimity had seen numerous eager and loud young girls dressed in skimpy dresses heading to the nightclubs, many of them tattooed, and nearly every one of them heavily tanned. She hadn't ever seen so many extremely tanned people, and she hadn't even visited the famous Greek islands yet. Even in the midday heat, the

Greeks didn't seem to cover up; their bare skin was left on display. It was a far cry from the sun-smart linen shirts and huge fedora hats she was used to seeing on the beaches of her home town, not to mention the spray tanning salons that couldn't keep up with clients wanting to wear strapless, summer dresses to attend a wedding, or pre-Christmas drinks, without the damage from the Australian sun. She was one of those people. Her honey glow looked like it was actually pale compared to the tanned complexions she saw around her. They had tans on tans on tans …

She stayed at the outdoor restaurant for a while, having met some female tourists from England who had let their husbands look after the home-front while they went on holidays. They laughed and drank and ordered more *mezethes*, and even offered to join her for lunch the next day.

Dimity was starting to fit right into the lifestyle of a solo tourist. She felt so mellow and slightly tipsy as she got ready for bed, taking off her makeup, and brushing her teeth, when suddenly it occurred to her — she had forgotten to call him! She anxiously looked at her phone for the time, toothbrush in hand. It was too late now. It was one o'clock in the morning in Amsterdam. She couldn't possibly call him then. He could be sleeping, and she was definitely not up for that heavy conversation this late. She needed sleep. *I'll call in the morning*, she thought, feeling guilty. She would call Malcolm in the morning.

***

Nicki sat comfortably in her seat on the Airbus A380. She would be in Greece soon. Her heart felt open, after being closed for so long — as though it had shut the door to the world. "It's a great idea," Cassandra and Connor had told her before she had left. She'd promised them that she would tell Marco. It was the right thing to do. He was hurting as much as she was, but he was right — she had forgotten who

176

she was, and who they were. It had been a week of confusion since she had left him that Monday morning. If she hadn't done something, she felt that her heart would not be able to cope with the excruciating pain. "I just need some time away for a while — to sort out who I am," she had told him.

"Nicki, I didn't mean what I said, I mean, I did, but I wanted to work it out together. I never told you to leave," he had said in a soft voice that Nicki didn't recognise. His confidence and passion seemed to have been replaced with confusion and despair. *Maybe time away will be good for both of us. I dragged him down with me,* she thought between tears, *my brave, passionate, larger-than-life Marco. It's the best thing to do right now.*

"Do what you need to do," he had said. "And Nicki," he had continued.

"Yes, Marco?" she had asked with anxious curiosity.

"Just … be careful. I wouldn't want anything bad to happen to you. We need to talk when you return."

"I know … we will. I need to do this now, though. Bye Marco." Nicki felt that her heart would break. It all seemed so final.

"We'll check in on the house then. It will be like old times, spending time here," Cassandra had said to Connor.

"Well, it *is* where you two met. I guess this place would mean a lot to you guys," Nicki had told them.

"Sometimes, we need to be reminded about what brought us together. Every couple needs to be reminded, especially when things get out of control."

Nicki had looked at Cassandra sceptically. She had felt that she was making a point, as she gave Connor a knowing look.

"Are you okay? Cassandra had asked her when she'd stood silently at the front door, ready to leave.

"It just feels weird, how one minute I was with Marco, and now I'm going to Greece. I feel bad for leaving, but happy at the same time. Does that make sense?"

"It makes perfect sense. Nicki, you still love him," Cassandra said, giving her an encouraging smile.

"Yes, I do. I'll always love him. I don't know how it all went wrong. How did his smile disappear like that? He brought so much laughter and light into my life."

"From the sounds of it, I think you both did." Cassandra had looked at her with compassion and understanding.

"Taking time off for yourself might also help you, and your relationship," Connor had then added. "It's okay to feel bad for leaving. You're allowed to feel however you're feeling. Love doesn't end, even though we feel that our hopes and dreams have ended."

"Thank you guys for your concern, and advice. You're right. I can't just pretend that everything is the way it's always been. I need time to think." With that, Nicki bade them farewell and headed out the door.

Nicki looked out of the window. It wouldn't be long before she was back in Ioannina. She hadn't even told Maria. Her sister would be so surprised. *Marco, I hope I find myself again, and I hope you find the light in your eyes again,* she thought as she imagined the mountainous terrain of Epirus, the Ionian Sea, the sunlight caressing her skin, healing her heart, lighting her life.

CHAPTER NINETEEN

The morning sunlight boldly intruded on Malcolm's plans to get some morning sleep. He had tossed and turned again; his sheets were in the corner of the bed in a messy pile. The clock on the console informed him that it was nearly seven o'clock. The glass of scotch was still on the oval glass coffee table in front of the lounge where he had sat for half of the night, thinking. She still hadn't called him. He couldn't get his head around how things had ended up this way.

He looked at the coffee table again, and noticed his sketches from the previous night. Feelings of inertia had led to a desperate need for an outlet. He had bought a sketchbook from the local art store, and went back to the hotel where he began sketching without thinking — designing and creating for no reason at all. He felt so liberated — to sketch because he just wanted to, with no plans, and no deadlines. The pencil glided smoothly over the paper; each stroke and each shade came together effortlessly.

He stood up from his bed, walked over to the table and looked at page after page of designs. A chair he had sketched with a unique aesthetic and smooth curves caught his attention. It was almost the shape of a woman's body. He looked at another sketch — a table that had a shape resembling that of a boat. He smiled to himself. It was amazing where his mind went when it was free to explore. Creating eased his uncertainty. He felt that he had something he could control, that was his. *I wonder if she felt like that?* he thought to himself. *Not having a creative outlet would have been difficult for someone so passionate about creativity.* A bout of guilt instantaneously dug at his heart, as he tensely played with his slight beard. Why did he expect her to be okay with it, if he couldn't be?

179

"I only wanted to surprise you," she had told him, tears streaming uncontrollably down her beautiful, soft skin. He didn't know what to do anymore! He couldn't wait idly indefinitely. Sketching began to give him new positive energy. It was time to take control of all aspects of his life.

Moments later, freshly showered and armed with hope and energy, Malcolm pulled on his navy chino pants and opened the cupboard to pick out a shirt. His hands brushed past the denim shirt he had been wearing that day, when he had noticed her in the foyer, her long tousled hair flowing freely, caressing the silky smooth skin of her bare shoulders. He took the shirt out of the cupboard, realising that it needed to be thrown into the laundry bag. He slipped a grey, striped v-neck t-shirt over his bare chest and placed the denim shirt in the laundry bag, stopping momentarily as a pleasant scent instantly reminded him of Dimity. He brought the shirt close to his nose. It was the smell of her perfume. She was wearing it the day he had last seen her; the very same fragrance she'd worn almost every day since that very first moment they'd met in his studio. The scent always drove him wild.

His mobile rang, snapping him out of his trance. He answered it, the shirt still in his hand. He couldn't miss the call. It could be Dimity. As he answered hastily, he realised it was his mum.

"Oh, hi Mum," Malcolm answered, impatiently.

"Hi Malcolm … I see you're too busy to give your mum and dad a call."

"Oh … sorry Mum … I've just been distracted lately," he answered irritably, peering through the blinds, looking down at some cyclists on the paved, busy street.

"So how are the girls? Are you still in Amsterdam? I'm surprised. Are your trips usually this long?"

Alex had obviously kept his mouth shut. His mother didn't seem to know anything about Dimity running off.

"No, I just have a lot of business associates to meet with. The girls are fine, Mum. Why do you ask?"

"Oh nothing,"

"Meaning?" he asked, his impatience growing quickly.

"Well, it's not like I get to talk to them much these days. I mean, they even hardly talked to your father and me at the dinner on Saturday."

"They ate with us, and then excused themselves because they had an important assignment to work on," he responded, running his fingers through his hair. He was beginning to regret ever hosting that dinner. His wife might have still been with him.

"Yes, but Dimity didn't even make sure that they said goodbye to your father and me. Your father was so offended. Has Dimity been saying negative things about us? I mean, she insulted me so much. I just don't know what has gone into her, Malcolm … and I'm worried about how she's raising the girls. I mean, they don't lift a finger in the kitchen. I think she is spoiling …"

"Mum, are you even listening to yourself? You're blaming Dimity for everything. I mean, why aren't you blaming me for any of it? I could have ensured the girls said goodbye to you and Dad. Anyway, this is getting old. I don't want to hear another negative word about Dimity, *or* our girls! Is that clear? I don't have time for this. How we raise our girls, and what Dimity does in her life — it's our business!"

"Malcolm … how could you of all people talk to me like that? It's Dimity. She's causing all the family to despise me …"

"Mum, I don't despise you. You know I love you … I know you suffer from high blood pressure, so I don't want to upset you, but I've been away so many times from the girls and from Dimity. I haven't been involved in any of the trivial family issues. I've been too busy making a name for myself. Dimity has been there on her own to deal with it all. I never wanted to hear it because it sounds so mundane —

181

so suburban. I thought as a family we were above that. I mean, you loved Dimity when you met her. You told me yourself. Don't you remember what you said about her? You said she was one of the sweetest and most beautiful girls you've ever met. You also said she was intelligent, and that we had many things in common, being in the design industry. You said she was perfect for me."

"Malcolm, your father and I are so proud of your accomplishments. I mean, everyone in our family thinks that you've achieved so much in your career ..."

"Mum, have you even heard a word I said? I don't need my ego to be stroked. I've been getting that from buyers and magazines for years now. I was talking about Dimity — the person who gave up a successful career to look after us, the person who does everything so that I can have time to achieve all these amazing things — to travel the world, to create. Don't you see? Everything I've achieved, I owe to her, to her generosity. The difference is that she doesn't get any recognition. She only gets judgment and insults. As for that beautiful house, that you keep admiring — she did most of the legwork. She organised the builders, the contractors, the whole lot, while I was busy focusing on my career. The girls have also turned out to be free-spirited, opinionated, intelligent students, and wonderful daughters, because of Dimity, so please, stop with the vindictive attacks against her. Don't disrespect my wife again!"

"Malcolm, I try to respect Dimity and I never said she hasn't been doing a great job with the girls. It's just, when we're there, she doesn't encourage them to be close to us. As for helping around the house, I'm sure they do, but it seems they don't when we're there, so they don't have to spend time with us. I don't pay attention to your father's beliefs in gender roles. I've always encouraged you and Alex to help around the house. Anyway, that's why I thought they might have heard something negative about us. I also realised Dimity had a successful career before she had the girls. I mean, your father and I always questioned her decision to resign. She has become so disrespectful of us lately though … well except for your brother, of course. He really has an acid tongue. I think *we* have spoiled him over the years. I just see how close she is to her parents and how close the girls are to them also and I guess I envy that in a way. I thought we would be close when I met Dimity. She respected me then."

"Well, I don't think the real problem is with you or Dad. I think it's with me, Mum," he answered, sitting on the side of the bed, suddenly letting his guard down. It had been an emotionally draining week. He was sick of taking the defensive stance. He was tired.

"Why would she have a problem with you? You treat Dimity as well as any husband would."

"I treat her well, but I think I've let her down. In fact, I'm certain of that. Don't worry about it. We just need to work a few things out. Dimity wants to be close to all of you. She has never been vindictive by nature. She just wants to feel included, and to not be left behind. It wouldn't be so bad if you, for once, gave her some credit, instead of always boasting about *me*. Maybe she would reciprocate, then. It wouldn't hurt. Anyway, I've got to go now. I have to make an important phone call. Don't worry, Mum. I'm sure one day you and Dimity will be close again; as for the girls, they love you and Dad as much as they love their other grandparents. They just love that Mr McKenzie has a boat. They always scored extra points for that — from when they were young. Oh, Mum … one more thing …"

"What, Malcolm?"

"Ease up with your so-called 'observations'. Maybe some people can handle them, but the rest of the world might find them blatantly rude … I mean, all Dimity was really doing is what you've been doing for years — except, she doesn't really think you're overweight. She just wanted to prove a point. I think she succeeded, don't you think? It hurts, doesn't it, when you're the one receiving the unwanted feedback or so-called *observation*? Bye, Mum. Say hi to Dad for me." He hung up the phone before his mother had a chance to respond.

Malcolm was soon out in the hallway and in a lift, heading to the ground floor. He suddenly felt recharged and needed to have some breakfast. He would call her after that, deciding he needed a lot of energy to try to mend their relationship, and have Dimity back by his side. Surprisingly, he felt better after talking to his mum. He knew the real problem was with him, and that Dimity and the girls needed him in their lives. He in turn needed them — more than he realised. Indefinite time away from her, and not knowing if he had lost her, had really put things in perspective. His designs meant nothing without them. After all, that was what he based his designs on — his muse was his family, and he loved creating comfortable, innovative, and cool designs that could be enjoyed with loved ones, where stories could be told, opinions voiced, artistic expression realised, and passionate, intimate moments shared between couples.

"Hi ... *Dimity*?"

"Hi Malcolm."

"How are you? I've been waiting for you to call," Malcolm said, grabbing his coffee at a trendy coffee shop a few streets away from the hotel. He missed hearing her voice.

"I'm okay. I'm sorry I didn't get to call yesterday but something had come up and ..."

"Oh really?" he asked, wondering what could have possibly come up that would not spare her a few minutes to call her husband. He couldn't believe how formal they were being with each other, as though they didn't know anything about each other's lives.

"Look, Malcolm, I know you've been stuck in Amsterdam for so long and it's not fair for me to keep you waiting. Maybe it would be better if you go back to Sydney and be with the girls. It turns out I might need a few more days. There's something I need to do before I leave ..."

Malcolm took a deep breath as he sat at the table, his coffee untouched, trying not to miss a word over the noise of the busy coffee shop. He became tenser with each word she uttered, and remained speechless for a few seconds. "What are you talking about, Dimity? I gave you time to figure things out. I thought that was the deal — I give you time and then we organise to meet so we can work things out *together*," he said with a tight jaw.

"Yes, I know, but I need two more weeks at the very least ... maybe more. You can tell the girls that you felt bad, that you missed them, and that my parents can't stay longer, so you decided to come home, while I continue the trip ... you know, since I don't get to travel much lately?"

Malcolm took another deep breath, trying desperately to control his anger, but even he had his limits.

"Just what games are you playing with me, Dimity? You're telling me you want to continue lying to the girls, so you can be on your own — wherever that may be, because you haven't even told your husband where you are — and you need to do this so you can sort things out between us, *on your own*? Tell me why I shouldn't be angry about that. Tell me how I should react. I just want to know one thing. Do you want fix things between us? Do you want our marriage to be how it used to be?"

"Of course I do, Malcolm. Please, try to understand. I mean, I'm always patient when you tell me you have to extend your trips. How many times have I had to be there for the girls while you did your own thing?"

"Oh ... now I get it. This is your revenge. You're still upset with me for all the times I left you and the girls. I can't believe what I'm hearing. Both situations are completely different. I extended my trips for work — not to intentionally be away from my family. I always miss all of you," Malcolm said, his jaw getting even tighter.

185

"I *do* want to be with my family as well. I'm not doing this intentionally to be away from you and the girls. Of course I want to fix our marriage. How can you say that Malcolm? I'm telling you it's not you … I realise it's me. I need time to find out who I am again. Maybe then I'll get my zeal for life back. I need to be on my own to figure out who I am. Maybe then we can try to talk about us …"

"Okay … now I've heard it all," Malcolm gasped in disbelief as he leaned back in his chair, running his fingers through his thick, wavy hair tensely. "'It's not you, it's me?' What the hell is that supposed to mean? Who are you talking to? I'm your husband of twelve years," Malcolm continued talking, as he stood up and walked out, into the street. "I'm the father of your children, the man you spent so many intimate hours with. Do you ever remember those moments, Dimi, or have you forgotten them all? I'm not some high school boyfriend you're *going steady* with. Please, don't insult my intelligence. I tried to be patient with you, but this is beyond a joke now. It's so damn obvious. You're trying to make a point, to show me what it's like when you're the one always waiting. You're also angry because I told you you're not that passionate woman I fell in love with. So, this is your revenge. Tell me though Dimi … do our girls matter to you at all? Do you care if they're worried? Do you know that Sam asked if we're getting a divorce? I mean, how can you not even tell me where you are? Don't you know how irresponsible that is?"

"*What?* I can't believe you're blaming me for everything again when I'm the one that's always there. Well, I can see nothing has changed between us since I left Amsterdam. So, I'm glad I'm taking more time *for me* … yes, that's right Malcolm, *for me*! It's true — I need it. Maybe then you'll all learn to respect me. I know you find it hard to believe that I might want to better myself, but it's true. I do want to serve another purpose in life. It's *you* who has forgotten that about me, and if that makes me selfish, so be it. As for the girls, how dare you accuse me of not caring about them! I love and care about them so much. I've always been there for them ..."

"Dimi, please ... I didn't want to get into an argument again. I just need to know where you are. I'm worried about you. We need to talk in person. It's difficult on the phone. We're just miscommunicating again. I need to know where you are ... at least tell me that?" he pleaded, trying to calm the situation down. She sounded so upset and he knew he was losing her again.

"I can't yet. I was going to actually tell you where I am until you started accusing me again. I thought you wanted me to be *that* woman again. Well, why can't you have some faith in me? I'll call you in a few days to catch up. Just go back home. You've been there too long. I've got to go. I'm late for something."

"Dimi, wait ... you can't do this again. I need to know where you are. I'm tired of these games ..."

"Bye, Malcolm."

Malcolm felt like throwing his phone in the bin next to him. He couldn't believe it had happened again. Why was she doing this to him? He couldn't take it anymore. His patience had run thin. Something had to give. He had felt so hopeful after he had talked to his mother, thinking that if there was any hope for his mum and Dimity, that surely there was hope for Dimity and him! He turned his phone off and placed it in his pocket. He needed to be free of it for a while. He tugged at his slight beard in frustration. He didn't know what to do next. Instinctively, he walked back to the coffee shop. He placed a few bills on the table and headed for the door, until he saw her. It was Julie Canei — the interior designer he had done business with. She was smiling at him from the counter of the coffee shop. She grabbed her coffee and walked over to him, giving him another warm smile. She had beautiful hazel eyes, and her smile was so sweet and infectious; Malcolm couldn't help but reciprocate.

"Hi … I didn't know you were still in town," she said.

"I had to extend my stay a bit longer," he replied. "So, are you still working?"

"No, my boss actually gave me a few days off. We finished earlier than we thought, so he insisted I see the city for the rest of the stay."

"Generous boss," Malcolm said, smiling.

"So … since you're practically a local, where do you think I should start?"

Malcolm was about to recommend a few places, but instead found himself saying: "Look, I have nothing else on, so do you want me to show you around?"

"If you're not busy," she said, hesitantly.

"Actually, I can honestly say I have nowhere else to be at the moment, so I'm yours for the rest of the day — if you need a tour guide, and some company?"

"That sounds great, Malcolm. I thought you were busy when I saw you. You looked intense. Is everything okay?"

"Well, it wasn't for a moment, but you know what? Everything is fine now," he said, as he guided her out the door.

Back in Ioannina, Dimity looked at the phone in shock. How did it happen again? How did their words get so tangled *again*? Looking at things from his perspective, she knew it looked like she was intentionally keeping her distance from him. It had started out like that, but it had become so much more. Dimity hadn't felt so energised and optimistic for a long time. There was something about not knowing what her plans were that was so liberating. She didn't want to feel guilty about it as she normally would, and she didn't need to be questioned about her love for her daughters. That was so far from the truth. She *did* feel bad for him though. He sounded so worried and lost.

188

She took one more sip of her *frappe*, put her sunglasses on, and made her way to the studio where she would meet Stavros and the other students. It was all so exciting — being in Greece, learning and creating. As she walked through the crowded streets, the sun on her back, she decided to call him again after her class. She didn't feel right about leaving things the way they were. But in that moment, she had to focus on herself. It was her time to do something for herself. Malcolm would have to understand it. He would have to accept it, the way she had.

Moments later, she stepped into Stavros' studio. "*Yiasou* Stavros," she said to the now familiar, olive-skinned, handsome Greek man standing at the counter amongst his beautiful creations. "I'm ready for my lesson," she said, smiling. "I'm ready to learn how to create something beautiful."

"*Yiasou,* Dimity. I don't think we'll be able to create something as beautiful as you ..." he replied, matching her smile, "... but we'll try. I'm good, but I'm not that good."

"I'm *positive* you say that to all the girls," she replied, matching his playful tone. For some reason she felt that she could really trust this man. He had such positive energy. His presence alone had inspired her when she had met him the day before. Something told her that she would enjoy her lessons with this talented designer.

"You know, you really need to learn how to accept a compliment," he said, as he led her to a big table where another man and two young women were waiting for the lesson to commence. "I mean, being in a creative field, you should know how hard it is not to acknowledge something that is extraordinary. It's almost impossible."

Dimity just smiled as she walked to the table. He was really good with words, but the strange thing was that she didn't even mind his direct flirting. She knew it was innocent. Besides, it was about time that she felt special again. It was her time to shine. It was her turn to create beauty in the garden!

***

Malcolm returned to the hotel lobby late that evening. It had been an interesting day. He hadn't laughed that much for a long time. Showing Julie the sights of Amsterdam had led to a tour of the city on one of the many boats, sipping Champagne as they admired the views from the canals. They had then visited a few galleries, the Museum Quarter nearby, and had caught the tram to visit some design studios. He had shared his thoughts with her over dinner, at one of the happening contemporary wine bars — how he missed focusing on the creative process, how it had all become business, networking, and promotion. He had explained that he had no time for anything else lately. She had listened patiently; she understood where he was coming from. She had been so understanding, *and* sweet; he couldn't help but compare her to his wife. He had then walked her back to her hotel room, where she showed him some ideas they had for his new lighting range. He had stayed a while.

Remembering that his phone had been switched off, he sat on one of the leather couches at the hotel bar, switched it back on and checked to see if there were any messages. He had been so angry when he had turned it off that morning in the coffee shop. Dimity *had* left a message; in fact, she had left several, saying they needed to talk. Then she had left a more detailed message:

Malcolm,

Sorry about before. I don't want to argue with you. I do love you, and the girls so much. I want you to know where I am. I can't say too much just yet, except to tell you that I'm in Greece. I just felt that it was calling me, I guess. I know it sounds strange, but I feel like this is where I need to be for now. Malcolm, you would love it here! Anyway, I'll keep in touch. I just need a bit more time. Please, try to understand. I want to be the woman you fell in love with — but I also want to be the woman I used to love being as well.

Dimity

She had left him a text message. She had contacted him so many times while he was enjoying himself with Julie. *She still loves me. She does want to make it work,* he thought to himself. *What is she doing in Greece, though? It doesn't make sense.* He had to go to her. He couldn't wait any longer. He felt so guilty. He needed her so much. Spending time with Julie had reminded him of what he was missing. He wanted to make it up to her. He needed to fix their marriage before it was too late — now more than ever. He had to get that passion back — *with her!*

He looked at his messenger bag on the couch. Without thinking, he took out the sketches. He had shown them to Julie over dinner. She was very impressed. *They're funky designs, even quirky,* he thought as he looked at them proudly. He began to place them back in his bag when he noticed a familiar looking young woman sitting at the bar with a group of friends. He recognised her. It was the woman he'd seen at the park who was eager to show him around Amsterdam, knowing that he was *Malcolm Stewart.* Instinctively, he took out a pen and signed all of the sketches in the corner. He then walked over to the young woman and greeted her.

"Hi," he said.

"Hi! Um … Malcolm Stewart!" she replied in surprise. She sat wide-eyed with rosy cheeks, flicking her hair back, words obviously failing her. She then turned to her friends and attempted to discretely tell them who he was.

He read her lips as she whispered, "It's *Malcolm Stewart.*"

191

Malcolm decided to speak. "So, I'll be leaving Amsterdam soon and I thought, since you were interested in my designs, you might like these." Malcolm handed her the designs. She held them without moving, the shocked wide-eyed stare still fixed on her face.

"Anyway, hope you like them," he said and then walked away feeling the young woman's disbelief as he made his way to the lifts. He smiled to himself. His heart began to feel light again.

CHAPTER TWENTY

After a few days in picturesque Santorini, Maria, Antonio, and Thomas had spent another few days on the island of Paros, where they enjoyed the pebbled beaches, eating alfresco at the many bars and family friendly restaurants by the beach, and relaxing listening to the chilled out trance music that seemed to be *all the go* in the trendy bars and outdoor cafes.

Thomas had so much fun in the water with Antonio, both at the beaches and at one of the hotel pools, which was also pleasantly surrounded with bougainvillea in bloom in fuchsia and cherry blossom, creating a lovely and cheerful display.

Maria lazily stretched her long, slender, tanned legs as she sat on a beach chair in the courtyard of their double-storey apartment in Mykonos that sunny afternoon. The white cobblestone pavers were prominent throughout the island, and also extended to the many apartment and hotel courtyards. It had been a wonderful three days thus far in Mykonos. They had hired a car and drove to the beaches. They had eaten at the many restaurants which overlooked Mykonos' famous windmills, and they had walked through the narrow streets way past eleven o'clock at night, shopping at so many interesting clothing, accessory, jewellery, and homeware boutiques, which were open until the early hours of the morning. They could hear the music coming from the nightclubs now and then. All the while, throughout all the noise, Thomas peacefully slept in his pram.

"Deep in thought again, I see?" Antonio walked over to her, and handed her a chilled *freddo cappuccino*.

"I guess I am," she said, taking the tall glass from Antonio. "How could I not be? Look where we are. You know I always considered my Greek background to be something that oppressed my growth as a person, like a label where you belong to something and therefore you must act a certain way. It's so different to the reality. I'm sure that if I got to know Greece the way I wanted to back then, and not the way my mother did, I would have accepted everything about myself a lot earlier. Maybe I wouldn't have become so stubborn and resistant."

"*You*, stubborn and resistant?" Antonio teased.

"Okay Antonio, I know I can be at times; well … most of the time. You know what, though? I've never felt so liberated in my life. It's my mother that made me feel like I had to be a certain way to appreciate my Greek heritage. She was always over the top, even compared to my other relatives."

"It's good to see you like this," he said, smiling proudly. "It seems like this trip is what you needed. I guess it's cathartic."

"I think you've been hanging around Cassandra and Connor for too long!" Maria laughed. "Cassandra sometimes drives me crazy with her counselling talk, but she does make a lot of sense. Speaking of counselling, I wonder how my sister is. I might give her another call later, to see how things are going. Anyway, our 'alone time' will soon come to an end. We'll have to go down the obligatory list of visits soon. I don't even know some of the people my mother expects me to go and see."

"We'll do our best, Maria. I think you'll enjoy meeting everyone and embracing their way of life. Look how accepting you're becoming already. You're going with the flow, more than you ever did around your incense burners and healing candles."

"Are you mocking my products? If it wasn't for your sister loving them so much, we wouldn't have even met."

"That's true," he acknowledged. "I guess we owe our marriage to your exfoliators and foot scrubs," he said, as he leaned over to kiss her. "Anyway, about what you said earlier … about labels and belonging to something. Is it really so bad? I mean, if you think about it, you're now my wife. Some would say that's a label. Is it really so bad to be called my wife?" he challenged, leaning closer to her.

"No, I guess not, if you put it that way. It feels really good to be called your wife, and to call you my husband. I guess some labels aren't so bad. Being called someone's mother is okay as well … but Antonio, I'm warning you right now. I will still be Maria in all other aspects of life, and if Thomas ever joins a soccer team, I will really lose it if anyone calls me a *soccer mom,*" she said, attempting an American accent.

'I'll be sure to warn anyone in advance," he said in a serious tone. "Just to get things straight though, you mean that it would bother you if everything you are as a person was summed up as being someone who drives their child to and from soccer training? I'm speechless," he teased. "Anyway, speaking of being my wife, and being in an exotic place, Thomas is still having his nap … so …?"

"So, what?"

"So, we'd better take advantage of it. That sounds healing and liberating to me."

"Antonio … do you ever stop? We have one more day in Mykonos. Shouldn't we plan to look at more of the sights before we leave?

They both stopped and looked at each other. Thomas' crying could be heard from the bedroom.

"Well, looks like our 'alone time' will definitely have to take a backseat right now," she said. "We better go and see how Thomas is doing. I want him to be well rested for the restaurant tonight."

"Don't worry. I've got it covered," Antonio obliged.

"Okay. Wait a minute … are you trying to score some points because I didn't take you up on your offer?" she called after him as he headed to the bedroom. Maria admired him in his relaxed cream shorts, and loose, checked, short-sleeved shirt, which revealed his toned, olive-skinned arms. She was used to seeing him in slim fitted chinos or jeans, and fitted shirts or polo tops, with trendy sneakers, so this was a rather different look. Together with his boat shoes, he looked like he belonged in Mykonos.

"Guilty as charged," he called out. "I don't want to tire you out — *yet.*"

Maria rolled her eyes, then smiled. But as happy as she felt on the inside, she still carried an uneasy feeling within her. It had been neatly hidden away in the background throughout their trip, but now that she had to begin visiting people she had never met before, she began to feel a familiar anxiety. She hated that feeling — as though she wasn't in control of her actions. *It's not all bad,* she reassured herself. She had already met so many relatives when she was a child, who she adored. Auntie Irene in particular had spoiled her rotten. She then remembered the invitations. She had to get answers from her Auntie Irene, Uncle Pavlo, or even Aliki. Her mother was hiding something. *Why did Mum keep those invitations from us?* She made a mental note to call them soon, to let them know that they would be visiting.

Her chest began to feel heavy again when she thought about her mother and the invitations. It evoked an unpleasant feeling in her stomach, this constant hold she had over her. Feelings of obligation resurfaced once again — her mother telling her she had to do this and that. Nicki never seemed to mind, and never had to deal with the wrath that was her mother. And no one seemed to expect John, in his grunge-hazed teenage years, to do anything that was considered Greek or even obligatory.

Her mind instantly went back to a Saturday afternoon when fourteen-year-old Nicki waltzed into the kitchen with Dimity.

"I won't be able to go to the Greek function tonight, Mum. Dimity and her sisters are going to this cool new

196

coffee shop, and they promised Dimity and me that we could also go next time they went. It's, like, the place to be seen."

"Don't worry, Nicki. You go with Dimity. Is Luca driving you home?"

"Yeah, so we're okay for lifts. See you later, Mum. We have to decide what I'm going to wear," Nicki had said to Dimity, and they giggled excitedly all the way back to Nicki's room.

"Well, I don't want to go *either*!" Maria exclaimed. "I was invited to go to the movies. Ella from my class asked me. Her parents will be looking after us. Why is Nicki allowed to miss the function and not *me*? Most of the girls from my class will be there. I'll be the only one not going and she's one of my closest friends ..."

"Maria, you're coming with me and your father. It's not safe. I don't even know her parents."

"Yes, you do. You met her mum at the Mother's Day school breakfast. You said that you liked her mother a lot ... that she was a decent woman ..."

"Maria, you're coming with us and that's all there is to it!"

"But Mum, it's not fair! Why do I always have to go to these things?" Maria had sulked all the way to her room, hearing excited laughter from Nicki's bedroom down the hall as she slammed the door behind her.

Maria suddenly admired the bohemian, green dress that she was wearing, with its creative print on the cotton fabric. She felt so relaxed and free in it. She could do anything in it — anything that she wanted to do, yet she still had an anxious feeling in her heart ... that she had to prove her *Greekness* — that she had to earn it somehow. It was ridiculous. Anyway, she had a relaxing evening with Antonio and Thomas planned for that night. For the moment, she was in control, and she would be free to enjoy her dinner by the sea with her family. She sighed contently at the thought of it.

Later that evening, they were sitting at another outdoor *taverna*, waiting for their mains to arrive. Maria's hair blew ferociously in the stubborn wind. Her wind-stung, slightly teary eyes gazed at the windmills in the distance. The sounds of the melodic Greek *hasapiko,* a blues style of tune, had invited some locals and tourists to dance in the centre of the cobblestone courtyard. She watched their faces, their relaxed attitudes. A healing, positive vibe exuded from their energy.

"Maybe I'll try some *retsina*," Antonio announced boldly, with smiling eyes. "I'm feeling adventurous tonight."

Maria gave him a wry smile. "I thought I'd have to take you to the doctor when you tried the *ouzo* the other day," she teased, feeling the salty wind in her hair. "I just love sitting here, having a drink, watching all the happy people go by." She felt pleasantly lethargic as she surrendered to the relaxed atmosphere.

Just then, the loud and sharp sound of a solo *bouzouki* abruptly interrupted the melodic *hasapiko* that had been playing through the speakers. Maria turned to see a man with the *bouzouki* sitting on a chair behind her. A woman adorned in an exotic Greek dancing costume appeared beside the man, and the energetic, seductive melody of a *tsifteteli* took over the whole courtyard.

"Isn't that that dance that's like a belly dance?" Antonio happily enquired.

"It sure is," Maria responded, remembering all the times she had to get up and attempt to sway her hips in circular motions. She felt a soft hand on her shoulder. It was the dancer. She was looking at her, reaching for her hand, motioning her to stand up from her chair — to dance with her — in front of all the other diners, who were suddenly all whistling, chanting for her to dance! Maria felt her cheeks becoming warmer. Her heart seemed to be beating as loud as the *bouzouki*. She just wanted to idly watch the passers-by. "I have to mind my son …" she began, looking at Thomas, who was laughing along with the music. She begged Antonio to intervene with her eyes. He knew she didn't do the whole Greek thing anymore. "Sorry, I don't dance like that …" she continued to protest. "Maybe the music is too loud. I'll move the high chair to the other side," she began to say over the music, looking at Thomas.

"I'll mind him. Don't worry, you go. Have some fun. Live in the moment and all that," Antonio shouted over the music, with smiling eyes.

"I can't," she said, her body feeling hot and flustered all over. This wasn't how her planned relaxing evening by the shore was supposed to be. Her eyes scanned the faces, cheering and screaming for her to get up. The noise of their clapping and chanting seemed to be getting louder the more she sank into her seat. She had no choice, but she *had* to have a choice.

The woman wasn't having any of it. Her hand was still reaching for hers. Her eyes were still coaxing her to get up. Without thinking, with the crowd's chanting guiding her, her silver sandals hesitantly made contact with the cobblestoned pavers. She had stood up. As though in a dream, the woman took her by the hand, a floral aroma exuding from her perfume. Her dress sparkled like the stars that blanketed the Mykonos night sky. She led her to the centre of the courtyard. The woman's sequinned dress, her copper bangles, and her earrings seemed to embellish the music, making subtle rhythmic sounds like a tambourine. Maria slowly surrendered to the woman's magical, alluring force, and she began to gently sway her hips from side to side, mirroring the woman's movements — like waves dancing in the ocean. It was as if there was magic in the air. The chanting, the cheering, and the happy faces gave her confidence, and her hips found a natural rhythm that she didn't know was possible. Maria's bohemian dress caressed her skin as she twirled around, her arms creating wave-like motions in the air, as she let go of all her inhibitions — all her resistance. She was a dancer — one who was accepted by the welcoming, loud crowd, by the woman's warm, mesmerising smile, by the look of contentment that had washed over Antonio's face, and her little boy's laughter. She had become one with the music, and the wild wind matched her liberated spirit. She felt the depth of the moment. People continued cheering, "*Bravo, bravo!*" As Maria looked at the woman, she realised that the dress she was wearing was similar to the bohemian dress Maria herself was wearing. The woman also had a kindred rebellious light in her eyes.

"You're very good at Greek dancing," the exotic woman said loudly into her ear. Maria felt her face beaming with pride, as the woman's floral perfume awoke her senses.

"Thank you," she shouted over the music as she continued to sway her hips. Why had she resisted this? She was a natural at it, and it was such a liberating dance. She danced her way over to Antonio. His sparkling eyes shone with happiness.

"You owe me," she said as she pulled him towards her, coaxing him to dance as Thomas looked on from his high chair, his eyes shining with humour. "You're feeling bold and adventurous tonight, that's what you said, after all," she teased.

Antonio stood up and twirled her around until her face met his. "You're so beautiful right now. This is who you are — wild at heart, free-spirited."

"I know," she said, as a sense of peace settled in her heart. She felt right at home. The cheering became louder as Antonio began to show some of his Latin dancing moves, and the sharp piercing sound of the *bouzouki* amplified the passion in her soul — in *their* souls.

***

It had been a pleasantly exhausting night. Maria glanced at the Greek Orthodox church of St Nicholas with the blue Aegean Sea in the background, which was so typical of the islands. Images of white churches amongst different shades of blue were something one could never tire of. Maria sat next to Antonio and leaned on his shoulder as they sat by the ocean. The sounds of laughter around them were so relaxing, as were those of the waves crashing on the shore. Her feet ached from her impromptu performance almost an hour ago, but her heart wanted to keep dancing to the rhythm of the island — to the natural flow of Greece.

It had been an exhilarating night in windy Mykonos. Soon they would be packing again, ready to head off on their next adventure. With Thomas dozing off to the music, amongst the buzz of activity around them — including the many kids with their families playing with glow sticks and toy windmills that spun ferociously in the wind — Maria felt so content. In the morning, they would head straight to Delos, to visit the ancient sites. It was all so surreal; so magical. A sense of pride filled her heart as she breathed in the atmosphere. She felt so beautiful as the wind caressed her skin. The smell of the sea was becoming so familiar, as was the smell of many Greek foods: *haloumi, dolmades, moussaka*. It conjured up so many images of her childhood: her mother's cooking, her parents' restaurant in Melbourne, their home in the inner west of Sydney. The more she remembered, the more Maria realised that the memories made her feel safe and secure. They had always been a constant in her life. Yes, she was a businesswoman, but she was also into leading a present-centred life. She was a mother, and someone's wife, she was Australian, but she was also part of all this — Greece was also part of who she was, and who wouldn't want to be part of such greatness?

CHAPTER TWENTY-ONE

The bus, or *leoforeio*, was another eye-opening experience for Dimity, to say the least. She marvelled at the driver, with his blasé attitude, a cigarette in one hand, the other complacently on the wheel, and a rudeness that would make her mother-in-law look like Mother Teresa. The way some drivers drove still gave her a sense of culture shock. "Don't worry, we'll get there," were words she would hear often, including from Stavros, who was seated on one side of her at the back of the bus. He had told her that usually meant, "We're lost," or "We'll get there, but we might be a few hours late — at best." The cigarette smoke wafting through the bus was enough to make her stomach turn, but the narrow-minded obnoxiousness coming from the driver's mouth was more toxic than any cigarette smoke. *"Chauvinist" was a word coined for him and his type*, Dimity had immediately thought when he greeted her with a lecherous smile, as his eyes fell to her chest. Rose, the English tourist sitting next to her, was also appalled. Stavros translated what the driver was saying to his co-driver about the female passengers exiting the bus. Rose, and her friend, Anastasia, were about to tell him what he could do with his cigarette, but Dimity helped them to curb their anger, after she curbed hers that is — with the help of Stavros. "Go with the flow," she kept telling herself.

Rose and Anastasia had been so impressed with Dimity's description of the glass and ceramic design classes she was taking that they had decided to sign up as well, helped along by Stavros making an appearance in all his glory. The ink had stroked the paper with their names as quickly as smiles appeared on their faces when they noticed how irresistible their teacher would be. Dimity did, in fact, have lunch with them as she had promised the day after they had met.

Anastasia, it turned out, had relatives in Ioannina, and Rose would also accompany her English-Greek friend for a few weeks. The three soon became good friends, and enjoyed learning all about glass and ceramics together, guided by the charismatic Stavros. Anastasia and Rose often joked that Dimity was getting too much attention from Stavros and that they couldn't compete with her, because she was beautiful and already knew so much about design, which of course scored points with their teacher. The fact that they were all married had taken a back seat. A bit of innocent flirting was okay once in a while, they had challenged Dimity, especially with a gorgeous, Greek, artistic, philosophical teacher like Stavros.

Dimity had enjoyed the last couple of days so much. Their first day of lessons had been an eye-opening introduction. Stavros explained that they wouldn't exactly be manipulating the glass — that took years of training, and they would leave that up to him. They would start with the ceramics work and focus on the actual painting and glazing of each piece. He would also show them how he designed and manipulated the glass in the fusion process to create the contemporary and unique formations back in his other studio, at one of the villages, where he also usually sat and designed, close to the rugged terrain of the mountainous region of Epirus. Dimity would at times stop and ask herself what she was doing in Greece, taking lessons in design. She had become so immersed in the surroundings, her sudden routine, and new friends, that she would just keep going, and allow herself to enjoy the journey without asking too many questions of herself.

She was a few days into the second week of her solo adventure. Malcolm was always on her mind. He hadn't called since she had told him she was in Greece. She remembered how angry he had been with her when they last spoke. The girls were also asking so many questions, thinking they were still together. It was becoming increasingly difficult to find excuses to explain why they were never available to both come to the phone when they called. Her parents were also very worried and were feeling so guilty when they couldn't reveal anything to Malcolm, who had called them on numerous occasions. They both felt for him, and could feel his worry. He had become like a son to them over the years. They couldn't bear to see them apart.

Alex had also called her, wanting to know what was going on, as had her sisters, barring in on the whole saga and offering advice, even going so far as to say that they shouldn't be examples to her, and that the adventurous lifestyle wasn't all it was cracked up to be. Luca and Andrea were always envious of her "real" relationship with Malcolm, and that's why they couldn't settle for just anyone. They wanted something like Dimity and Malcolm's romance. She had now upset their fantasy, and ruined their hope that a romance so sacred as theirs could never be destroyed.

"You have to get back together, or there'll be no hope for the rest of us," Andrea had pleaded.

Now, she and the other students were heading to Stavros' second studio in one of the nearby villages. They would continue working on the sketches they had already started designing. Dimity and the other ten students had already practised drawing a design, and once they were all complete, they would be made into vessels or vases. It was so exciting, sitting outside and gaining ideas from the mountainous terrain about texture, colour, and tone. Dimity had proved to be one of his best students as she was very familiar with many design terms. She even felt obligated to help some of the other students who were having difficulty grasping the techniques, thus becoming Stavros' right hand student.

"Amazing," Stavros had said, smiling to himself as he shook his head from side to side.

"What is?" she had asked, perplexed, during one of their lessons, as she made her way to the sink.

"Your desire to help people. You're amazing, Dimity," he had said, his face becoming serious as he looked intently into her eyes.

Dimity smiled awkwardly. She walked back to the table, brushing his observation aside. It was who she was. She didn't know how not to help someone who needed help. It was one of the qualities Malcolm had always admired about her. The light that once again filled her heart had heightened the need to help people again. She felt that she had nothing to offer anyone else for a while, as she couldn't even help herself. Something had begun to re-awaken inside her.

They were finally on the right road. It was wide and winding, and would lead them to their destination. With one turn into a narrow exit, they were now amongst the mountains that she had admired from afar, in Zitsa, one of the many villages that was known for its authentic old-world charm, its famous, ancient monasteries, its vine-harvesting, and its wineries. As they drove up the steep hill, Stavros said something to the driver in Greek, and the bus came to a sudden and rough halt. They all stepped out onto the rugged dirt road, as Stavros dealt with the fare. Dimity was glad to see the back of the crass driver, and was instead greeted by a donkey basking in the late morning sun.

"Hello, donkey," she heard Rose say. "I'll bet you're a lot more refined than that ignorant and socially inept driver."

The donkey looked away, not bothered by the interruption, as though it was used to it from the locals, or the holiday-makers who rented houses in the village. It was a different world from the town of Ioannina. Her eyes scanned the area through her sunglasses. She noticed that the quaint local shopping centre nearby consisted only of a few shops, which sold the necessary staples, a *souvlaki* eatery known as a *Psistaria*, a few local *tavernes* and *kafeneia*, and even a cosy bookshop.

"This is amazing, Stavros," Rose exclaimed. "So are you an outdoor type of guy at heart?"

Anastasia looked at Dimity and rolled her eyes at Rose's obvious flirting. Dimity had to admit, Stavros looked hot in his denim pants and loose t-shirt, which revealed two small tattoos on his toned right arm. His short dark hair and olive skin accentuated the green in his eyes. He oozed an arty, rebellious, yet intelligent and philosophically, sensible vibe.

"Next, she'll say, 'that's why your hands are so strong'," Anastasia whispered in Dimity's ear.

Rose overheard her friend's remark. "Well, I can't let Dimity, with all her design knowledge, get all the attention. It's not enough that she looks like a model …"

"Need I remind you that you are happily married," Anastasia reminded her.

"Oh that …" she said, laughing. "Come on you guys, you know I'm joking. It's just a bit of innocent fun."

"So, this is my studio and workshop," Stavros said, proudly pointing to a house perched further up on the hill. "It's behind the main house."

"It's lovely, Stavros," Rose commented.

"It's so old-world. I can see why many from the town would come here to get some peace. It's also not as hot up here," Dimity added.

"Speak for yourself," she heard Rose giggle to Anastasia.

"Yes, in the afternoon, there is a nice breeze," Stavros informed them, as they heard bells from wandering goats in the distance.

They all looked around for a while. Many of the other students seemed mesmerised by the landscape. Dimity heard them speak passionately about designing and creating in such peaceful yet rugged surroundings. A lot of the students were tourists; others were art and design students

206

from the local university, who wanted to excel in their chosen field.

Dimity looked toward the mountains in the distance.

"You're wondering about the mountains?" Stavros asked her, standing next to her. "It's Albania. You can also see one of the smaller vineyards behind the old church further up … near my workshop."

"That's amazing … that another country is just there in view. In fact, all of this is amazing, the whole experience. It's surreal for me … to be here, designing again amongst all this," she said, looking at him excitedly.

"You really miss working in the design industry, don't you? I can see how it's still part of you."

"I guess it never left me," she responded, looking earnestly into his eyes. She had filled him in about her decision to take time off away from her work, but had not gone into specifics.

Just as she brushed a strand of hair away from her face, she caught Stavros looking at her hand — at her wedding ring.

"So where is he?"

"Sorry?"

"Your husband … the lucky guy. Where is he?"

"Um … he just got caught up with some business," she stammered. "He's actually an industrial designer."

Stavros looked at the mountains again.

"So, aren't you going to ask me anything about his designs, being in the industry and all?" she asked curiously.

"The only question I have is how any man that married someone as intelligent and beautiful as you can be away from you for more than a day. He's a fool, that's what I think," he said, turning and looking at her intently.

"Well, it's not entirely his fault," she responded, feeling that she had to defend Malcolm, seeing as he had tried to call her and find out where she was. She didn't feel comfortable telling Stavros the details. She also didn't want anyone else criticising Malcolm. He was the opposite of what he accused him of being. It hurt her. But Stavros wasn't buying her reasoning.

"He's a fool," he continued, and before she could respond, he guided her to the studio with the other students. She surrendered and followed him inside, with Rose close behind her, staring at her curiously.

***

Nicki stepped onto the rough ground. It all looked so familiar. She breathed in the warm air, and marvelled at the huge, old stone wall. It was the very street where she had spent her days working all those years ago, going from here to the island, Nissi, with the tourists. She had told the driver to stop so she could have a quick look before she headed to her holiday house in the nearby village where they had lived for a time as young girls. She wanted to live close to nature — to reflect.

Nicki suddenly recalled their reaction when they learned they would be living in the village. "I can't believe we have to live in this old place! Everything is ruined and broken. Look at that horrible old wall," Maria had said to her as they sat with fallen faces in the taxi, despondently peering out of the window.

"I can't believe they made us leave our school and Dimity," Nicki had whispered in her ear.

Nicki smiled at the memory. She then imagined her younger self waltzing into the travel agency with her sun-kissed skin, in her summer dress, eager to learn and start the day. The Greek lifestyle had agreed with them very quickly.

The sound of pebbles and dirt under her sandals became louder as she walked more quickly, eager to see if the travel agency was still there. The small rocks massaged her feet through the thin soles of her shoes, and dirt crept in between her toes. Her eyes met the building's old wooden door. She stepped up onto the old concrete steps, the same steps that had led customers to a quaint little space filled with laughter, expectations, and the promise of adventure. She peered into that space, but it was eerily quiet. She could see a man inside, painting the walls, and desks and computers covered with sheets. *After all these years, it's still here*, she thought to herself. She wondered if any of the people she knew back then would still be there. *Very unlikely*, she speculated, realising nearly twenty years had passed. The sign was still up, even if renovations were being carried out.

"Excuse me, Miss Rossi? I need to get back to the airport after I drop you off," her driver called out.

Miss? she thought. "It's Mrs ..." she said softly to herself, before turning around to head back to the taxi. She took another glance at the travel agency, her heart raced with anticipation — to see all the things that she saw as a young girl once more. *This is exactly what I need right now*, she told herself as she felt the intense sun on her face.

CHAPTER TWENTY-TWO

Malcolm stepped onto the rough ground. His grey denim shirt shielded him from the intense heat. He had landed in Athens a few hours ago, without any specific plan, but he took comfort in the fact that Dimity was at least somewhere close by.

Facing one of the greatest historical sites known to mankind — the Parthenon on the Acropolis — he felt the need to take in some history and culture. He didn't have a plan, and didn't even think she was ready to see him yet, so he had decided to see the ancient sites as soon as he had settled into his hotel.

His first stop had been at one of the jewellery shops in the five-star hotel, where he was drawn to the display window; diamonds and pearls shimmered in the light, instantly reminding him of her. He wanted to make her feel special again. He had let her down. He knew the pendant he had chosen would look so beautiful on her, so he had purchased it, as expensive as it was, wanting her to have nothing but the best. She deserved it. His appreciation for fine, beautifully crafted things was always part of who he was as both a designer and a person. Dimity had to know how he cherished her — how much she meant to him.

Marvelling at his surroundings, he walked over to the south side of the Acropolis and breathed in the city. The view was spectacular, but as right as it felt to be there, it also felt wrong that they were both in Greece but not together.

Moments later, he was at Plaka, in one of the many taverns, having a beer to cool down. He felt the scorching heat all over his body. It then hit him — why Dimity had chosen Greece as the country to do her soul searching. He had gone over it a thousand times in his mind, until it finally occurred to him. She was feeling lost and betrayed by him, and perhaps even by life. The last time she ever really felt like that was when her friends had suddenly left her — for Greece! She had shared the story with him on numerous occasions, telling him they had been so close, that life had been great with her closest friends, until suddenly the world changed in the blink of an eye. He remembered the words she had used to describe how she had felt — *abandoned, left behind.* That's why she came to Greece. She felt betrayed and abandoned once again, but not by her friends. She felt that *he* had left her behind this time. The person she thought that she could rely on had made her feel so alone.

He needed to remember where her friends had lived. It was a village near a town named *Ioanian* ... or something like that. They spent a lot of time in the town itself. Instinctively, he took his phone out and searched for places in Greece with names that were similar. He combed his fingers through his hair, feeling relieved. He finally knew where Dimity was. She was in Ioannina!

***

The rest of the week went by quickly for Dimity. Surprisingly, Malcolm hadn't called, only leaving her a message about the girls. It had already been a full two weeks since she had left Sydney, bound for Amsterdam. It was so strange that she had instead spent many of her days in a remote Greek village, hearing the timber chimes from the verandas of the holiday houses close by, caught in the lovely afternoon breeze. The coolness of the village was as nice as Stavros had said it would be, especially after an extremely hot day. They had spent many afternoons in Zitsa, and in fact, Stavros had selected one of Dimity's designs for a vase to make into a glass structure — her very own design. She was sure Malcolm would be proud of it. It had been up to her to add the finishing touches.

She also enjoyed Rose and Anastasia's company and was glad that she had met them. They accompanied her to many of the historic sites, and they had just spent the previous day at ancient Dodoni, near Ioannina, which they had found out was apparently also famous for its cheese. They often had breakfast together, sometimes in the courtyard of Dimity's hotel, where they had the best view of the lake, and sometimes at the local restaurants. Their late night dinners had also become a ritual, as had their walks along the lake. Rose had even persuaded Anastasia and Dimity to dance the night away at one of the many nightclubs, which also had a lit-up, outdoor pool with a bar at its centre. She had also been grateful that Mihali, the hotel concierge, had allowed her to stay longer on such short notice, and thus accommodation had been taken care of for at least another week. Stavros had told her she could rent one of the holiday houses in Zitsa if she didn't have anywhere to stay. She had entertained the idea for a moment, imagining how glorious it would be to wake up and be embraced by mountains, hearing the bells from the goats each morning, and taking strolls to the wineries nearby.

Saturday morning marked another warm day in Ioannina. They were all walking and talking casually after they had just visited the main local travel agency to see Eleni. They had made some inquiries regarding which was the best way to get to Igoumenitsa — a beautiful beachside town approximately an hour-and-half away from Ioannina. Rose and Anastasia couldn't stop talking about how much fun they were having taking design lessons, and couldn't believe how amazing Dimity's vase had turned out. They told her it looked so professional and that she must have done something like that before. Dimity had told them that art had been her forte back at school, and that she and her friend Nicki had in fact topped the class with their tapestry and paintings. Rose was envious that she would be getting more attention from Stavros after making such an amazing piece.

"Speaking of Stavros," she heard Anastasia say, "there he is." The man who had been the topic of conversation for the last half hour was suddenly standing right in front of them.

"Hi girls, what are you all giggling like teenagers about?"

"Oh, we just saw the most handsome man," Rose replied deviously.

"And where are you all off to … the beach?" he asked, completely failing to realise that the handsome man was, in fact, him.

"Yes, we are in fact heading to a beach in Igoumenitsa. We just came from the travel agency to ask how we should get there," Dimity informed him, deciding to be the mature one.

"I've been there so many times. It's so picturesque. You will all definitely love it there."

"So, do you want to join us, Stavros?" Rose asked, innocently.

"I'm sure Stavros is busy," Dimity interjected, feeling slightly embarrassed by Rose's relentless flirting. She had now taken the innocent *just being sweet* approach.

"Actually, my sister is looking after the shop today, and it's Saturday, so there are no lessons on. You know what … I think I might join you. Better yet … if you're interested, I could drive us all there," he offered, looking at Dimity intently.

"Oh … okay," Dimity managed, looking at the ground, breaking the stare.

"That's wonderful," Rose said, taking Stavros by the arm, her English accent suddenly sounding more like she was from aristocracy than it did before.

"Just give me a few moments, ladies, and I'll be with you," Stavros said, letting go of Rose, or rather, freeing himself from her grip. He then headed towards his shop.

Dimity suddenly felt awkward. She had planned on swimming in the clear, pristine water, enjoying a day at the beach that had looked so glorious in the pictures, but she didn't plan to spend the day in her bikini in front of their design teacher, who did have the body of an Adonis. Part of her was happy that she had been working out. She also felt slightly guilty that she wanted to impress this Greek man who had somehow become part of her life in the last two weeks. She had told Malcolm that she had wanted to spend time *alone* — *alone* being the operative word. She was enjoying herself, though, and she *would* be going with Rose and Anastasia also, she told herself.

***

"It's not fair," Rose agonised, eyeing Dimity's orange bikini. "Dimity is so toned. Is there anything you're not good at or don't look good in? That bikini looks so hot on you."

"You *do* look hot," Anastasia added. "Now Stavros won't stop looking at you even more. I mean, the way he looked at you earlier … well, it was intense …" she said, and quickly pretended to look for something in her bag when Dimity gave her a defensive look.

Dimity could feel her cheeks becoming warm with embarrassment at Anastasia's words. She never paid much attention to Rose's cheeky comments, but Anastasia was more quiet and observant, only speaking when she really needed to. Dimity decided to dismiss her words. All Greek men seemed to be direct, and Stavros was also an artist. Most artists were passionate and intense. She knew this from experience, being married to one.

"I'll race you to the other side!" Stavros yelled.

214

"Okay!" Dimity yelled back. She had just managed to beat him in a swimming race, and she took on the challenge to swim back to the other side.

"Okay ... you win," she called back, while she simultaneously tried to catch her breath as she made her way to their belongings on the beach.

"Sorry, I couldn't let you beat me. I guess it's my male pride," he said with a laugh. "You're really fit. I could tell you were athletic the moment I saw you in your bikini. You obviously work out. So what other sports are you good at?"

"Oh, cricket, a sport that's popular in Australia ... I guess, tennis maybe? It's been a while that I played any sport. The last time I played cricket was when I got my husband out and the girls wouldn't stop ... anyway, I walk a lot," she digressed, feeling she said too much. She couldn't talk about her family to him. She felt it was wrong.

"Why do you do that?" Stavros suddenly stopped walking as Dimity sat down on the beach chair. "Why do you always change the subject when you talk about him?"

"What do you mean? Um ... I guess I miss him. He travels a lot for conferences and exhibitions ... a lot of work-related things and ..."

"And you're here, in Greece, holidaying ..."

"Like I said, my husband was supposed to join me, but his plans had changed so he felt bad if I missed out," she managed, feeling self-conscious as Stavros studied her for a while. He didn't seem convinced.

Finally, he smiled as though he had just uncovered something. Dimity smiled back as she dried her hair with her towel, trying to convince him that she was okay with all of it.

"Okay, I get it. I'm prying too much. You don't have to worry. I'm just glad to be spending the day on this beautiful beach with a beautiful woman. You know, you really do have the sweetest smile, especially when you get defensive." He looked deep into her eyes.

Dimity self-consciously laid the beach towel out on her chair. She then tied her long damp hair into a ponytail and placed her fedora on her head, pretending she wasn't bothered by anything he had said to her. She sat back on the chair. She tried to tidy some loose strands underneath her hat as she looked at the scenery around her.

"It *is* beautiful here," she noted, looking out at the clear, blue water surrounded by mountains. "So what's over there?" she asked, looking into the distance.

"That, is in fact Italy," Stavros responded, sitting on the beach chair beside her.

"You mean, we could just catch a boat and before we know it, we're in Italy? That's amazing," she said, excitedly. She turned and looked at Stavros. He was smiling at her. *He does have beautiful eyes*, she thought. She had been drawn to Malcolm's intense, dark blue eyes when she had met him in his studio. She had found them friendly yet seductively intimidating at the same time. Stavros' eyes seemed just as seductive, the way he looked at her. She was starting to feel that something had changed between them.

Dimity glanced in the direction of a coffee shop at the left side of the beach, and saw Rose and Anastasia walking towards them holding refreshments. They were whispering something to each other.

"So, how have you two been getting on," Anastasia stated rather than asked, when they finally reached them.

"Great," Stavros replied.

Rose looked at Anastasia with a knowing smile. Her pupils looked dilated, as though they were shocked about something. Dimity looked away. She suddenly became self-conscious of her bikini as her damp ponytail caressed the skin on her chest. She flicked it away, and reached for her top from her beach bag. Stavros placed his hand on her shoulder.

"Are you okay?" he whispered in her ear.

"I'm fine," she smiled at him, trying to convince herself, as she felt sensations run rampant over her body the moment his hand touched her skin. It had been so long since she let a man touch her. It had been so long that she let Malcolm do such a thing. It awoke a desire in her. It was Malcolm — she missed him. *I should call him sooner than later*, she told herself. He meant the world to her.

CHAPTER TWENTY-THREE

"*Yiasou* Maria. It's so nice to see you." Maria's uncle, Nikos, from her father's side, greeted her with a kiss on both cheeks at the bus depot in the town of Agrinio. "*Yiasou* Antonio. He's a very good-looking man, Maria!"

"He's okay," Maria replied, messing Antonio's hair.

"That's what they tell me," Antonio said, a smile sweeping across his face.

"So is this little one," Uncle Nikos then said, patting Thomas on the head. "*Ti omorfoulis.*"

"It means he's a stunner," Maria translated. "Your English is great, Uncle Nikos."

"It's okay," he said proudly. "Now, let's get going. Your auntie has a feast awaiting us in the village. We're staying at our holiday house in a village nearby, around an hour away from Agrinio. That way you can visit your father's uncle in the morning. He and his wife live on a steep hill near our holiday house."

"Sounds exciting!" Maria said, deciding to go with the flow. She suddenly couldn't wait to see everyone. A new energy was emerging from within. She was also looking forward to seeing Nikos' wife, *Theia* Katerina, as well as Aliki, and finding the answers she needed.

"Have some homemade wine, Antonio," Uncle Nikos shouted as he tended to the food on the grill.

"After you try some of my *pita* — it's made with fresh spinach," *Theia* Katerina said to Antonio.

Maria looked around the table. Her cheeks were warm from the glass of wine she had consumed. The long outdoor table was laden with food, fruit, and salads. She looked at the warm, friendly faces of her younger teenage cousins.

218

"Stelios, go put the music on," Uncle Nikos called out to one of his three sons.

Maria felt the sun on her face. She admired the old brick on the house. It looked so rustic.

"Maria … e*lla koritsi mou.* Help me with some of the salads," her auntie called out from the kitchen.

Maria stepped inside, where *Theia* Katerina was taking a huge tray out of the old rustic stove. The kitchen floor was made of concrete and there were pots and pans everywhere. It looked so cosy — like something from a fairy tale. She smiled as she noticed a cat lazily relaxing on the sunlit front steps.

"Come, help me with the salad," her auntie instructed with a smile, handing her a peeler. She hadn't seen her in years and she was making her feel so comfortable — like they knew each other well.

Maria began to peel the cucumbers, looking outside into the courtyard and a thicket of tall trees in the distance.

"Now you can help me with the *skorthalia,"* she told her with a warm smile. "You used to come and help me in the kitchen when you were younger. Do you remember? How is your mother, Effie?"

"She's fine," Maria answered with a forced smile.

"Your mother, she was a fun woman. She made me laugh, but she always had to have her say."

Maria nodded as she pressed the garlic in the old-fashioned wooden garlic presser with all her might. Thinking of her mother made the task easier. *Maybe I need an old wooden garlic presser to help me release frustration back home.*

"*Elate na fame.* Come outside you two, or the flies will have a feast."

Maria smiled at the scene outside. Antonio and Thomas were dancing to the Greek music. Her teenage cousins seemed to be in a heated debate with their dad. Maria added the pressed garlic to the rest of the mixture and, after some intense stirring, transferred the dip into a serving plate.

"Thank you, Maria. You know how to cook Greek food?"

Maria was about to say, *"I don't usually cook Greek food,"* but refrained. "Actually I plan to cook more of it."

She walked over to the table, which was drenched with sunshine, warmth and heartfelt laughter.

They poured more wine. They sang some old Greek folk songs. They ate and they ate. It was such a relaxing atmosphere. Maria felt languorously mellow as she sat in the shade.

They then decided to go for a walk. A herd of goats from the neighbour's house caught their attention. It was amazing how she had visited the same house as a little girl with Nicki and John. Now Thomas was here, taking little clumsy footsteps, walking on the same dirt path. It led to one of the few taps in the village, the source of water for many of the households in the area.

"So we're going back to Agrinio tomorrow afternoon. We'll sleep here tonight. The rooms have been renovated and are air-conditioned," *Theia* Katerina informed her. Maria continued walking, liking the sound of spending the night with nature all around her.

"It will be fun to see Aliki again," Maria said.

"Aliki?" her aunt queried.

"Yes, my cousin Aliki in Agrinio. She and her parents live close to you, don't they? We lived in their house for a few months when I stayed in Greece as a young girl. I've been calling them to make plans to visit, but I always seem to miss them."

"Yes, her parents still live near our house in Agrinio, but Aliki lives in London now. She married an English man and now they live there."

"Oh ..." Maria managed, her jaw instantly dropping, her heart suddenly beating anxiously. "Oh ... well, I can still see Auntie Irene and Uncle Pavlo then," she said, her anxiety increasing as she looked at *Theia* Katerina's perplexed expression.

"Um … no you won't be able to see them either. They actually go away this time of year. They won't be back for a while …" She trailed off after meeting Maria's expression.

"My mother didn't tell me this. She would have told me if …" Maria's face felt hot. *Surely Mum didn't know,* she thought to herself. *Of course she knew. She kept this information from me also, just like she kept the information about the invitations.*

"Um, no … your mother knows all this," her aunt began, stopping suddenly when she saw Maria's bemused, worried expression. "I'll take the rest of the food inside before the flies get to it," she said nervously.

Just what was her mum hiding? Her anger began to surface and her skin became itchy from perspiration. She felt dizzy, like she was about to faint. She looked at a stream nearby and took deep breaths, trying to calm her anger. As she turned around, she met Antonio's confused eyes. She had dragged him and Thomas all the way to Greece to get answers, and her mother didn't tell her that the people she wanted to see wouldn't be there. That's why she was okay with her visiting their relatives. What was she keeping? Why was she, once again, a pawn in her mother's games?

Later that evening, Maria marched into the bedroom of the old house, her shoes nearly making a hole in the delicate, old timber floorboards as she paced up and down the room.

"She deliberately didn't tell me! *Do you believe her?* Once again, she's controlling me and everyone around me. She didn't even tell me that Aliki was living in London, and that Uncle Pavlo and Auntie Irene would be *away — on holidays!* She knew I wanted to catch up with them. There's something really strange about this. I knew there was … that's why I came all this way …"

"Maria, quieten down. Everyone will hear you."

"*How can I calm down?* I was right. She's up to something. I had a hunch the moment Nicki showed me that unusual bag — a bag that sparkled with uniqueness and acceptance, something my mother would know *nothing* about!"

"Maria, didn't you agree that you wouldn't let her get to you like this?"

"But to not tell me? She always acts like she can do no wrong. No wonder she suddenly didn't care if I came here. She probably realised that they wouldn't be here. This just proves what I suspected … that there's something going on with her. Now I won't even get a chance to talk to them …"

"So, what are you saying? That you're not enjoying yourself? That you aren't discovering that aspects of your Greek background actually agree with what you stand for?"

"No … that's not what I'm saying. It's just that …"

"That you're having the time of your life, just like you did back then when your parents dragged you to Greece all those years ago. Was it so bad? Apart from losing touch with Dimity, was the rest of it so bad? I mean, your face lights up every time you talk about that time in your life. As far as I'm concerned, I think your mum keeping those invitations from you has liberated you."

"What? You're saying my mum did me a *favour*?"

"No. All I'm saying is that you're finally accepting and not resisting aspects of who you are. You realised that your background is not to blame for the lack of choices you had as a child."

"You're right about that. The more I see of Greece through my eyes, the more I realise how its ethos is synonymous to my own. I just felt that I needed to find out why she hid the invitations. I don't know … I felt like, for once, I would have full control … to let go of this constant fear that has pulled me away all my life … the fear I keep fighting. I have always felt that everything I ever did, or still do is wrong in her eyes. It may look like I'm this strong, decisive person, but I keep questioning myself, just like she always does. She thinks that she knows how I should live. Well, it's wrong to hide something like that from the family.

Why should she get away with everything? I felt that I could finally live freely, without her words in my head ... to prove that she isn't right about everything, about how I should live ... and that by talking to my uncle and auntie, I would be taking the control back again — for once. I'm waffling. I know, it doesn't make sense ..."

"It makes perfect sense, but sometimes we find answers when we least expect them. Even if you didn't get the answers you thought you would get, you learned a lot about yourself." Antonio looked at her with familiar, pleading eyes.

She felt warmth in her heart when she looked at him. He was right. She wouldn't let her mother control her life any longer. By worrying about her hold on her, she was actually allowing her to control her.

"But, to not tell me? I told her I wanted to see them, and she didn't say anything ... how I can I let her off the hook for that?"

"Maria, just let it go." Antonio pulled her close and lifted her chin so his eyes met her own.

Maria looked into Antonio's affectionate, kind, brown eyes. A smile appeared on her face. She began to caress his freshly shaved chin. He was right again — they *were* having a great time. "You're right, Antonio. I'm sorry. Who cares about why she does the things she does. It's like Cassandra ... and now *you* say ... 'we might not be able to control other people's behaviour ...'"

"'... but we can control how we respond'," Antonio continued, gently pulling her close in his arms.

Maria held on to him. Her brain said that he was right, but her heart had other ideas. The anxiety threatening her peace was still there. But she had to try to live in the moment. She had to do it for Antonio and for Thomas.

CHAPTER TWENTY-FOUR

The next, slightly overcast morning, Nicki walked towards the holiday house she had booked in the village where she had spent many glorious days all those years ago, on the outskirts of the Ioannina. She needed to gain some perspective and she knew that Maria and Antonio would be arriving in a week to spend time there. She couldn't wait to surprise them. *Maybe we could all even spend a day at the vineyard nearby. We spent so many days as children there*, she reminisced. She looked at the donkey that seemed to be admiring the view of the mountains that faced Albania.

As she walked towards the old but renovated house, she noticed that the door of the property a few houses down was open. An older woman was holding a ceramic vase. She was taking it to the back of the house, which had some type of storeroom. A young man appeared next to her and seemed to be in deep conversation with the woman. He then walked towards a car parked in front of the house, holding some type of vessel. She noticed he was lean and fit, and had some tattoos on his arm.

As the man drove off, Nicki knocked on the door of the house in which she would be staying. Her uncle Yianni, who used to own the hotel and restaurant all those years ago, and had taught her parents many useful things about running a business, would be there to greet her. He owned the house, which he had renovated for holiday-makers.

"*Yiasou* Nicki. *Ti kanis?* How are you? You have grown so much since I last saw you," he said with a warm smile. "Come inside. You must be tired."

Nicki followed his direction and noticed a woman packing up a vacuum cleaner. "It's been a while since we used to run around your hotel, trying to help behind the front desk. I hear you've sold it?"

"Yes ... I'm too old to worry about it now. Besides, I'm renting out some holiday houses now, like this one."

"Well, you've really freshened it up," she said as she looked at the white walls, new grey rugs, and modern furnishings. "Although, I thought the house we had lived in was further up from here."

"You're right. It's over there," he said, pointing to the house where the older woman and young man had walked out of with the vases. "I sold it. I regretted it though ... soon after. I can't keep away from these mountains. The view, it doesn't leave you."

"You're right. I haven't forgotten it, and it's been almost twenty years since I was a fifteen-year-old girl," she said, breathing in the fresh air.

"It's been that long? Did you see the old travel agency you used to work in? My son, your cousin, Peter, owns it now ... with his wife, Angela. I'll take you to see them later, after you relax. I've got some jobs to do around here; taps are leaking, door locks need changing. I'll see you in an hour. The fridge is full. Enjoy yourself!"

"*Yiasou, Kyra* Sophia," he called out to the older woman next door, who was walking out of the house with another vase in her hands. She nodded and smiled. Nicki caught her eye and smiled back.

That afternoon, Nicki waited outside the travel agency in Ioannina, at the bottom of the ascending road that led to a spectacular view of the mountains. Her uncle had given her a lift, and she would meet her cousin and his wife there. They wanted to show her around, and Nicki would have dinner with them later that evening.

"Hi, my beautiful Australian cousin. How are you?" said a young man with a slight beard and wavy dark brown hair. It was her cousin, Peter, who stepped outside to greet her.

"I'm okay, my handsome Greek cousin," she said with a smile.

225

"Come in. I'll show you how the place looks now."

She stepped into the small space. The smell of fresh paint greeted her.

"Hi Nicki, I'm Angela," said a petite woman with flawless skin, and thick, lustrous, dark brown hair held back with a hair clip. "I've seen photos of you from when you worked here." She guided Nicki to an off-white wall covered with photos in contemporary black frames. "There you are, when you worked here," she said with a smile.

"Wow," Nicki said, as she looked at a youthful, enthusiastic-looking blonde girl in the photo, sitting behind a desk. It was her, when she had worked there as a teenager. There was another photo of herself and some tourists at Nissi, when she had helped out with the tours. "Interesting shorts," she said, laughing aloud as she saw herself in high-cut white shorts that were stylish at the time, but now looked hilariously dated.

"You look great," Angela said. "As you do now," she continued, making her way to the phone, which had been ringing persistently for a while.

Nicki looked around. There were travel brochures in bundles spread throughout the shelves that seemed to have just been sorted. Computer screens were on; cables lay in a messy pile. "You look really busy."

"We've been flat out since we took over. We're still learning a lot and we've just renovated. Sorry about the paint smell. *Oh no!*" Angela suddenly shrieked. "I have that meeting with Eleni. She works for the tourist board and helps out in one of the main travel agencies. Who will pick up Poppy from school?" Angela became flustered.

"I've got the meeting with the bank manager and the air conditioner needs to be fixed," Peter informed her.

"Well, we can't spend another day without air conditioning," his wife said, her worry clearly getting worse. "*Mafti ti zesti, then boro na thoulevo.* I can't work in this heat."

226

"Having a comfortable work environment is definitely a must," Nicki replied.

"What will we do about Poppy?" Peter queried.

"Um … I'd pick her up … but I don't know where the school is," Nicki offered with slight apprehension in her voice.

"We couldn't let you do that … you're on holidays. How's … Marco … is it? He isn't with you?"

"Um … he couldn't take time off, but Maria knew I could, so she asked me to come along," she managed, scratching her nose, and flicking her hair awkwardly.

"That's too bad. We'll make sure you're looked after," Peter said.

"I better get ready for the meeting. Eleni is being so generous with her time. She knows so much about the industry. You still work in travel, Nicki?"

"Yes, I do in Melbourne. It all started here … my desire to work in the travel industry," she said, looking around the small space.

"I love seeing the excited smiles on people's faces," Angela said.

"So, who will pick up Poppy?" Nicki then enquired.

"Maybe … I can pick her up before the bank but then …" Peter trailed off.

"Oh … you need a babysitter? I can help … if you feel comfortable with that?" she offered, her voice trembling slightly.

"Would you? It would only be for a while … I'm so embarrassed. You've caught us at a bad time," Angela said. "Of course we're comfortable with you minding Poppy. We'd be honoured and so grateful."

"Maybe I can pick her up with you before the bank meeting, and then you can head back here and let her play in the courtyard at the back of the office." Peter suggested.

"That should work," Nicki said, her apprehension slowly fading.

"*Yiasou*. See you soon," Angela called out from the small space as Nicki and Peter stepped out into the street.

"You and Marco? You haven't had any of your own yet?" Peter then asked with a gentle voice.

"No ... not yet," she quickly answered, feeling a twinge of pain in her heart.

"Maybe one day? They can be a handful," he said.

"They can, but I don't mind that," she said, as they continued walking.

***

"Come on, Poppy. I'll show you. Just hold the bat in your hands and then swing it like this," Nicki demonstrated.

The little girl looked at her with a smile. She took the small plastic cricket bat from Nicki. Nicki bowled. Poppy swung the bat, completely missing the ball, which hit the old wall behind her.

"I missed!" Poppy wailed.

"That's okay. Your mum will take you home soon when her meeting is over, but we can play another day. How does that sound?"

It had been an enjoyable afternoon teaching Poppy how to play cricket. She was glad to have found the bat at a local toyshop on their way back from the school.

"Yes ... I want to play with you again. Mum and Dad never have time to play with me anymore," Poppy said solemnly.

"Parents can be busy at times." She smiled at the little girl.

Nicki peered inside the old wooden framed window of the travel agency. Angela was shaking hands with Eleni.

"Let's go in now. I'm sure you have homework to do," she said with a grin. She saw Poppy's face fall the moment she uttered the words. "It shouldn't be that much, though?" she reassured her. "You're eight years old now ... right?"

"Yes ... but I ... am nine next," she answered slowly and proudly, slightly struggling with her English.

Nicki's heart felt warm. She gave Poppy an affectionate smile.

They stepped back inside and Angela rushed towards them.

"Nicki. Thank you so much for minding her. I'm so embarrassed that I imposed on your time."

"I can reassure you that I was more than happy to help. Poppy was so great, and she's becoming an excellent cricket player as well. I'll teach her many Australian things."

"Did you pat a koala?" Poppy awaited Nicki's response with wide eyes.

"I sure did," she replied. "I'm really impressed with her English," she then said to her mother. "I didn't know that English was part of the curriculum."

"I also go to dance class!" Poppy exclaimed, twirling like a ballerina.

"Yes, and you have a lesson tomorrow afternoon straight after school, so you can't be late. We need to get back and sort some things out, especially with the electrician ... after your lesson."

Nicki looked at Angela's flustered face. Then she looked at the piles of papers on the desk. Without thinking she sat at the desk and began sorting them.

"What are you doing? You're not here to work ..."

"Honestly, I don't mind. It brings back memories." She noticed the other desks with chairs where the clients would be seated. The chairs were facing a blank wall. "May I make a suggestion?" she asked, placing the paperwork down. "I think it would be better if the clients faced *this* wall. They can see all the brochures from here," she said, walking over to the desk and changing the chairs around.

"Yes ... you're right. We've been so busy; I didn't even think of that."

"You could also …" Nicki began, but then refrained. "I'm sorry. I've been in the industry for so long …"

"No … feel free to make any suggestions. You might teach us something."

Right then, Peter walked in. "Okay, what have I missed?"

"I learned how to play cricket," Poppy said, happily.

"That's great. Sounds like you two had fun," he said, smiling at Nicki. "The chairs look better on that side," he then said to his wife. "Nicki's idea," Angela said.

"Well, looks like you've come here at the right time. You're a godsend. You know what … let's finish up here, and then head out to dinner. Our treat, Nicki."

"Okay," Nicki replied, feeling appreciated.

Hours later, Nicki stepped into the old holiday house in the village. "Bye. See you tomorrow," she called out to Peter and Angela as they beeped their horn. "*Yiasou Kyra* Sophia," she then called out to the woman next door.

"*Yiasou*, Nicki," the woman replied. She had met her properly earlier in the day, when her uncle had introduced her. *Kyra* Sophia had told her to let her know if she needed anything, and to not be too shy to ask for help. Her nephew apparently conducted design lessons in the studio behind the main house, the house she had first seen *Kyra* Sophia come from, and the one where they had lived as children back when their uncle owned it. Apparently *Kyra* Sophia's nephew rented the main house from time to time.

Nicki placed her bag on the sofa. It had been a fun but exhausting day. She had laughed so much over dinner in one of the many restaurants in Ioannina. Nicki felt happy — like she had a purpose. She felt that she had passion inside of her — *"passione"*, as her husband would say. *Marco*, she thought as a vivid image of his face entered her mind. *Marco. How is Marco?*

CHAPTER TWENTY-FIVE

Maria sat on an old wooden bench in one of the villages not too far from the holiday house. After that particular visit, they would all head back to Agrinio, where they would stay at Nikos and Katerina's family home. She was amazed at how much fun she was having, meeting everyone, seeing how her parents grew up. It was turning out to be a remarkable experience. It was amazing visiting both relatives who lived in the hip and contemporary areas of Greece, and those who still lived in the same old stone houses from years gone by, who still had goats, made most of their own products, picked their own olives, and collected water from the spring not too far from where they lived. She loved all of it, but one thing — she just couldn't get used to the threat of encountering a scorpion. Antonio told her that she looked like she was walking like she was in a minefield. She was plagued with worry that she would step on a scorpion any time they took a walk through the fields.

"I can't believe you grew up in Australia," he had teased.

"*Efharisto*," Maria said, as she accepted a refreshment handed to her by her father's uncle. She took a sip of the water and placed the spoon full of the vanilla nougat-like substance in her mouth. It brought back so many memories,

"I used to have this all the time," she said, turning to get Antonio's attention. He was seated across the table from her, in the courtyard next to the old house. "Even in summer, in Sydney, we would eat and drink this when it was a hot day, and whenever visitors would come over."

She then translated what she said in Greek so that her father's uncle and auntie, who were well into their eighties, understood. They had been so hospitable. They had even insisted that they try some of the corn that they grew themselves, and had cooked it on the grill for them. Maria could sense they were getting tired, so she looked at Antonio as she finished her drink. He picked up on her cue, and began to pack up Thomas' belongings.

"*Efharisto*," he thanked them.

Maria took over, explaining that Thomas needed to have another nap and told them that they were so happy to see them again. As she walked to the entrance of the courtyard, which was surrounded by the tallest trees she had ever seen, she felt a tear stream down her face. It was a sacred moment, and she knew that she wouldn't be seeing these people any time again soon.

They walked over to the car, where Uncle Nikos was waiting. He had driven them to the remote house, which was perched high on a steep hill.

She sat in the back seat with Thomas strapped securely next to her. Antonio was in deep conversation with her uncle about how much torque the car had, as they slowly made their way down the very steep, rugged hill. Maria smiled at the scenery as they drove past, feeling each bump of the dirt road, holding Thomas tightly. She smiled until she remembered her mother's betrayal. *How could she lie to me again?* She had treated her with such disrespect, like her views and feelings didn't matter — like she was still a child that she could control.

"So, how is Nicki doing?" Uncle Nikos enquired.

"She's fine. In fact, the last time I spoke to her, she sounded happy," Maria replied. Nicki had sounded happier than usual and was being very mysterious. She didn't want to say any more to her uncle, though. It was too soon. Maria hoped that she wouldn't need to — that she and Marco would work it all out.

That late afternoon, they were driving through Agrinio, down narrow, busy streets lined with many fashion boutiques, shoe and jewellery shops, and many cake shops — known as *zaharoplasteia*.

232

As they drove past another busy street lined with apartment complexes and houses, she suddenly felt nostalgia for a time gone by.

"There's something about this place. It looks familiar," Maria said.

"You remember it?" *Theia* Katerina asked. "It's familiar because you lived here, in the house next to that apartment block. You were here for at least two months. This is the house. This is your Auntie Irene's and your Uncle Pavlo's house."

"Oh," she said. "I didn't know we would pass it on the way to your house."

Her heart felt heavy again. How could her mother not tell her that they wouldn't be there? She looked at Antonio's content face and tried to calm down. It didn't matter. She wouldn't let her get to her anymore.

***

The next morning, Maria and Antonio decided to take a stroll along the streets of Agrinio and have a bite to eat at one of the outdoor coffee shops. Thomas was enjoying his time in the pram, holding one of the toys they had collected from the ice creams they would often buy for him. Thomas was always excited to see what toy would be next. The latest was a monkey with a soccer ball.

Antonio and Maria were treated like royalty as they casually strolled along the narrow streets. Everyone seemed to know her uncle and aunt, who were very gregarious and warm. They would constantly stop to talk to their many friends and acquaintances, amid the noise of the traffic and the many scooters that surreptitiously sneaked their way between cars and trucks in the crowded streets. Everyone seemed to own one, and the noise emanating from them could be heard constantly throughout Agrinio. They had become part of the background noise the night before, when she had sat on her uncle and aunt's veranda, overlooking the town.

As they made their way to one of the local eateries, Maria suddenly stopped at a street corner.

"Maria, are you coming?" Antonio asked, placing his hand on her shoulder.

"This is the street, isn't it? The street we came out from yesterday?"

"Yes, I think it is," Antonio answered. "Why? Are you okay, Maria?"

"Yes, I just thought it would be great to revisit it again … to imagine myself playing here as an eleven-year-old girl. Antonio, do you mind if I just take a walk for old time's sake? Can you order something for Thomas? Don't worry about me, I'll eat something soon."

"Maria, it's about the invitations, isn't it? You know that they're not even home," he said with a worried look on his face.

"It's not about that. I really want to see the neighbourhood," she said. "It's surreal just being here."

"Sure," he finally said. "I can see it means a lot to you. Don't worry about Thomas. I'll make sure he eats something. We're just going to be at the restaurant across the road," he said as he saw her aunt and uncle grabbing a table on the other side of the busy street in the *plateia*, the centre of Agrinio. "Take all the time you need." He kissed her on the lips. "I just don't want her to get to you anymore …"

"I promise you. It's not about that," she tried to convince him.

Antonio's face softened and he gave her a warm smile. "Okay. I believe you. Just don't get lost."

"I won't." She headed in the opposite direction, waving to her aunt and uncle and blowing a kiss to Thomas.

She walked slowly down the familiar looking street. It had been so long ago, but it strangely almost looked the same, apart from some new apartment complexes. Some of the old houses were still there, standing humbly amongst the concrete giants that towered over them. She held her nose for a slight moment as an awful stench took her by surprise. Yes, she remembered the many bins that would line the streets, full of rubbish due to strikes. Old lettuces and carrot peelings surrounded one of them; the overflow stank in the heat and humidity of the gruelling summer, flies buzzing as they hovered over it.

She could feel the perspiration on her face as she walked, smiling to herself as she remembered Auntie Irene feeding the neighbourhood cats the leftovers from the many lavish dinners and lunches she cooked for her family. As a child, she would look at the cats eating it all up until it was all gone. She always thought of Dimity — the way she would try and save any lost or neglected cat. She felt so relaxed walking in the heat, smelling the humidity in the air. She had opted to wear a khaki summer jumpsuit, and flat sandals. She had added some of the byzantine-inspired jewellery she had purchased during her stay in Athens, and felt so beautiful and happy in her own skin, walking with her very long, rich auburn curls flowing freely from side to side.

There it was — Auntie Irene and Uncle Pavlo's house. She looked at it for a while. *What if they're still here?* Just as she was about to ring the doorbell, she heard a female voice behind her. She turned around and came face to face with a familiar-looking, young woman with shoulder-length dark brown hair, who must have been her age. They both looked at each other for a while.

"Hi ... I'm Maria ... I'm from Australia," she said, her heart racing.

"Maria ... from Australia?" the woman spoke, obviously confused.

"Aliki?"

CHAPTER TWENTY-SIX

"I can't believe the person I'm looking at is actually my mother — my very strict and rigid mother!" Maria gasped.

"It's her, together with my mother. They met at university. They were full on hippies. I mean, look at what they're wearing!"

"How short is my mum's skirt in this picture! I'm so glad I ran into you, Aliki. This is the first time I ever laughed when looking at a photo of my mother."

"Well, apparently they were quite the rebels. Do you know that they had taken the initiative to set up many of the student demonstrations while they were at university? My mum goes on and on about it when I try to act like I'm too cool."

"Oh, my mother doesn't even mention anything about her university days," she said, wondering why that was the case. Why would Auntie Irene be proud of those days, while her mother never talked about them?

"Oh, so you didn't know that our mothers were the coolest girls at the University of Thessaloniki?" her cousin asked as she handed her an orange juice.

Maria was sitting in the lounge room of her Auntie Irene and Uncle Pavlo's house. She remembered some of the rooms, but the entire house had been completely modernised, with contemporary lamps and rugs throughout.

"How's London treating you?" Maria suddenly digressed.

"It's a dream come true living there … It's such an exciting city."

Maria cleared her throat awkwardly. "Um … Aliki … I've been meaning to apologise for not responding to the wedding invitations. Do you know that they somehow …"

"Don't worry about it, Maria. I know all about it. I know that Auntie Effie has been distant with my parents. I understand. Anyway, do you remember when we played outside on this street when we were little girls?" she asked, also digressing.

Maria didn't understand what Aliki meant, about her mother keeping her distance. Why would she do that? Her cousin obviously knew. She had to find out. She opened her mouth to speak, when Aliki interjected.

"I'll bring some more albums out," said Aliki. "You should see some other photos with our mothers. I can't believe you haven't seen any of them."

"Wow," Maria mused as she opened one of the older looking albums. "Who are these cool hippies?" She looked at two women who appeared even cooler than her mother and Auntie Irene.

"The girls in that photo? Those cool hippies are also our mothers," her cousin explained. "It must've been at the peak of their coolness," she said with a giggle.

"Who would have thought? My mum being so cool — so carefree? This is so weird." Maria continued looking at the photos with wide curious eyes. "And the cool guy that's always next to my mother, the one with the jeans, and denim jacket?"

"Oh … that's Stelios, you know the one that was a soccer star that your mother dated — well, without her parents' knowledge, I would think. It's tragic though … what happened to him. Maybe that's why your mother never talks about those days. Maybe she's still torn about what happened. I suspect that's why my mother and she severed ties. I heard my mother saying that your mother never wanted to talk about that time. Maybe my mum being in her life is a constant reminder. I hope that's not the case, though. I mean it would be sad if she hasn't made peace with it yet."

Maria didn't have any clue what her cousin was talking about, but she just nodded, looking as though she did. She wanted to know more. "It would be sad. I don't know. She doesn't talk much about it. She must have been close to Stelios … I mean, from what she's told me."

"Of course, they were in love. He and your mum were the star couple. He was also cool, but athletic as well. He always had dreams of being a professional soccer player. It's sad that he was even offered a position that same year, to play professionally. Look, here's a picture of them on the scooter. They always rode together, attending cool parties, you know … during the disco days."

"Disco days? My mum attended discos and nightclubs? You mean the ones that don't have any Greek dancing, right?"

"Definitely! From what I hear from my mother, your mum never conformed to anything. If someone told her black, she'd say white. That's what happened that night. It's really sad, isn't it? You know, I still have the newspaper article."

"Oh, can I see it … if you don't mind, that is?" Maria had an uneasy feeling in her stomach. She felt bad for lying to her cousin, but she was also eager to find out what Aliki was actually talking about.

"Oh … that's awful! How tragic!" Maria gasped as she looked at the newspaper article from 1978. It was about an accident concerning Stelios, who had a promising career as a professional soccer player. Well, according to the article, he *had* had a promising soccer career, but they didn't know how long it would take him to recover. It was a miracle that he wasn't killed as his scooter had collided side-on with a truck, and he hadn't been wearing a helmet. That was the most vital concern, for family and friends, the article went on to say. The article also mentions that a woman was somehow responsible for the accident.

"Are you okay, Maria? I'm sorry to bring this up again. It was all a long time ago. I thought it would be fun to see some old photos, and now I've upset you. Let me pack them up, and we can go out onto the balcony and I'll make us a *frappe*. I want to know about John and Nicki, how they're doing. My mum would probably get upset if she heard I took out the newspaper article. I'm supposed to be housesitting while she's gone. Maria, are you okay?"

"Yes, it's okay Aliki. I asked you to show me. So, who is the young woman pictured here? The picture is a bit blurry."

"That girl? That's your mum; she's crying in this picture. She felt so guilty. I guess she still hasn't recovered from the experience. That's why our mothers aren't on speaking terms. My mother used to always try and talk to her about it — she was concerned that she had bottled it all up. Your mum didn't want to hear about it, so she shut herself off from us. I thought that if we sent an invitation to my wedding and to my son's christening, it would have repaired their relationship. That's why I'm glad that I ran into you."

"Why would my mum feel guilty?" Maria blurted out when her cousin finished her sentence, forgetting that she was supposed to know the information.

"You know … if she had attended the function that she was supposed to have attended instead of going with Stelios … You do know the whole story, Maria … don't you? I hope I haven't revealed anything that you didn't already know?"

"Yes, I do. I just forgot all the details. My mother told me a while ago, but she doesn't talk about it anymore."

"That's a relief! Well, like I was saying, your mother was supposed to go to a function for the church. It was some Greek dance to raise money or something like that. You know, something your mother would have refused to attend, and that she did! Apparently she got into a heated argument with her parents that night."

"So, I don't understand, why would my mother feel guilty, though? It's not as though she made Stelios go on his bike. I mean, the woman they mention in the article is responsible."

Her cousin looked at her blankly. "Maria, the woman they mention in the article is your mother. That's why he was heading to her house. Your mother had told him to go on his bike. The woman they mention on the article is your mother. Did you think there was another woman involved as well?"

Maria suddenly felt dizzy. She started to perspire even though the air-conditioner was on. She needed some air. She couldn't breathe. She could hear her cousin's words as she continued looking at the article.

"She had begged Stelios to take her for a ride on his bike. He had refused at first, as he had to wake up early for training. They would make their final decision that next day — to see if he would be accepted for the team. Things were looking good for him — well they were, until ... but you know most of this anyway. I can see I've upset you. Do you want a glass of water?"

"No, it's just a sad story. I forgot the details. I couldn't remember why my mother had called him that night. She didn't want to do something her parents enforced on her. She had rebelled against them. So, do you know what happened to Stelios after that?"

"Oh, he apparently had been so devastated. It took a year for his leg to heal, but it was never the way it used to be. He had fallen into a depression, and turned to alcohol, so that had become his next challenge — to stop drinking. Your mother and he had ended their relationship straight after the accident. He wouldn't talk to her, or anyone for a while. Sad story!"

"Yes, it is," Maria said fighting back tears. "Anyway, I really have to go back to Antonio and Thomas," she said, looking at her mobile. She had been there for hours. There were messages from Antonio on her phone. "Oh no. Antonio's been calling," she said. "I had called him and told him I wouldn't be long. We'll try and fit in a visit before we leave," she said as she stood up.

"Yes, that would be great. I would love to meet your husband and see your child and for you to meet my children and my husband. Maria," she then said, as Maria walked to the door. "You did know the story, didn't you?"

"Yes, I did Aliki. Don't worry. You're right, my mother hasn't recovered from it. She had only mentioned it once, and I had forgotten aspects of it. I want to help her. I think she might need to finally let go of the guilt." She tried to hold back her tears.

"I hope I haven't upset you too much." Her cousin's blue eyes were filled with concern.

"No Aliki, you know … you've actually helped me. You've helped me find the missing piece."

"Okay … I hope that I *have* helped. Bye, call me to make sure I'm here before you leave. You've got my number."

As Maria walked out of the house, tears began to stream down her face as quickly as her footsteps touched the footpath. In between sobs, she noticed a church. Instinctively, she crossed the road, wiping her tears away as she stepped inside. She walked over to the candle stand, and without thinking, lit a candle. She wanted to do it, for her mother — and her pain.

As she stepped outside, she took a deep breath. She had been right all along. Her mother was relentless when it came to following rules and obligations, more than any of her relatives had been. It wasn't because she wanted her to do everything the Greek way. It was because of her guilt — and her belief that had she obeyed her parents that night, everything would have been fine. She had raised her with fear — her sister not so much, because it was Maria that was the most rebellious and stubborn of the two daughters. *She* was the one that was like her. *She* was the one that refused to listen!

***

Maria arrived back at Uncle Nikos and *Theia* Katerina's property. She had begun to feel as though something had been lifted from her — the burden she had felt from resisting her mother's interference slowly ceased to torture her. She was seeing things from a new perspective, and felt nothing but empathy for her mother. She had been carrying the guilt all her adult life and had kept it hidden from her children, as though she was ashamed of the person she used to be. She feared that the same thing would happen to Maria.

Maria empathised with a mother's need to protect her child. She was a mother now as well, and knowing the real woman that was her mother, she realised that she could really get along with her if she let the guilt out.

She knew Greece could help her embrace her heritage, but this discovery had definitely been a game changer. She had even felt compelled to immediately call Nicki; however, she had refrained, and decided to sit with the information for a while. It didn't feel right to run and tell her sister.

She saw Antonio sitting alone on the small sofa.

"I already put Thomas down for the night," he said, not looking up from his phone. "Your uncle and aunt stepped out for a while," he said in the same unfeeling tone.

"Antonio, I'm sorry I got back so late."

"I'm glad you found your way back. I was worried about you. I left messages."

"I messaged you. I told you that I was with Aliki. I was there longer than I thought I would be. You won't believe what she told me."

"About the invitations?"

"Well, yes. I found out why my mother wanted to keep us away from them … why she can't stop interfering in my life."

Maria told Antonio everything about the accident.

"That's a sad story," he finally said when she had finished talking.

"Do you see what this means? It means that I can be free of her … now that I understand why she is so relentless." Maria's excitement began to fade as she looked at Antonio. "Why aren't you excited for me, or even shocked about what I found out? It's so sad …" Antonio then looked at her. She looked at him with questioning eyes. "Are you angry with me for visiting my cousin? Why are you being so distant with me?"

He stood up from the couch, and walked over to her. He placed his hand on her face. "Maria, of course I'm happy for you. I'm just tired. I didn't know why you were taking so long. I'm glad you found out why she interferes in your life, and it is a very tragic story." His face appeared lighter again. "Now can we continue with our holiday, and start living like we always wanted to live?"

"Of course, we can Antonio. Once I find out if Stelios is okay … what he's doing with his life. My mum won't be free of the guilt until she knows what happened to him. I thought we'd extend out stay so I can find out as much as I can …"

Antonio abruptly released his hand. He walked back to the couch and then turned around. Maria had never seen him so tense. He was always the mediator — the calm and supportive one.

"Okay …" he began. "You want us to rearrange our trip just so you can find out things about a stranger from your mum's past. Maria, we came all the way to Greece, out of nowhere, just because your mother hid some invitations, and now you want to rearrange our trip … forget it. I have to go to sleep."

243

"How could you be so cold about this? I thought you of all people would understand."

"*Me* of all people? Yes, because that's *me*. Good old Antonio. He'll understand. I've been understanding since we got married. If your mother doesn't say something, you worry why she didn't. If she says something, you worry about what she said. I mean, what happened to the free spirit that you always wanted to be — that you were finally becoming. How much more understanding can I be, Maria? I mean your mother's been treating me like I'm a good-for-nothing sinner. Me, the one who would help the poor, even if we had nothing ourselves. I lived through hard times, in a chaotic family. We were all tight — close, but I wanted to be free — to not live in their shadows, with their dreams. I wanted to do it my way … and then I saw you standing behind that counter in your shop … with your wild hair … I've told you this before. I'm tired."

Maria watched him walk into the bedroom. She sank into the couch and curled her knees to her chest. He was right. He *was* always the supportive one. He had been criticised by her mother for so long, and he charmed his way and proved that he was worthy of her daughter.

An hour later, Maria looked up from where she had been sitting the last hour. Wiping away a tear, she looked at Antonio through blurry eyes. He was holding a piece of paper as he entered the room.

"I did some research," he said as he walked over to her, and sat beside her. "It turns out Stelios lives not too far from Agrinio."

"What? You actually know where he lives? I thought it would take forever to find anything about him."

"It wasn't hard at all because he and his wife are quite known for their humanitarian work. There were contact details on his website. We can go to the address on the site, and take it from there. I can't promise that they'll let us see

244

him or tell us anything. It's on the way to Ioannina anyway," he said as he stroked a strand of hair away from her tear-stained face. "Come on. We better make plans."

"Antonio ... how did you find ... I mean ... I thought that you said ..."

"Forget what I said. I should have been more sensitive to your feelings. I realise now that this is exactly what you need to do, so that you and your mother can mend your relationship. You're right, it's a sad story, what your mother went through. It explains a lot. It explains a lot about how she treated you. It also explains a lot about how she treated me. You know what though, you actually take after her."

"I know," she said, and she wrapped her arms around his shoulders and ravished him with soft kisses. "I love you so much. Thank you ... for understanding."

CHAPTER TWENTY-SEVEN

Dimity couldn't believe another week was coming to an end. It had officially been three weeks since she left Amsterdam. Time had sure passed quickly. Three days had been and gone since their day trip at Igoumenitsa. She had told Malcolm to give her another week or two, and he had kept his word since their last talk. They only texted each other about the girls, and he always ended his messages by telling her how much he loved and missed her. He also asked her to make sure she called him soon.

Rose and Anastasia had continued attending the design classes with Stavros, which were coming to an end in the next week, as would their stay in Ioannina. They all promised each other that they would keep in touch when they parted ways. Rose had also said she would miss seeing Stavros every day, but she was sure there would be many more gorgeous Greek men at the islands, not to mention the tourists. Of course, her husband was the hottest one of them all, she had reassured them.

Stavros had also been great to her. He really was an artist and a very patient teacher as well. Dimity still couldn't believe that he didn't sell any of his fine art online. She was sure it would be a success with international consumers. Attending his classes had been beneficial in regaining the confidence she had been lacking over the years — confidence to design again.

It was now early morning and she was getting dressed to take a stroll by the lake and buy something for the girls, as she had noticed some gorgeous and unique shoes and dresses. She placed a copper bangle on her wrist that worked perfectly with matching mid-length earrings, and her pastel pink and white summer midi dress and sandals. A touch of watermelon-coloured lip gloss did wonders for her

246

now tanned complexion, and, after running a comb through her silky hair, leaving a soft fringe swept to the side, she was ready for her morning shopping trip in Ioannina.

She walked down the stairs she had come to know so well during her stay in the hotel. "Hi Mihali," she acknowledged the concierge as she stepped out into the cobblestoned, sun-drenched courtyard that overlooked the mountains and the lake, where many guests were still enjoying their breakfast.

"Looking lovely as usual," Stavros called from across the courtyard, as he walked in her direction holding a big paper bag with his shop's logo on it.

"Oh, Stavros! I was just stepping out to do some shopping. I'm surprised to see you here."

"Well, I just thought that I would come over personally and show you your masterpiece. You know, it really is. You must have done this before. I'm very impressed."

"Oh … in that case, maybe we should go over there," she offered, pointing to a hill that was a few metres away from the hotel.

"*Endaxi*," he said smiling at her. "Let's go."

They walked towards the hill in silence. Stavros appeared to be deep in thought. Feeling awkward, Dimity began to talk.

"So, I'll miss attending your design classes when this is all over. I mean, it's been great for my confidence, to finally get back into interior design. I suddenly have this sudden need to place beautiful things where they belong," she said, as she sat on the hill beside Stavros.

"And where does this beautiful creation belong?" Stavros asked, looking deep into her eyes.

Dimity brushed the comment aside, unsure if Stavros was referring to what was in the bag. "I really think that if you branch out more, your designs would be a success with even some of the interior design companies," she said. "Designers are always looking for unique, quality pieces for their clients. I should know. I used to be one once upon a time." She looked out at the lake. "I mean, my husband did just that with his furniture and lighting designs and he is known internationally now. His brand has become known to clients …"

"So where do you fit into that, Dimity? Are *you* known? I mean … does your husband even know how lost you really are? From where I'm standing, I see a beautiful, sweet woman — alone, here, in a place where married people usually travel together, or with family or friends. Why isn't he with you, Dimity? And don't tell me it's because of work. You know I wasn't convinced the first time, and I don't believe that for a second now."

Dimity kept her eyes on the lake. She didn't know what to say.

"Anyway," he continued. She knew he could sense her uneasiness, the same way he had at the beach a few days ago. "Let's get to the reason we're here. I wanted you to see your completed vase, before everyone else saw it," he said, as he took out one of the vases she had been working on for the last two weeks. It was spectacular. It had finally dried from the last coat of glaze, and it really did look like a masterpiece. The colours she had chosen consisted of deep browns and gold, blended together with white throughout.

"It looks great, doesn't it? Since you're really passionate about design, I also wanted to give you this. I remembered how much you liked it, so I thought I'd make another one for you, that's similar to the one you clumsily dropped to the ground. You looked so shocked when I first met you."

"Stavros … this is so amazing," she said as she looked at the vessel, which was almost a replica of the one she had first seen that day when she had walked into his shop. "You don't have to do this. I mean, I broke it …"

"That's the look," he said looking at her intently. "That's the worried, adorable look you gave me that day when you broke it. All I wanted to do when I saw how concerned and

248

sweet you were, was to take you in my arms and tell you that it was okay."

Dimity looked at the grass this time. She then turned to look at Stavros. He was still looking at her intently.

"Stavros, I appreciate it so much …"

"Dimity, forget the vessel." He became serious as he placed it on the ground.

Dimity turned to look at the vessel, its beauty reflecting in the sun, mirroring the lake and the mountains. Just as she was about to look up, she felt his hand on her face, as he guided it close to his. He moved closer as his lips gently stroked her lips. She looked at him. He then began to kiss her, gently at first, and then with more urgency. What was happening? *Stavros* was kissing her! He was kissing *her* — Dimity, a married woman, with two beautiful daughters. She could feel his sensual soft lips on her lips, his warm breath. It had been so long since she had been kissed like that. She hadn't allowed it. She was too hurt; too let down. Part of her had guiltily enjoyed being desired — the way Malcolm used to desire her — but she never expected it to go this far. She knew Malcolm still loved her. He told her, time and time again, that he wanted to get the passion they had for each other back — that it was still there. Of course it was. The chemistry between them had been so potent — so intense. It had been like that for years.

His lips had parted from hers. She was numb all over. She had let him kiss her. She had never anticipated it, even though she saw the signs, but she had chosen to dismiss them. She couldn't believe she had let another man kiss her! *Who am I?* Malcolm had always been the only man for her. He was sexy, confident, intelligent, creative, and intense. They had shared so many meaningful, intimate moments together. They had created two precious daughters, and yet she was in Greece, with another man, that she had allowed to kiss her. Feeling as though she was in a daze, she looked into Stavros' intense green eyes, which stood out from his olive complexion and light stubble. She finally spoke, between short heavy breaths.

"Stavros ... I can't do this. I never do this. This isn't who I am. I'm married, and I have children ..." She became more anxious as she spoke, realising the severity of what had just happened. "Yes, you're right ... we're having some problems, but I love my husband. In fact, I can't imagine life without him. It's taken me going to another country to realise that. I thought I needed to be somewhere else to figure it all out, but I now realise, all I need is to be with my family. I've been away from them too long. I wanted to do something for myself — to be the one doing something exciting. I've been the one ensuring that their lives and his career run smoothly every day. I gave up my career, my passion. I realise that's just a small part of the problem. I miss being creative, but most importantly, I miss being a family, and spending time together. The rest can work itself out in time. I just need to talk to him ... to explain it all ..."

"It's okay," he said looking straight at her. "I'm a grown man. I understand. You're still in love with him. So then, Dimity, my question again is, why are you here — *alone*?"

"I ... I don't know. Stavros ... I'm sorry ... I have to go. I have to talk to Malcolm. I've kept him waiting too long. He's been so patient with me ... with my antics. He's been trying to fix our relationship. I'm the fool, Stavros — he's been great considering I left him just because of an argument."

"Dimity, you don't need to apologise. I should be the one apologising. I just let my feelings for you get the better of me. It was a lapse in judgment. I've caused you pain. You don't have to feel guilty. You were caught off guard. Just go make things right with your husband. I had convinced myself that your relationship was beyond saving. I couldn't understand why you were here without him. You looked so lost in the beginning. I thought you were searching for something new."

"Stavros, it's my fault. Sorry if I've led you on in any way. I smile a lot. It's just who I am. Everyone says that about me. I even got in trouble at school for smiling in class. The teacher actually thought I was mocking her when she was trying to discipline the class."

"Dimity … stop, relax. It's okay. It's not your fault. Yeah, your smile is … well, it can melt hearts, but please, don't blame yourself for being who you are. I don't want to be responsible for that. It's my problem — not yours. I just have to find a way to deal with my feelings. I simply can't have you. I have to learn to accept it. Your heart is with someone else. You belong with your family. Please, don't change who you are, because who you are is one remarkable woman."

"Thanks Stavros," she said, still in a daze, as she stood up.

She walked quickly back to her hotel room, leaving Stavros behind looking despondently at the lake. She couldn't worry about him right then. She needed to focus on saving her marriage. She had to focus on Malcolm, and how she had upset and confused him over the past few weeks. He must have been so worried about her. What she did to him wasn't fair.

CHAPTER TWENTY-EIGHT

Dimity's heart beat uncontrollably. She was afraid — not just of Malcolm finding out, but of herself and what she had done. She never would have anticipated being in such a situation. She had travelled all the way to Europe to mend her marriage, but she wasn't with her husband, and she had been spending time with another man — a man who had developed feelings for her, only she had refused to see the truth. She had gotten swept up in the adventure, the attention, the adulation. She had let it get to her head.

None of it felt real. *Why am I even in Greece?* It was as though someone had paused her life for the last few weeks, and shown her a movie. Her real life couldn't be on pause forever. What was she hoping to gain from being there? It started out as an adventure — to be the one leaving. Secretly, she had also wanted Malcolm to see what it felt like — to have no choice. However, she began to realise that she did have a choice — she always had a choice. She had only begun to resent her life over the last year or so, realising time had passed quickly by, and needing to know if she would ever get her turn on centre stage. *Why didn't I talk to Malcolm and try to work things out — together? Instead, I shut him out. I caused the passion in our relationship, that at one stage seemed indestructible, to suffer.* She had sabotaged her relationship the same way she had sabotaged her career — the same way she had sabotaged the friendship she had with her best friends. She had given up trying. Now, she expected to solve all her problems by acting like a spoilt teenager, running off and kissing another man?

She knew she was being her accommodating, nice self again — always smiling, always laughing, giving Stavros the wrong impression. He had always refused to believe that Malcolm hadn't joined her because of his work commitments. He had been right. He had assumed that their relationship was beyond saving. He was wrong about that. She had never given up on Malcolm and saving their marriage. Did she give that impression through her actions, changing the subject every time he mentioned her husband, her reluctance to talk about him … her continuous smiling? It was in her nature to be like that. Even her dad kept telling everyone about the cats —how she would always feed any abandoned cat to the point that it wouldn't leave. As much as they had warned her, she had refused to listen.

"Dimity, hi," Rose called out, waving to her as she walked up the road to the hotel.

"Hi … Rose," Dimity answered, feeling flustered. The last person she wanted to run into was Rose. Her competitive flirting with Stavros had made her feel uneasy over the last week, as did her curious stare whenever Stavros would compliment her.

"Dimity … are you okay? You look like you're dazed. Did you have a sleepless night?"

"I'm just a bit tired. I think I need to go and eat something," she said, hoping Rose would take a hint.

"Oh …" Rose said, looking into the distance. "What's Stavros doing here … near your hotel?" she asked, turning to look at her, the shock in her eyes evident.

"Oh … he just dropped off my vase," she stammered, realising that she forgot the bag with the vase and the gift.

"But it's still with Stavros," she continued.

"Oh, I forgot them, I mean … it," she corrected, not wanting Rose to know he had also given her a gift. "I …" Dimity struggled to complete her sentence.

"Aren't you going to go and get it? To tell you the truth Dimity, I'm surprised he couldn't wait until tomorrow to give it to you … when we have our next lesson. Look, I didn't want to say anything, but I feel I need to warn you. I think Stavros is really into you. I mean, I think he is falling for you, in a serious way. Dimity, I know you're sweet and you are really gorgeous. I mean, it's been hell being with you sometimes — in a good way that is. You get all the free drinks at the bars and all the attention from the waiters … Anyway, I digress. I know you want to make things right with your husband. You've been telling us that since we met you. So, I think you need to be careful. Unlike Anastasia and me, you're here because you had a disagreement so I know that you're probably feeling vulnerable. I know, being married for so long, how easy it could be to get swept away, especially when a hot, artistic Greek man worships the ground you walk on, and especially when you feel that you're not getting that type of attention from your husband. For Anastasia and me, it's always been innocent flirting. We even tell our husbands about all the hot men we see. I just want to warn you. When you cross that line … well, you might not be able to turn back."

Dimity couldn't speak. As genuine as Rose was in her concern, she wasn't in the mood for a lecture. She didn't need anyone warning her. She had already seen it for herself, and she felt so stupid for not having stopped it earlier. The last thing she needed was Rose telling her that Stavros was falling for her. She already felt guilty.

"Look Rose, thanks for your concern, but I know what I need to do. Anyway, I really need to go now. Did you want to tell me anything else? You were walking towards the hotel."

"Only that Anastasia and I are going to have lunch at Nissi with some of Anastasia's relatives. Did you want to join us?"

"Um … no, I really feel tired, but thanks anyway. I've already been to the island and seen the museum," she managed, trying to hide the fact that her heart was racing and her mind was still on the hill where Stavros had kissed her. She had to process it. She couldn't deal with anything else.

"That's okay … I hope I haven't insulted you, Dimity. You probably think I'm jealous, but like I said, I was just having some innocent fun. I love my husband so much …"

Dimity was finding it hard to balance as she stood there listening to Rose in the late morning heat. She felt light-headed. "Rose … I really have to go," she said, and began to make her way to her hotel. "Rose …" She suddenly turned around to face her again.

"Yes?"

"I *also* love my husband — *so much*."

As soon as Dimity stepped into the cosy one-bedroom suite, her mobile rang. *What if it's Malcolm?* She couldn't talk to him just then, without gathering her thoughts.

"Hi … Samantha?" she answered in a daze.

"Hi Mum, how are you? How's the trip going? Are you and Dad having fun?"

"Yes, Sam, we're having a wonderful time. Except, we miss you both so much. I can't wait to come home. I mean, your dad and I can't wait to come home, as wonderful as it is. So how's everything over there? Are you having fun with …"

"It's weird that you're not here, Mum. You're always home with us. I don't know … it just feels weird to be waiting for you to come home. We're used to waiting for Dad, but not you. When are you both coming home?"

"Trust me, it will be very soon now. Besides, I'm sure your grandparents need to get back to the south coast. It is strange being away from both of you, for me as well. Is everything going okay with school?"

"It's okay, but we have to do so many chores on the weekends. Granddad said we need to do extra around the house because it's not fair if you always do most of the chores. He was impressed that we tidy our rooms and set the table, but he thinks we might need to free your time more. I can't believe how much you do for us. No wonder you're always tired. I mean, you even help so much at our school."

"Well, I'm glad that you're both helping out," she said, feeling so guilty about what had just happened, as she stepped towards the window facing the hill, which was now empty.

"So, where's Dad?" Sam digressed.

"Oh … Malcolm? Sam, sorry, you missed him again. I can't believe every time you call, he's out buying something," she blurted out, feeling like the worst mother in the world.

"So everything is okay with you and Dad?"

"Yes, honey, why wouldn't it be?" she asked anxiously.

"I don't know. Grandma keeps saying that we should free your time by helping out more, and you and Dad being away … it's like they are preparing us." Samantha sounded worried.

"Everything is fine, sweetie. You don't need to worry. Your father had told me that you mentioned something similar to him. We both couldn't be happier though. Please, don't worry. Everything is fine," she said, trying to convince herself.

"Okay, Mum. If you say so. Oh … and Mum?"

"Yes, sweetie?"

"I think you're really cool. I mean, everything you do for us …"

"Thanks sweetie … say hi to your sister," she said as she hung up the phone, shocked that her eldest daughter didn't react to her calling her "sweetie". She also thought she was "really cool" — her mother, who no longer had a glamorous career, had just been promoted to "cool" status, which, up until now, had solely been their father's title. Her daughter had just called her cool and she had just allowed another man to kiss her! Feeling like the biggest hypocrite on earth, she walked away from the window, and sat on the bed. Her guilt began to feed her paranoia. It was as though everyone suddenly knew that Stavros had kissed her!

Why was she still there? She already had her cool and sexy designer — her husband.

Still, travelling and being on her own did give her perspective. Like Eleni had told her as she drove her to the hotel in Ioannina, "That's what it's all about, perspective." Maybe her life had been on pause, not to see some movie, but to gain clarity about what really mattered to her. By being there, she had discovered that she was more than able to be creative and to try to renew some type of career. She had regained her confidence to get out there. She was starting to think that an online business would be the way to go — a place where different forms of art and homewares could be accessible. She was sure she could call some old friends in the business. Malcolm could also help her — and why shouldn't she allow him to help? She had been too proud. She had helped him over the years, so why was it so shameful to use some of the business and creative knowledge he had acquired over the years?

As she forced herself off the bed, she realised that the most important piece of insight that she had learned was when Stavros' lips were on hers, kissing her passionately — she learned that there could really be no other man for her but Malcolm. No one else would feel right. Malcolm was the only one that could make her happy, but the only thing standing in the way of their relationship was *her*. She didn't know how she would make things right again. One thing she knew was that as rewarding as her detour in Greece had been, she had overstayed her welcome. Her real life couldn't remain on pause indefinitely. Too much was at stake. It was time to go home, to her precious family.

***

Malcolm Stewart walked down the descending road that had led him to a steep hill. He admired the old architecture as he walked, trying to figure out if the buildings were from the Ottoman or earlier Byzantine period, his digital camera on hand. The town was so full of history, and he had decided to take some photos of the remnants from the old buildings, and also of the mountains and the lake. He always took advantage of anything that he felt inspired him to create a piece of furniture, or a light fixture.

He had been there for two days, after having spent most of the week in Athens. He had respected her wishes about giving her more time, not wanting to have another disagreement. He wanted her to be ready this time, desperately needing them to work things out for good. But at the same time, he hoped he would run into her before he called her. He didn't realise Ioannina would be so big. He had even bought her another gift — a pair of earrings he knew she would love. He wanted to make sure she knew how much he loved her.

Later that day, he sat back on his bed in the five-star hotel he'd booked for a few days. It was all he could find, having at first been drawn to some of the more rustic hotels. His jaw had dropped in amazement when he had entered the foyer. He had seen many hotels in his long and successful career, but he was really impressed with the attention to detail, and the unashamedly opulent and contemporary magnificence he found himself standing in. Instantly, he thought of Dimity, and her ambition to work on a hotel project. Feelings of guilt consumed him again, bringing him right down from his euphoria.

After having a sip of water, he picked up his camera and began to look at all the amazing photos of the town. *So spectacular,* he thought as he rubbed his slight beard, his blue eyes intently focusing on a picture of the mountains and the lake. He zoomed in to see an old rustic building in the distance, stopping as he realised that a couple had been included in the picture. They were sitting on the hill further away from where he had taken the shot. His heart suddenly beat more quickly. "It can't be ..." he softly murmured to himself, his face becoming warmer. Without thinking, he took out his laptop and downloaded the photos onto it, hoping a larger screen would help him see the photo more clearly. He then went back into the photo to have a closer look. The picture was clearer; in fact, it was very clear. His suspicions were right. *It's Dimity*. What he thought was just a happy couple, romantically sitting on the hill, overlooking the lake, was in fact *Dimity* — his wife who needed time away from him — smiling with another man!

His heart pounded as he looked away from the screen and leaned back on the pillow, taking deep breaths to steady the tight feeling he had in his chest. "It's come to this ... seeing her with another man ..." he said aloud. Daring himself to look at the screen again, making himself face his reality, he studied it carefully, trying to see what the picture would tell him. Pictures could usually reveal the truth, he always knew that, as could eyes. Her eyes looked carefree, as though she was being taken on an exciting journey, one of passion. The cool looking man with the tattooed arm was holding some type of object, and she was looking at it with a smile. His eyes ... he knew that look — what it meant when eyes like that looked at a beautiful, kind and passionate woman. They were intense. He couldn't mistake it; he was attracted to her.

He began to breathe more slowly. He had to give her the benefit of the doubt, and to trust her. The man with the tattoos ... he wasn't so sure of. It was in her nature to be kind, to be friendly. As he focused on the object, he realised it was a vase. He zoomed in closer, and looked at the bag next to the man. It had some type of logo on it, with the words "Live & Create", and then something in Greek. It was the name of the shop. *Why would Dimity look at a vase with such interest, and why would a man give her a vase, of all things? Does he know that much about her?* She was looking at it as though it was a diamond, like it was something more than just any vase from any shop. He couldn't think anymore. He had to move quickly. He had obviously given her too much time. She had to listen to *him* now — and what *he* needed. Enough was enough! Part of him was so angry with her, but the other part felt so sad that he had let her down to that extent that she would try to find solace in someone else. He trusted her — she wouldn't cross the line. One thing he was certain of was that the games had to stop right then. There was no way he would allow some other man, who hardly knew his wife, to come between his family!

CHAPTER TWENTY-NINE

Nicki waited patiently for the school bell to ring. Poppy would be coming out of class soon. She felt the early afternoon sunlight on her face as she waited on one of the school benches. She had picked Poppy up for three days straight and she recognised some of the parents. She smiled at a little boy who was waiting with his mother. She had seen the woman at the dance lesson she had taken Poppy to. She'd volunteered to take her that afternoon as well.

Nicki watched the other parents arrive — some with tennis rackets, and various bags containing extra-curriculum activities. She was beginning to get used to the flow of her temporary life in Greece. She loved looking at the mountainous landscape in the distance as she waited.

"Hi Poppy. Are you ready for your dance lesson?" Nicki asked, her face beaming with happiness as Poppy approached her looking tired and hot. "Do you want me to carry your school bag? I'll buy you a drink on the way to your lesson." Nicki held Poppy's hand and began to lead her towards the busy street. It felt right helping out. Angela and Peter were in over their heads. She wanted to help. A rewarding feeling of pride took over her — minding Poppy, helping out with the travel agency; it all felt so good. Peter and Angela were so grateful for her suggestions. She would help them for a while longer. A car horn beeped and Nicki grasped Poppy's hand tighter. They then crossed the road at the pedestrian crossing. She noticed some of the children from Poppy's school at the coffee shop situated nearby. One of the fathers had met his children and his wife there. *He must have finished work early and they planned to have an afternoon snack together*, Nicki speculated. A bout of regret made her heart feel heavy, like it usually did when she would watch parents with their children. It was different this time,

261

though. She envied the idea of family, but her heart hurt even more when she saw the man greet his wife with a warm, passionate embrace. He picked her up in the air, and the little girl laughed as she looked on. *That's how Marco used to be with me.*

A while later, Nicki waited for Poppy at the dance studio. They were having a break, so she took out a magazine she had purchased at the airport in Sydney, feeling the need to catch up on all matters relating to fashion, to uncover what styles were on trend. Was orange *really* the colour of the season? Spending time casually perusing through a style magazine hadn't exactly been on her radar the last couple of months — or years, for that matter. It seemed like every time she picked up a magazine or scanned celebrity news on the internet, there would always be a story speculating if a celebrity was pregnant or not, or worse, there would be a feature article on a celebrity who'd just had her *fourth* child, with many photos of them as a family, posing in different rooms in their perfect homes.

That afternoon, waiting for Poppy, she felt free and content. She was enjoying looking after her and a bit of gossip and fashion advice would go well with her *freddo espresso* while she waited. Besides, she needed some wardrobe inspiration. She had neglected herself lately. As she flicked through the pages excitedly, noticing so many clothes that she loved and could imagine herself in, her eyes landed on a section about Melbourne Fashion Week. Pictures of models, celebrities, photographers, fashion bloggers, fashion stylists, make-up artists, and hair stylists were spread across the pages, each of them making a statement and oozing attitude and effortless coolness. Her heart almost stopped when she noticed a familiar looking woman. She had jet black hair, with a blunt fringe, and a touch of red on the ends, her eyes conveying that she was part of the scene — part of the team that contributed to steeping the models in fabulousness and edge, just like she had — like she always had. The cool looking woman had always been unconventional and a fashion rebel. *It's her — Luca — Dimity's older, and very cool sister!* she thought, her heart beating rapidly. She was one of the make-up artists at Melbourne Fashion Week! Dimity — their best friend, who they had lost … her constant regret in life. She thought she would never see her again, even in today's cyber-world where people could be re-united with second grade crushes. She'd never been unable to gain even the slightest clue in regards to finding her … but now Luca, as she was simply now known, her surname no doubt omitted to add to her mystique, was staring out at her from a magazine. *I have to call Maria! Maria will never believe it!*

A half hour later, Nicki saw Poppy walking towards her. "You were so graceful, like a swan!" Nicki said, giving Poppy a hug, and grabbing the bag with her dance clothes. "Now, we need to head back to the office, and then we're eating dinner together at the village where I'm staying."

"Yay!" Poppy cried. "I love being with you. You're so fun," she said in her adorable Greek accent.

Nicki's heart felt warm. Her eyes became teary as she looked at Poppy. *What if I can't ever have this?* The fear came back, making her feel tight. *What if Marco and I never have this? Marco.* She saw his face in her mind again. *We're not even together. What if I never even have Marco in my life?* The anxiety began to deepen at the thought, until she felt her heart palpitate fiercely. *I have to calm down*, she instructed herself. Taking a long deep breath, the palpitations began to slowly ease, and as she looked into Poppy's concerned brown eyes, a calmness began to take over. She placed her hand on her chest, to make sure her heart rate was back to normal.

"Let's go," she finally said, a smile slowly forming on her face again. Looking into Poppy's innocent eyes made all her problems disappear.

That evening, Nicki sat at a table outside a quaint local restaurant in the square in the village with Peter, Angela, and some of their friends. Taking another sip of the local wine that Zitsa was known for, she smiled, looking at the people around her. The moonlit sky lit up everything in the courtyard, illuminating the laughter in everyone's eyes. It was such a healing environment. She was beginning to feel again — she had a purpose for the moment. She would take Poppy to school the next morning before the weekend, and she would help Angela and Peter out at the office. On Saturday, they would go to Nissi together.

As she took another sip of wine, feeling the night air on her face as the wind picked up, her phone rang. It was Cassandra.

"Hi," Nicki answered, and walked away from the loud, jovial group to hear her.

"Hi Nicki. How are you going?"

"I'm fine. Actually, I'm enjoying my time here so much. Would you believe that I'm helping out at the travel agency I used to work in, and I'm taking my cousin's daughter to school every day. It's been fun."

"Wow, sounds like you have a routine over there. So, you work at the agency every day?"

"I'm helping out. I'll be there tomorrow again … all day until I pick up Poppy from school, and all week next week."

"Where was that agency again? I just want to know because the location sounded so nice. Maria kept talking about it."

Nicki explained where it was, confused by Cassandra's queries.

"Well, it's great that you're seeing that there's more to life out there, and that you can contribute — you have so much passion, kindness, and joy in you. It's great that you are unleashing it all again," Cassandra said emphatically.

"Yes, it is."

"So you're okay with looking after Poppy … Is that her name?"

"Yes, I'm enjoying it so much," Nicki replied.

"That's great. It might be hard to say goodbye …"

"Yes, it definitely will be," Nicki answered with apprehension. She felt like Cassandra was warning her.

"Marco is probably missing you so much. It's great that you're finding yourself, though. You might then be able to find each other again. Do you think that's possible?"

Nicki looked at Peter and Angela giving each other a kiss. "I guess, anything is possible," she said, remembering Marco's words to her. She had begun to lose faith in those words, but maybe he knew something she didn't. Maybe they weren't just words.

"Yes, Nicki," Cassandra said. "Anything is possible if you truly believe it — if you want it badly enough."

CHAPTER THIRTY

Dimity slipped into a long summer skirt with a side split that revealed a slender, tanned leg that Monday morning. It was the fourth outfit she had tried, but realised it too looked playful. She didn't want to give the wrong impression. She had to end things with Stavros — the design classes, the outings, seeing him. It had to stop right there and then. But whichever outfit she put on couldn't erase the uneasy feeling she felt inside. Dimity felt so nervous to even see him again. Whichever outfit she chose, exuded a carefree, summer spirit — some made more of a statement than others, so she tried to choose something that made less of a "look how fabulous I look" statement. Knowing she was being silly, she decided to leave the skirt on. She had to admit — the Greek sun had made her look even more radiant. She had a luminous glow on her face and body. She finally added a black tank top and decided to throw a printed kimono on top.

Moments later, she was standing nervously outside Stavros' shop — the shop that had fortuitously changed her life.

"Hi Stavros," she greeted him with an awkward smile.

"Hi Dimity," he replied, looking straight into her eyes. "I believe you forgot this," he said, pointing to the bag with the vases.

Dimity awkwardly scratched her nose as she began to talk. "Yes, I did forget them. I ... I actually just stopped by to tell you that I have to end my lessons. I realise the girls back home have missed me more than I thought, and I promised them I would get back as soon as possi ..."

"Dimity, stop ... please. You don't have to feel uncomfortable around me. I've scared you. What happened yesterday has made you end your lessons with me. I'm sorry. I know I was out of line."

"No, it's not just that. I realise that I've put my life on hold for so long," she said quickly, clutching her cross body bag tightly as it rested on the side of her hip. Her heart raced as she looked into his unconvinced eyes. "You're right about my husband and me … We had a few problems, but we need to work it out. I can't do that if I don't tell him how I feel. I just realised that it's time to move on. I did enjoy being here though, and attending your lessons. I'm sorry if I've given you the wrong impression. Maybe it's because you really inspired me. I mean … my confidence has come back. I can't wait to delve into a project and get back into the workforce when I get back to Sydney," she said, her trembling fingers nervously playing with the side tussle on her bag.

Dimity met Stavros' green eyes as he suddenly extended his toned, tanned arm towards her face. He began to stroke the side of her face affectionately, only to stop abruptly when she broke the stare. Dimity looked down at the counter, avoiding eye contact with him.

"Dimity … you know, you're not to blame. It's not your fault. You were just being yourself. I should have known better. You're a loyal person who is genuinely trying to find some answers. That's what makes you so attractive — the fact that you want to reach for something more than just settling. You want to have a happy marriage — not only to pretend to, like many do. It's all good. There's just one thing that I can't accept though," he said, in a business-like, professional tone.

"Oh … what's that?" she asked, her breathing slowly becoming lighter as she looked into his eyes again.

"Just as I don't want anyone buying something that doesn't bring joy to their life, the same goes for my lessons. I can't let you go without finishing the vessel you started

267

working on. At least complete that before you end your stay here."

Dimity smiled at him. She looked at Stavros' warm, infectious smile and didn't want to disappoint him. He genuinely cared about his work and his lessons. "I guess, it won't hurt if I complete it," she found herself saying, the tension between them subsiding.

"Endaxi! I've got to step out and do some errands. Do you mind being here on your own for a while? I won't be long."

"No, it's okay. I'll just get started on completing the vessel."

"It is an interesting looking motif. You really are talented, Dimity. Anyway, I'll see you soon," he said, before turning once again to face her. "And Dimity … one more thing. Don't ever change who you are. It's so refreshing to meet someone so kind and generous. We've got enough bitter people out there. Keep smiling, okay? I'm sure that's what attracted him to you … what attracted Malcolm … that's his name, right?"

"It is. Okay Stavros. I hear you," she replied as she watched him walk out into the busy street, closing the door behind him.

Dimity took her bag off from her shoulder and sat back in the chair. She looked at the vessel in front of her. She admired the motif and the colours that she had chosen. Feeling proud of herself, she took off the kimono that she had thrown on top of her relaxed, silk tank top, wanting to be comfortable to continue her work. Feeling inspired, she then grabbed the brush and dabbed it into the paint.

"It's really interesting. The colour combination works really well," a deep, familiar male voice came from beside her.

His hand gently grabbed the piece of paper with her design on it, momentarily brushing her hand as his own swept past. She sat fixed to her chair, speechless, gazing at the Swiss-made watch on his wrist as he leaned over her to look at the sketch — the watch *she* had gifted him.

"I knew you were good at art, but I never knew you could sketch like this. It's really amazing. So, what else are you keeping from me that I don't know about? I thought I knew everything that I could possibly know about you, but the last few weeks have really surprised me," he said, looking at the sketch. He then looked at her. His blue eyes were deep with emotion. He looked at her searchingly.

"Malcolm …" she finally said, sitting up from her seat to face him as he straightened up, standing with the sketch in his hands, still awaiting her response. "How did …"

"How did I know you were here? Oh, I worked it out. I guess I do know a lot about you after all. There are some missing gaps, though. I thought we might have that conversation we've been meaning to have since I saw you in Amsterdam, and maybe then I might get the whole story. I knew you were here, Dimity, because you were feeling betrayed and abandoned. The last time you felt like that was when your friends left for Greece — for Ioannina. Am I right?"

"You remember? You remember about Nicki and Maria leaving for Ioannina? I haven't mentioned that for so long …"

"You'd be surprised what I remember, especially when I know it's something that means a lot to you, or if someone's hurt you. Unfortunately, that someone, this time, is me."

Dimity looked away. The emotion she had felt that day in Amsterdam came back to her. She couldn't bring herself to look at him. So much had happened in the last few weeks. The words they had said to each other suddenly came back to her mind. Then she thought of Stavros — and how he had kissed her.

She felt his strong, smooth hand on hers as he gently took it into his. Her whole body shivered. It was as though they were strangers.

269

"So am I right, Dimity?" he asked, this time touching her face.

She looked down again. She could feel all the emotion deep within her, threatening to spill out.

"Dimity ... please, look at me. So this is what it's come to ... that you can't even look at me ... you can't tell me how you feel?" he asked, gently stroking her bare arm.

She freed herself from him and walked a few steps away. She didn't know where to start. She was feeling so much inside her but she couldn't put it into words ... and then there was the guilt — the kiss between her and Stavros. She stood there for a while, suddenly flinching when she noticed Stavros at the door. Instantly sensing that something heavy was happening, Stavros motioned that he would be back and then he left as quickly as he had appeared. She instinctively looked at Malcolm. He was staring at the glass door tensely.

"So, who exactly owns this shop? Was that the owner?" he asked, noticing the "Design lessons" sign.

"Yes, he had to do something so he had stepped out for a while ..."

"So, what's his name?"

"Um ... Stavros ... his name is Stavros ..." she trailed off, as he began to slowly look around the shop.

"He must really trust you, to leave you here — alone. And these are all his creations?"

"Yes, they're all his," she answered nervously, wondering if she should tell Malcolm about the kiss. How would he react? It was as though he could sense something, the way he was talking, asking her what else she was hiding.

"You know, I have to say, he has some really interesting work. I mean, some of the techniques he uses to manipulate the glass in the fusion process take a lot of work and talent. You were obviously inspired by him — I mean to go as far as to take design lessons from him."

"Um … it happened suddenly. I broke a vase … I mean a vessel, and when I offered to pay … well, he told me that he also offers design lessons …" she quickly blurted out.

"Dimity … it's okay," he said, walking over to where she was standing. "You obviously needed something that I couldn't give you, and you found it here — from an industrial designer — in Greece."

"Malcolm, I know it looks weird, that I'm here, taking lessons, but it just felt like I needed something in my life …"

"Something more than I could give you? Stavros could though; he brought the light back in your eyes, the passion back in your soul. I mean, look at you — you're glowing. Did I even tell you how incredibly radiant you look?" he asked her, combing his fingers through her hair. She momentarily closed her eyes as her body tingled. Once again, she couldn't bring herself to look at him.

"Malcolm, Stavros did inspire me. I noticed his work in the window and I was really drawn to it …"

"Like you were drawn to my work?" he asked, looking searchingly into her eyes, as she momentarily dared to look at him.

"Yes … I mean … it wasn't like that … and it also wasn't some contrived plan that I engineered to get back at you — I see you with a pretty interior designer, so I get close to Stavros …"

"Dimity, it's okay. You don't have to hide anything from me. Just let me in. You just need to talk to me … to tell me what you're feeling. We need to have this conversation if you want to save us. You do want that … don't you? I want it more than anything. I *need* to have this conversation. You can't keep me waiting any longer. Haven't you punished me enough?"

"Malcolm … I don't want to punish you. I just needed time to figure things out," she said, looking away again.

"Dimity, just look at me — it's *me*, Malcolm: the guy you met at the studio all those years ago. Do you remember that

271

day? I remember it clearly. You looked so desirable. I couldn't stop looking at you — the same way I can't stop looking at you now. Every time I looked into your kind eyes, I felt so blessed to have met you. It's okay. I'm here now. We can work it all out. I know I've let you down. We both got lost somehow along the way. I just feel so guilty. I'm also so envious that this Stavros guy brought you back. You're different. You looked so focused, and driven when I saw you. I'm just upset that I couldn't do that for you. Dimi …" He gently lifted her chin up so that she faced him. His blue eyes looked intently into her hesitant ones. She couldn't commit to them. She couldn't completely let go and look back. He didn't break the stare. She looked into his eyes again, this time daring herself to keep the stare going, until the tears began to spill out, slowly at first and then uncontrollably. She couldn't stop crying. He caressed her hair with his hand, pulling her close to him. Gently stroking her face, he kissed her tears.

"It's okay, Dimity. I'm here now, and I'm not going anywhere until I show you how much I love you, the way I should have in Amsterdam."

"I don't even know why I'm crying. I just feel so … lost, and … I don't even know why anymore. I feel lonely. I feel like I have it all. I mean, I know it looks like that on the outside, but on the inside, I feel so lonely, and …"

"Abandoned?"

"Yes, I feel like I've been left behind — *again*."

"I should have supported you more, to make it easier for you to go back to work. I know how much you loved your career. You were so passionate when I met you. How could I have expected you to be completely happy without it? I shouldn't have listened to you when you told me you were fine. I let you convince me."

"It's not just work, Malcolm. It's part of why I'm feeling like this, but I realise it's more than that. I miss being a family, spending time together, being part of each other's

272

lives. I miss *you*. I mean, when will it be the way it used to be? I feel like I have nothing. I know it can be difficult to have it all, but I feel like I don't have the best of any world. It wasn't supposed to be like this … I don't know who I am, or who I'm supposed to be anymore. I just feel that it'll never be my turn. I know it sounds silly," Dimity blurted out between heavy sobs, her body trembling as the hurt spilled out.

"Dimi … please, stop crying. I can't bear to see you hurting so much. You're trembling."

"The way you were looking at her … it tore at me. When did you stop looking at me like that? When did you stop defending me to anyone that criticises me? Do you know what its like to have given up a promising career, only to be judged when becoming a mother? I mean, I feel like I'm under a microscope every day, and the worst part is that I actually cared about negative comments from people like your mother, because I felt that if I wasn't good at something, then what did I have to show for it? I became so competitive. I helped so much at school, I tried to be the perfect cook — the perfect everything. I even cared obsessively about the girls and their education, consumed with worry about whether they excelled as much as they could … but that's not who I am. I've always considered myself to be an artist, not someone bound by rules and conventions, or someone who just cares about mundane domestic issues. I would never have cared about anyone's negative judgment if I was confident in myself — if I didn't resent my choices. I guess the resentment made me spiteful and maybe even a little vindictive. You know that's not me, though. That's why I feel so lost."

Malcolm stroked the tear-soaked hair away from her face. He looked into her eyes, and moved closer towards her. "Dimity … I wanted to be part of your life, but you shut me out. I know I wasn't there for you and the girls as much as I wanted to be, or you needed me to be. I got caught up in the business side of things. That's not who I am either. I know what I need to do now, though. I've had my turn to reach my potential. I've become an international brand, but I miss the time I had with you and the girls. I miss creating, and having the luxury to divide my time to fit everything and everyone I love in it. You're right about a lot of things. It isn't fair to expect you to take care of the tedious tasks all the time, and not get acknowledged for anything. We're both parents, and we both have aspirations, but I know we can find a solution. It's not too late, but you need to include me in your thoughts. We can work everything out together, as a team. I'm nothing without you, Dimity. Don't you know that by now?" He looked at her pleadingly.

Dimity's heart beat faster when she saw his expression of desperation and fear. She listened quietly to each heartfelt word.

"What I've achieved is because of you, and the girls," he continued. "I even told my mother that. You know, I told her everything you've done for me ... that I wouldn't be the man I am today without you. Knowing I have you all in my life is what inspires me. I want to be close to you like we used to be. You couldn't resist me back then; you were always so responsive." His expression conveyed deep emotion. "I know we still have that deep connection. Just don't shut me out anymore. Remember what you said to me at our last south coast holiday? You said you loved me and you wanted me to promise you that we would have many more moments like that. I told you that we only needed each other — and the rest would follow. Well, nothing's changed since then. We *do* have each other, so everything else can be fixed. I want to keep that promise, Dimity. The intimacy between us was so strong."

"I remember. We can't always be like that though. It was just me trying to live in the past ... and we were on holidays anyway. The rest of the year is different ... we have so many responsibilities ..." she trailed off, looking at the ground.

"I don't believe that for a second. I know it can still be like that ... even when we're not on holidays. You just have to let me near you. You need to start trusting me again, and let me know what you're feeling. That's the only way we can get that connection back," he said, stroking her bare shoulder, his eyes deep with desire. "You look so beautiful, Dimity. The fabric, your skin ... is so sensual, just like you've always been," he said softly.

"It's from an Australian designer ... I mean ..." she stumbled, suddenly feeling hurt again as she remembered his words back in Amsterdam.

"You're thinking about my comments again. That was a stupid thing to say. You know that I've always admired you in beautiful clothes. I didn't mean that. I was reacting to what you said about that night ... the night when I couldn't keep my hands off you," he said with vulnerable eyes, the hurt obviously still stinging.

"*That* was a stupid thing to say. I'm also sorry that I hurt you so much. That night was the most sacred night of my life. I have no regrets about that. Malcolm ... you need to know that ... I didn't mean it," she pleaded with him.

"I know, Dimity. I never really believed you meant what you said. I couldn't mistake the love in your eyes, whenever I touched you, whenever I held you close in bed. It was like that for many years, until recently."

She studied his face. He was looking at her so seductively — the way he always looked at her when he wanted her.

"I miss holding you in my arms, showing you how much I love and desire you. You know I need that in my life. You distanced yourself from me to the point that you couldn't even look at me a few minutes ago. Now, looking into your beautiful eyes, I see the Dimity I fell in love with — the Dimity I never stopped loving. I just know she's hurting and she's a bit confused, maybe even scared. You know we can achieve anything together. You know that, don't you? I can't imagine spending my life with any woman but you. Just let

275

me show you, Dimi — like you used to." He touched her face and then her soft lips with his thumb.

"So, does that mean you recognise me now? I mean, you said you couldn't touch someone ... that that's not how you're made ..."

"Please, don't remind me of what a jerk I've been. You have to believe that I know you aren't vindictive, or intentionally cruel. I know you too well. I always have."

He then looked down and took something out of his pocket. It was a small, elegant, silver box. "Speaking of beautiful things, I had to buy this for you. It reminded me of you when I saw it. It had a presence about it. Its beauty is unassuming, and it exudes warmth and substance, just like you do — like you always have."

She took the box from him and opened it. "Malcolm ... is this a diamond pendant? It's probably so expensive ..." she gasped.

"Shh," he said, placing his finger on her lips, his slight beard caressing her face as he leaned close. He then took the pendant out of the box and placed it around her neck, kissing her gently on her bare shoulders and neck as he clipped it on. "You know I want the best for you. You mean more to me than anything. Fearing that you would give up on us, and imagining my life without you ... it tore at me. Life wouldn't have the same sparkle." He smiled, acknowledging the pun. He looked at the pendant that sat just above her blouse. "I was right. It looks beautiful on you." He then became serious. He leaned towards her and began to kiss her gently on her lips.

"Malcolm ... there's something I need to tell you. It's Stavros," she said, feeling that she couldn't keep the secret from him.

Malcolm suddenly pulled away from her for a moment.

"What about him?" he asked, his demeanour slightly changing, as he anxiously waited for her to continue.

"He ... he," she looked away.

"Tell me, Dimity. You need to tell me everything. What happened? Is there something going on between the two of you? I need to know. I mean, I know you looked so happy with him on the hill …"

"What? You saw us on the hill?"

"I had taken a photo, not knowing that you were both in the distance. That's how I found his shop — from the logo on the bag. I know that he inspired you and I'm fine with that. I'm glad to have you back, to see the passion in your eyes again, but if there's something more …"

"He kissed me … and I let him. I was shocked though. It had happened so fast that I became numb. He thought our marriage was beyond saving. He apologised straight after. I told him that our marriage wasn't over — that I had to get straight back to you and work things out — that I love you so much …"

Malcolm stood there holding her hands. His eyes had darkened. His jaw was tight, and his toned arms were tense.

"So, that's as far as it got? He kissed you?" he finally asked, his demeanour once again changing so he looked at her with affection. He was obviously relieved she didn't cross the line — that it was just one kiss that Stavros had initiated, catching her off guard.

"Yes, you know there's only one man for me, Malcolm … it didn't mean anything."

"It's okay … really. I trust you. I knew you were just being yourself. Of course he found you irresistible," he said, suddenly smiling. "As long as that's all it was," he continued, moving closer to her. "We've all done things we regret."

Feeling relieved and surprised at how quickly he forgave her, she looked at him without inhibitions.

"Besides, once you remember how good we are together, you'll forget that it even happened." He moved closer to her.

She felt his warm breath, his soft lips brushing her own. They pressed harder on hers as he began to kiss her with

277

intensity, his rebellious hair caressing her forehead and face as he stroked her hair and bare shoulders. She held onto his neck, her whole body becoming weak as his beard caressed her skin. She shivered. It had been so long. Their lips abruptly parted. Malcolm's smooth yet masculine hand caressed her warm face gently as he searched her eyes in between short heavy breaths. Her heart felt like little butterflies were fluttering within it. She smiled at him as he guided her close to his chest, wrapping his arms firmly around her waist, pulling her even closer to him. Dimity could see the emotion on his chiselled face as she looked up at him. She instinctively stroked his face, combing his dark wavy hair away with her fingers. They sat there for a while, looking at each other, communicating without words.

"Come on, let's get out of here," he finally said, softly. "You've been here too long. Besides, we need to start that second honeymoon we were supposed to have in Amsterdam, don't we?"

"Malcolm? Did you really say those things to your mother? She would have really been shocked."

"Actually, she was really supportive of your career and wants to be close to you. You know, I think she just wants to be included."

"And not be left behind?"

"Oh, she also said that you and I were made for each other, or something along those lines."

Dimity smiled as peace filled her heart. Malcolm wrapped his arm around her and guided her to the door. As they stepped outside, arm in arm, her pendant glistening in the sunlight, she noticed Stavros waiting at the street corner. He looked at her. He smiled approvingly. She smiled back at him, knowing he was okay, that he understood. She had her husband back — she had her family back! All the rest would follow, because they would face it together, the way they

always should have. She was finally starting to see clearly —
she did have it all!

CHAPTER THIRTY-ONE

Nicki sat back comfortably in her chair, ready to help out with some Monday afternoon paperwork. She looked at the computer screen on her desk. She then turned around and momentarily watched Poppy playing behind her, her long hair tied in a braid that she had made for her that afternoon after picking her up from school. Angela and Peter were busy with clients. Nicki momentarily gazed out of the window, at the rugged terrain in the distance, and then at people scurrying busily by, carrying on with their day, shopping or having a bite to eat in the street, enjoying another glorious, hot summer's day in Ioannina. She then thought of the weekend — how fun it had been to have the red and white ferry take her to Nissi. It brought back so many childhood memories.

She began to sort out the paperwork, until she instinctively lifted her head, sensing that someone was approaching her.

"Excuse me, I need some help with accommodation. I'm planning to holiday here but I haven't booked anything yet. Can you help me?"

Nicki looked up into a pair of olive green eyes. She noticed his tanned complexion, and how his thick, long fringe fell freely onto his forehead, standing out from the shorter strands that were neatly gelled back in place. "*Marco?*"

"Yes, that's my name ... did I even mention that?" he innocently asked, a smile appearing slowly on his face. "Like I said, I was hoping you could help me. You *do* work here, don't you?"

Nicki continued to stare at him. *What was he doing here? Why was he pretending that ...*"

"Um ... so, can you help me? You *do* help customers with queries?" he asked as he looked at Angela and Peter who were, in fact, helping customers with queries. "Well, in that case, since you can't help me, I was hoping you could join me for a coffee ... *or something?* I'd love it if you could show me around ..."

"Marco ..." she began to say, but then stood up and smiled at him. He looked so adorable, standing there with a mischievous grin, the way he had looked the day she had met him.

"Um ... I'm just stepping out for a second," she called out to the others as they looked at her inquisitively. Grabbing her bag, she guided Marco to the door.

"Yes, I can join you for a coffee ... *or something,*" she said, giving him a warm smile.

The glorious sunlight greeted them as they stepped outside.

"So, have you been working here for long?" Marco continued.

Nicki grinned at him. "No, I actually just started last week. I'm helping out. My cousin and his wife just took over the business." Nicki decided to go along with whatever game Marco was playing.

"Oh ... and have you worked in this particular industry before?" he asked, obviously trying to stifle a smile.

"You could say that," she said, suppressing her own.

"Well, I'm sure you get many men asking you out. I'm sure I'm not the first."

"I have been known to attract the odd uni student now and then," she said with a laugh.

"I can see that happening. I really can."

They walked into a cosy indoor coffee shop. Marco took charge and led the way. Nicki sensed that he had been there before. They both sat at one of the tables by the window, overlooking the busy street.

"So, where are you from?" Nicki asked as she settled in her chair, still following his cue.

"I'm actually from Melbourne. I thought, why not just jump on a plane and head for Greece? For some reason, I felt that I might meet the love of my life here — my soulmate," he said, suddenly serious.

Nicki's eyes instantly locked with his. She broke the stare when the waiter appeared beside them. Marco was still looking at her when she turned to ask him what he would be ordering. Her heart melted.

He finally looked away, and took a quick glance at the menu.

When the waiter walked away with their orders, Marco continued. "You know, you really have the most beautiful smile. So, are you seeing anyone? You're not married ... are you?"

Nicki paused to think for a while, scratching her head as though she was deep in thought. She was still puzzled by his behaviour. "Um ... let me see ... am I seeing anyone at the moment? No. You're looking at my ring?" she innocently queried. "I just wear this to deter potential suitors ... you know, with my smile and all. I'm not actually married or anything like that." Nicki giggled like a teenager. She forgot how much Marco could make her laugh.

"Thank God. I was beginning to worry. This calls for a celebration. How does Champagne sound?"

"I thought that we were just having coffee, or are you one of those guys who gets women drunk?"

"No ... far from it. Some women, in fact, find me to be irresistible and even great husband material."

"They do?" Nicki said, looking sceptical. She then became serious. "I can see that," she then said, looking at him with intent.

They stepped out of the coffee shop an hour later. Nicki felt pleasantly tipsy from her glass of Champagne. When she had arrived in Greece, it had been a while since she'd even had a sip of alcohol. Now, she did have a little wine here and there. Peter and Angela had insisted she try many of the wines from Zitsa on offer at dinner, and she had obliged, just as she had now. Besides, it wasn't like they were still trying. Her thoughts instantly trailed off.

"Are you okay? You did enjoy yourself ... didn't you?"

"Yes, I did." She gave him a warm smile. She couldn't resist his charm, the way she couldn't in the old days — the carefree days.

Right then, Nicki jolted as the sound of an electric guitar pierced her ears. "Oh my God! *What is that*?" She turned around to find a whole band behind her. Before she knew it, one of the guitarists began to sing the lyrics to "I Was Made for Lovin' You" — *in Greek*, with intense passion.

"*Kiss ... in Greek*?" Nicki cringed, and felt her cheeks colouring as crowds of people gathered around them. She then began to laugh.

"Well, it was short notice. I was hoping for a jazz band or a Frank Sinatra impersonator. The manager from the coffee shop booked them for tonight. They're having a retro-themed party. Sorry?"

"Forgiven," Nicki said, laughing hysterically.

Marco began to laugh as well, as she leaned on his chest between laughter. They were now away from the crowd, and Nicki felt her back press against a wall. Right that instant, she felt his hand on her hair and his other hand around her waist. His lips felt soft. He kissed her gently, but his eyes revealed intense feeling. Nicki looked deep into them. She saw her reflection. Her heart began to beat wildly as though they really were on their first date. She smiled at him. "Just who are you, Marco Rossi?" she asked, just as she had when they first met.

Marco paused for a moment. He answered with a smile. "I'm the man of your dreams ... and you're the love of my life. We're soulmates ... you and I."

The song ended. As they walked hand in hand through the busy crowd, the piercing guitar sound began again. Marco looked at Nicki as she began to laugh. "I think that's the only song they know," he said, matching her laughter.

"I love it," she then said. "The lyrics ring true."

After walking for a while, they both stepped back into the office.

Poppy came running towards her. "Can you help me with my English homework?"

Angela looked up from her desk and immediately went to introduce herself to the handsome man Nicki appeared so taken with. Peter soon followed, while Nicki helped Poppy.

"Okay? See? You've learned it already. You're becoming a little champ at English," Nicki said as Poppy's whole face beamed with pride.

She walked back to Marco who was looking at her. "You're great with her," he said softly.

"She's adorable."

"So, you're okay … with leaving her?"

Nicki took a while to answer. She finally spoke. "You know what, Marco? I think I will be okay. I have a strange feeling that things are going to change." She then walked outside, taking a deep breath. She felt Marco's hand on hers. He turned her around. "It's okay … Nicki. Please, you don't have to hide anything with me."

Nicki's eyes suddenly became teary. She looked down at the ground. "I'm going to be fine, Marco. Do you know how I know this?"

"How?"

She looked up at him again. "Because I realise that I have so much love inside of me … so much passion and I just feel that it's been wasted. I can offer so much … I don't know … working here, helping out has helped me see who I am … what I can bring to the world. I was so shy when I was young. Maria was the confident, outspoken one.

284

Working at the agency brought me out of my shell all those years ago … and then I met you, and you made me laugh at myself … you made me want to celebrate who I was … who we were. I don't even know what I'm trying to say."

Marco took her hand in his again. "Nicki … you'll make a great mother one day … this I'm certain of. I mean … we haven't even explored all our options yet. You will give that smile to some little boy or girl one day … all that love. Don't you see … the reason you laugh at all my antics? It's because of who you are … how you see the world — with love, and light. You say that I had light in my eyes. That's all because of you."

"Marco … sorry for everything I said …"

"Shh … you don't need to apologise. Like I told you all those years ago — we can fix anything. Nothing is impossible … *comprendere?*" he asked, his face giving way to a warm smile.

"*Comprendere,*" Nicki replied, as she messed his hair up affectionately.

***

That afternoon, Maria waited patiently and nervously in the foyer, waiting for Stelios Harris to arrive. She had to find peace for her mother. She had to ease her mother's guilt, and the only way she could do that was by finding out if Stelios' life had turned around. Her mother's constant interference in her life had become an unhealthy obsession. It was proof that she was living in fear; she had to protect or deter anything like that from happening again, especially to her rebellious and unconventional daughter.

Maria looked up as heavy footsteps on the marble floor interrupted her thoughts.

"Maria?" the man said.

"Yes," she said, standing up and reaching for his hand.

"Remarkable," he then said. "You remind me so much of your mother. Come into my office. I have a lot to tell you."

Maria followed the man down the marble corridor.

A long while later, Maria stepped into the car, hugging a letter in her arms. She would give it to her mother, as Stelios had instructed her to, just as he had wanted to after he had let his anger subside all those years ago. He wanted her mother to know that he didn't blame her — that he was fine. In fact, he was doing great. Mr Stelios Harris had married and had three children with his wife, who was a humanitarian. They lived by the water, and he had done so much for soccer on an international level: coaching, commentating, organising events. He had obviously fought his demons and accomplished so much in an industry he loved. She was sure her mother would find solace in that knowledge, and she would tell her as soon as she got back to Sydney. How to initiate the subject would, however, be challenging.

"Let's go," she said to Antonio.

"So you have the answers you need?"

"Yes … I do, Antonio. I have all the answers I need."

Right then she heard her mobile beeping. Nicki had left a text message. Maria hadn't heard from her for a while. Her sister had been acting very mysteriously lately. Apparently she had seen someone from their past in a magazine, and that *someone* was Luca — their best friend's sister — from the old neighbourhood in Sydney! Maria found herself smiling at the thought of seeing the McKenzies again. They had been a big part of their lives growing up. *Dimity*, she thought. *I wonder how life turned out for our dear friend.*

CHAPTER THIRTY-TWO

"Would it be so bad to work with me, Dimity? I mean ... surely you've thought of it before. You're good with the business side of things, dealing with clients etc ... well, as long as your dealings aren't like ours were!" He smiled wickedly from across the table, which overlooked the lake. "It might be difficult to get any work done of course ... we need to take that into account," he continued in the same playful tone.

Dimity smiled at him from across the table. They had decided to have a drink after leaving Stavros' studio. Malcolm couldn't stop telling her how much he loved and missed her, even telling her that the small table they were seated at created too much distance between them, which was apparently unbearable because she looked so enticing. It was painful not sitting next to her, unable to touch her. Dimity felt so desired. Malcolm wanted her to know how much he loved her, and even gave her another gift — an expensive set of pearl earrings from an exclusive Danish jeweller. She had told him that he shouldn't have. He had replied by stopping to kiss her as they made their way to the coffee shop.

"I was thinking of maybe starting a business where I could introduce interior designers to new talent, you know ... like homewares, paintings ... maybe an online business. It might be interesting and rewarding. I mean, it's a shame that a lot of talent isn't recognised. Some of Stavr ..." Dimity looked down and played with her drink.

She felt his hand on hers. "Look ... it's okay. You don't have to feel uneasy. I'm okay with it. I trust you. I know you were caught off guard. I just love seeing you so passionate and optimistic again." He leaned over and kissed her gently on the lips. "Let's forget about him though. As much as I love how much he's inspired you career-wise, if it's okay with you … I'd rather talk about something else, like you and me?"

"Well, I haven't dismissed working with you entirely. It might actually be fun, and it would be easy to work around the girl's schedules. It could be a win-win situation. You'll have more time to create; I'll help you and maybe even start my online business. I mean, we're still young, and I'm sure I can get in touch with some of my colleagues from the past. I've started to follow them online and keep up to date with what they're doing. I think Susan is working in the Eastern suburbs."

"I love seeing you like this! It's been a while. I told you … if we have each other, everything else will follow, and we can make it happen — together. We both signed up for it. It's okay to ask for help, and it's okay to work with me. I love the idea of being close to my family and having the time to create again. You're right — it can be a win-win. I don't know why we didn't think of it before."

"Because I was being proud, and I thought it was like feeding on scraps, I guess … you know, that I'd be riding on your coattails … I thought I had to be the perfect mother, and that that meant always being there for the girls. You were also branching out and making a name for yourself internationally. I didn't want to distract you."

"I can't believe you felt like this. You should have come to me. You know I would do anything for you." He caressed her hand.

"I didn't always feel like that. In the beginning, I didn't mind. In fact, I loved seeing you thrive, and I loved that I was fortunate to be able to raise the girls. Now that the girls are older and more self-sufficient, I feel that I need to do something — to get out there again. Even making a vase — it made me realise how much I crave creativity in my life. At school, I topped the class in art; back then, being a designer was all I had."

"It was all you had when your friends left for Greece. I mean … that's why you chose this place instead of any other. I've always said, you're too sweet for your own good. I should have known better, Dimity. We both crave the same things, and I should have known you would regret resigning."

"It isn't just that, though. I missed you, and I didn't want to admit it to myself. I felt like I was being selfish, that I had everything financially …"

"I get it, Dimi … you felt abandoned. The script had been changed, and you had no warning about it. You felt that you were left to make things right — on your own. That can't happen though, because the script changed because of what we did together. We created two beautiful girls together, so we should have planned the next scene together too … you realise that now, don't you?"

"I understand that we're good at being creative together. And yes, our greatest creations have been our daughters," she said, smiling. "I also understand that what I've been craving is not so unattainable. It's in front of me — I just have to reach out and touch it," she said, placing her hand on his face. Right then, Malcolm's phone rang.

"Speaking of the girls," he smiled, kissing her hand as it made its way towards his lips. "It's Olivia."

Dimity leaned back on her chair, feeling content as she admired her husband speaking to their daughter.

"Hi sweetie, how are you? Yes, your mum and I are fine. In fact, she's sitting next to me as we speak," he said, smiling proudly. "You can speak to her after you speak to me."

"I'd better go to the travel agency to organise the accommodation for the islands," Malcolm said, getting up from his chair.

"What are you talking about?" Dimity asked as she hung up the phone after speaking with Samantha.

"Well, we can't leave Greece without seeing some of the islands," he said, a shocked look on his face.

"Okay ..." Dimity said, liking the sound of his plans. "I have to go to see my friends, Rose and Anastasia. They're leaving soon, so I'd better tell them that my sexy husband has come back to whisk me off to the islands. I also need to pick up some souvenirs."

Malcolm looked into her eyes contently. He moved closer to her and kissed her. "Did I tell you how spectacular you look?"

"I think you've told me at least ten times just over coffee."

"I also knew how desirable you'd look with those earrings," he continued, stroking her arm. "Well, I'd better go." He looked at her regretfully.

"Are you sure you don't want me to go with you?"

"No, I also have to sort something out with my accommodation at the hotel. You go and do what you have to do."

"Okay, there are a lot of things I need to take care off as well. Rose and Anastasia were supposed to meet me at a place called Kouvenda — a really happening coffee shop just down the street. We're not going to see each other after today, so that might take a while."

"Okay, I'll call you as soon as I'm done," he said, kissing her on the lips softly, and then more intensely. Her body shivered all over as his beard tantalised her soft skin. "I've missed you so much Dimity. I can't wait to show you how much I love you." His eyes suddenly conveyed deep, intense desire. "You're the only woman for me. Don't ever forget that. We'll get that chance soon." He looked at his watch. "I better go."

"Okay ... bye." She wondered what he was up to. "Just don't buy more gifts. You've already spoiled me so much," she called after him, but he was already too far away to hear her.

CHAPTER THIRTY-THREE

Nicki couldn't believe how connected she felt to Marco, resting in his arms between the sheets, the late afternoon sun lighting up part of the room. She looked at the light on the bed, and hope filled her heart again. As much as she couldn't bear the thought of not having a baby, the pain would be far more unbearable if she lost the love of her life. She and Marco had so much love to give. They would find a way — together.

"What are you thinking?" he asked as he stroked her bare back with his lips.

"How lucky we are to have each other — to bring the best out of each other again. We reached crisis point, and now we …"

"… we're stronger than ever," he finished. "Which reminds me …" He reached in the pocket of his jacket, which had been placed hastily on the chair earlier. "I have something for you."

"Oh … a gift?" she queried, looking at the small box he handed her. "Is it a ring? I already have one, you know!"

"Yes, you do, and I'm happy to see you're still wearing it."

"So what is it, then?"

"Open it."

"Okay," she said excitedly. She unwrapped the box and opened it. "Keys? They're our house keys," she said, perplexed.

"Yes, they are, but they're magical house keys. You see, they have the power to change our lives, to give us hope for the future — our future, Nicki. All you need to do is turn the key, and you're home, where you belong …"

"Marco … I acted hastily … leaving you like that. I mean, it was really unfair to you. Of course I'll turn the key and come back to you — to our home. I have a question, though. What you did earlier, acting like you didn't know me …"

"That, I'm afraid, I can't take complete credit for. You know those two counsellors who are also engaged … they were asked to mind the terrace house?"

"Cassandra and Connor? That was their idea?"

"It sure was, which reminds me. I have to take care of something." Marco promptly stood up from the bed, walked into the bathroom and stepped into the shower, leaving her alone with her thoughts.

She then remembered Cassandra's bizarre phone call. That explained everything.

Ten minutes later, Marco stepped out of the bathroom. "Why were you acting like you didn't know me?" she asked again, as he dressed.

"Oh … they suggested that I come here and remind you about what attracted you to me. She knew you would be working there today, so the rest is history." He leaned over to give her a kiss on the lips, before heading for the door.

"Where are you going?" she asked, baffled by his urgent actions.

"I have something I need to take care of. Leave your phone on," he said hastily. "You might want to tell Maria and Antonio to get here earlier if they can. Bye!"

"Bye!" she said, wondering what he was up to. With Marco, she never knew.

That same afternoon, Dimity walked past the shops that she had admired on so many occasions during her stay in Ioannina. It had been a surreal experience, and nostalgia began to set in. It was exciting to be spending time with Malcolm here — to share the experience with him. She reminisced about the very first day, when she had seen the hotel situated by the lake as she bade Eleni farewell, and the day she had stepped into Stavros' shop. She realised so much had changed within her since then. Then, there was Stavros. She hoped he wouldn't be a sore point in her marriage and that Malcolm was really okay with what had happened.

She also looked forward to the village dance, the *panigiri*, later that night, and she was sure Malcolm would be happy to escort her there and meet her new English friends. It was the night that the village came together, and Rose and Anastasia had insisted that they all meet there that night. They couldn't wait to meet her husband, they had told her, and since they had to have a late lunch with relatives and didn't have much time to chat, they thought it would be a great time to say their farewells there.

Her mind instantaneously went to the village — to Zitsa. She had told Rose and Anastasia that she really wanted to see it in the day time one more time. She had to go back there! She had to see it — now, in the afternoon, when the breeze would seduce the mountainous landscape with its mystical presence.

Dimity admired the scenery. The breeze was as lovely as she remembered it, and had eased the intense heat from the relentless, unapologetic summer sun. The gentle, soothing music from the timber chimes created positive vibes that enveloped her. The donkey also looked content, half asleep in a patch of shade.

"Y*iasou* Dimity." It was Stavros' auntie, *Kyra* Sophia.

"Y*iasou Kyra* Sophia. I thought I'd see the village one more time before I leave. It's so beautiful here."

"You can go in if you want, and sit on the veranda. I just cleaned the main house a bit for Stavros. He rents it out sometimes, now that his parents live in the city. He's always too busy to tidy up so I help him out when I can. I'll just go and finish making my *spanakopita*. Maybe you can have some when it's ready," she said, smiling warmly. "You are such a beautiful and sweet girl. Stavros says so many nice things about you."

"Thank you. Your nephew is a very kind and talented man. He'll make someone very happy one day."

Dimity decided to take one more look at the studio/workshop at the back. She walked into the small space, with the big table in the centre, inviting artistic experimentation. She reflected on the lessons that had taken place, where they each sat; Rose flirting while Stavros demonstrated how the glass could be manipulated, his strong arms on display. She had been bothered by Rose's constant, somewhat jealous stares, but she had been wrong about her. They had all been taken on a short, creative journey, and they had been caught up in the landscape, the lessons, and of course, in Stavros. She had learned a lot from him; she now knew she still had what it took to achieve what she wanted, and that as talented, nurturing, and attractive as Stavros was, there was only one man for her.

She decided to take a walk on the veranda, via the main house. She breathed in the air as she stepped outside, taking casual strides as she wrapped her kimono around her mostly bare shoulders. It felt beautiful. *She* felt beautiful. As she neared the entrance of the house, she noticed a woman standing in the distance, admiring the view of the mountains — just like she had. She was wearing a white dress, and had a light blue bandana on her head. There was something familiar about her. She had seen her before. Her slightly wavy hair sat just below her shoulders, and was a silky, light brown colour. Dimity walked closer towards her, needing to know more. The pretty woman turned around. She was smiling as she looked at something. It was *her!* Dimity would recognise her anywhere. Dimity followed the woman's gaze. A man was approaching. *Malcolm?* It was Malcolm, walking with a picnic basket. He was also smiling. He was walking — but not towards *her* — he was walking towards the pretty woman with the big smile on her face, the woman who had passion when she apparently didn't, the one that was with him in Amsterdam. It was *Julie Canei* — the interior designer!

Her heart raced. Her legs trembled, as she looked at the man who was her husband but seemed like someone else — someone *she* didn't recognise! She touched the pendant he had given her; it had felt so delicate just moments earlier, but now felt as if it was choking her. She gasped for air. She had to move, but she couldn't. They couldn't see her there. Summoning energy, she turned and headed back towards the entrance of the house, feeling dizzy and struggling to balance. She closed the door — and closed them out — wanting to erase them from her mind. It started to make sense — the jewellery, the overwhelming compliments, telling her he felt guilty and that he had let her down, wanting to plan the travel arrangements *without her*. *"We've all done things we regret,"* he had whispered before he had kissed her — when he had found out about her and Stavros! He had accepted what had happened so quickly, taking her by surprise. *No wonder! It all makes sense. Of course he forgave me because he was the one having an affair!*

She instinctively walked to the window, needing but not wanting to know more. She couldn't believe it! They were heading to the house — the house she was in! Trembling all over, tears streaming uncontrollably down her face, she walked into the lounge room. Hysterically, she tried to bolt the door. She couldn't let them see her! She finally got the bolt loose and shut the door forcefully. She then stood there, unable to move, as she stared at the back of the door. She couldn't believe her eyes. It was looking her in the face — the beautiful church against a blue backdrop, the intricate flowers, the boats in the distance, the hours of effort and dedication. She couldn't mistake it. It was just as she remembered it — just as she and Nicki, with Maria's help, had woven it, thread by thread on the loom — together, as a team, for their Year 10 art project. It was the tapestry — the *Greek tapestry*.

Wiping away her tears, taking deep, slow breaths, she took the tapestry in her trembling hands. As she turned it around, her heart felt warm as she read the names: *Nicki Salas and Dimity McKenzie*. Nicki had penned their names proudly on a late rainy afternoon in her bedroom, as they shared Greek shortbread biscuits that Mrs Salas had freshly baked. Tears began to roll down her face. Her heart filled with joy and regret for what could have been.

The voices were now getting closer. They were coming from the back of the house. Dimity hastily went to place the tapestry on the lounge chair, turning to look out of the back window as she did this. The look on Malcolm's face stung her heart. He gave it freely to *her* — to this Julie woman who had ruined her world as she knew it. She looked at the lips that had kissed her almost two hours ago. His hair fell freely, flirting unashamedly as it landed on his face. She always thought it made him look rebellious. She finally managed to place the tapestry on the chair, stopping instantly when she noticed a small folded piece of paper tightly fastened to the back. Nervously, she took it from where it had been for so long. Anxiously and hastily, she unfolded it and read the text. It was from one of Nicki's uncles … stating that it was for the Salas family. A sticker was on it. It was from the post office. Dimity couldn't believe her eyes as she read what she could from the note. The word STRIKE stood out. *There was a strike. They never got the letters I sent them! They never knew that we were moving!* Hysterically, she unfolded another piece of paper. Dimity's heart sank once again with regret. The letters that she had written to Nicki and Maria, telling them that she missed them, and that she would be moving to the south coast, never made it to them. *They didn't get my letters because of a strike at the local post office!*

"Oh no!" she cried. The footsteps were getting closer. As she looked out of the window, she noticed *Kyra* Sophia walking behind them, towards the house with a plate that was carrying the spinach pastry she had promised she would offer *her* — *Dimity* — *"the beautiful and sweet girl"* as she had described her, or as Malcolm had just told her — the one that was *"too sweet for her own good"*. There was no escaping them. She had no choice. She took a deep breath, and walked towards the back door. With the letters still clutched tightly in her hands, she opened the door.

"Dimity?" Malcolm greeted her with a smile, looking surprised.

"Hi!" the pretty *Julie* woman also greeted her. "I just have to get this ... sorry," she continued, smiling warmly at her as she answered her phone.

Just what game were they playing? Did they think she was so daft that she would think they weren't there together? Malcolm didn't know anything about the village. She didn't even tell him she would be there.

"So, is this the place where you took the lessons? What a coincidence!"

Dimity just stood there, not knowing what to say.

"Dimi ... are you okay? Did something happen? You look frazzled."

"Don't worry," she heard Julie saying to the other person on the line. "We'll talk about it when I get back to Sydney. I love you too. Don't forget to have a break in between lessons. I miss you!"

She could feel Malcolm's stare as she listened in on her conversation. Her eyes were still on Julie. His stare became more intense as she continued to look away from him, and look solely at *her*. Dimity's eyes felt tired. *She* felt tired, and confused. What was happening?

"Dimi ..." she felt Malcolm's cool hand on hers, as he moved closer. "Are we okay?" he whispered softly in her ear, his warm breath caressing her face. He sounded worried and confused.

She turned to look at him. Her eyes couldn't hide the emotion, the despair, the hurt.

"Sorry Dimity, that was my boyfriend calling. He's finding it hard to take time off for our long weekend away. I'm so glad to finally meet you. Malcolm has told me so much about you. So, you're also an interior designer?"

"Um ... yes ... I was ... I mean I am," Dimity began to talk, her thoughts still in a haze. She could still feel Malcolm's concerned stare. Overwhelmed with emotion, she finally turned to Malcolm and met his eyes. They looked worried — almost afraid. He moved closer and placed his arm around her, instantly sending shivers throughout her shocked, numb body.

"Yes, Dimity is an interior designer. You two should have a lot to talk about," he said, holding her tightly, as though he was afraid that he would lose her again.

She looked at the picnic basket he was still holding in his other hand.

"Oh, I thought we'd have a picnic here in the village. I heard you were here so I thought it would be nice to have some wine and a light late afternoon snack — you know, the way we used to," he added, looking deep into her eyes. "Maybe we can even walk to one of the nearest vineyards. There's also a really famous monastery ..."

"You knew I was here? How?"

"Rose and Anastasia. I met them at that place, Kouvenda, you told me about. I thought you might still be there. It didn't take too long to sort out the travel arrangements. I met another one of your friends, Eleni, from the main travel agency. She was very helpful. Rose and Anastasia seem very fun also. They told me you'd be here, in Zitsa, and gave me directions to the house."

"What? But they had to see some relatives ..."

"They decided to order some food from the coffee shop to take with them. Dimi, that's why I'm here ... to have a picnic. I thought I'd surprise you."

"But what about Julie?"

Julie cut in. "I can't believe I ran into your husband here … in the middle of nowhere. I mean … talk about a small world. I'm here to spend some time with my friend, who's holidaying here with her son and husband. She actually lived here for a while as a young girl. I was telling Malcolm that this is the house she lived in, and that we'll be renting for a few days."

"A friend … which friend … I mean, what's her name?" she asked, realising that Julie would think she was weird. Every time she ran into her, she was flustered. She then looked at *Kyra* Sophia who stood looking into the distance as a taxi pulled up.

"What are you holding?" Malcolm asked gently, caressing her arm as he spoke. "Dimi … please, you're scaring me. Why do you look so shocked and hurt? What's going on with you? I feel like I'm losing you again. Please, clue me in," he continued, as Julie walked towards the taxi. A man and woman got out of it. The man was carrying a small child, and the woman was wearing bohemian clothes. Her lustrous, auburn hair looked as free as she did as the breeze picked up. It was the couple she had seen at the Acropolis, in Athens. She had looked familiar. It couldn't be!

"I can't believe we're here, Antonio. I remember it so vividly," Maria exulted as she waved to her friend. Julie was standing on top of the hill upon which the house was perched. She noticed another man and woman standing outside the house. An older woman was also there with a plate in her hands. Maria had just received another message from Nicki. She wanted all of them, including Julie, to go to the small courtyard behind the old church near the house they used to live in. *Why does Nicki want us to go there?"* she thought to herself. It was so weird.

"Dimity?" Malcolm touched her hand again.

299

"You're not losing me Malcolm," she said, as she looked at *Kyra* Sophia, who was now talking to the man with the child. "Sorry if I'm being mysterious. It's the tapestry. I found it, Malcolm. I found the tapestry that Nicki, Maria, and I made all those years ago. They never got my letters. Would you believe it? There was a strike and they never got them. I knew the village where she had lived was small and close to the town, but I never thought it was *this* village."

"Are you saying you found letters in this house that you wrote for Nicki and Maria? You mean this was the actual house? That's amazing! No wonder you're so shocked. I was so worried ... about *us*."

"You don't need to worry," Dimity said, her heart beating with excitement as she turned to look at the woman who was nearing them. "It's Mar ..." she began.

"Maria!" Julie called. "I'm so happy to see you. How's the trip so far?" Julie ran over to greet her while the man talked with *Kyra* Sophia.

"*Maria* ..." Dimity called out, unable to contain her excitement. "Is it really you? Nicki's younger and devious sister?"

Maria looked perplexed as she stood next to Dimity. They all paused for a while.

"Well, you definitely know Maria with that description. I guess there's one in every family. My sister isn't a walk in the park either," Julie teased her obviously close friend.

Maria was taken aback with the sudden realisation of who stood before her. She gasped. "*Dimity McKenzie,* from number 28 ... our best friend ... in the whole wide world! I can't believe it. Will this holiday get anymore surreal?"

"Well, you won't believe it until you see it ..." Dimity stuttered, her heart beating much too fast and her thoughts tangled with excitement. She walked into the house and brought out the tapestry that had meant so much to all of them — that had been part of their lives.

"It's the tapestry that Nicki and I completed together … the one that you also helped with! Maria … this is it! Can you believe it?"

"*The tapestry?* Nicki drove us all crazy when we forgot it. No one could find it when we asked about it when we got back home. You're right. I wouldn't have believed it unless I saw it. *The Greek tapestry* is back where it should be. Well, then, it's your turn to keep it. Wasn't that the deal? It stays with us for a while and then it stays with you?"

"You're right, but that also means I have to hand it back to Nicki!"

"Speaking of Nicki," Maria said. "She told me to meet her near that old church on the hill … over there." Maria began walking, with everyone following close behind.

Nicki felt like her heart would explode with joy as she turned to peer at the nearest vineyard in the distance, its rows of robust vines climbing a steep, lush green slope. She then looked around the cobblestone courtyard and the old church, and at the Justice of the Peace who stood before them, ready to commence proceedings. "I can't believe you organised this so quickly. The pink roses look so beautiful. How did you know there was a wishing well here? I didn't even see it. I think you've outdone yourself." She was ready to pledge her undying love to Marco. They would have a new beginning. She daydreamed of things to come.

Marco looked at something behind her, and smiled broadly.

"What is it, Marco?" Nicki turned her head with curiosity.

"Our guests have finally arrived."

"Hi Nicki!" Nicki heard a young woman call. She turned around. The woman was waving to her. The man next to her was holding some sort of painting. "It's me. It's me … Dimity. And I found something. I guess it's my wedding gift to you," she said with a laugh.

"*Dimity?*" Nicki exclaimed, her eyes wide as saucers. "I can't believe it. It's Dimity, Marco. Did you know about this? Did you plan this too?" She turned to look at her husband.

"Plan what?"

"That Dimity would be here. Our best friend from the old neighbourhood ... and she found the tapestry that we made together."

"Sorry, but I can't take credit for that either," he said.

The Justice of the Peace cleared his throat.

Marco straightened his shoulders. The guests all listened quietly as the ceremony began.

It was soon time for them to pledge their vows. Nicki became serious. She took a deep breath and looked into Marco's eyes. "Marco ... I love you so much. We may have strayed for a while, but the lesson I've learned today is that whichever path we all take, we can all create a beautiful picture together. We were all meant to return home." Tears formed quickly as she glanced at the tapestry and then back at Marco, who was giving her a knowing smile.

"Yes, and like I always say, Nicki: '*Abbiamo sempre bisogno di passione nella vita*'. We always need passion in life," he said, moving closer. He kissed her passionately. Wrapping her in his arms, he continued to kiss her. Nicki heard whistling and applause, and then a familiar tune — an electric guitar. "*Kiss?*" she queried, with a smile. "*Kiss* ... in Greek *again?*"

Marco gave her an innocent look. "It was short notice," he said as everyone congregated around them to congratulate them.

Nicki felt the light in her eyes, and she saw it in Marco's again too. She looked at the gold coin he had given her and then at the wishing well. She placed the coin in his pocket. "I don't need it," she whispered in his ear. "I have what I want already. You're a wish that keeps giving. You keep giving me love, hope and passion."

"Together, who knows what we can achieve," he told her. As she looked first at Marco, her confident and sincere soulmate, to Maria, her wonderful sister, and to Dimity, the best friend she now had a second chance with, she knew she had returned home.

***

"So, it was quite an eventful day, wouldn't you say?" Malcolm asked Dimity, as they walked towards the hill where they would have their picnic.

"You can say that again," she said, holding his hand contently, the relief freeing her heart. They had all agreed to catch up at the *Panigiri* that night. Who would have thought she would be catching up with Maria and Nicki, and spending time with Julie — *Maria's best friend*, not the woman having an affair with her husband — at the village dance, of all places? It was as though life had come full circle.

"It *is* beautiful here, Dimi. I can see why you didn't want to leave." He stopped walking for a moment.

"Malcolm … what is it?"

"Now I know! I knew it wasn't just the tapestry, although that was quite unbelievable. Your reaction didn't quite equate though. Your eyes looked so hurt, and vulnerable, as though someone had betrayed you. I can't believe it. You thought I was here to have a picnic with Julie — not you! I can't believe it …"

"I didn't know what to think," she said, feeling guilty that she had jumped to conclusions. Right then, she felt Malcolm's cool, strong hand clasping hers as he pulled her towards him.

"You know what that means, don't you?"

"What?"

"It means that I'll really have to show you how much I love you. I can't believe you thought that. It breaks my heart to think that you were in there crying because you thought

303

I betrayed you. My sweet, beautiful, Dimity," he said, looking into her eyes. "Don't you know that I don't work without you? I *will* have to prove it to you, because there is no way that I'm going to lose you again," he said, leaning over and kissing her gently on the lips. He then looked at her intently for a while as they both felt the warm and gentle breeze on their skin. They stood there for a while, in each other's arms. The timber chimes, and the bells heard from the goats in the distance, complemented the ambience they felt in their souls.

"Just don't buy me anymore expensive gifts. I have everything I need already," she finally spoke.

"Don't worry. What I have in mind won't require any money. It might take all night though — maybe even up to the early hours of the morning, because judging from what just transpired, I obviously have a lot of convincing to do."

CHAPTER THIRTY-FOUR

The clarinets could be heard from the mountains above, as could the *bouzoukia*. Dimity looked at Malcolm, who was in animated discussion with Rose and Anastasia. Everyone was seated at one of the many outdoor tables in the stone-paved square at the heart of the village. Antonio had also joined them. Dimity smiled as she looked at her new friends talking to her husband. She smiled as she remembered Rose tapping her on the shoulder, commenting on how gorgeous Malcolm was. Julie had also been a breath of fresh air. They did have so much in common — more than she could have imagined. Julie had picked up on Dimity's assumptions, and felt so bad for her — apparently knowing too well what it felt like when someone you loved seemed to be having too much "fun" with someone else. They talked for a while about interior design, her time in Amsterdam, how Malcolm was so generous to show her the sights, and, of course, about Maria and Nicki.

"Looking lovely again." The voice was familiar to Dimity. It was Stavros.

"Stavros … how are you?" she asked him, looking instinctively in Malcolm's direction. He was still talking to the others.

"You know, I can't believe your husband is *the* Malcolm Stewart. Now I feel worse than ever. It's bad enough I fell for someone who was clearly taken, but when that *someone* is Malcolm Stewart's … Dimity, he's always been an inspiration — I mean, his work is so innovative and his methods are so unconventional. Look, he probably hates the sight of me … but please tell him I would never have kissed you …"

"Stavros, relax! Malcolm is cool with everything. If you really want the truth, he really liked your work. He said you're very talented, and that it takes a lot of effort and dedication to make the formations that you make."

"Unbelievable … I kiss another man's wife, one who inspires me — *his wife* — and he likes my work! He must really be confident with his marriage and your love for him — *or* he can't blame another man for falling for you — as it's really difficult not to. Anyway, before I get out of line again …" he continued, looking in Malcolm's direction, causing Dimity to also look at her husband, who was looking down at his drink, "I thought I'd give you your last incomplete masterpiece. I also left the other vase and the gift I gave you with Mihali, the concierge at your hotel. You forgot it again. Anyway, I thought Malcolm and you could complete this one together."

"Thanks Stavros. I'll never forget my stay here. Your work has inspired me so much. Maybe I could sell some of it through the online business I'm planning on starting."

"That sounds very impressive. I'm sure you can do it, and I would definitely love for you to sell my work. You are an artist at heart, and artists sense things; they know when they've found a good thing. Oh … Dimity … one more thing."

"What's that?"

"Your name, I finally remembered its Greek derivation. It means *thread.*"

"*Thread?*" she replied, smiling.

Stavros smiled back and then looked towards Malcolm again. He acknowledged him with a nod. She then walked towards Malcolm, looking at him curiously. He reciprocated the gesture and also acknowledged Stavros with a nod — like one artist respecting another.

"Malcolm …" Dimity needed to know if he was okay with her exchange with Stavros.

"What is it, Dimity?" he asked, looking up at her.

"I just wanted to say one more goodbye to him. He also gave me my incomplete vessel. He thought we could work on it together. He also feels so bad for crossing the line because you've been his design inspiration for so long. Oh … and he also told me that my name actually means *thread*. Anyway, he's really a big fan, and wouldn't stop complimenting your work."

"Did he compliment *you?*"

"Malcolm … it wasn't like that …"

"Because you look so incredibly sexy tonight. I can't stop looking at you," he smiled, as he pulled her gently towards him, seating her on his lap. He looked at her affectionately, as he placed his masculine hand on her bare knee. "You know what … I actually feel sorry for him," he said, as he stroked her hair.

"You do? Why?"

"Well, he can't have you. I'm sure he'll take a while to get over you. As for your name, he's right — it's from a Greek word used to name a double-threaded cotton fabric. The fabric had a feminine, sensual feel to it, but it was really strong at the same time … just like you are."

"How do you know all that?" Dimity was astonished.

"You know me Dimi … when I'm interested in something … I find out as much as I can."

Dimity gave him a warm, affectionate smile. She felt so valued and loved.

Right then, she heard Maria's voice. "Dimity … come and have a dance with us. You remember how much I love Greek dancing, don't you?" she laughed.

"Go … be with your friends," said Malcolm. "I know you have a lot to catch up on. I mean … you came to Ioannina to make peace, and you did — in all aspects of your life."

Maria waited for Dimity to join her. She couldn't believe she was back in her life — that the McKenzies had reappeared. Nicki had *just* told her that she had seen Luca in a magazine, and now they were here with their childhood best friend. She stretched her arm out and placed it on Antonio's shoulder, as she waited for her to join them to dance the *hasaposeviko* — one of the dances she had refused to dance all those years ago, when she'd been chosen to be the lead dancer. It was the fifth dance she would take part in, and she couldn't believe how much she actually enjoyed it — when she wasn't being stubborn and defiant.

"You're quite the Greek dancer," Antonio teased. "I'm glad it's summer. I mean, it would be funny if your stockings tore accidentally. It *would* be ironic."

Maria just smiled. He was right. It *would* be funny. She held Dimity's hand and proudly let the music take her away, without any resistance.

"Nicki … Nicki, look what I got!" Poppy ran towards her. Nicki walked over, leaving the circle of dancers.

"Wow!" she said, looking at Poppy's new bangle. "Marco, take a photo of me and Poppy."

Nicki smiled happily with Poppy.

"That's perfect," Marco said.

"So was my time here," she said, looking at Poppy. "I'm going to miss you so much," Nicki said, as tears began to form in her eyes.

"Nicki … are you all right?" She felt Marco's hand. She turned to him and saw his worried expression through her tears.

"Come on … let's go," he said. "I knew it would be difficult for you."

"No … I mean, it is, but not for that reason. It's been the best time staying here … minding Poppy. I learned a lot about myself … what I have to offer, how rewarding it is to look after a child. I know I will one day … one way or another … I'll share the love I have inside of me."

"I'll make sure of it," Marco said, his eyes conveying concern. "Let's go for a walk," he then said, as Poppy ran back to her parents.

"I'll say one more goodbye tomorrow, when I say my goodbyes to Peter and Angela," she said softly.

"Come on," Marco said, taking her hand in his. "It's a magical night. Look at the stars!"

Nicki looked up at the sky. She could feel Marco still looking at her. "I'm looking," she replied.

"So am I," he said.

Nicki gave him a puzzled look. "What do you mean … you're looking? You're not even looking at the sky."

"I don't need to look at the sky to see them. I can see them … in your eyes. They're glistening like diamonds." His face gave way to an affectionate smile.

Nicki smiled back. "Well, they tend to sparkle more when there's light around them. There's so much radiating from here right now," she said, pointing to his heart. "Diamonds need light so that they can reflect it back."

"It's great that we can reflect it off each other again," he said, his face suddenly serious.

"Well, getting to know you again has brought back the romantic side of me. I mean, we're still at the dating stage, aren't we?" she asked with a laugh.

"Yes we are," he replied, smiling again. "We better continue our date then." He wrapped his arm around her shoulder. Nicki leaned her head on Marco's chest as they walked arm in arm under the glittery night sky.

Dimity was having so much fun holding Rose and Maria's hands, dancing the night away. By the time the music stopped, they were all exhausted. Dimity's new black heels weren't helping her keep up with the quick pace of the dances, when it was already a challenge learning the steps and keeping up with everyone, even though she remembered some of the dances Nicki had taught her so many years ago. Still, she kept the shoes on because she felt sexy in them. They wrapped high around her ankles, and complemented her red ponte dress, which fell just below her knees, hugging her figure as though it was made for her. She felt so free and beautiful — inside and out. They all let go of each other's hands as yet another Greek dance called the *kalamatiano* came to an end, and stood in their spots talking for a while, smiling and laughing. Dimity flicked her hair away from her face, her gold bangle caressing her summer skin. She caught Malcolm looking at her. He had finished talking to Antonio, who had left to tend to Thomas, who had been sleeping contently as one of Maria's aunties watched over him. Malcolm looked so sophisticated in his navy suit jacket and v-neck top. She was very familiar with that look in his eyes. She could feel its force as she walked over to him.

She felt the heat from his hand as he pulled her towards him. He led her away from the noise, from the people. She could feel his desire as she walked beside him holding his hand, not saying anything. Words weren't needed, and they walked together silently, each of them feeding off the other's desire.

"Malcolm … is this the hotel you're staying at? It's so opulent. I can't believe how magnificent it is. It's beyond words."

Malcolm looked at her proudly as she looked in awe at the hotel he too had found spectacular — even though it had felt empty without his wife by his side. Now she was with him, he knew that she would love it.

"I've always wanted to be involved in a project …" she began.

"Maybe you will be one day, Dimity. Anything is possible."

"It's majestic. I've never seen anything like it. Have you, Malcolm? I mean it's …"

"Dimi, you can see the hotel in the morning … I promise you."

"I mean … my hotel is charming but this takes five-star to a new level."

"Dimi … please," he took her by the hand. He needed her so much.

She stopped talking when she looked at him. Malcolm could see that she knew — she knew how much he needed her. She took his hand and walked with him to the lift. He waited for the lift, trying to hide the intense feelings inside of him as two guests stepped out of it and they entered.

Dimity watched as the door closed with the "Do Not Disturb" sign on it. Her face felt warm. He looked so confident and worldly. Sensing his urgency, she walked over to him. She needed to be with him. He pulled her close.

"You drive me crazy … even after all these years. Did I tell you how sensual you look? I mean, you're glowing," he said softly. "It's been so long since I've touched you." He stroked her hair away from her warm, soft face. He began to kiss her. His kisses sent electric sensations throughout her whole body as his lips worked their way to her neck. They then made their way to her mouth. He began to kiss her urgently. His beard caressed her skin. His cologne drove her wild with desire. She'd missed this. She had shut him out, but she was now ready to give in to the desire — to give in to him.

***

Malcolm Stewart woke up in the king-sized bed. It was definitely too big for one person, but this time he wasn't alone. He was with his wife, who was fast asleep in his arms.

He jolted as he heard a knock at the door. It was the continental breakfast he had ordered the night before.

Realising the "Do Not Disturb" sign was still on the door, he quietly went to bring the tray in the room.

Dimity ate another strawberry fed to her by Malcolm. She had woken up to him handing her a glass of orange juice. As she took a few sips, leaning on the pillow, he had placed the glass down onto the tray, and began feeding her the delicious fruit from one of the many serving plates, kissing her in between.

"You know Malcolm, you *are* spoiling me," she said, as he sat close to her, stroking her hair as she took another sip of her orange juice.

"Well, you deserve it. I'd do anything for you, Dimity. I finally have you back. Anyway, this is just the beginning. We've got the islands next."

"And then we go back home? I think the girls really miss us. Are you sure my parents were okay with our plans to extend our trip?" she asked, as he kissed her bare shoulder.

"They couldn't be happier. When they heard you and I were spending time together on the Greek islands, they offered to mind them for as long as we wanted."

"So, we'll be gone for another week?" she asked, as the luxurious, satin sheet she had been wrapped in began to slip down.

"A week and four days," he continued, as he kissed her neck. "I forgot to tell you. We're stopping over in Amsterdam."

"What?" Dimity looked into his eyes. The sheet slipped down to her waist.

"We still have to get Samantha … what was it now? Some cool bangle that's all the rage," he said, as his toned, tanned arms pulled her close to his bare chest. "Olivia wants one too, of course."

"Of course," she smiled in a haze as he began to kiss her, allowing the desire to once again take over.

CHAPTER THIRTY-FIVE

Maria sat in the kitchen of the North Sydney terrace house. It was Saturday evening and it had been a week since they flew back to Australia. Her father was upstairs getting dressed for the dinner party that Dimity and her husband were hosting.

"Effie ... where's my suit jacket?" she heard him call out to her mother, who was applying the final touches to her make-up. Her parents had decided to fly up from Melbourne to see their grandson and to catch up with Dimity and her family. Even her brother, John, and his family had agreed to come along, and were all staying at the terrace house in its many available rooms. It would be a reunion from the old neighbourhood.

Maria nervously looked at her mother as she walked into the kitchen. She had been anxious all day. She had to do it — she had to tell her mother what she had found out.

She took a deep uneasy breath, and then cleared her throat. "Um ... Mum, I forgot to tell you ... I ... I ran into Aliki in Agrinio. It turned out she *was* there ... from London ... housesitting, and visiting friends." She looked at her mother anxiously. "Well ... anyway," she continued, when her mother didn't respond, instead choosing to clean the already clean bench top with a sponge. "She showed me some photos. I didn't know you were so cool. I mean, some of the clothes you wore were so out there. The photo of you and that guy Stelios ... that was so cool. Um ... would you believe he's actually involved with the International Soccer Federation, and he's married to a humanitarian who raises awareness for different minority groups? He travels with his wife, spreading awareness. I think he's doing really well for himself. He even has three intelligent kids who are also successful ... and he came from *your* neighbourhood ...

from *Agrinio*," she added awkwardly, knowing she was overdoing it. But the words were out there. She did it. Now she had to know what effect they would have. "Oh," she continued, "and it was so nice meeting him."

Her mother looked up abruptly, stunned. Her eyes were teary; her lips trembled.

Maria continued. "I have a letter for you. He wanted you to have this. In fact, he wrote it a while ago. Here."

Her mother slowly reached out to take the letter in her trembling hand. She walked out of the kitchen, hugging it close to her heart.

"I have to go and get my bag," she said in a serious tone.

"Mum ..." Maria began, as her mother walked out, wondering if it was the wrong timing for such an intense conversation.

At least twenty minutes later, Mrs Salas walked into the kitchen with her handbag, and a beautiful, unusual wrap around her shoulders. Maria had never seen it before. It almost looked like something she would wear.

"We'd better go. It's rude to be late, you know. Your father is already waiting outside, and John is already there. It is exciting to see the McKenzie family again," she said, smiling.

"Okay Mum, let's go. I'd better get the *baklava* I made," Maria announced proudly, looking into her mother's eyes. She was certain she had shed a few tears.

"You know Maria, it looks really good," she complimented her as she took the plate out of the fridge.

"Almost as good as yours, Mrs Salas," Antonio said as he walked into the kitchen.

"You really are the best son-in-law," she said with an affectionate smile, letting her guard down.

As Maria looked on, she knew her mother seemed more relaxed — and she also knew that it was only the beginning. Her mother knew that Stelios was doing well. Maria knew she hadn't ever tried to find out anything about him because she was too afraid to revisit the whole tragedy. It seemed she was glad that someone else did it for her — especially since the outcome was positive. In time, Maria would give her all the details regarding her meeting with Stelios.

"Oh, is Nicki already there?" her mother asked.

"I'm not sure," Maria replied, the smell of her mother's hairspray suddenly making her stomach turn.

"You know, Mum. You shouldn't use hair spray," she blurted out.

"What? I always need a bit of hairspray when I go out," she replied defensively.

"Well, maybe in the 80s it was okay, but your hair looks better without it. Besides, it's bad for the environment. I'll give you one of my organic hair products from the shop," she said, as she walked to the play area to get Thomas.

***

Everything was going smoothly. The caterers served entrees to the vibrant guests who were all conversing in different rooms of the house, some stepping out onto the veranda to enjoy the pleasant stillness of the night. The sounds of the *bouzouki* could be heard in the background, and complemented the relaxed and accepting atmosphere. As she looked around, Dimity saw that it was just as she had imagined it. She loved witnessing joy and hearing the laughter and conversation. It was so exciting being back where she belonged and feeling content and at peace with life and with herself.

"Dimity, you've outdone yourself. I mean, a *bouzouki* player? That should put a smile on my mother's face. Maybe we won't hear her insults," Alex added wickedly. "I must say though; she has been on her best behaviour. I mean she really loved the necklace you bought for her from Greece. I can't believe Luca and Andrea are also here. I mean … Luca has worked with some of the best photographers, and being in the industry ... I thought she might be able to help me out a bit. I don't want to be taking photos of houses for a real estate company forever. Besides, maybe she could also introduce me to some of the models," he laughed. "It's hard out there. I mean ... you and Malcolm might have found each other again ... but the dating scene is tough. I think I'm ready to settle down, but where can I meet someone as wonderful as you? I'm glad that uptight brother of mine finally realised what he has." He eyed Malcolm as he walked over to them.

Malcolm wrapped his arms around Dimity. "I always knew what I had, little brother. But I don't know if meeting models and settling down quite mix. I appreciate you caring so much about our relationship though. You know, I could help you find a job for one of the design magazines if you want ..."

"Thanks Malcolm, but I'd rather take photos of models than furniture, as cool as it is, and the thing about models isn't true, bro. A friend of mine is engaged to a model," he continued, and then grabbed a goat's cheese pastry from one of the caterers. "Oh, there's Andrea. She's in marketing. She might have some suggestions," he said, walking away.

"The caterers are doing a great job," Dimity acknowledged as she turned to Malcolm, her head spinning after trying to process everything that Alex had said. "You know, I could host a lot of these dinner parties, if I don't have to do any of the work." She smiled.

"Well, everyone seems to be enjoying themselves. I think it's because you're such a great host, making sure that everyone is happy."

"Well, you know I don't like anyone to feel left out. It's in my nature," she said, becoming worried as she spoke.

"What's wrong now, Dimity?" Malcolm looked concerned.

"Do you think we should have invited Julie … since she knows Maria and Nicki?"

"Dimi, please, relax. She had something on anyway. Don't worry. Even my mum looks happy, and I don't think it's just from all the sparkling wine she's drinking. It was a great idea to bring some bottles home from Zitsa."

Dimity looked at Sylvia, who was laughing at something her father was saying. Mrs Salas was also laughing. They seemed to be getting along so well; Maria and Nicki's parents and her own reminiscing about the past, with Malcolm's parents joining in on the conversation. As her eyes scanned the room, she noticed a blonde, blue-eyed woman walking down the hallway towards the open-planned lounge room, after being let in by Samantha, who was proving to be a responsible host.

"Nicki! Malcolm … it's Nicki!" she cried. "Hi Nicki, you look so beautiful in that dress." She hugged her friend warmly.

"Thanks Dimity. You look spectacular in yours," she replied. "I can't get over how gorgeous your house is. It's wonderful!"

"Hi Dimity," Marco shook Dimity's hand with a firm grip.

"Hi Marco," she replied with a warm smile.

"It is beautiful," Stan, Dimity's father-in-law, interjected. "It pays to have two designers in the family. You and Malcolm always made a great team." He nodded at them and walked to the kitchen to get more drinks for everyone.

"Thanks, Stan," Dimity called after him.

"Your father-in-law is sweet," Nicki said, as Dimity guided them both to the veranda, where John and his wife were talking to Maria, Antonio, and Luca.

"John … is it really you?" asked Andrea. "I can't believe you became a dentist. I remember the old days, when you were always listening to Soundgarden … or was it Pearl Jam? Did you know we could hear it even from *our* house?"

"Yeah ... I guess it would seem strange that I actually have my own practice if you knew me as a teenager, but you know what, the music got me through those years, and my studies. Anyway, it's under the name Anthony J. Salas, if any of you are ever in Melbourne and in urgent need of a dentist," he replied proudly. "I thought it had a nicer sound to it."

"That explains it!" Dimity interjected, shocked that she had in fact found him on the internet. "I saw that name when I tried to find out if you were all still living in Australia. It was you after all, John."

Later that evening, Dimity walked into the main dining room that overlooked the beautifully lit garden, where splashes of pink and white created magic. The table that Malcolm had designed and made stood in the centre of the room, dressed beautifully with plates that were abundantly full with mouth-watering food. Wine glasses glistened amongst the gentle flames from the many candles that were strategically placed across the table, waiting to be filled. Amongst all this, she could hear laughter and conversation, and at the centre of it all, hanging proudly on the wall above the Carrara marble fireplace, was the Greek tapestry. Its blues, white, and magenta added colour to the otherwise very neutral aesthetic of the contemporary setting. Despite it being a complete contrast, Dimity felt that it belonged there, adding its unique beauty to the rest of the house.

"Your skin looks amazing," she heard her mother say to Mrs Salas.

"Oh, thank you," Mrs Salas replied, slightly embarrassed, but equally grateful for the compliment as she placed her hand on her face. "It's that new cream Maria has in her shop, from suppliers in Greece. It has olive oil in it. She's devoting a whole section to Ancient Greece." Mrs Salas beamed with pride. She then directed her attention to Nicki and Marco. "I'm so glad you two are back together. I knew you were too in love with each other," she said, slightly emotional.

"Connor and Cassandra were very helpful," Marco said.

Mrs Salas looked deliriously happy to be there. She seemed to be having a wonderful time. Dimity sensed that everyone was enjoying themselves. *Maybe I should have invited Cassandra and Connor*, she thought. Even though she didn't know them, they meant a lot to Maria, and they had helped Nicki so much.

"What are you worried about now?" she heard Malcolm's voice.

"Oh ... I was just thinking that maybe we should have invited Cassandra and Connor as well. I've heard so much about them, I feel like I know them ..."

"Dimity ... stop worrying," Nicki said, overhearing. "You always were so considerate, always thinking of others, and you haven't changed. They would be honoured to attend such a wonderful dinner party, but they didn't expect to be invited. Besides, they're probably organising their wedding, which should be soon."

"I think they had to postpone the wedding for a while. They're both so busy with the practice," Maria corrected Nicki.

"Oh ... well, maybe counsellors have relationship problems too."

"Why do you say that?" Maria asked.

"I just know when two people want to be together, they don't let anything stand in their way," she said, turning to Marco and giving him a kiss on the cheek.

Maria looked at her sister happily. She was right, though. It was odd that Cassandra and Connor were postponing their wedding.

"Anyway, that's my wife, always thinking of others," Malcolm interjected, wrapping his arms affectionately around her. "That's why I fell for her when I met her — well, apart from the obvious."

319

Dimity heard Olivia and Samantha giggling in the background. Feeling embarrassed with Malcolm's public display of affection, she whispered in his ear, "Malcolm, both our parents are watching."

"Do you know how sexy you look when you get flustered?" he teased, stroking her hair. Sensing her uneasiness, he decided to back off a little.

"Did I tell you about a time when Dimity would pick up any lost kitten she could find? She would feed them and I couldn't get them to leave." Her father began to tell the story he had told so many times.

She caught Sylvia looking at her.

"Nicki and Dimity made this. It's beautiful, isn't it?" Mrs Salas then said proudly, looking at the tapestry.

"I can't believe it's back in our lives," Mrs McKenzie mused. "It is a masterpiece, considering tapestries can be complicated."

"You should see some of their paintings," added Mr Salas. "They were top of the class in art."

"What about the vase on the console … you made that while you were in Greece?" marvelled Alex. "I can't believe how talented, sweet, and gorgeous you are Dimi."

"Oh stop," Dimity said modestly, a blush creeping up on her face. "Nicki's the one who encouraged me to try art. She had always been artistic."

"Hey you two, don't forget I helped as well. I did this bit!" Maria stood up and pointed to a small section of the sea.

Everyone laughed with her.

"Yes, that you did, sis," Nicki said. "Maybe I did encourage you to try art, but you were the one that motivated us when things became challenging. Dimity always looked at the positive side of things. She always made sure that I never gave up. From the moment that we met her, she made sure I wasn't left out at school. I was new and so shy. She *is* talented, and generous," Nicki became emotional.

320

"She is," Sylvia suddenly said, looking at Dimity straight in the eyes. "You are a wonderful woman, and I couldn't be happier that my son met you."

Dimity was speechless. Her heart felt warm with emotion as she heard all the kind words. Looking at Malcolm, who was standing at the door holding some wine glasses, she replied, "Thanks Sylvia. I think I should be thanking you though, for doing such a great job at raising such a wonderful man." She walked over to her mother-in-law and gave her a hug, feeling Malcolm's appreciative stare.

"Okay, everyone, before we all break down in tears, let's eat," he ordered.

"Did you know that tapestries were only owned by the wealthy in ancient times?" Dimity heard Marco say to Nicki.

"Yes, that's what we learned while studying the history of art," Nicki said. "That's why we had to make a tapestry."

"The tapestry of life," Antonio then offered. "Isn't that the analogy that is used to describe how complex life is, yet how beautiful the overall picture can be?"

"That's right," Malcolm said. "I guess, as complicated and intertwined as every thread is, the end goal keeps one going."

"Yes, and every thread is important," Nicki added. "Even if the warp threads are hidden by the weft threads, they are just as crucial to the end product; the loom keeps the warp threads strong so that the weft threads can be interwoven, which are the only threads on display, " Nicki offered proudly, as Malcolm gazed over at Dimity, nodding his head in agreement.

"Yes. There's always someone behind the scenes," said Malcolm, his eyes still on Dimity.

"And even if you make a mistake, you can undo it and head in the right direction again. Sometimes you're given another chance to make things right." Maria looked at Nicki, and then at her mother. "After all, as I recall in my tapestry lessons from you two, the weft threads are discontinuous and don't have to go from edge to edge."

"And every colour adds its own unique quality, just like in real life. They all have a turn in contributing," Luca joined in, her black and red hair being a case in point.

Dimity instinctively looked out into the garden at her words.

"When I look at it … I also see different points of origin leading one to different paths … but no matter where one starts on the tapestry, they lead to the same end point," Nicki said contemplatively.

"And the end picture or point can be just as rewarding to reach, and as beautiful — no matter which direction one *chooses* or is unexpectedly steered towards," Dimity added.

Everyone took their places at the table, which was abundantly rich with food and drink, and intellectual and warm conversation. It was a place where everyone was accepted and respected — just the way she had imagined it.

"Oh … Grandma," Samantha suddenly said, looking at Sylvia. "I need to show you my school design project that Dad helped me with. I did most of it myself though," she added. "I honestly think it looks okay!"

"I can't wait," Sylvia said, taken aback. "I'll be honoured to look at your work."

"You're wrong about something, Sam," Malcolm advised his daughter with a smile. "It's a lot better than okay. If you're going to sell your prototype to buyers, there's no room for modesty, especially when the end product is something you believe in."

"Okay then … it's exceptional, a masterpiece, even better than a *Malcolm Stewart* original," she said in a loud voice.

"Much better," Malcolm said, as the room filled with warm laughter.

EPILOGUE

Dimity sat on the bench and placed her hands on the timber picnic table, awaiting Malcolm's response. They had dropped the girls off at their friend's house, across the street from the park. Dimity had led Malcolm to the bench as they casually walked and talked on that gloriously sunny Sunday morning in November. As they sat at the bench, they lost themselves in a discussion regarding Malcolm's need to meet with some new suppliers, as he wanted to use the latest renewable materials for his next line. For a while, he had been pressed for time, and didn't completely explore all his options. Having cut back on some of his business deals, he was now excited to delve into that side of things. He also knew it was smart to take a step back and re-group so he could research new methods, which would benefit his designs in the long run. Dimity would help him with a lot of the buyers and suppliers. He knew that she was also busy setting up her new online homewares business, so they always found themselves discussing who would do what on which day.

"Okay then ... you could meet with some of the buyers, and maybe I'll go to see Olivia perform at her mock trial debate, since one of the meetings is scheduled then."

"Oh ..." Dimity said apprehensively, feeling that she had to be at the debate. It was still hard to completely let go.

"What is it? You're feeling bad about missing the debate, aren't you?"

"Well, yes I do ... but I've seen so many of them. I'm sure Olivia would want you to see her in action too. I also have to meet Meagan that day. I can't believe how much she's helped me. I'm so glad I got the nerve to call her after working for her all those years ago. She was so excited to hear from me. I have a whole list of interior designers who know about the site already. She's also keeping me up to date with changes in the industry, even with suppliers. I still can't believe I'm doing this," she said, smiling proudly, "and that she's also offered me a job at her new design company. I must admit, it *is* tempting, but I feel like I need to do this now. Besides, it also gives me a chance to even create something of my own. I realise that as wonderful as interior design is, art is where it all started for me. You can relate to that, Malcolm, can't you?"

Malcolm leaned over and kissed her gently on the lips.

"What was that for?"

"I just couldn't resist. I've missed seeing you like this. I can't believe that I didn't see how much you needed this. I'm so glad you agreed to start out by working with me again. We can both help each other — and get to meet other needs as well. I did warn you that I might find it difficult to work with you though, when you look so radiant. I guess that's one of the perks of the job," he continued playfully, his blue eyes teasing her.

"Well, try to control yourself," she smiled. "We have a lot to organise. The next couple of months are going to be so busy. It was definitely a good idea to turn the downstairs room into an office. Just don't look at me like that when we're with clients," she ordered.

"Like what?" Malcolm asked, defensively.

"Like you ... you know what I mean," she said trying to resist a smile.

"Oh ... you mean the look I give you before I do this?" he asked, as he leaned over to kiss her again. "Is that what you mean?"

"Yes," she said, running her fingers through his hair.

"Well, I don't think you should be too concerned about *me*," he said as he sat next to her on the bench. "That Ricardo guy we met on Monday couldn't stop looking at you, and I know what he was thinking. It definitely wasn't about LED lighting."

"Well, that's always been a problem with me I guess." She stifled a smile. "It *is* difficult getting so much male attention."

Suddenly, she heard a male voice from behind her calling her name.

"Dimity?"

She instantly turned.

"Boris!" she exclaimed. He was standing with a group of people at the entrance of the Bavarian Bistro.

Malcolm also looked at the tall, young man.

"Hi Boris," she called out. "Nice to see you!" He nodded and smiled at her, before turning and walking into the bistro with his friends.

"Boris?" Malcolm looked at her inquisitively. "So this is what you've been doing when I've been working? I mean … how many guys have you got under your spell? Let's see … first there was Stavros, now a guy named Boris. Ricardo couldn't keep his eyes off of you …"

"There was also an Australian English Professor … I met him on the plane when I was going to see you. He actually said that you were a fool if you didn't work things out with me. There was also an American waiter, who said I was really beautiful …"

"Okay, okay … I hear you. Well, they were all right. You *are* beautiful, and a lot more. And I *was* a fool for not working things out with you in Amsterdam," he said, looking at her seriously. "Being with you here … it's how I always wanted it to be, Dimity. These last few months have been so great, going away with you and the girls, sharing our interests, our passions together."

Dimity kissed him on the lips. She felt so much for him, and couldn't believe that only a few months ago she had pushed him away.

"You know, Malcolm … that was the guy I told you about … Boris. He's the one that told me that the ship can survive without me … that I should swim … remember?"

"So, you're saying if it wasn't for him, you wouldn't have flown all the way to Amsterdam to see me?"

"That's right."

"So, I guess he saved our marriage! Speaking of men liking you, I just spoke to Stefano. You remember him, don't you? He thinks you're a remarkable designer, and is really excited to talk to you about your future goals. You'll be making waves in the design world before you know it."

"Well, you're not the only *rock star* in the family. It's about time I got some attention!" she challenged him with a smile.

"Yes, I guess it is about time, Dimity. It's about time you got all the attention you deserve," he said, his blue eyes deep with emotion. "Stefano can't wait to see you again, when we go to London for the design exhibition."

"Oh, when is that on?"

"Sometime in January, before we head off to Milan."

"I thought …" Dimity began.

"We're *both* going," he said, clasping her hand, when she looked at him in shock. "Dimity, if you want to be back in the industry, you can't miss all the important furniture and design exhibitions and conferences. Besides, we won't have any problems with child-minding, because we're all going."

"Oh! Wow!" Dimity exclaimed. "In that case, I wouldn't want to fall behind with what's happening in the industry." A smile began to form on her face. She loved Malcolm's new carefree attitude. She was fine with his plans. She had no problems with spending time with her family in one of the most beautiful and culturally rich cities in the world. "We're also visiting Nicki and Marco in Melbourne in a few weeks," Dimity reminded him. "They felt the need for a get-together, and they want us to see their house."

"It all sounds good to me," Malcolm said. "Nicki has also been good for you. I really like hanging out with her and Marco. Maria and Antonio are also really fun."

"They're great, aren't they?" Dimity enthused. "I'm so lucky to have them in my life again."

Malcolm nodded. "So am I."

***

Maria looked at Antonio, surprised and bemused at the scene in front of her. It wasn't every day that she saw her mother and mother-in-law dancing together to Latin music in a South American club. Antonio's parents, who were visiting from Chile, had been staying with them for a few weeks in Sydney, and they thought it would also be exciting for them to visit her parents in Melbourne, so they could see more of the country. But she never expected this! Her mother was getting along so well with Mrs Reyes; they had been going shopping together, eating at restaurants, had gone to the Yarra Valley vineyards together, and were now dancing in a nightclub, sipping margaritas in the early hours of the morning.

"Mum ... don't you think we should get back home now?" She nudged her mother on the dance floor. "Nicki and Marco are at your house minding Thomas. I'm sure they want to get some sleep. I should have organised for him to sleep at their house, but they are renovating their veranda so ..."

"Relax, Maria. Nicki and Marco love the time they spend with Thomas!" she shouted in her ear.

"Yes, but he's sleeping now so they have nothing to do," she persisted.

"I'm sure they'll think of something ... the way those two have been lately ... I'm sure there'll soon be a little boy or girl on the way," her mother shouted again, the same way one of her girlfriends would in a nightclub back in the day.

"Mum!" Dimity was shocked at her mother's response, not only because of the image it conjured up of Nicki and Marco on their parents' couch, but because of the sensitivity of the subject.

"Maria, relax. You think I don't remember how your father and I were in the early days …"

"Mum, I think you've had too much to drink," she continued.

"We're just getting started," her mother-in-law said with a heavy accent, and then winked at her. "Maria … relax … your sister is not so guarded about that topic anymore. She just wants to take each day at a time from now on, and see what happens. She's changed. So has Marco."

"I don't think we should be discussing this here," she shouted back in her mother's ear. "Antonio and I are tired. We haven't slept much …"

"You go!" cried Mrs Salas, as she kept dancing.

"Don't worry. We'll catch a taxi later!" exclaimed Mrs Reyes.

"Okay …" she said apprehensively as she walked back to Antonio.

"Kids, they worry so much these days," she heard her mother say.

As she headed out the door with Antonio, she turned and looked at them again. Her father was also dancing. They were completely oblivious to anything around them.

"Let's go, Antonio," she said. "I think we're cramping their style. Let's go get some sleep. We need the energy. I'm sure our mothers have a lot planned for tomorrow. I think my mum wants to take your parents to one of the Greek nightclubs next."

"Don't worry … we'll have a word with them when they get back," he teased as they walked to their car.

"Yes, maybe we should!" Maria said sternly, stifling a smile. She looked back at the club, the vision of her mother dancing fresh in her mind. She smiled, and warmth filled her heart. Lately this was happening more and more often — she would catch herself smiling when she thought of her mother. Maria had finally realised that her mother had let fear control their relationship, and that she genuinely wanted what was best for all her children. The more time she spent with her mother, the more she saw herself in her. Who knew her mother was so free-spirited at heart? It was just like Nicki kept telling her: "Just when you think you know someone …"

"Maria … is everything okay?" Antonio asked.

Maria nodded. She looked at her husband lovingly, the warmth in her heart enveloping him. "Yes, Antonio. For the first time in my life, I can honestly say that *everything* is okay."

ACKNOWLEDGEMENTS

This book was so much fun to write. I was fortunate to have travelled to many of the places I mention in the book. I'd like to thank my husband for being my travelling partner on all our wonderful adventures, for his IT expertise, and for his continuous encouragement in writing this novel. My children are also a constant inspiration, and I hope to prove to them that dreams can come true with perseverance, dedication, and hard work.

A special thanks, again, to the team at Bespoke Book Covers, for their beautiful cover, and for being so helpful. A huge thank you to my editor for her suggestions, and her encouragement.

I'd like to also thank my friends and extended family for taking an interest in my writing and for their encouragement in writing this book.

Finally, thanks to all of the wonderful readers who have read my books. I hope they have touched your life in a positive way. Please feel free to note your thoughts by writing a review.

ANTHEA SYROKOU is an author who grew up and resides in Sydney, Australia.

Anthea's love for writing was planted at a young age when she studied Greek mythology. Her love for literature continued well into her teenage years when she enjoyed reading novels by many of the great English writers.

As a young adult, she immersed herself in reading women's contemporary fiction and writing about topics, that many could relate to, in a witty, light-hearted way, which became a passion — one that she takes very seriously.

Anthea has a BA degree, majoring in psychology and industrial relations, and a diploma in counselling. She also studied Greek literature at university and has worked in direct marketing, and insurance and investments.

As well as writing fiction, Anthea also writes articles and posts on everyday issues; often adding her dash of humour.

When she isn't writing or reading, Anthea enjoys spending time with her family, travelling, yoga, and escaping to the vineyards. A quiet house with some jazz playing in the background, surrounded by a few lit scented candles is her idea of relaxation. Anthea lives with her husband and their two sons.

For more information, please visit **antheasyrokou.com**